third watch

the middle east

FIRST CENTURY A.D.

Mount Hermon +

GALILEE

• Caesarea Philippi

Mediterranean Sea

Chorazin •
• Bethsaida
Capernaum •
Magdala • Sea of Galilee
• Tiberias

Jordan River

SAMARIA

Jericho •
Jerusalem • + Mount of Olives
• Bethany
Bethlehem •
• Herodium

PEREA

JUDEA

Dead Sea

IDUMEA

← to Alexandria, Egypt

↑
N

BOOK THREE

<svg>fish icon</svg> A.D. CHRONICLES™

third watch

NEW HANOVER COUNTY
PUBLIC LIBRARY
201 CHESTNUT STREET
WILMINGTON, NC 28401

Tyndale House Publishers, Inc.
Wheaton, Illinois

BODIE & BROCK THOENE

Visit Tyndale's exciting Web site at www.tyndale.com

Coyright © 2004 by Bodie and Brock Thoene. All rights reserved.

Cover illustration © 2004 by Cliff Nielsen. All rights reserved.

Cover designed by Rule 29, www.rule29.com

Interior designed by Dean H. Renninger

Edited by Ramona Cramer Tucker

Published in association with the literary agency of Alive Communications, Inc., 7680 Goddard Street, Suite 200, Colorado Springs, CO 80920.

Scripture quotations for Parts I, II, and III section pages, 1 Kings 18:21, and Matthew 16:15 as well as verses/portions of verses, are taken from the *Holy Bible*, New International Version®. NIV®. Copyright © 1973, 1978, 1984 by International Bible Society. Used by permission of Zondervan Publishing House. All rights reserved.

Some verses/portions of verses are taken from the *Holy Bible*, New Living Translation, copyright © 1996. Used by permission of Tyndale House Publishers, Inc., Wheaton, Illinois 60189. All rights reserved.

Some verses/portions of verses are taken from the *Holy Bible*, King James Version.

Some verses/portions of verses are taken from the *New American Standard Bible*, © 1960, 1962, 1963, 1968, 1971, 1972, 1973, 1975, 1977 by the Lockman Foundation. Used by permission.

This novel is a work of fiction. Names, characters, places, and incidents either are the product of the authors' imaginations or are used fictitiously. Any resemblance to actual events, locales, organizations, or persons, living or dead, is entirely coincidental and beyond the intent of either the authors or publisher.

Library of Congress Cataloging-in-Publication Data

Thoene, Bodie, date.
   Third watch / Bodie & Brock Thoene.
     p. cm. — (A.D. chronicles ; bk. 3)
   ISBN 0-8423-7512-0 — ISBN 0-8423-7513-9 (sc)
   1. Jesus Christ—Fiction. 2. Bible. N.T.—History of Biblical events—Fiction. I. Thoene, Brock. II. Title III. Series: Thoene, Bodie, date. A.D. chronicles ; bk. 3.
   PS3570.H46T475 2004
   813'.54—dc22   2004009719

Printed in the United States of America

10 09 08 07 06 05 04
 7   6   5   4   3   2   1

To all our friends at University of the Nations, YWAM, Kona—
For all your love and prayers—
Aloha and Mahalo Nui Loa.

The Spirit of the Sovereign Lord is on me,
because the Lord has anointed me
to preach good news to the poor.

He has sent me to bind up the brokenhearted,
to proclaim freedom for the captives
and release from darkness for the prisoners,
to proclaim the year of the Lord's favor.

ISAIAH 61:1-2

Prologue

"Who do men say that I am?"[1]

Yeshua of Nazareth tossed out the question one evening as He camped with His talmidim near the spring where the river was born. His disciples sat around the fire roasting quail on sticks for supper. Their shadows loomed against the rock face. An owl hooted from a tree outside their circle. Smoke stung Levi Mattityahu's eyes. John stirred the embers.

"What are the rumors then?" Yeshua asked. "Tell me. Who do men say that I am?"

His talmidim were so used to Him by then that they hardly glanced up from the flames as they replied, "No one knows for sure who you are: Prophet. Liar. Lawgiver. Rebel. Rabbi. Heretic. Good Man. Bad Man."

Such bland, insignificant definitions were like shadows on the rocks. No substance. No strength. After all, it took no commitment to call Yeshua "a good man."

But upon His *next* question the gates of eternity hinged. "Who do *you* say that I am?"

It was Shim'on who blurted out the answer around a mouthful of quail meat. Shim'on, licking his fingers, who spoke the truth straight-out and got it right on the first try. This surprised everyone, including Shim'on.

"Who do *you* say that I am? . . ."

Shim'on was a fisherman, not a poet. He said what he said so plainly that it seemed as if he believed it. But Shim'on did not believe it. Not really. Or at least he could not comprehend the complexity and significance of what he had just declared.

Perhaps at the time no one could comprehend what Shim'on's answer truly meant. No one. Not yet.

Even now, after everything, the vastness of Yeshua's identity and what He holds in His hand is impossible for the human mind to grasp.

> *He is*
> *the One who knows the beginning*
> *and the midpoint and the end of times.*
> *He knows*
> *the force of the elements,*
> *the organization of the universe,*
> *cycles of seasons and years,*
> *position of stars,*
> *personalities of men and beasts,*
> *powers of winds and thoughts of all men.*

It is written that an hour is coming when every knee will bow and every tongue confess that Yeshua Messiah is Adonai, the Lord.[2]

For every soul that moment will come.

Look! Yeshua approaches the shore and calls out The Question! You do not answer Him, yet the boat draws nearer. Its keel scrapes onto the sand. He steps into the water, wades to shore, takes your hand, looks you in the eyes and asks: "Who do you say that I am?"

Eternal destiny depends on the answer. You know the truth. Oh, yes. There's no denying it now. You know.

No excuses. Not like before.

But there was a time when Yeshua lived on earth among men and the only creatures who recognized Him were those fallen angels cast out of heaven with the Great Deceiver to rule this world. Demons possessed men, dwelt within mortal bodies, and held them in bondage.

Controlling the human mind, they whispered lies and fear and hope-lessness and rebellion and suicide to their human hosts. They peered out at the world through human eyes. They committed adultery, stole, cheated, and murdered with human hands. They lied, boasted, gos-siped, slandered, and blasphemed with human tongues.

And then The Light came to earth as the prophets foretold in Holy Scripture. Born as a man named Yeshua, which means "Salvation," He lived among us.

The Angel of the Lord. El Shaddai. Adonai. The Way. The Truth. The Life. The Living Word of God. Savior. Messiah. Redeemer. The Anointed One. El Olam. Ancient of Days.

So many names of grace and beauty to call Him—as many names as there are human needs to meet. And so The One Lord of All Eternity came to our world to ask each heart The One Question: *Who do* you *say I am?*

This is the story of the battle between The Truth and the Father of Lies. Each fought mightily for the souls of mankind.

Those who witnessed the conflict firsthand could not comprehend how ancient this war was, nor what the outcome meant for generations yet to be born.

On the day before Yeshua arrived in the Decapolis, unseen whisperers who served the Prince of Darkness knew The Light was coming to their shore. They had seen Him in heaven and remembered how He, The Lord of All the Angel Armies, had cast them out. They trembled because of it.

Before the citizens awoke in the land east of the Sea of Galilee that morning, demons flew from their lairs and looked west over the calm surface of the lake.

Yes. Truth was coming! The One, the Enemy of Evil, had turned His eyes upon the Prince of this world and his legions at last!

They hissed in terror to one another. The end of their dominion was threatened. They must band together to fight!

Stir it up! Stir it up! Summon the winds!

Though their voices were inaudible to the human ear, the tremors of spiritual fury and defiance oppressed the souls of mortals with unexplained dread.

The people of the ten cities feared disaster, though they did not know how or why or by whom. All agreed, however, that something sinister was coming to the land of the Decapolis.

The air crackled with omens.

The sky was bloodred at sunrise.

Flies swarmed. Goats miscarried.

A mad dog, snarling and frothing at the mouth, staggered through the marketplace of Gadara. Pandemonium! Pursued and stoned by the people, the creature collapsed, convulsed, and died beside the well.

By the well, mind you! A very bad sign!

At that instant, outside the city, the Madman of Gadara ran shrieking from his limestone cave, the tomb of the priest of Molech. He climbed the bluff above the town, rattled the broken chains on his wrists, and began to howl. Dancing and weeping, he recited incantations and pronounced curses on the heads of the citizens who had killed the dog.

The old hag, prophetess of Gadara, saw a vision of the god Pan, the bloodied horns and cloven hoofs covered in human gore. In her vision Pan, ancient god of all the Pantheon, galloped through the tombs and rallied the souls of the dead to fight for him.

Fight what? Fight whom? the people asked.

The dream was a portent, the prophetess warned. The One, The Judge of All, The Executioner was coming soon to the Decapolis to destroy their way of life.

The sullen day ended.

Heaven and earth, water and wind grew dark and violent. People huddled in their houses. The night sky poured down rain and hail. Water swept away spring gardens and knocked blossoms from the branches of fruit trees. Soil turned to mud, which oozed over the terraces. Stone walls tumbled. Roofs leaked. Streets became bogs. Children screamed in their sleep that the Madman of Gadara was coming to devour them!

Sheep in the pens crouched together in misery. Birds perched under dripping eaves. The herd of two thousand swine, being fattened to feed the Roman garrison in Syria, grazed in the rocky fields above the lake. They were dangerously restless.

Six fearful swineherds drew swords against an unseen enemy. They huddled in a shallow cave above the sea and prayed to their gods that daylight would come soon.

Had there ever been such a gale upon the Sea of Galilee? The roar of the storm was punctuated by the crash of a thunderclap.

What was that on the crest of a breaker? Yes! There! A small open boat near to sinking!

Driving rain pounded the faces of the herdsmen as they stepped from their shelter and strained to observe the drama.

Lightning arched from cloud to cloud, illuminating the life-and-death struggle of a doomed vessel tossed by monstrous swells.

The herdsmen bellowed to one another: "A followin' sea washin' over her stern! She'll be swamped!"

"The fools! They've packed her to the gills with passengers! Look there! How many in the boat? She'll never make it. Nay."

A blazing monochrome pulse burned the image on their retinas. Threads of silver rain slashing the shredded sail. Hull lifted up and poised for destruction. A plunge from the crest, twenty feet down into the trough. Rudder high and useless, out of the water. Panicked faces of a dozen men about to die. And there, upon the outcropping, the Madman of Gadara cheered the lightning bolts, urged the waves to greater heights, ranted in favor of destruction for the travelers!

Storm light flickered and winked off. Darkness. Cries of terror and calls for mercy were carried on the gale. Above the sound of their pitiful entreaties were the clearer, stronger incantations of the Madman: "Come wrath! Rise! Rise up! Come wrath and torment! Up from the pit, old enmity! Kill him! Kill him! Hold back the time! Keep sealed the Abyss! Drown him, ancient powers! Into the sea! Into the sea! As he did to the chariots of Egypt, do now to him! Bury him! Bury him beneath the sea!"

Surf boomed against the pebbled shore at the base of the cliffs. The herdsmen watched the dance of the Madman.

"He's the evil himself, Madman is! Look at him! Naked as a buzzard! Flappin' in the deluge! Enjoyin' the distress of fools!"

"It's an entertainment. The gods themselves are havin' good sport with 'em. They deserve what they get. Crossin' on such an evil night."

"The moon is full behind the clouds. Madman roams about, cursin' the world when the moon is full."

"Here's a sword for his belly if he comes near me or my hogs."

"Pity him. The storm's got him all stirred up."

"And the hogs as well."

"Me too."

"Aye. Wish the clouds would part. I could do with moonlight."

"Wish we'd have another bolt to see the sailors die by."

"We'll see them drowned on the beach come mornin'."

"Aye. We'll need to bury 'em before the hogs have 'em for breakfast! Or Madman strips the bodies. You know what a mess that would be."

"The fools."

"Perhaps their deaths will appease the gods."

"Better them than us."

"Out on the sea on a night like this. What were they thinkin'?"

Shafts of lightning exploded from the clouds, blasting the water all around the craft and illuminating the last seconds of life for the unfortunate victims.

"Won't be long now!" one of the watching herdsmen muttered. "One more breaker over the stern and she's sunk."

An instant of moonlight broke through the clouds and then . . .

The swineherds saw Him.

A fierce man, plainly visible in the bow. Hair and beard and clothes swept by the force of the storm. Arms stretched out fearlessly as if to embrace destruction. Head thrown back and mouth wide in a defiant shout!

From the boat a luminous beam flashed skyward, up from His right hand like a sword, deflecting a forked spike of descending fire and piercing the underbelly of the storm! And then the retreating wind howled like a thousand demons. Towering waves shuddered and collapsed beneath the weight of His command. Clouds splintered and broke, rolling back at His roar: "Shalom! Peace!"

And there was peace.

"*Raphah!* Be still!"

Tranquil silence.

"And know that I AM . . ."

A bright moon floated in the star-filled sky. Land and sea glistened quiet, clean, bright, and obedient. The little ship, suddenly set right, sailed on across the water in the silver path of the moon's reflection.

The Madman of Gadara sank to his knees with a tortured scream. "No! No! Not yet! Not yet!" Sobbing, he crept from the outcropping and slunk into the shadows of his cave.

The swineherds conversed in a cautious whisper.

"Did you see that?"

"Aye."

"Have you ever seen such a thing?"

"Never."

"The wind! The wind!"

"Never."

"And now look! Still afloat! Headin' right for us! To our shore."

"Strange. Strange."

The Madman's incoherent wails brought them to subdued silence for a time. Then the whispers began again.

"Madman's worse than ever. You know how he gets when he's upset. We'll have to warn the townsfolk to go the long way 'round. Haven't seen him this bad off since his little sister died and his brother brought news of it to his cave."

"Aye. Terrible. Terrible."

"Somethin's up."

"Wish I was home in bed."

"Great Pan, god of us herdsmen, protect us!"

"Suppose that boat's a phantom?"

"Aye. Perhaps a vision."

"The passengers, tormented spirits!"

"Shut up, will you? They look solid enough to me."

"I'll be glad when it's day."

Sand rasped under the keel as the craft drifted ashore. On one side a husky figure jumped out and splashed through knee-deep water with a mooring line slung over his shoulder. The man who had authority over the surf and surge stepped off the fishing boat onto a boulder, then onto the beach.

Amidships a pair of dark-haired men, brothers by their looks, leaned together near the mast. "'Where is your faith?' he asked us," one of the men quoted.

"Aye, where indeed?" the other man repeated. "Thought we were dead for certain! John . . . who *is* Yeshua? He gives orders to the wind . . . and water . . . and they obey!"

"Who is he?" one of the swineherds unconsciously echoed.

"No business of ours," another swineherd cautioned. "Such as us mixin' with wizards and phantoms? Not likely!"

"Wait!" a third herder called. "Look at Madman. Headin' straight for 'em!"

Bounding from rock to rock like a goat, chains clanking, hair and beard fluttering in the wind, Madman darted from moonlight to shadow in a headlong plunge from his perch. Appearing and disappearing, his speed amplified. He also seemed to be multiplying, a host of demons streaking shoreward.

"Should we shout?" a swineherd wondered aloud.

"Worse'n the storm, he is. Wish they was back in the gale, they will."

"Should we shout?"

"Too late."

Madman was already there, crouching on the last ledge above the strand, like a lion ready to pounce.

The husky man saw him, clenched his fists, bellowed a warning. "Watch it! Look there!"

The men who looked like brothers grabbed up oars and waved them like clubs. "Stay back, you!"

Others huddled together in the boat.

The man who had calmed the storm motioned with the same gesture He had used on tempest and billow. Then He stepped forward to confront Madman.

Screaming an inarticulate cry of pain, as if scalded or pierced with a dagger, the lunatic jumped—or tumbled—landing mere paces away from his opponent . . . and fell facedown in the gravel. At the top of his voice he shouted, "What do you want with me, Yeshua? What? You who are bar El Olam, bar El'Elyon, bar ELoHiYM. The Son of the Most High God . . . what do you want with me?"

"Come out!" Yeshua directed. "Leave him!"

"What? What'd he say?" a swineherd wondered. "What'd Madman call him? Who did he say he was?"

"What did he . . . how did he know the Master's name?" John queried, dropping the oar and grabbing his brother's arm. "Ya'acov, how could he know?"

Moonlight welded Yeshua and Madman together: the one an upright flame of burnished silver, the other a lumpy shadow prostrate before Him. When the two outlines merged, Madman writhed in agony. "Don't . . . I beg you . . . don't torture me!"

"What's happening?" a herdsman asked. "Can't see."

"What is your name?" the onlookers heard Yeshua demand.

"That's rich, that is," one of the swineherd commented. "Madman don't even—"

A wavering, garbled note, like a flurry of discordant trumpets or all the flutes of a panpipe blown at once, responded. *"Legion,"* it whistled, grunted, groaned, and rasped. *"Because we are . . .* many."

"Legion," the voices said. *An army corps,* the Greek-speaking ones heard.

"Leshon," it pronounced. *Accuser, Slanderer,* the Hebrew-speaking ones heard.

"Did y' hear that?" the men on the rocky slope asked each other.

"Did you hear that?" the men in the boat concurred.

"Too right!" were the replies. "Made my hair stand up, it did."

"Shh!" others urged.

The reply came from Madman's lips: *"Don't send us into the Abyss,"* a pleasant baritone pleaded.

"Not into the pit," a husky voice implored, using Madman's throat.

"Not before the time!" an owl-like screech begged, forming the request with Madman's tongue.

Yeshua, stern-faced, implacable, spoke no word that was not a command. He accepted no argument. He regarded the man and disregarded the voices.

"Let us go into the pigs," a sweet childlike voice suggested.

"Yes, into the swine," an oily tenor agreed.

"Eh? What'd he . . . they . . . it . . . say?" a herdsman questioned.

Yeshua raised His hand. "ELoHiYM commands you: El HaYaM . . . into the sea!"

Madman's body quivered from the top of his Medusa-like locks to the horn-hard soles of his bare feet. Spasms that began at opposite black and jagged fingernails met in the middle of his scarred back. Madman's spine arched. Then he sagged, like a sail when the wind dies away.

The moon, drifting lower, illuminated the upper reaches of the cliff. Caves in its face were revealed as eye sockets in a skull.

Approaching dawn aged the blackness of night to gray.

"S'pose he's dead?" one of the herdsmen guessed. "Well, I'll be—"

"Wait!" another cautioned. "It ain't over . . . yet."

On the tableland above the precipice the herd of pigs stirred. A boar hog lifted his snout, snorting with alarm. A pair of shoats left off foraging among the fallen acorns. They chased each other in a frenzied whirligig of squeals and grunts. Two sows who, seconds before, had lain side by side, bellowed, bared slavering fangs, and slashed at each other in fury. Soon the whole herd was on its feet, milling and screeching.

"Gotta stop this before . . . ," a lone voice observed.

"Who?" two swineherds inquired in unison. "You go then."

The herd swirled and rampaged with all the fury exhibited by the storm. Then, simultaneously, two thousand pigs turned to face the lake and broke into a run. They gained momentum as they thundered down the slope.

The herdsmen of the hill and the men gathered around the boat watched in astonishment as the pigs never hesitated or broke stride. Two thousand hogs flowed over the edge of the cliff. The rumble of their galloping charge became a roar of successive crashes. Cascading like a waterfall, the moving mass spilled into the embrace of the lake. Spray jetted up toward the heights in near continuous fountains. Then they were gone into the depths.

El HaYaM . . . into the sea, just like the Egyptians drowned in the sea. And once again ELoHiYM, the Lord God, used the depths as a judgment.

Herdsmen and fishermen were transfixed, staring at the ripples, as if expecting an eruption to prolong the disturbance.

Not so Yeshua. Having whipped off His cloak, He covered Madman with it, raised the shuddering form with strong hands on the man's shoulders, looked deep into clear eyes.

The static moment lasted a single beat longer, then was broken by Yeshua's shouted directions: "John, bring a spare tunic. And oil and bandages. Ya'acov, get a fire going. Shim'on, bring something to remove these shackles." And to the man He asked again, "What's your name?"

This time the reply, in a voice shaking with emotion, was "Nefesh."

But the herdsmen did not wait to hear the reply. They scattered in all directions. Two ran toward Gadara; two went toward the country estate of the hogs' owner. And two simply faded into the hills, vowing to find another line of work.

Dawn broke over the land. It illuminated the far side of the lake first, then spread eastward with a rush, dispelling the last shadows from the country around Gadara.

Within an hour the entire population of Gadara, save one, alerted and alarmed by the excited reports of the swineherds, crowded onto the strand. Only the prophetess refused to come along. She sent the warning, "Get rid of him," but she herself remained indoors, with shutters latched and door bolted.

Fingers stabbed the air. "Up there's where we watched from," the herdsmen related. "There's where we first saw Madman. And there, right there below the cliff, that's where the herd . . . vanished."

The audience followed the story intently, until one, an innkeeper, demanded, "So, where is he then? Where's Madman?"

"He's . . . he's right there," the reporter insisted, sounding as if he doubted his own words.

Seated beside Yeshua, bathed, dressed, sandals on his feet, eating a meal of bread and broiled fish, was the former madman. Ignoring the stares and speculation, Nefesh engaged Yeshua in earnest conversation.

The innkeeper peered closer. "It is him," he confirmed.

The crowd murmured, pushing the innkeeper forward.

He cleared his throat, approached Yeshua, and addressed Him diffidently. "Sir." He tried on the title conveyed by the witnesses. "Son of God Most High. I want . . . that is, the town thinks . . . we all want to ask you somethin'. Would you please leave us? Meanin' no disrespect, of course. Would you go away from here? After you've finished your breakfast, of course," the innkeeper added hastily.

Yeshua nodded.

John and Ya'acov grimaced and shook their heads sadly.

"Take me with you," Nefesh implored.

The demons asked Yeshua if they could go into the swine.

The townsfolk asked Yeshua to leave them and go away.

But Nefesh—restored, healed, in his right mind—wanted just to be allowed to stay near Yeshua forever.

Yeshua smiled. "Not yet. I cannot stay, but you can be my witness here. Go home. Tell everyone how much God has done for you today."

Nefesh smiled back, even if a little sorrow remained in his eyes. "I will, Lord. Yeshua, Son of the Most High God. You can count on me."

PART I

As soon as Jesus was baptized, He went up out of the water. At that moment heaven was opened, and He saw the Spirit of God descending like a dove and lighting on Him. And a voice from heaven said, "This is My Son, whom I love; with Him I am well pleased."

Then Jesus was led by the Spirit into the desert to be tempted by the devil. After fasting forty days and forty nights, He was hungry. The tempter came to Him and said, "If You are the Son of God, tell these stones to become bread."

Jesus answered, "It is written: 'Man does not live on bread alone, but on every word that comes from the mouth of God.'"

MATTHEW 3:16–4:4

It was a miracle she was alive. Everyone said so. A miracle. Ordained by Yahweh. The life of Zahav was important to the Almighty. She was born to accomplish something.

Every Jew who worshipped in the synagogue of Caesarea Philippi knew the details of her brother's death and of the murder of her righteous grandfather at the hand of Herod the Great thirty years before.

Children at the Torah school sat on the edge of their seats when her story was told. It was like this:

Zahav's mother, eight months pregnant, hiding down a well with her tiny son as Herod's soldiers searched Beth-lehem and slaughtered every male child under two years old.

The whimper from the child as the captain drew water to wash the blood of the innocents from his hands, his face, his sword.

Discovery!

The fight as Zahav's mother resisted. A blow to her face, which knocked her down! The blade of the Samaritan plunging into the little boy's heart!

The heart of the mother, breaking.

Breaking.

Yes. It was quite a story. And a true one.

So Zahav had been born in a cave as her mother and father fled Judea, carrying nothing but a single Torah scroll, wrapped in clothes that had belonged to their slaughtered son.

And marring the newborn girl's face was a crimson birthmark in the shape of a hand. It was as though the brute who had struck Zahav's mother had somehow slapped the infant within her. The wound of Herodian brutality, and thus the memory of that terrible night was imprinted indelibly onto the face of little Zahav.

Her mother, looking at the disfigured cheek, had cried out. She insisted the baby be named Zarev, like the melted wax of a candle, because all light had melted from her soul.

But the baby's grieving father took her from the arms of her mother. He wrapped the child in his prayer shawl.

And then a miracle happened. Tiny fingers grasped the fringes of his tallith, pulling the knots and single azure strand of the fringe up to her mouth as if she were kissing the ineffable Name of the One God after a prayer!

Yes. A miracle. Who could deny it?

For a baby born only minutes before to kiss the tzitzit of her father's prayer shawl where the letters of Yahweh's name are woven! Yes. A wonder! Who had heard of such a thing?

It was a sign of hope sent from heaven by way of this precious one. She carried with her the promise to the grieving parents that God was still God. The infant sons of Beth-lehem who had perished at the command of Herod now lived in heaven with the Lord. The infant's soul had embraced her brother when he arrived, and he had whispered a secret to her as she departed. Why else would a baby know the command of the Lord about the fringes and fulfill the command even in such horrible circumstances?

Thus encouraged, the father had cradled his daughter and emerged from the cavern. The night sky was frosted with stars from horizon to horizon. He kissed the newborn's marred face and lifted her high before the throne of El Olam!

"Blessed are you, O Adonai, King of the Universe, who has sanctified us by your commandments and has commanded us to wrap ourselves in fringed garments. My daughter shall not be called Zarev! She is Zahav, 'Shimmering like Gold,' just as the golden promise in your Torah shimmers like a bright star to guide us!"

After some days, mother and father and newborn daughter fled north from Judea to the foot of snowcapped Mount Hermon. They came to the village of Paneas, which later was called Caesarea Philippi.

There was a derelict synagogue in the village. It had been built 170 years earlier by Jewish refugees before the Maccabee rebellion. The synagogue had no Torah scroll. It had no rabbi. Only ten old men survived in the congregation. The city was infested with apostate Jews who had fallen into pagan worship. So many had turned from the Lord. Barely enough faithful Jews remained for a single minyan to gather and pray. These ten had been praying for a miracle. Praying for a rabbi to come. Praying for a rabbi with a Torah scroll.

And the miracle came. . . .

It was just past midsummer in the seventeenth year of Emperor Tiberius. Tonight Mount Hermon loomed up against the backdrop of starry skies. The scent of pine wafted down from verdant slopes.

Zahav, spinster daughter of Eliyahu, Chief Rabbi of Caesarea Philippi, sat on her window ledge and inhaled deeply. It was hot. But the breeze from the mountain was nice.

This was Zahav's favorite time of day. It was, in fact, the only hour she could have a single uninterrupted thought.

Shops below her second-story balcony were shuttered. The rattle of carts and the lowing of livestock passing in the street had ceased. Dickering merchants, squabbling children, harried mothers, and the endless discussions among talmidim about the meanings of Torah portions had fallen silent at suppertime.

Thirty years had passed since Rabbi Eliyahu had arrived in Paneas with one Torah scroll, a wife, and a baby. The village had blossomed into a city. Rabbi Eliyahu and his wife had four other children after Zahav. They had dwelt in exile, but in peace.

The tetrarch Philip was a son of old Herod. But Philip was, in temperament, more like a docile ox than a rampaging bull.

Philip had survived the familial slaughters of his father by laying low and rarely offering an opinion more controversial than which wine tasted best with mutton or fish. Philip ruled his subjects with the same benign neglect that he cherished. Taxes were negligible. The trade route from Damascus to the sea brought commerce and visitors as never before.

Now the synagogue of Caesarea Philippi flourished in the midst of the pagan north country. The Jewish Quarter of the city had a population of three thousand Jews who worshipped the God of Israel in Rabbi Eliyahu's synagogue. There was a Torah academy and a kosher inn, where religious Jews traveling the Damascus Road could stay and eat with confidence.

Outside the Jewish Quarter lived three thousand apostate descendants of Abraham.

The two groups of Jews did not mix.

Zahav's work had continued until very late. And all evening her father had read Torah aloud as she wove the tzitzit . . . on four woolen prayer shawls. No one could make a tallith the way Zahav made a tallith. Everyone said so. God forbid, anyone in the congregation should buy a tallith from anyone but the rabbi's daughter. Zahav knew something about prayer shawls and fringes, didn't she? After all, she was the infant who kissed the fringes of her father's prayer shawl when she was merely minutes old.

Now Zahav considered her reputation as she finished off a plum with a luxurious slurp and pitched the pit onto the empty street.

Of course the legend of her birth had grown until she had not simply kissed the fringes but also recited the Shema. Then the Ten Commandments. After that, in the voice of Mosheh, she had commanded her father to go north with his Torah scroll to the synagogue of Paneas. They would live there and be happy. Someday Messiah would come visit. Zahav would give Him a prayer shawl.

Over the years considerable effort had been made by the rabbi to dispel these legends. To no avail.

The tales were interesting and good for business. Every mother of a bar mitzvah–age son felt the same about it. God forbid, any tallith but a tallith made by the hands of Zahav should be worn for a son's bar mitzvah celebration!

Always somebody else's son. Never Zahav's. Somebody else's wedding canopy. Never, never Zahav's.

That was the price Zahav paid for the handprint that disfigured her face. She could never fall in love. Not permitted. Never marry. Never. Unthinkable. Never have children. By rabbinic law, such a birthmark excluded her from marriage and a family.

She would remain the daughter of the chief rabbi of Caesarea Philippi until she died. She would always be the infant who spoke and kissed the tzitzit at the hour of her birth.

She could not admit it to anyone, but she was lonely. Yes. Lonely.

Bearing the reminder of Beth-lehem's grief so plainly upon her cheek. The loss of those children. The deaths of so many little ones. The sorrow on Zahav's face never completely left her heart. As if they were her little boys somehow. Her arms were empty; she felt empty. Lonely. Dead before she died; buried though still walking around.

But never mind, she told herself. She had so much to be thankful for. The evil hand that had struck her mother had marked Zahav low on the left cheek. Behind Zahav's veil the disfigurement was nearly impossible to see. Her eyes were a pretty brown, Papa often told her. Very nice eyes. Pretty. As long as she did not remove the veil.

Often travelers, complete strangers, arrived at the door to inquire about purchasing a tallith from her. They had heard about her from this person or that, you see, and had seen her work. And so . . . very nice, it was.

Zahav felt their curious stares boring into her as they imagined the brand of that evil time bearing witness behind her veil. She tried to console herself. At least it had been good for business.

Not much consolation, to be sure.

But her hands were always busy—weaving, creating beautiful gifts for other women's sons. Other women's husbands.

Zahav's papa was proud of her. Her four younger siblings had married and set up their own homes. When Mama died five years ago, Papa had turned the management of the household over to her. What did it matter if she had no husband? no children? It was ordained, wasn't it? From the very beginning. Papa believed that. Told her she was meant to live as a spinster and manage his house. She was taught to read and write Hebrew. Allowed to study Torah with him in the evening. Why should she need a family of her own when she had Torah and the respect of everyone in the community?

Zahav searched the stars. Beautiful. Who could she tell? She wished someone sat beside her so she could talk about the stars. About what she felt when she looked at them.

"Adonai. Do you see me here?"

Somewhere, from inside a little house in the deserted labyrinth of streets, a baby cried.

A baby.

Zahav sighed as she listened. Leaning back against the window frame, she pictured a young mother wrapped in the arms of a sleeping husband. She could see them nestled together. Sighing in unison. Stirring at the baby's cry.

She could almost see herself, moving his hand from around her waist. Almost.

What would it be like? Slipping from bed to nurse her baby. . . .

The shop of the flute maker was just beyond the boundaries of Caesarea Philippi's Jewish Quarter. From the cot in the corner of the downstairs room Diana whispered, "Play your flute for me, Alexander."

Her eyes fixed on the instrument lying amid the clutter of unwashed dishes. The chaos that defined Diana's approaching death expanded each day, tumbling out from the center of Alexander's grief to the perimeters of the house where he fashioned and sold musical instruments.

The shop had closed three weeks earlier, when Diana could no longer climb stairs. Now only one neat square remained in all the space that was theirs. The place where she lay. Her domain. Tidy. Organized. She would have it no other way. Clean linens and nightgown every morning. The bowl of fragrant roses to combat the scent of physical anguish. Fresh water to wash her spindly body. Each day less and less of her to wash. Less and less. He did his best.

"Please," she rasped, her thirty-six years looking like one hundred. "A song for me, Alexander."

What good was music now? What solace could she find in a song? What comfort in melodies that only brought back memories of happier days?

Alexander stroked her thinning hair. What could he do? What? He left her side, lifting the guttering candle to retrieve his instrument.

Light fell briefly on the four-year-old boy huddled in the corner. Their son. Their only son. Hero. The child they had longed for, waited for.

Alexander had forgotten to put him to bed. Forgotten, he was there with them in the room.

"Still awake, Hero?"

Hero could not acknowledge his father's words.

Flute in one hand, Alexander passed the candle slowly before the boy's eyes. He was awake, yes. Conscious, yes. Sometimes it was hard for Alexander to tell. But tonight Hero was awake. Aware.

Arms clasped around his knees, the child began to rock as though he heard a melody. But Hero heard nothing. Not his mother's words as she labored to ask Alexander again, "One song before I sleep. Please, Alexander."

Alexander lifted the flute to his lips and began "The Shepherd's Bride." He had written the song for Diana when they were eighteen, when he first knew he loved her. In the beginning their lives had overflowed with so many dreams.

But five stillborn babies over twelve years had nearly destroyed Diana's ability to hope. During those dark days she had forbidden Alexander to play her song.

And then a dream came true. On the day Hero was born, Alexander joyfully stood at her bedside and performed as never before. How could he have imagined his infant son could not hear him? that Hero would never hear a note of his father's music?

Now perhaps the familiar tune would comfort Diana in the final days of her life. But Alexander was the one who needed comforting. After three bars he paused, then tried to go on. He could not. Swallowing hard, holding back emotion, Alexander lowered the instrument.

"I can't . . . I . . . can't anymore. Forgive me. Maybe later, eh? I'm sorry. Oh, Diana."

There was pity in her reply. "Later. Later. Yes. Play it another time. You're tired."

Hero's frightened eyes lapped up the grief of his father, the torment of his mother. Even without hearing, without fully comprehending, the boy seemed to grasp the meaning of the scene before him.

Alexander moved the candle to the table, stooped, and caressed his son's cheek. "Dear Hero," the father murmured. "You know, don't you, Hero? You knew long before I noticed. She was pale. Thin. I didn't see it. But you. You notice everything, don't you, Hero? Even without hearing. Without speech. You clung to her, cried for her when she left the room, knowing she would leave us soon forever. Your eyes are ears and tongue enough if anyone takes the time to look at you. I look in your eyes and hear your sorrow. What will become of you, Hero? How will you bear her going?"

Hero rocked more violently. He moaned.

"Alexander? What will become of him when I am gone?" Diana did not take her fevered gaze from the child.

"Don't . . . Diana . . ."

"I have to know. He needs so much. So much . . . mercy. And the world is never merciful to the wounded."

Alexander choked back the urge to cry out, "And what about me? Who will love me? Where is mercy for me?" Head bowed, exhausted from the ordeal, he stood stiffly, towering over his son. "You know I'll take care of him."

"He can't sleep alone," she reminded him. "So afraid. Poor baby. Poor Hero. Will you hold him when he is afraid?"

Alexander acknowledged with a nod and went to her side. "There's time yet, Diana. Another day."

"No. No. I'm so tired."

"Don't go . . . to sleep. Not yet! Diana! Don't . . . sleep . . . yet."

"You should rest awhile too, Alexander."

"No. Please. I can't sleep." He had not let himself drift off for more than minutes in two days. He feared she would leave him if he slept. "I'm not tired."

From the shadows behind them little Hero sobbed quietly. It was as though the child felt the imminent approach of death. He crept toward his mother on all fours like a whipped animal.

Diana put out her arms to the boy, pulling him onto the cot with the last of her strength. Fingers stroking the towhead, she whispered his name over and over. "Hero. Hero. My boy. My boy. Mama loves you. Always . . . Hero. Remember . . . Mama . . . loves . . ." Her breath on his cheek soothed him.

Pan, god of fertility, nature, and song, Alexander prayed silently, addressing the patron deity of the city and his guild. *You, Pan, oldest of all the Pantheon of gods. I see now that you take pleasure in our misery!*

Haven't I done everything you asked of me? So long we waited, she and I. So many years we begged you for this child. We offered our baby to you if you would not kill him like you killed all the others. So many stillborn babies before our little Hero breathed and wailed and suckled at her breast. And you, god of music and musicians, benefactor of my fathers, you gave us false hope! For your amusement you made my child deaf and mute. Pan, god of nature, you struck our lamb dumb, and now you fill him with panic at your will. Now you take his mother from him when no one else can comfort him but her! I see now how false you are. How you love our suffering. Liar! How cruel you are!

Hero wept quietly as he lay beside his mother and stroked her face with trembling fingers.

Urgent instruction tumbled out of Diana's mouth. "Alexander! You must tell Hero every day that my spirit lives . . . in Elysium. Somehow he'll hear you! Tell him . . . to dream . . . dreams of me . . . there in that place. A beautiful place where . . . where . . . there reigns an unknown god of mercy. Oh, if only there was such a place and such a god who would love us like a father! The god of your fathers. Tell me. Please tell me about him!"

"I know so little about—"

"Oh, that such a god would have mercy on me!"

"I know . . . nothing . . . about the god of my ancestors."

"Alexander! I'm afraid! What if . . . what if . . . I never see you again? What if Hero's nightmares are not dreams at all?" Diana stared in horror at the niche where the idol of Pan grinned mischievously down at their anguish.

Alexander stooped by her side, placed the flute on her pillow, and embraced her and Hero together. He could not let her know how frightened he was, how terrified that the end was inevitable. A few days, the doctor had told him. She could not survive longer. What if there was no Elysium? No life after life. No peace. No place for meeting. No eternal music. What if the long sleep of death offered visions like those haunting Hero each night? What if final sleep meant an eternity of nightmares, darkness, and demons?

"Diana! Don't be afraid." Alexander wiped away tears with the back of his hand and lied to ease her panic. "I know, my darling! I know you will be there among the gods!"

"No! No! They've deceived us!"

"I'll follow you later, and I'll find you walking in green fields with the sun on your face! Beside a pool of water reflecting a golden sky. Listen, Diana! I'll play my flute in that place and you'll sing with me! Someday Hero will hear the music of his mother and father and dance for us!"

She stiffened and arched her neck as a spasm of pain coursed through her. Her eyes locked on Alexander's face, pleading. Then she looked beyond him, above him? She embraced Hero's cheek with her left hand. Pointing skyward with her right arm she cried, "See, there! Hero! Look . . . Alexander!"

The illness spoke through her. She was hallucinating again, as she had for days and would until the end came.

He begged. "A little more time. How will I manage? Please! Don't leave me! Diana! No!"

She whispered, "Alexander. Won't you let me sleep?"

He stroked her hair. "Not yet. Not yet. You must not . . . no. I can't bear it if you leave us tonight. A few days. Stay with me as long as you can."

CHAPTER 2

Forty miles to the south of Caesarea Philippi, the Bethsaida estate of Manaen and Susanna bar Talmai was silent, slumbering in the swale of the countryside across the Jordan from Galilee. Insects trilled from the bar Talmai orchards and vineyards three miles north of the village of Bethsaida.

Susanna opened her eyes. Her young husband's place on the bed beside her was vacant, cold. How long had Manaen been awake?

He stood at the open window, his back to her, as if searching for the first glimmer of dawn. His chest was bare; a towel was tied around his waist.

"Manaen?"

The muscular physique of a wrestler was framed by starlight. Beyond him, Orion hung low in the eastern sky. The constellation proved a fitting backdrop to Manaen's brooding, since the starry hero of ancient legend had also lost his eyes in a quarrel over love.

Manaen did not move or acknowledge Susanna. She gazed at his silhouette and smiled. Patting the bed she whispered, "I was dreaming the statue of a Greek god came to life and appeared to me. He had your face. Your body. Your voice."

"And my eyes, too? Stone blind?"

Susanna ignored his bitter comment. "Orion. You know the story."

"His eyes put out by a king because of some quarrel over a woman. The daughter of the king, I think it was."

"And his sight was miraculously restored. I can't remember how. Something about true love."

"True love is blind. I'm proof of that."

"Married six weeks and I can't get enough of you. It's good I didn't know about love before the wedding. I would have gone mad with desire. You've made me wanton, Manaen."

The breeze from the Sea of Galilee stirred the curtain around him. She turned down the sheet and sighed. Dark hair tumbled over her shoulders. Her voice was languid, inviting, as she coaxed him. "Manaen? Come back to bed."

He did not move. Did not reply. His face was fixed. Blind eyes stared toward the east as he waited for a sunrise he could not see.

"Manaen?" she soothed, knowing that she could comfort his grief at the loss of his sight with the softness of her skin and the scent of her perfume. "Will you come back to bed? back to me? Love?"

"It'll be morning soon."

"Yes. Yes. Soon. But there's time. Servants are still asleep. Come back to bed. We can play together awhile."

He seemed not to hear her. "I dreamed a dream last night."

"Of me?" She would not yield to his melancholy. She would draw him back from the darkness that engulfed his soul. They would make love and he would forget everything but her!

"I dreamed of dawn. I could see again. See the sun rising over the mountains. Stars fading away as the sky ripened like an apple. A hundred shades of red."

"It's hours until daylight."

"For me, it's forever."

"Come back to bed. I'm the only light you need."

"And I dreamed about . . . about my brother."

"Demos? A nightmare then." She sat up, disappointed that he would not be tempted away from self-pity.

"Maybe not a dream. A memory. We were boys again. Swimming in the waves of Tiberias. Stealing grapes from the royal arbor and cheese from the governor's cold shed."

"Your brother always was a thief."

"Not always. I was the thief. Younger but braver."

"And Demos the more devious."

"A better liar," Manaen conceded. "I stole the cheese, and Demos managed to lie our way out of trouble. He saved my hide that summer."

"So he could steal your life . . . and your inheritance . . . and my love when you had grown to be a man."

"He was my brother until Father died. And then . . . he changed." Manaen raised his fingers to the scarred orbs that had been eyes. "Susanna, every night I feel the dawn approach. I sense it, hear it before it comes. As the third watch slips away I wake up as if I'm waiting for something . . . something. The wind from the lake. Birds beginning to stir. I dreamed it last night. A cruel dream. Sunlight. Golden. Bright. Like a starving man dreams about food."

"Demos only stole your sight."

"He may as well have taken my life."

Susanna flared. "And then? What about me? What would've happened to me? If you had been killed, your brother would've . . . you know what he would've done to me. In his life it was said that he out-Heroded the great Herod. A legend of perversion . . . everyone in Yerushalayim knows what sort of monster your brother was. His one interest in marrying me was so he could steal my property and keep me prisoner. He would have auctioned me off as entertainment at his orgies. And I would have paid a ransom to get free. What do I care about orchards and vineyards? If I could've given them all up to be with you I would've done it. Do you think they mattered? I'm sick of your self-pity. What about me, Manaen? Isn't my love enough?"

"If I could just see your face, Susanna! See you."

"Do you know you close your eyelids when we make love? Your hands aren't blind. They've explored my estate and know each secret turning more intimately than two eyes ever could. Your lips know by heart the path leading to the well of my pleasure. Oh, my love! You lift the cup and drink your fill until my thirst is satisfied and there's nothing left to offer you but my sighs. Have I ever left you thirsting? What are two eyes compared to other senses? Come back to bed, Manaen."

"Outside our bed I'm chained by darkness. You think I don't hear the whispers in the marketplace? Herod Antipas and his court have returned to the Galil. His servants and spies are everywhere. In

Bethsaida I recognized the voices. They recognize me. No doubt they're carrying tales of blind Manaen bar Talmai back to the royal villa. Herod Antipas and Herodias have something to amuse themselves over supper."

"Can't you be happy? We're together. It's everything we hoped for! Prayed for! For a year Herod Antipas forced us apart, pushed your vile, perverted brother on me so they could get my father's estates! And I held out. Waiting, always waiting for you to come for me! Demos is dead now. Be glad of it! We've won! We're together! I love you."

He turned to her, stumbled to the bed. His eyes were seared over, marbled white from the red-hot blade of a knife. "Look at me! How can you love this?"

She threw her arms around him and pulled him close, stroking his back, running her fingers through his thick thatch of dark blond hair. "If you love me, Manaen, don't mourn for a light you can't see! Or for a brother who would have brutalized me and killed you . . . if you hadn't killed him first!"

"I'm sorry!" He groaned and touched her cheek. "Sorry."

She kissed his forehead, eyelids, nose. Her lips lingered on his mouth. "Come back to bed, will you? Please?"

Breathless, wanting her now, he raised his face to hers. "Sorry. Sorry. I don't mean to. I . . .you know, Susanna . . . I love you! I do love you. More than light . . . more than . . ."

"Yes. I know. I know." She silenced him with kisses. "Come back to bed. It doesn't matter if the sun never rises."

Who could have known what the year would bring?

Sometime earlier that year the *am ha aretz*, the people of the land, had sensed Yeshua's imminent departure, the wrapping up, the setting of all things in order.

The opposition was growing. Too soon the ones in charge of the world—the ones who always won, no matter what the contest—would put an end to Him. By next summer something extraordinary would be over. A gaping chasm would remain where He had been.

Little houses bloomed on the hillsides of the Galil like white bunches of flowers. Inside each dwelling the question was asked over the supper table, "But . . . who is he? This carpenter from Nazareth. Who?"

Wondrous stories of mighty deeds were shared over garden fences and market stalls. He had fed five thousand with five loaves. Four thousand with seven loaves. He had healed cripples and deaf mutes. He had made lame men walk and by His word had raised the little daughter of Ya'ir from her deathbed in Capernaum.

"But . . . who is he?"

And then on Shavuot in Jerusalem, He had given sight to a young beggar named Peniel, a fellow blind from birth. The one who had sat at Nicanor Gate and greeted families during pilgrimages year after year. And the beggar, fully sighted, had faced the mighty Sanhedrin, looked them full in the eyes, and declared in sworn testimony that Yeshua was, and that He could, and that He wanted to! Peniel refused to deny what had happened to him, even upon pain of excommunication!

The last event and the boldness of an ignorant beggar had pushed the authorities over the edge. How could they keep such a thing silent?

Perhaps it was all merely a wild tale. Who had ever heard of such a thing? Where had the beggar gone off to? Herod's guards were searching for him. Everyone was looking for him. No doubt to put out his eyes again and then cut out his tongue so he couldn't talk. That would keep the incident quiet.

Perhaps there was no blind man. Maybe it was a rumor turned loose like a sheepdog to nip the heels of the flock and draw the ignorant and the desperate into an elaborate charade.

Shortly after that the lepers began to arrive home. Healed. Whole. Ten fingers. Ten toes. Noses. Ears. Arms. Legs. Mouths speaking of One who had descended into the Valley and . . . and . . . set them free. They continued to arrive like the dead returning alive from an open tomb after years of absence. Hundreds streaming out from the Valley of Mak'ob. Familiar faces, beloved ones, given up for dead years ago, suddenly showed up at the door of every synagogue with two doves to offer as the law of Mosheh required for sacrifice of healing!

Since the time of Elisha no leper had been healed in all of Israel!

"Who is he? Is he Elisha then?"

The edict of the Sanhedrin in Jerusalem forbidding the mention of

Yeshua's name or attendance at His teaching was posted throughout the District of Galilee and read aloud in synagogues.

Yet His fame grew. The forbidden name was on every tongue.

"Can't talk about him? On pain of excommunication? Why? What are they afraid of? What are they up to? Why do they fear him so much?"

Jerusalem and the Sanhedrin were a long way off. And the question became more urgent: "Who is he?"

For a time the roads were never deserted. Everyone knew someone who had met Yeshua or someone who had heard Him teach and seen His wonders.

Then those who had not yet gone to see for themselves decided they must go. At first people flowed toward Him like a river seeking the sea. So many strangers asking strangers in unknown places where He might be. And then the steady flow became a torrent of desperation tumbling down a ravine, tearing out centuries of messianic expectation by the roots, heaping debris of misunderstanding at Yeshua's feet.

"Who is he?"

Hopeless tangle of hopes.

Who could sort Him out? Rabbis? Scholars? Who could define for the common folk what His coming meant, or tell them for certain who He was? Who could say what He was supposed to be if He really was The One?

"Who is he?"

But when they found Yeshua, His teaching sounded strange. He called Himself The Way, The Truth, The Life, The Bread of Life! Manna come down from heaven! He told them that only if they made a meal out of His flesh and drank His blood could they live forever.

They did not understand what He meant.

They noted that there were no more tricks with the barley loaves. No free lunch after all.

The Pharisees, seething, commented that the hum of His novelty might finally begin to die away in the Galil. After watching Him heal a paralytic or two there was nothing worth walking so far to hear. These miracles belonged only to the ones who were healed. The show was over. Unless a person was sick and in need of healing, there was nothing to be gained along His path of righteousness except sore feet and blisters and perhaps a guilty conscience brought on by His preaching.

Instead of tens of thousands, the crowds who sought Him came in thousands.

Gossip said Yeshua had traveled across the lake to Gadara. The people of the Decapolis had asked Him to leave after He cast a sort of spell on their hogs. Even the swineherds had wanted Him to go away. This news had greatly pleased the high priest.

That summer there were seventy students whom Yeshua called out from the hundreds who had followed Him faithfully in the early years. Seventy was the maximum number of talmidim that custom dictated sit under the personal and intense tutelage of a single rabbi. Yeshua had sent everyone else home and gotten down to the business of serious teaching.

Those learned rabbis who taught in the Yeshiva schools of Jerusalem and Hebron consoled themselves that the great star of Yeshua of Nazareth was perhaps in decline. After all, the talmidim Yeshua selected to study Torah with Him were mostly undesirables who would never have been accepted into a real academy. They were former beggars, common middle-class workmen, tax collectors, sinners of every variety. In short, they had nowhere else to go and nothing important to do.

Upon the return of a pair of ragged beggars to Jerusalem the rumor swept around the Temple Courts that Peniel, the blind beggar of Nicanor Gate for whom everyone had been searching, was one of Yeshua's beloved seventy!

Caiaphas, high priest of the Temple in Jerusalem, reddened with indignation when he heard the news. "Pathetic! A sham! It would be laughable even, except that allowing an ignorant beggar boy to presume—to imagine—he could intelligently discuss Torah is a dishonor to the Law and the Prophets! Who does this Yeshua think he is? Who?!"

West of the Jordan, in the Upper Galil, it was Shabbat eve, an hour before twilight. The day of rest would soon begin. Seventy talmidim formed the core of Yeshua of Nazareth's students in the camp. Many others—mothers, sisters, and wives of the elite band—came and went, providing for the needs of the talmidim with regularity. The grounds bustled with preparation. Enough food cooked to last through tomorrow, clothes washed and gathered in after being dried in the sun.

Peniel ben Yahtzar had completed his assigned chores. He hopped nimbly across a table-shaped rock wedged at an incline between a pair of upright boulders. From its peak he surveyed the surrounding countryside. A white-walled town, on a knoll about a half mile distant, stood out from its rustic surroundings like a lantern in a dark tower. Beyond it sprawled the blue of the Sea of Galilee.

Every morning Peniel woke with wonder at new things to see, new uses for the sight given him by Yeshua of Nazareth. He marveled at the harmony of the colors displayed: azure overhead lightened to pale turquoise at the rim of the bowl of sky where heat waves shimmered. Tawny shocks of wheat lay heaped beside a threshing floor of dark gray stone. Threshers, clad in tan smocks, finished their work and retreated beneath the canopy of the apple orchard.

Peniel felt as if he had been waiting all his life. Before now he had not known what or who he had been waiting for.

Yeshua of Nazareth! Messiah! Anointed One! King of Israel!

The village on the knoll, he had learned, was Chorazin. It was two miles northwest of Capernaum, on a prominent ridge at the head of the Sea of Galilee. A center of wheat farming in the north, Chorazin also straddled the main east-west trade route through the Upper Galil, connecting Trachonitis with Lebanon.

While others of Yeshua's talmidim labored in preparation for Shabbat, their leader conversed alone with Mary, His mother, beneath a nearby tree on the edge of the apple orchard.

Peniel stared openly at mother and son. He was struck by their resemblance: hair color, eye color. Yeshua's dark brown hair was like hers in the way it framed His oval face. Sun-streaked copper shone in His hair; seams of gray accented hers. Each had cheerful brown eyes flecked with gold. They dressed simply, like the *am ha aretz* who flocked to hear Him teach. Yeshua's outer homespun robe was striped green and tan. Mary's cloak was plain indigo, proper for a widow. And yet both mother and son had a dignity of bearing that somehow set them apart.

There was more than the physical similarity between the two, Peniel noted. There was a convergence of mannerisms. When Yeshua spoke, Mary dipped her head, and while listening, her chin pointed slightly to the left. Then, when Mary talked, Yeshua attended in the same attitude of interested concentration.

What was Mary saying to Yeshua?

"On their way to join his family in Alexandria. They came together to take baby Isra'el. Jekuthiel and Deborah with their sons. They'll be safe in Alexandria. I gave them the name of my cousin there. And later, Lily and Cantor . . . so happy, the two of them. Lily returned this to me." Mary passed a crumpled note to her son.

Yeshua opened it, studied the writing, then grinned and said something Peniel could not quite make out.

Mary laughed aloud with joy at Yeshua's remark and patted Him gently on the shoulder. Yeshua spread His broad hands and continued with a story about the Valley of Mak'ob meant only for her ears.

But Peniel had seen the lepers for himself. He did not need to hear the words to know what had happened when Yeshua descended the narrow path and went to redeem the forgotten people. Yes, Peniel had seen it all from a distance. For a day and a night he sat on the rim of the canyon high above the dreadful place. One by one the people came out—healed, whole, restored again to the world. Jekuthiel. Deborah. Their little son. All the others. Every one. Finally, at the very last, Lily and Cantor.

And Peniel knew who had restored their lives. He knew what it meant.

Mary understood as well. She grasped Yeshua's hand in thanks.

Peniel's head bobbed in silent agreement. Oh yes! The things his new eyes had witnessed!

Behind Peniel, his best friend, Amos, clambered onto the rock and slapped him too hard on the shoulder in greeting. "The ox doesn't know how strong he is." Peniel rubbed his shoulder.

Once small and bent in body, Amos stretched long legs in the sunlight and stared at his big feet. "Ho, Peniel! Life is a dream, eh? But don't wake me up. I'm as tall as Shim'on the fisherman, you know. Tall as him and twice as smart."

Shim'on bar Jonah—brawny, ham-handed, with a tangled mop of curly brown hair—put his fists on his hips and glared up at Peniel and Amos. "Did I hear my name blasphemed? What are you two up to?"

Peniel admitted, "Listening. Watching. Admiring the rabbi and his mother."

Shim'on shook his fist. "Admire something else. Get off of there. Didn't anyone ever tell you it's not polite to stare?"

"No," Peniel answered truthfully. "No one."

Shim'on squinted. "Point taken. Well, then. Ain't anyone ever told you that it's not polite to listen in on other people's private conversations?"

"No one but you ever told me such a thing, Shim'on. I'm Peniel. You know me. I love a good story. I sat at Nicanor Gate in the great Temple of Yerushalayim and begged since I was old enough to hold a begging bowl. Oh, the things my ears saw! The words men spoke before me like I wasn't even there! Plots and plans and sins by the bucketful! And they never imagined I could hear them because I was blind."

Shim'on roared, "Well, Peniel ben Yahtzar, you're not blind now!" Then to Amos he added, "And you! Amos the dwarf! It's plain as the nose on my face that the Master made your ears as big as your feet. So get down and quit your listening to private words between the Teacher and his mother, will you? They've precious little time together these days. She's going back to Magdala soon and there's plenty to catch up on!"

Amos slid down and scowled at Shim'on's retreating back. "Lucky for him I don't know how strong I am yet."

Peniel also complied, though he could not see what harm they were doing. He trailed after Amos, who sat beside Judas Iscariot.

Dark-complected, with his beard oiled and combed, Judas rebraided his turban, neatly tucking in the folds. He offered Peniel and Amos a few almonds. "Don't see why you let that Galilean fisherman order you around like that. Who made him the overseer of the rest of us?"

Peniel, whose life had been spent in Jerusalem before joining Yeshua's band, had to agree that Shim'on sounded very Galilean and, for that reason, very uncultivated by Judean standards. The big fisherman freely substituted *Hets* for *Khets*, putting hard sounds where none belonged and improperly softening other consonants. No, there was no disguising the fact that Shim'on was a Galilean.

But then so were most of the talmidim. Judas, who both looked and acted like a more polished southerner, was one of the exceptions.

Peniel shrugged. He liked the good-hearted if brash Shim'on and would not be drawn into a petty rivalry. There was jealousy enough among the band of Yeshua's followers.

Peniel attempted to redirect the conversation. "His mother seems a good sort. I admire such a mother. Very kind, she seems. Very interested in her son. Proud of him. With reason."

Judas shrugged. "Time enough for pride when he publicly declares himself king."

Amos hummed his agreement. "I'm tall enough to make a good soldier, don't you think? Maybe an officer, eh? I would look very fine in a uniform. Marching into Yerushalayim beside the king's chariot. Sword in my hand!"

"God help us if you ever have to fight." Judas spit a shell into the fire.

Amos scratched his beard. "Hmmm. Yes. Point taken. Well spoken. Never mind. I wouldn't want to fight. A man should stay alive if only out of curiosity."

Peniel hugged his knees and scanned the camp. Every one of the talmidim had set his eye on a particular government post. Competition for important positions in Yeshua's future kingdom was fierce among the Twelve of the inner circle. Judas claimed the office of treasurer, though Shim'on said privately that Judas Iscariot would steal the commandment not to steal if he could make a profit on it.

Amos stretched his arms toward the sky, admiring the length of his reach. "What will you be, Peniel?"

Peniel had not thought of it much. He was not qualified for anything like a civil post. A Scripture popped out of his mouth almost unbidden: *"I'd rather be a doorkeeper in the house of the Lord."*[3]

Amos approved. "Well spoken! Good choice. Entirely fitting, since your entire life has been spent at a door."

Judas' eyes narrowed. "Doorkeeper, is it? Why not ask him if you can be a priest? Keeper of the keys to the Temple Gates? Why not assistant to the high priest? John will most likely be appointed *cohen hagadol*, the high priest. Yeshua will be filling those places as well when Caiaphas and Annas are gone and their rabble with them."

Amos awkwardly clapped his hands. "Good thought! Peniel, the blind beggar of Nicanor! Think of it! You! Assistant to the high priest! Now won't that be a sight! Won't that show all of the high and mighty!"

Judas shifted his weight uneasily. His face hardened. He muttered, "He must declare himself soon. While they're still filling the roads. While they're still curious. Willing to fight. One sign is all it will take." He stared above the treetops at the sinking sun.

Shabbat had arrived, and yet the camp of Yeshua's talmidim was not at rest.

Before leaving her room, Zahav traced the blue letters of the most recent title she had embroidered on the prayer shawl she hoped someday to give to Messiah: *Yahweh-Shammah, "The Lord Is There."*

Today was Papa's birthday. For several weeks Zahav had been working on a new tallith for the old rabbi to wear at services today in case Messiah came. She had just given it to her father last night. He had been so pleased he had wept.

Now she whispered, "Messiah. I had hoped you would come to Papa before today. He was up all night. I heard his prayers, asking you to come. Yahweh-Shammah, may your spirit be here with Papa now, today."

When she arrived, the synagogue of Caesarea Philippi was packed.

Zahav shifted Dori's weight from one hip to the other. Her nephew was a good-natured two-year-old, almost a contradiction in terms, she knew. Sucking his thumb, he clung placidly to her arm with no wiggling, but his weight alone was enough to wrench Zahav's shoulder and back. What did her sister Rebecca feed these children? They were as rotund as the pygmy hippo Zahav had once seen displayed in an itinerant caravan of curiosities.

Perspiration beaded on Zahav's forehead and trickled into her eyes. Since she was holding the hand of her niece Deborah on the side opposite Dori, there was no chance for Zahav to wipe her face. Lifting her chin, she tried in vain to locate any whiff of cool air. The women's gallery, on the second story of the synagogue, attracted and trapped all the hot air in Caesarea Philippi. Though it was early Shabbat morning, the temperature had climbed through the first half of the service.

There was Papa, presiding in the hall below. In honor of his birthday, he would perform the Hagbahah, which means "to rise up." Wrapped in the prayer shawl Zahav had made for his sixty-seventh year, how fragile he seemed! He fingered the fringes tied on the four corners of his tallith. Ten knots tied in series of two knots each, for the Ten Commandments. Between the pairs of knots the single blue thread was wrapped around the cords of the fringe to represent the numerical equivalence of each of the four Hebrew letters of Yahweh's name.

Two knots. Ten wraps; the letter Yod
Two knots. Five wraps; the letter Hay
Two knots. Six wraps; the letter Vav
Two knots. Five wraps; the letter Hay
Two knots.

YHVH, representing the infinite name of Yahweh, The Almighty. Zahav could weave The Name into the fringes of a prayer shawl in the dark. She did so frequently. It was a way to pass the lonely nights.

She skimmed the congregation below her. Nearly every man and boy was wearing a tallith she had made. But none was as elegant as Papa's. The stripes were indigo, like lines of writing across a clean sheet of parchment. Hidden within the stripes Zahav had embroidered raised pomegranates, like those that the Lord commanded be carved on the pillars of the Temple and also on the robe the high priest wore on the Day of Atonement. The Hebrew word for pomegranate came from the root *ramam*, which meant to "exalt and lift up." Papa, who was slowly going blind, could one day touch the embroidery and count the letters in the fringes and with his fingers still read the message to exalt and lift up the Holy Name of Yahweh! The fabric of his tallith was as white as the snow on the mountain.

To every Jew a prayer shawl served as a reminder of the Tabernacle in the wilderness, the tent where the presence of the Lord dwelt among men during forty years of Israel's wandering.

It was a suitable gift for a man who had worshipped the Lord and lived in exile from his beloved Jerusalem for so long. Zahav had put aside the tallith she had been making for the Messiah in order to complete it.

Papa waited in the open space before the ark, the Aron HaKodesh, containing the Torah scrolls.

On the floor was a finely figured mosaic. The pavement, worked in different shades of agate, onyx, and marble, depicted a pair of seven-branched candlesticks, a brace of ram's-horn shofars, and the outline of the entry to the sanctuary in Jerusalem. There was even a representation of the starry curtain within the doorway that hid the interior of the house of ELoHiYM Adonai from prying eyes.

Papa's eyes rested on the Aron HaKodesh. Within the Aron HaKodesh, the lambskin Torah scroll wound around two wooden roundels tipped with pomegranates. It was adorned with a gold crown and mantled in purple cloth covered by a gold breastplate. Papa taught his assembly that the Word of Yahweh was a king, living and present among them, worthy of adoration. It was also a symbol of the heavenly King promised to Israel.

Three blessings were recited by other members of the congregation in preparation for the Hagbahah.

Papa seemed not to hear them. Perhaps he was thinking about the Temple Mount. A line drawn through mosaic floor, ark, and the synagogue back wall would lead eventually to the Holy of Holies, though that was more than a hundred miles away. Perhaps he reflected on the days when the family had resided and worshipped there.

He appeared cool and serene.

Zahav was neither cool nor serene. Given the fact that she was the only one among the three sisters and two sisters-in-law who had no children, Aunt Zahav was always pressed into service to assist with the nursery duties. Off to her right, Zahav heard smacking, gurgling noises as Rebecca nursed Aaron, her youngest.

As usual the women's gallery was packed, even though it encircled three sides of a space forty feet on a side. Also as usual, sixteen of Zahav's fellow worshippers were family, counting sisters, nieces, and nephews still too young to join the men below, but not counting cousins of all degrees.

Zahav stole a glance at Rebecca. Such a contented face. She smiled down at her little Aaron. Five of the youngest generation belonged to her. Rebecca was large, taller than Papa, but then, so had Mama been.

Rebecca was broad of face, shoulders, and hips. Her smile, Papa said, was like Mama's. Her build was from Mama's side of the family too. Never flurried, or anything other than patient, Rebecca seemed expressly made by the Almighty in both temperament and physique for bearing, wrestling, and rearing children.

Rebecca nudged Zahav. "Here he goes." Then she shushed her buzzing brood.

Zahav pressed her face close to the lattice so she could see it clearly.

Papa opened the Aron HaKodesh to reveal the beauty of the Word, crowned in gold and clothed in glory. He bowed and gathered the scroll into his arms as if the Word were the infant King whom he loved.

Was he remembering his dead son? Zahav wondered.

He carried the scroll to the bema, a reading table in the center of the synagogue. Reverently he placed it on the table. There he undressed it, removing crown, breastplate, and royal mantle. What remained when the kingly garb of the Word was laid aside was a scroll, made from the skin of perfect, unblemished lambs. Upon this lamb-skin, holy to the Lord, the Word of Yahweh was inscribed. A long strip of linen cloth was wound about it as final protection. It was at this stage that the Word appeared like a baby wrapped snugly in swaddling clothes. The King of Heaven had descended from His great throne to be born on earth and live among men.

Yes. Everything meant something.

Papa removed the shroud, opened the scroll to the day's reading, and grasped a wooden roundel in each hand. Then he performed the Hagbahah. He lifted the open scroll high above his head and turned slowly to present it to all the congregation.

And then he began to read a Parashah for the day.

For Papa to read such a Parashah on his birthday? Papa, who had lost a son to Herod's command?

How curious that the Lord had chosen such a Parashah at the service when Papa was chosen to lift the Word before the congregation! Everyone knew what the story of baby Mosheh in the basket meant to Papa. In ancient days Mosheh, the infant deliverer of the Hebrew people, was saved from death while so many other little boys died. And the same thing had happened again in Beth-lehem some thirty years ago!

Papa had spent his life waiting for the Deliverer to come show Himself. But the infant king he had seen in the lambing cave at Beth-lehem had not returned.

No one moved. Silence was absolute.

"From Shemoth, the second book of Mosheh . . ."

Papa's voice was strong as he read the passage detailing the death of Hebrew babies in Egypt. Zahav's eyes brimmed with tears as Papa came to this verse:

"But when the child's mother could hide him no longer, she got a papyrus basket for him and coated it with tar and pitch. Then she placed the child in it and put it among the reeds along the bank of the Nile. His sister stood at a distance to see what would happen to him."[4]

Papa glanced up to where he knew Zahav watched him from behind the lattice. His slight nod was an acknowledgment of her presence. Then he proceeded with the reading.

"Pharaoh's daughter opened the basket and saw the baby. He was crying, and she felt sorry for him. 'This is one of the Hebrew babies,' she said.

"Then his sister asked Pharaoh's daughter, 'Shall I go and get one of the Hebrew women to nurse the baby for you?'

" 'Yes, go,' she answered. And the girl went and got the baby's mother. Pharaoh's daughter said to her, 'Take this baby and nurse him for me, and I will pay you.' So the woman took the baby and nursed him. When the child grew older, she took him to Pharaoh's daughter and he became her son. She named him Mosheh, saying, 'I drew him out of the water.'"[5]

Thus ended the Parashah.

Never taking his eyes from Zahav, Papa replaced the Torah scroll on the bema. He bowed and kissed The Name she had woven into the fringes of his tallith.

"May the Word of the Lord be lifted up and exalted among the nations!"

The midsummer sun beat down on the Galilean hillsides and on the villa of Herod Antipas. Beneath the shade of the arbor the air was cool and pleasantly fragrant. Dark clusters of grapes, swollen almost to bursting with juice, hung tantalizingly over the tetrarch's head. Black-

and-yellow wasps, like living motes of sunlight and shadow, droned lazily in and out of the trellis.

The north breeze sighing across the Sea of Galilee into the city of Tiberias carried the smells of harvest. Mingling with the dusty tang of the last of the wheat crop was the spicy aroma of the first crush of this year's vintage. This summer promised to be exceptionally fruitful for the province of Judea, especially so for the tetrarchy of Herod Antipas.

For all the agreeable scenery, the delightful smells, and the bounty of the land, the ruler of the Galil was not cheerful. Herod's sallow face was dour. His puckered expression and wrinkled brow were more akin to a neglected raisin than to the fruit of an optimistic future.

His confrontation with his trusted servant and paid assassin, Eglon, was not going well for either of them. "You mean after failing miserably you want to be exempt from trying again, is that it?" Herod accused.

Eglon's brutish brow was damp with perspiration far in excess of what the afternoon's heat demanded. The sides of his tunic were both sweat-stained and clinging, as if he had not changed his clothing in days. The eyes in his ferretlike face darted nervously around, hopping past his master's angry stare faster than the wasps that flitted above. "It's not . . . I failed, yes, but that's not it. He's not human, that one. I can't explain, but I think maybe he shouldn't be killed . . . maybe . . . *can't* be killed."

Herod snorted. "Yochanan the Baptizer was called a prophet. *His* head fell to your ax, didn't it? His blood spurted scarlet, didn't it? Isn't his cousin just the same?"

Eglon's head twisted from side to side, as if, even against his will, a negative reply was unavoidable. "My lord, Simon the Pharisee—"

Herod interrupted impatiently. "Yes, I know. He interfered. Kept you from striking. One man—a bloated Pharisee at that—your excuse for failure?"

Eglon looked haunted . . . hunted. "Simon . . . had leprosy."

Herod spat between his fingers and made the sign against the evil eye but replied disdainfully, "What of it? You mean a leper frightened you and you missed your aim?"

"Simon was . . . healed."

Herod slapped his palm onto the table, making a wineglass jump. "Absurd! Lepers are never cured. It's not possible. You're imagining things . . . or lying."

Once again Eglon's face described a tortured spiral. "First Simon the Leper . . . then . . . hundreds."

"What're you saying?"

Stronger, more firmly, Eglon beat one fist into the other hand. "Hundreds of men . . . women too, and children—all claiming he came to them in the Valley . . . healed them. Crowding into village after village. Priests baffled . . . having to look up the cleansing ceremony. Never needed it before . . . and now, all at once, all of them."

"Preposterous!"

"They were recognized." Eglon trembled. "Family . . . friends . . . running to meet them. 'I thought you were dead,' they said. 'Never expected to meet you this side of *olam haba*,' they cried out. Hundreds testifying that he healed them."

"Impossible. A hoax."

Abruptly Eglon requested, "Send me away. Anywhere. Send me away from where he is . . . before he curses me. If he can remove *tsara'at*, he can curse with it too!"

Despite the warmth of the day Herod Antipas shivered, and the hair on the back of his neck stood upright. "Get out of here, then. You go with the next caravan to Machaerus. Report to the warden of the lowest dungeon. You're now his servant."

Eglon fell to his knees and pressed his cheek against the hem of Herod's robe. "Thank you! Thank you."

"Get out," Herod bellowed, dismissing his retainer. "Go before I change my mind and have *your* head on a pike."

Eglon bowed repeatedly as he backed out of Herod's presence. "He's not human." The assassin disappeared behind a screen of vibrant green grape leaves. "Not . . . human. Yeshua of Nazareth is more than just a man."

The final service of Shabbat was read and the day of rest ended. Work began again at sunset when the new day began. Shops opened briefly in the Jewish Quarter. Music drifted through the streets. Meals and social gatherings were held.

The synagogue was deserted except for Papa and Zahav. Zahav always remained behind to straighten benches and sweep floors, dust the bema and the Aron HaKodesh, and trim the lamps so everything would be ready for the new week.

She removed the veil that hid her disfigured face.

This evening Papa stayed with her. He sat on a bench near the bema and ran his hand over the nearly invisible embroidery on his new tallith. Then, contemplatively, he fingered the knots and wraps of the fringes.

Zahav polished the menorah. "Did you enjoy your birthday, Papa?"

"Such a gift you have given this old man." His voice sounded so weary.

"You'll sleep well tonight."

"Zahav. Daughter. Such a good girl you've always been."

She rubbed a smoky streak from the silver candlestick. "Me, Papa? I'm no girl. Nearly thirty-one. How many children did Mama have when she was my age?"

He would not be deterred. "For almost thirty-one years you've been up in the women's gallery. Yet you read and study Torah with the passion of ten talmidim in the academy."

"I wasn't born a son."

"You might have been dead like your brother at the hand of Herod if you had been."

"So I'm a daughter. And the silver on the menorah is brighter for it."

"Come sit." Papa patted the bench beside him.

"Almost finished."

"Daughter, come sit beside me. There is something I must say."

She sighed. The delay in cleaning would mean she was hours later going to sleep. Tossing the polishing cloth to one side, she descended the steps and sat beside Papa in the darkening hall.

"What's this?" she asked.

He patted her hand. "I must share with you a vision. A dream I had."

Papa's dreams were always good. Mysterious and echoing with the voices of angels.

"Papa. A dream. Last night?"

"Yes, last night. And then this morning, at the morning service." He looked toward the Aron HaKodesh, which was nearly invisible in the darkness.

"You were asleep?"

"Dreaming last night. Wide awake this morning. Flooded with light." His brow furrowed in thought. "All my life I have been part of the Rising of Torah. Since I was a boy I loved the Parashah. And now for my birthday I have been given a gift from *olam haba*, as it is written in the prophet Joel: *'I will pour out my Spirit on all people. Your sons and your daughters will prophesy, your old men will dream dreams, and your young men will see visions.'*"[6]

She was silent as she considered the importance of what he was telling her. "Papa?"

"Yes. A vision. I did not understand it last night. But now . . . it came to me clearly. Everything means something."

"You've always said so, Papa. You are the rabbi and that is what you've always said. A thousand times. Everything means something."

"But even a rabbi does not always know exactly what the meaning of a thing is. Unless the Lord shows him."

"And today he showed you something." She clasped her hands in her lap.

He nodded slowly. "Today I saw something. Very . . . wonderful, Zahav! And something very terrible. I understood something I have not understood before. Something else I do not understand." He cleared his throat. "Thirty years ago your mother and I brought you to this place when we fled from Herod. Your mother carried you. In my arms I carried the Torah like I would carry my son. It was the very same scroll I read from this morning."

She knew the significance of this. The scroll had been in the family for centuries. "Yes, Papa. Precious. From the time of Solomon. Hidden in a cave in Beth-lehem when our ancestors were exiled seventy years in Babylon. I remember."

"More than that. The scroll is made from the skins of Passover lambs sacrificed in the Temple of Solomon. In those days the Shekinah Glory of the Lord dwelt in the Holy of Holies where the Ark of the Covenant rested."

"I remember, Papa."

"Today I saw it. I saw what it means, Daughter. Here in my exile I understood something I had not understood before."

"I'll try to understand."

"Listen. Listen to me." He leaned forward and began to speak with an urgency that frightened her. "Last night as I slept, I dreamed that I opened the doors of the Aron HaKodesh and looked into it. I did not see Torah scroll, crown, purple covering. No! When I looked, I saw the face of a king there. A great king. Ancient and wise. But very distant from me. So far away I could not hear his voice. The king wore a crown like the one that crowns our scroll. He was clothed in purple and on his chest there was a golden breastplate. Like the one that covers the scroll. In each hand he held a rod topped with pomegranates. I wanted to fall on my face before him, but I heard a voice say, 'The Hagbahah must be accomplished before men will see and know the identity of the king.'" Papa shrugged. "And then I awoke. It was morning. I puzzled over the meaning of the dream."

"You were very quiet this morning. I thought you were missing Mama."

Papa continued, "I was puzzled until in the service today I opened the Aron HaKodesh. Then all became clear! Everything we Jews have practiced every Shabbat! Every time we remove the Word of God, carry it to the bema, and undress it! I understood it!"

Zahav stared at him. "Tell me, Papa. So I'll understand as well."

"Inside the Aron HaKodesh, there were the crown and the purple vestments covering the sacred scroll. I remembered the dream and thought, *Here before me is the Word of the Living Eternal King of Heaven inscribed upon a Passover lamb!* So I reached in and picked up the lamb-skin scroll and carried it to the bema as though nothing unusual was happening to me." He took her hand and gazed into her eyes. "And then I heard a whisper: 'Remove the crown! Set aside the glory of heaven! The great King must leave his throne before his word and truth can be revealed to men.'

"And I took the crown from the scroll and laid it to one side. The royal vestments I removed from it. And when I came down at last to the linen cloth that wound around the lambskin scroll, I looked and for a moment—just a moment—I saw a baby lying there before me on the bema . . . yes! A living baby lying there! I recognized his face! I saw again the baby I had seen lying in the manger . . . in the lambing cave of Beth-lehem! He was wrapped in swaddling clothes when we came to see him . . . wrapped up like a Torah scroll! No crown. No glory. No power. A tiny thing. Bleating like a lamb. Yes! Innocent. Like . . . a Passover lamb."

Papa's shoulders slumped forward.

Zahav asked, "Would you like to talk later, Papa? Are you all right?"

He raised his hand to prevent interruption. "Let me . . . Zahav. If I am able. Listen! When I finished reading the Parashah, I returned to the altar and placed the scroll upon it to dress it again in glory! But when I wound the linen wraps around the scroll . . . I saw . . . before my eyes . . ." He faltered. Eyes brimmed with sorrow. "How can it be, Zahav? How can it be that what happened to my son can be for nothing? Come to nothing?"

"What, Papa?"

"Ah. I dare not . . . dare not . . . speak it." Like a child finding comfort in a familiar blanket, Papa traced the pomegranates embroidered into his tallith. *"Raman!* 'To rise!' I must contemplate the meaning of raman and speak no more of the vision . . . or I will fall into despair!"

Papa leaned on Zahav's arm as they made their way home from the synagogue. She would get up before daylight and return to finish the cleaning. Tonight her papa needed her.

Zahav removed Messiah's tallith from its basket and held it on her lap. She had embroidered so many names and titles of Messiah along the hem over the months. What name should her fingers write upon the fabric tonight? She closed her eyes and imagined the baby in Papa's stories, born in Beth-lehem, as a man. He would be thirty-two years old or thereabouts. Close to her own age. What color were His eyes? His hair? What would the Messiah, Son of the Living God, look like? What would His voice sound like?

She could not think of anything so wonderful. Perhaps He was near. On the road to Caesarea Philippi even now. He would come to the house of the rabbi who had held Him as a baby. Zahav would fix Him supper and give Him the prayer shawl. She smiled. It had been a good day after all. Papa had seen a vision. Something good was bound to happen.

Immanu'el! "God-with-us!"

Are you coming soon? Zahav's heart cried out. *Do you walk, unnoticed, through the streets of a great city? Do you speak to a lonely man beneath a tree? or feed an abandoned child huddled in a doorway? O, Immanu'el! God-with-us! I am watching for you! Speak to me!*

 ne day after dismissing Eglon, Herod Antipas brooded beneath the grape arbor while the afternoon shadows lengthened. The statue of a faun laughed at him from a decorative stone grotto; it suggested solace for Antipas' disquiet in the form of an uplifted wine flask.

His thoughts were interrupted by a soothing voice. "Is my husband troubled? Your guests are arriving while you sit here fretting. Don't you feel well, Antipas?"

Antipas' wife, Herodias, glided around the corner past the figure of Pan. Dressed in a shimmering green only a shade lighter than the grape leaves, she blended with the sinuous pattern of the vines. Subdued by the sheltering canopy, her coppery hair darkened till it resembled the somber crimson of the grapes.

This was the woman to whom Herod Antipas owed everything. He had gained the enmity of his half brother by stealing her. He had infuriated his former father-in-law, King Aretas of Nabatea, by rejecting the king's daughter to marry her. Finally Herod Antipas had achieved nearly universal condemnation for murdering the only widely recognized prophet of Israel—at Herodias' request—in the last four hundred years.

Antipas sucked his teeth and lied. "It's nothing. News of border raids by the Nabateans. I shall complain to Governor Pilate."

Herodias waved a graceful hand dismissively, suggesting slyly, "Is my lord certain his thoughts aren't occupied here in the Galil? Poisoned by a sorceror from Nazareth? And Eglon such a failure. But see: I conjure up a cure."

Herod Antipas winced when she clapped her hands. At her command a man and a woman appeared, flanking her.

Herodias introduced the couple. "Shamen and his wife, Ona, newly come from Alexandria. I give them to you."

Antipas' lower lip stuck out and his frown deepened. The pair were dressed as common folk and indeed their appearance reinforced the conclusion that they were peasants. Shamen, whose name meant "lusty," looked anything but vigorous. Narrow-framed, potbellied, with a fringe of gray hair protruding at the neck from a not-too-clean turban, Shamen beamed as if simpleminded and bowed repeatedly.

Ona scarcely matched her description. Plump-visaged, with form to match, her thin hair was the color and texture of dead ashes into which grease had been spilled.

"I didn't know we needed more kitchen drudges," Antipas scoffed. "Doesn't Kuza hire the scullery help, or are you displeased with the state of the dishes? I'll have him flogged if you like."

Herodias' chin flashed dangerously. She hissed, "I warned you Eglon was the wrong choice to deal with the Nazarene. He was a club when something more subtle is needed."

"So you thought of these?" Antipas mocked.

Coldly, Herodias demanded, "Question them. Shamen, where was your last service?"

"With the Empress Julia, your ladyship. Some twenty years. In Rome and here in the East as needed."

Antipas' ears pricked up. Julia, widow of Emperor Augustus Caesar, who handpicked her son, Tiberius, for the throne, had recently died. Many in the empire breathed easier at her passing. Julia had assassinated those who stood in the way of her ambition. It was rumored, but never openly spoken, that she had poisoned her husband when he opposed Tiberius for the succession.

Antipas peered more closely at Shamen's face. The man's smile

never reached his eyes. They remained dark, cold, impenetrable—
a viper's eyes. "Were you ever in Syria?"

Shamen's grin broadened even further. "When the great general
Germanicus met his untimely end?"

Germanicus, military hero of the Empire, had been poisoned while
campaigning in Syria about a decade earlier. He had been Augustus'
preference for an heir and had the support of the army.

Julia had not allowed him to live to oppose her son.

"How clever of His Highness to think of it. But proper credit
belongs to my wife."

Herodias laughed. "You begin to understand, Antipas? And this is a
matched set. Ona was *born* in Alexandria. And she was trained by the
temple priestess of the Serapeum."

Ona fluttered one hand modestly. "I have eased the passing into the
next world of some . . . threescore."

Herod Antipas brightened. "Forgive me, Herodias. One mustn't
judge a scroll without knowing its contents, eh? And are you willing
to . . . *investigate* Yeshua of Nazareth? These things we hear: miracles,
healings . . . invulnerability?"

"Anything Your Majesty requires." Shamen bowed.

The sound of flutes and pipes trilled from the garden terrace. The
evening's entertainment had begun.

Antipas suggested, "I'd like to propose a test. There is a bit of
unfinished business." Summoning Shamen to his side with a heavily
jeweled forefinger, Antipas whispered in the assassin's ear, adding, "It
must be outside my territory, you understand?"

"Consider it done," Shamen responded.

Cheerfully Antipas concluded, "Come, Herodias. Let's go to our
guests. We'll talk more of this later."

The voice of darkness counseled Manaen bar Talmai's heart more
strongly every day until even his soul had become blind.

What good was he now? He was nothing! Helpless!

Manaen clung tightly to the bony arm of Hashim. The two made
their way toward the drying barn, where enormous trays of almonds
were being salted and roasted.

"It was a fine harvest this year!" Hashim's treble voice quaked as he gummed the good news of the crop to his youthful master.

Hashim's tone was unchanged since Manaen's boyhood. The steward of the bar Talmai estates had always seemed ancient, Manaen mused, as he remembered the features of his Nabatean bondservant: Missing teeth. Faded eyes, which had long ceased to have any definable color. Face cracked and tarnished like a leather shoe left out too long in the sun. Wild grizzled hair escaping from a carelessly wrapped turban. Gray beard caked with almond salt and stained by decades of drinking wine or barley beer in preference to water.

Today the darkness said, "So this is what Manaen the wrestler has become! It used to be, not so very long ago, that men would step out of his way when he passed. Handsome, wealthy Manaen. Women would stare at him in admiration. Now a frail old man leads him!"

"Aye! Fine big nuts they are too. Nay, Manaen, my lad!" Hashim caught himself. "Pardon, sir. It should be Lord bar Talmai I'm callin' you, eh? Eh? I'll remember you're not a boy by and by. Be patient with me, sir. You and your brother was boys before you was men. Couldn't tell one of you from the other. And that is how I knew you first, eh? Eh?"

"You're forgiven, Hashim. As long as you remember which bar Talmai brother I am."

He was the blind brother. The stumbler. The one who couldn't find his own way from the back door to the barn without help.

"Aye, Manaen. No mistakes on who is who and which is which. Only when you was sprouts did you seem alike. Night and day between your hearts, eh? Eh? Night and day. My second wife always said you was the light of your father's house."

Manaen recited his well-learned lessons of bitterness. "And now the light of my father is condemned to live in darkness."

"Praise to the God who made day and night that you are alive."

"Praise him if you like, old man. But don't praise him in my presence. I'm chained in a prison. There aren't stars in this night. And the sun will never rise for me again. The blade of Eglon, Herod's executioner, made certain of that."

The old man cleared his throat uncomfortably. "Eglon. Same as he who cut off the head of the Baptizer?"

"The same. I saw it."

"The head of the Baptizer?"

"Yes."

"Then you're lucky to be alive indeed."

"Lucky?"

"Aye. Well, what I mean is . . . there is no justice in the courts of Herod Antipas, eh? Eh? Bad as his old butcher father, that one. But you and Lady Susanna are safe across the border in King Philip's country. No need to fear Philip. Never heard of him puttin' a man's eyes out. They say if Yochanan the Baptizer had stayed to King Philip's bank of the Jordan he'd be alive today, preachin' condemnation against Antipas and that harlot of a wife of his, eh? Eh?"

"If I'm lucky I'll die before I hear their names or speak of Herodian politics or religion again."

"Aye. Politics. A pain. The very thing we must discuss. So now, about politics and the harvest of your orchard! The shakers and pickers never had such an easy time of it in the trees. Nay. Never. Send the lads up the trees, give a shake, and it was rainin' down fine, big, healthy nuts onto the gatherin' cloths. Hardly a wormy or a gummy nut in the lot. You're a rich man, judgin' by what's in the barns, and we've not yet carried one basket of samples to Bethsaida market."

The aroma of roasting almonds made Manaen's mouth water as they stepped into the barn. "You never forget such a scent as roasting nuts. I dreamed of almonds and beer when I was . . . in prison." The vivid image of squalor and starvation seeped into his mind, overwhelming the more pleasant sensation of memory.

Hashim scooped up a handful from a drying tray and pressed the warm delicacy into Manaen's palm. He coaxed, "Aye. There are days when I'd rather have a bowl of warm salted nuts and a beer than a woman."

This was an extraordinary confession coming from a fellow who had enjoyed three wives and sired twenty-one offspring. Hashim's grandchildren and great-grandchildren now numbered something like the nuts in the drying trays. It would take too long to count them all.

Manaen's mouth was dry as he remembered bread tossed onto the filth of his cell floor.

"Well?" the old man urged in an impatient tone. "Will you not eat it? Try it? Taste! Eat! Taste and know how you have prospered!"

Manaen forced his mind back from the brink of despair, burrowed his nose into his palm, inhaled deeply, tossed an almond into his mouth, and crunched it between his teeth. Mimicking the merchants in the marketplace he took his time, pretending to savor the flavor as if it were a glass of fine wine. But he barely tasted it. "Ah! First quality. Delicious. Extraordinary! Hashim! You are a master of almond roasting."

"It's in the knowin' of how much salt to soak them in, you see. But the trees! The trees! Ah, it's a blessin', it is!"

A mocking, Manaen thought. What blessing were trees he'd never see? Aloud he said, "Never has an almond been so large or tasted so sweet." Then he forced himself to add quietly, "You've done well for the house of bar Talmai."

Pleased with his master's praise, the old man demurred. "Nay. Wasn't your servant Hashim that done well. Almonds are favored by the Almighty: almond blossoms carved into the golden lampstand. The rod of the first high priest was of almond wood! Aye, The God preserved the fortune of your father and your father's father for you, lad. That's it. Give credit to The God for preservin' your almond orchards and your life from those who rule the Galil west of Jordan. Aye! All of you but your eyes was rescued!"

Manaen was overwhelmed with the irony of it. In Hebrew, *shaqed*, "almond," was near enough in sound to *shaqad*, which meant "alert, sleepless, always watchful." *The God of the Jews never misses anything; he's forever paying attention.* Wasn't that the way the rabbis explained the connection?

So where had this *all-seeing* God been when Manaen lost his *eyes*?

Give credit to a God who preserved a worthless, useless, *sightless* life . . . to profit from growing almonds?

Absurd!

Oblivious to the torment on Manaen's face or in his thoughts, Hashim rambled on, "Saved you are, and out of reach from that devil Herod Antipas, who was in league with your brother, Demos! He who would have stolen these lands and killed you to get at what is rightfully your inheritance. And now you're home in the kingdom of Philip. The one good son of the great butcher King Herod. Philip's mother was of my own clan, I hear. A distant cousin to be sure, but of good blood."

The orchards and vineyards Manaen had inherited stretched out across the hills beyond Bethsaida. Located in Gaulanitis, or the Golan, the bar Talmai estate bloomed along the eastern bank of the Jordan River as it poured into the Sea of Galilee.

Hashim opined, "But it was politics I need to talk with you about. Merchants travel far for such a delicacy as your harvest, eh? Eh?" He hesitated, patted Manaen's hand in sympathy. "And now? And now . . . I'm sorry to tell you. A message come this morning. Kuza, steward of Herod Antipas, will be arriving in Bethsaida in a boat big enough to carry away a trove of bar Talmai almonds. Antipas has always got the first of the bar Talmai harvest."

Manaen flared. "I'll refuse to sell to him."

"Can't do that. No. No. Can't. You're here safe and sound in King Philip's land, but you can't go insultin' King Philip's half brother now. First of the best, that's what's kept Antipas from tryin' to take King Philip's lands."

"I'm forced to do business with him? Even though Antipas blinded me for sport?"

"Antipas is a swine. Everyone knows that. But King Philip would take a dim view of one of his subjects insultin' his half brother. Refusin' to sell him Bethsaida nuts. King Philip's got to keep peace in the family, you see, or get swept away."

"I would poison the lot of them if I thought—"

The old man jerked down hard on Manaen's arm and hissed, "Shut your mouth about such things. Poison? Poison? You never know who might be lurkin', eh? Eh? Antipas will finish what he set out to do with you. That is, he'll slit your throat and blame a sicarius."

Manaen clenched his fists as the darkness roared in his head. *Dead. Yes. I'd be better off.* "Take me back now, Hashim," Manaen wearily instructed the old man.

"There now. You're white as a ghost. You needn't fear a sicarius, eh? Eh? Must be terrifyin' to be in the dark. I didn't mean to set you on edge. Just that, since you can't see and all? Watch what you say, eh? Eh? That's all. Herod Antipas' assassins move as freely as anyone across this border. And his spies are thick as fleas in Bethsaida. Don't indulge yourself by insultin' Herod Antipas, no. Not that. It's like kissin' a cobra and expectin' to live."

Manaen no longer valued his own life, but he certainly did not want to die at the hand of one of Herod's hired murderers.

Hashim added one more layer of fear to his caution as they shuffled back to the house. "Promise me you'll keep your mouth shut about Antipas and the crop and poison and the like. For the sake of your lady Susanna, you must do it."

The sun was hot and high overhead. The teaching of Yeshua on the Torah portion was about to come to an end.

In Capernaum, at the northwest corner of the Sea of Galilee, Peniel sat on a stump beside Amos at the rear of a large crowd. Perhaps as many as a thousand—Peniel had difficulty gauging numbers—had come to hear Yeshua of Nazareth. Before dawn the crowd had blocked the door of the house where Yeshua stayed. The synagogue could not contain the multitude longing to get close enough to touch the fringes of His tallith.

Finally, they overflowed from the open courtyard, where Yeshua stood, into the shade of a grove of mulberry trees. Beside Peniel and Amos was Levi, former tax collector who had once been in the employment of Herod Antipas. Mary, mother of Yeshua, approached Levi. She carried a newborn baby in her arms.

Peniel heard snatches of what she whispered in Levi's ear: "Must see him right away . . . born last night. Cleft lip and palate. Worst I've ever seen. Can't nurse. He'll die soon unless . . ."

Yeshua's glance acknowledged His mother's arrival. He gestured for her to come forward. Mary, with a handful of other women, cared for unmarried mothers and unwanted children in nearby Magdala.

She made her way to her son.

Yeshua embraced her, then gathered her precious cargo into His arms. Pulling back the blanket He studied the little face. His brow knit in consternation at what He saw. His big hand caressed the child's head, then covered him in His tallith. He laid His cheek against the infant's cheek and summed up the day's instruction in a gentle whisper that was somehow heard by the crowd. "So I tell you, sell what you have. Give it away. Give to those in need. First share what you have and all you are with these little ones whose angels are always before the throne of Yahweh. These who are dearest and most loved by my Father. They cannot care for themselves and have no ability to repay your kindness or thank you. And yet your heavenly Father will see what you do for them. Fulfilling such a mitzvah will store up true treasure for you in heaven! Only there will your treasure be safe—no thief can steal it. And no moth can destroy it. And remember this, wherever your treasure is, there your heart and thoughts will also be."[7]

The lusty bleat of the newborn sounded out. Whole. Healed. Healthy. Hungry.

Thus ended the lesson. Yeshua smiled and brushed His lips across the forehead of the baby. With a nod, He returned the child to the arms of Mary. She gazed down at the baby with satisfaction. Mouthing the words "Thank you, Son," she covered the infant's face to protect him against the sun and made her way out of the milling throng.

The crowd began to break up. Snatches of conversation drifted in the wind. Complaints mostly, Peniel noted.

"I came all this way to see a miracle and he tells me to sell everything."

"Give away what I have? Then who would feed me? Why didn't he do something? Show us?"

"Not much going on today."

". . . would have liked it if he would have . . ."

". . . came to see a sign, not to stand in the sun and get a lecture!"

It occurred to Peniel that no one except those few who knew the purpose of Mary's coming would ever be aware of what Yeshua had just accomplished.

Levi paused in writing on a wax tablet. He scratched his neat black beard with the tip of the stylus.

"Are you recording everything? Everything?" Peniel inquired.

Levi nodded, not wanting to be distracted.

"You caught that?" Amos inquired. "He did something . . . something . . . for the baby."

Levi nodded and continued to write. "All the books in all the world couldn't hold everything that Yeshua did."[8]

Peniel observed, "Ah. To know how to read Torah. And to write about Yeshua!"

Levi finished his recording and glanced up sharply at Peniel. "I never thought . . . you speak so well, Peniel. Like an educated man."

Amos philosophized, "A few big words and ignorance is covered up."

Levi glared at Amos. "Shut up, will you? I'm asking Peniel."

Peniel shrugged. "You know me. I'm Peniel. All ears I was. Learned by listening to the rabbis teach as I begged at Nicanor Gate. But no. Can't read. Can't write."

Just then a stranger joined them. Peniel shaded his eyes against the glare of the sun.

"Kuza, my old friend," Levi exclaimed, shutting the wooden case of the writing tablet and grasping the newcomer by both arms. "Have you left the service of Herod Antipas at last? Come to join us?"

Kuza appeared uncomfortable at the question. At the name of Herod Antipas Amos scowled and shook his head.

Levi said, introducing the steward, "Yeshua healed Kuza's son."

The recollection brought no joy to Kuza's face. If anything, the man looked more troubled than ever.

"Levi," Kuza said in an urgent whisper, "I've been sent by Antipas. Would you ask Yeshua something for me? Herod Antipas wants to see him. Wants Yeshua to come . . . invites him to Tiberias to speak with him privately."

Surprise and suspicion chased each other across Levi's face, and Peniel knew his own expressions mirrored those sentiments.

Amos broke the silence. "Not safe! A Samaritan dog named Eglon was on the prowl. Out to kill Yeshua! Eglon belongs to Herod!"

Still holding Kuza's arms, Levi said over his shoulder, "Yeshua knows how to deal with this." Leaving Kuza beside Peniel and Amos, Levi approached Yeshua.

"You're steward to the tetrarch?" Peniel repeated.

Kuza nodded without speaking.

"And Yeshua helped your boy?"

Again the curt bob of the head.

Peniel followed Kuza's gaze. It lingered with sorrow on Yeshua.

After a time Levi rejoined them. "The Rabbi says to tell that fox Herod that his time has not yet come."

Kuza's head bobbed with relief. Peniel sensed that he had discharged his errand and would be pleased to report Yeshua's refusal to Antipas.

Thanking Levi, Kuza turned as if to go. Then he paused and leaned closer to Levi's ear. "Warn him, will you? From me. Tell him it isn't safe. The same madness runs in Antipas' veins as was in his father's. Cruel and dark. Yeshua—and anyone he loves—should leave Antipas' territory."

Levi pressed his lips together. "Thanks. Yes, I will. Tell him, I mean."

"If I hear more, I'll try to get word," Kuza promised. And then he melted into the crowd.

5

CHAPTER

Diana clung to life many days longer than the doctor believed possible. This was evidence of the strength of love. At last, as Alexander slept, she slipped away.

Friends, relatives of Diana, and members of the musicians' guild began to arrive early in the morning to pay respects. Alexander sat on the floor at the foot of Diana's bier and cradled Hero on his lap. Trays of donated food and pitchers of wine kept the visitors satisfied.

Alexander could not eat. Little Hero clung to him, refusing to be separated even when Aunt Flavia offered to take him outside to play for a while.

The din of music and conversation gave the cluttered house an atmosphere of celebration rather than mourning. Too much. Too many. Too loud.

Alexander longed for silence and solitude, for a few moments alone to say farewell to the only woman he had loved. But it was not to be.

From a niche in the wall, the idol of Pan grinned impishly. Carved by Alexander's grandfather from a lump of ebony too obstinate to be used for a musical instrument, the image was now a member of Alexander's family.

Four generations had passed since a righteous Jew named bar Dan had fled from Jerusalem during the slaughter of Jews by the Greek ruler Antiochus Epiphanes. Bar Dan had moved his clan north to the obscure village of Paneas at the foot of Mount Hermon.

Antiochus had eventually been defeated and Jerusalem recaptured by Jews fighting with the family of Maccabee. But even after the great Temple was cleansed and restored, bar Dan never returned home to Judea.

The Jewish heritage he had longed to preserve for his descendants had not been destroyed by foreign edict, persecution, or sword. For bar Dan's grandchildren, the Jewish way of life had simply eroded away beneath the constant dripping of cultural assimilation and neglect.

As Caesarea Philippi was built upon the foundations of Paneas, many of the original Jewish settlers had adopted more than a new name and town. Wanting to fit into the Greek-thinking society of the province, the descendants of bar Dan espoused the god of the city as well. So no one among his Jewish relatives had protested when young Alexander bar Dan married Diana, the daughter of a Greek tin merchant.

Many Jews in Caesarea Philippi remained faithful to Torah and the teachings of Mosheh. There was a synagogue and a Torah school just up the street from Alexander's shop. Those religious Jews considered men like Alexander apostates and somewhat lower than swineherds. In return Alexander regarded the religious Jews as intolerant and ignorant. They deserved any abuse or persecution that came their way.

Alexander utterly rejected the God of his fathers. None of the other deities reacted with the kind of jealousy exhibited by the One God of the Jews. After all, Alexander had grown up where Pan worshippers mingled freely with other cults. Dionysus had followers in Caesarea; so did Mithras of the Persians and the storm gods of the Syrians. Veneration of the emperor was also present and growing in popularity as a way to combine divine assistance with political practicality.

But for residents of the city there was a special pride in belonging to Pan—the ancient, secret, and powerful force of nature. Even the vanished Canaanites had worshipped their god of fertility in this place. They had called him Ba'al-Hermon, "the lord of the mountain," but he had been Pan just the same.

Alexander's music, the outpouring of his creativity and what he regarded as the best of himself, had always been devoted to the service of the cloven-hoofed god. Though by heritage Alexander was a son of Abraham, Isaac, and Jacob, he was culturally more Greek than the Greeks.

Insistent knocking sounded from the front of the shop. The music and conversation continued as Aunt Flavia opened the door.

"We're looking for Alexander bar Dan."

The quiet female voice of Flavia replied, "He's . . . mourning . . . his wife . . . dead . . ."

"All the same, we need to have a word."

"But I must protest. He's in mourning . . . unavailable."

"A summons from Tetrarch Philip. We'll have a word with him if you please."

"Not now. Can't it wait?"

Alexander stood slowly. Mercifully, Hero had fallen asleep. Alexander shifted the boy in his arms and carried him into the shop.

Two uniformed officers from Tetrarch Philip's personal retinue stood arguing with Flavia.

"Sorry, sorry." Alexander shaded his eyes against the glare. Then, giving Hero to Flavia, "Will you take Hero? He's sleeping now. I'll handle this."

Flavia nodded unhappily and retreated to the living quarters.

"You haven't come to mourn." Alexander gestured for the visitors to come in out of the sun.

"Clearly."

"But I do know you. You're Diomede, the tetrarch's master of entertainment."

The palace official inclined his head slightly. "And you, Alexander the flute maker, are commanded to appear at the palace tonight to play for the tetrarch and his guests."

"Tonight? But I . . . my wife, you see. Tomorrow is her funeral and . . ."

"It's a matter of extreme political urgency. An important visitor to the tetrarch, you see? A foreign visitor who heard you perform two years ago. He has made a personal request of Tetrarch Philip that you play again for his delegation. You'll perform tonight. Or, if you prefer, move away forever. Which is what you'd need to do when it became known you refused your tetrarch's request. Nobody'd buy from you after that."

"My son is very sick . . . very distressed. How can I leave him?"

"Find someone to watch him. That woman seemed eager to help. Leave the boy with her. Be at the palace before sundown. Or leave the territory forever. I think I know which you'll choose."

"Wait here," Alexander and the other musicians were told. They stood on a walkway atop a wall outside Tetrarch Philip's banquet hall. The view from the height was sweeping. From that vantage point Philip's home overlooked the three mountain valleys in which Caesarea Philippi nestled.

Facing southward, Alexander saw a panoramic expanse of stairstep terraces descending toward the Sea of Galilee. Behind his left shoulder loomed the even greater bulk of Mount Hermon.

Perched on a rocky outcropping a thousand feet higher than the town of Caesarea Philippi and across an intervening valley from it, Tetrarch Philip's palace was part mansion and part fortress. Just as his father, Herod the Great, had built easily defensible redoubts at Machaerus and Herodium, so Philip had learned his lesson well.

Philip's province was peaceful, with less of the turbulence that disturbed his brother-monarch Antipas'. Even so, Philip understood the wisdom of being prepared for war. Not far away to the east were the Parthians, always looking for ways to encroach on the territories of Rome. Southward of Philip's holdings, in a crescent-moon shape, lay the desert kingdom of Nabatea, whose raiding tribesmen were noted for their willingness to break treaties at a whim.

King Aretas of Nabatea was a powerful monarch, ruler of an independent client-state of Rome. Though surrounded by swathes of barren wasteland, Nabatea's capital, Petra, was enriched by trade in spice, silver, and precious incense. Four major caravan routes converged in Petra, connecting the Rose Red City with Egypt, the Gulf of Persia, Damascus, and the Mediterranean. The main route north, known as The King's Highway, was patrolled by Nabatean cavalry . . . and taxed by them accordingly.

At the present the Nabateans had no quarrel with Philip. But they were on the brink of war with his half brother, Herod Antipas.

When the quartet of entertainers was finally ushered into the dining chamber, the meal was already in progress. Alexander recognized Philip, reclining in the center position of the low table. The tetrarch of Gaulinitis was tall, thin, fit, and relaxed in his appearance. To Philip's right was a richly dressed man in a sky blue turban and the flowing striped robes of Nabatea. To the left of the tetrarch was a Roman centurion. The Roman's short-cropped hair and clean-shaven face, broad shoulders and crooked nose, made him look more campaigner than courtier.

"Anyone know who the guests are?" Alexander gestured with his flute toward the tetrarch's companions.

The harpist indicated the desert chieftain. "The hawk-nosed one is Rabell, the son of King Aretas. Brother to the woman Antipas sent packing when he married Herodias. The Roman is his escort. Marcus something, I think his name is."

Surrounding the principals and ebbing away in importance to both extremes of the horseshoe-shaped table were attendants and courtiers from both royal households.

Only the Roman officer was unaccompanied.

At a signal from Diomede the musicians began to perform their first tune, a love song. Alexander alternated between flute and panpipe as the music required.

Despite the music, the din of the dinner party did not slacken; none of the guests stopped eating, drinking, or conversing to listen. Because of the performers' place on a balcony behind the high table, Alexander was privy to snatches of discussion without trying to eavesdrop.

Rabell, the Nabatean prince, waved one bronzed hand over his swarthy features as if to confirm an oath. "And I tell you again. My sister's honor will be avenged. Your brother . . ."

"Half brother."

Rabell swatted away Philip's correction like an annoying insect. "Your brother, Antipas, sought the alliance to my father's house, not the other way around. My father, the king, was against it. So was I. But Caesar would have it so. And Antipas dismisses her, a princess of royal blood, like an unwanted slave! It is not to be tolerated. In my country Antipas would not live two days."

"Which is why Tetrarch Antipas won't visit your country." Philip's lean face possessed a smile but also wary, watchful eyes.

"What is more, my sister believes that witch, Herodias, was going to poison her. You know my sister escaped? She did not wait to be murdered!"

The Roman centurion tapped a silver ring on his wine goblet. "My lord Rabell, Tetrarch Philip knows this. All Judea knows it. The emperor knows it. We are not here to review past . . . errors . . . but to find a way to prevent war."

The Nabatean prince peered into his goblet as though the future were written there. "Perhaps the districts ruled by Herod Antipas will fall of their own accord. There are whispers of open rebellion among the people! Rumors that a true king of Israel prepares an army in the wilderness to storm Jerusalem and take the land by force. As in the days of the Maccabees, it is said. A deliverer will come and drive out the interlopers. He will cleanse the Temple of the Jewish One God. That is the rumor we hear."

Alexander knew that in this statement the seeds of all Roman fears were watered. Yet the centurion remained unperturbed. "A true monarch preaches peace and justice. Peace will come when men's hearts are turned to righteousness. That is what men of every nation long for."

Rabell smoothed his eyebrow with one finger. "A strange philosophy to spring from the mouth of a centurion, Marcus Longinus. You are more a diplomat than a man of war. Or are you a follower of the late lamented Baptizer as well? I salute you." He raised his glass in a toast.

The soldier returned the gesture. "There is a time for war. But I pray for the king and his kingdom of peace."

With the clink of cups Philip added to the toast, "May our lord Caesar make certain there is peace. Any who violate the peace will surely see Marcus Longinus and his legionaries in a light less than diplomatic."

Alexander turned his attention away from the posturing of politics. He fretted for Hero. How was Aunt Flavia managing? Would the child sleep till his return? Hero was bound to wake up frightened at his father's absence.

Unconsciously Alexander rushed the tempo of the tune. Lysander, the harpist, glared at him. Alexander recognized his error and shook his head in silent apology.

Rabell warned, "Nabatea is not an easy nut to crack! In our canyons of red stone we have defied armies before. We Arabs alone have never been conquered by Rome. King Aretas, my father, has ruled for over forty years."

The centurion explained patiently, "We're here to seek Tetrarch Philip's aid in preventing *you* from attacking Antipas." Then turning his attention away from the Arab and speaking to Philip, the Roman officer continued calmly, "Lord Philip, Rome would like you to mediate this dispute between your half brother and King Aretas. You're at peace with both. Surely there are compromises that will satisfy King Aretas' honor—"

"My *sister's* honor!" Rabell rapped his knuckles on the table.

"—and prevent war."

Philip sighed. "I will do what I can. Some trade concessions might be worked out. Perhaps Antipas will agree to settle the boundary dispute between Perea and Nabatea."

Both Rabell's hands flashed past his turban in exasperation. "None of this is possible unless Herodias, that orange-dyed harlot, is kept out of it! It was Herodias' idea to kill the Jewish prophet because he spoke against her treachery. May the gods grant that her venomous intrigues take no more innocent lives. That Gorgon! That Medusa! It should be her head on a platter, yes?"

Alexander was relieved when the set was completed. Even so, he was not allowed to go home. This was merely a break while other groups performed; then Alexander would be on again.

The wrangling, the drinking, and the music would mingle for hours.

Walking home in the third watch of the night, Alexander interrupted the sleep of the city.

Over a wall a dog barked frantically at his footstep. From an open window a child cried for its mother. A disembodied lamp moved from room to room, searching for the reason of the disturbance.

From now on, when he heard a dog bark after sunset he would remember this night. He would remember Diana dead. He would think of her washed and dressed and paler than the moon, lying on a plank. He would remember how he was forced to perform for pompous politicians as though she were not dead! As though anything in the world mattered more than the fact that she was gone.

Alexander walked on. He took a shortcut through the Jewish Quarter of the city. Past the synagogue where his distant relations prayed to their One God. Invisible being. Cruel and cold and caring for no race but the Jews.

Once, after it was plain Diana was dying, he had come by night to this vast dark building and made a prayer to the One God his ancient fathers had believed in. *If only she can live*, he had begged. *If only she won't leave us! Then I would believe in you! I would! I would offer you everything!*

Alexander's supplication had gone unheeded. What did he expect from an invisible and silent being? He paused outside the synagogue that his great-great-grandfather had helped erect. Moonlight illuminated a loaf of bread, a cluster of grapes, carved in the lintel above the entrance. Bread and wine. Food for the soul.

A distant longing stirred in Alexander. An ancient memory, not his own. A wanting to know. A wishing he knew.

But the temple of the Jews was silent. No One God spoke to him from the darkness. When morning came, those whose lives revolved around this place might be aware of the funeral of the apostate Jewish flute maker's wife. They would say it served him right. He had received a just judgment from God. They hated Alexander, rejected him. These righteous ones, the chosen people, were the ambassadors of their One God. They were His snarl and frown of disapproval. Their voices declared the hatred of their invisible Lord for any who were not like *them*.

There was no room for compassion for Alexander the apostate. Hero was worse than a dog to them.

Zahav heard the footfall of the shadowed figure who glared up at the synagogue. From her window she saw him standing at the corner. His clothes were Greek. She could make out that much detail, but little more. His stance was defiant, head thrown back, as if daring a bully to fight.

What was a Gentile doing in the Jewish Quarter at such an hour? Lost, perhaps? Or drunk? Or maybe someone who intended to break into the synagogue and steal one of the candlesticks, or strip the golden crown from the Torah scroll in the Aron HaKodesh?

Vandalism and burglary of synagogues were common occurrences outside a twenty-mile radius of Jerusalem.

Zahav set aside the tallith she was working on and considered whom she might get to help her discourage the thief.

And then she heard a sob. Distinct. Human anguish. A fist rose up toward the heavens as the stranger sank to his knees in the deserted street.

Who was he? Surely not a Jew. No one from the congregation. Why was the stranger weeping? Why had he come here, within sight of her window, to shed tears in the dark?

Gazing silently down at the man, Zahav picked up her work again, endlessly weaving the Name of her God, even as she sought to comprehend the One who answered to that Name.

Two knots. Ten wraps.

Two knots. Five wraps.

Two knots. Six wraps.

Two knots. Five wraps.

Two knots.

Her hands braided a prayer for her loneliness—and for the grief of the stranger.

O God! O God! O God! The knots of my life! The tangle of myself! O God! The fetters that hold me here! O God! O God! Help me!

There was no answer.

The man beat his breast and bowed his forehead to the ground as he wept, but no angels descended to embrace him. No sages emerged from the synagogue to comfort him with wisdom.

Stars winked down, bright and beautiful like tiny flames, and yet their silvery light offered no warmth or comfort to Zahav or to the man she watched.

Perhaps Zahav was dreaming, seeing a vision as Papa sometimes did. Was the anguished fellow in the dust of the street real? Or was he, perhaps, the vision of everyone?

Yes. Everyone.

She whispered, "I'm sorry for you. Whoever you are. Phantom. Are you myself? Looking for answers when there are no answers? Each night my hands write Yahweh's name like a love letter. The fingers of my soul are weary from writing. But life is what it is."

Two knots. Ten wraps.

"We have a lot in common, you and I. We are alone tonight. Calling on the name of a God who doesn't answer. You call with your voice. I call with my fingers."

Two knots. Five wraps.

"But perhaps the One we're looking for doesn't care to be found by the likes of us. Stranger, I have no answers for my own life. How could I hope to reply to your sorrow?"

The man cried out loud, "Oh, God!"

"There's no one here by that name. No one at home for the likes of you or me."

Two knots. Six wraps.

Two knots. Five wraps.

Two knots.

Alexander wiped his eyes with the back of his hand. What had he been thinking? Not even the Almighty God of his ancestors, the one who had parted the sea, could raise the dead. Diana was gone.

Alexander climbed slowly to his feet and stood swaying in the street. No nearer to an answer than he had been twelve years ago when he and Diana had buried their first stillborn infant. Dead was dead. She had left him alone now to bear every burden without her to comfort him. Life was hard and confusing.

Why live it then? Why continue to hope?

Because the uncertainty of death was more frightening. What if there was no Elysium? no eternal place shining and peaceful where the dead might sleep on the riverbank for ten thousand years?

The dog barked. Alexander lowered his head and walked on.

The light remained on in the shop. There would be a group sitting beside Diana through the night. He hoped Aunt Flavia had managed to care for Hero. Poor little fellow. He was much worse off than Alexander because he would never understand the finality of his mother's going.

Alexander tried the latch. The door was bolted. He knocked and called to Flavia to let him in.

Haggard and angry at his late arrival home, she opened the door.

Lamps flickered at the head and foot of Diana. Skin gray like ash! Lips painted red. Cheeks rouged. The corpse did not look like her.

Flavia spat, "It's about time! Everyone's gone home. I was ready to take the boy to my house."

"Sorry. Sorry. I couldn't get away. Where is Hero?"

"Over there!" She gestured toward his cot. He was trussed up hand and foot. A gag was in his mouth. Eyes wide with terror blinked at Alexander!

"What! What's this?"

"He went mad! Tried to climb up beside his mother! Struck me as I rouged her cheeks! The others left! Left me alone to deal with it!"

"What have you done to him! What! What!" Alexander rushed to the boy and frantically struggled with the knots.

"He's a wild animal, I tell you! Look here! See my hand! He bit me! I tied him up! No choice!"

"Get out! Get out!" Alexander took the frantic child in his arms.

The door slammed and she was gone.

Two days after Yeshua's refusal to oblige Antipas, Kuza stared at the daggerlike shape of the shadow on the sundial's face. The steward was waiting in the courtyard of the Tiberias palace for his meeting with Herod Antipas. Kuza was glad to have the chance to prepare himself for the encounter with the tetrarch. Even so, his anxiety would not diminish.

Herod Antipas was a strange mixture of ego, curiosity, and suspicion. He had been intrigued by the preaching of Yochanan the Baptizer, enjoying the notion that a true prophet in the manner of Elijah of old was alive in his domain.

Then, when driven to it by Herodias, he had cut off Yochanan's head in a fit of wounded pride, fear, and obsessive mistrust.

Antipas expressed interest in Yeshua's teaching and the reported miracles of healing, but it was not safe to be the object of his inquisitiveness for long. The ruler of the Galil was perfectly capable of flipping between inquisitiveness and malicious attack in the space of a single day.

The tetrarch clearly was getting more and more suspicious of everyone. His royal father had descended into a madness of mistrust, murdering wives and sons and thousands of innocents before he died. Was Antipas going the same way?

All too soon, before the shadow of the sundial on the greenhouse wall had advanced one more peg toward evening, Kuza was in front of his master. Kuza found Antipas seated on the second-story balcony. A pitcher of wine was beside his right hand and a half-full goblet in his left.

"Well?" Antipas demanded as soon as Kuza appeared. "When can I expect this prophet to come? Tonight? Tomorrow?"

"He will not come, Lord Antipas."

"Will not come? One of my subjects and he refuses?"

"As he is a holy man, entering here would defile him."

Antipas exploded with rage, knocking over the jug. The attending slave leapt forward with a towel. "He dines with harlots and publicans and . . . and . . . lepers! And he refuses to meet with me because *that* would defile him?"

When the decanter fell, Kuza automatically bent to retrieve it, expecting a blow around his ears. Drops of bloodred wine draining from the table spattered the hem of Kuza's robe.

The tetrarch shook his wineglass like a club. "When the Galil hears of this, what will be said about me? Me, Kuza? Is it right for your master to be made a laughingstock?"

"It's not you, Lord Antipas. It's Tiberias. This place. Built on an ancient cemetery. No pious Jew will enter here. But perhaps you could . . . go see him?"

"So I can be refused to my face?"

Kuza anticipated that objection with a shake of his head. "Go in disguise. He's teaching near Capernaum. Hear him speak before revealing your identity; then decide if he's worth bothering with. Offer to meet with him privately. That way you can get your questions answered."

Antipas' pendulous lower lip trembled with agitation and his eyes gleamed. "Yes, that's it. See for myself. If he is Yochanan the Baptizer back from the dead, I'll know it, won't I? And if he's just another crackpot country preacher, I'll know that too. Very well, Kuza. I'll do it."

Papa was up praying earlier than usual this morning. Zahav heard his eighteen blessings for the day. She hurried to wash and dress.

He called her before breakfast was prepared. He wore his finest clothes, and his beard was braided.

"What is it, Papa? Have I forgotten something? A wedding? What?"

His fingers brushed the air exuberantly. "Go to the butcher. A fine leg of lamb. The best! The best!"

"Papa? What is it?"

"You were sleeping last night after Mordechai brought me this. I didn't want to wake you." A scrap of parchment fluttered in his hand. "Visitors are coming today. Your mother's brother! From Beth-lehem. His son-in-law with him. Such a meal you will cook for them! Like your mama, may her memory be blessed, would have made."

A meal like Mama would have made. Almost impossible. No one cooked like Mama. Papa would have to settle for a meal like Zahav could make. Nothing as fine as Mama's dishes. Maybe Papa wouldn't notice.

So much she had to do today! The one day in the week she could purchase light linen from Egypt used for the tallith katan, the fringed undergarment worn by male Jews from childhood. Now there were two separate markets she would have to go to. The butcher *and* cloth merchants. How could she manage?

"You'll manage?" Papa tested the expression of irritation he must have seen cross her face.

How long had it been since she had seen Papa so happy? "Of course, Papa. A wonderful surprise. How many?"

"Two. Only two."

"They'll stay with us?"

"Of course! Of course! Your uncle. Your mother's brother. My old friend. These thirty years and you've never met him. And now! They can have your room, Daughter, eh?"

"Sure, Papa. I'll sleep in the workroom."

Zahav hurried up the steep steps to tidy her bedchamber for Papa's guests.

The small home where Zahav and her father lived shared a common wall with the Caesarea Philippi synagogue. Papa often made a joke of it, saying it was right and proper for his home to lean against the back of the synagogue, just as his whole life depended on Torah for support.

His congregation was prosperous enough to provide larger accommodations for their rabbi. They would have liked to build him a large villa overlooking the Jewish Quarter. He was famous. He was beloved. It would have been fitting.

But Papa refused.

His sons and daughters were grown. His wife dead five years since. Papa felt no need of any grander space than one bedchamber for himself, one for Zahav, an adjoining workroom where she made talliths, a kitchen, and one large room for entertaining guests. Any more than this, he said, would unfairly cause Zahav extra work. She already had her own business in prayer shawls to manage.

Zahav reckoned Papa had another motive for staying put in such a cramped space. He had lived here with Mama from the beginning. Their memories were here. The raising of two sons born after Zahav and also two daughters. When the twelve grandchildren came for dinner with Papa and Aunt Zahav, Papa said he liked them buzzing close around him like bees in a hive. Filling the space where he and Mama had lived for twenty-five years. Since Mama was gone, grandchildren occupied the place her death had left in his life. New memories blossomed in the garden of the old.

The squared and beveled ashlars with which the synagogue and the rabbi's house were built had been quarried from Mount Hermon. This was a feature from which Rabbi Eliyahu drew parables about life and God.

The snow that formed the source of the Jordan River had first fallen to earth on the granite of the mountain whose Hebrew name meant "The Mountain Set Apart."

Yes, it was true that the pagan nations had changed the name of the great mountain of the Lord to Paneum and glorified the pagan pantheon on those heights. But the ancient stones were washed each season in the tears of Adonai. The rock itself, like those children of Israel who worshipped the One True God, remained holy to the Lord and set apart in spite of what the world proclaimed. The truth announced in the living word of Torah was immutable granite.

Inviolable.

It was an important lesson for the three thousand faithful Jews of Caesarea Philippi to remember, since so many Jews had intermarried with the Gentiles and fallen away from the commandments. The stone synagogue and the rabbi's house were a Jewish island in a sea of forty thousand Gentiles who populated the city.

Sometimes Zahav lay in bed in the early morning and studied the familiar patterns of the mason's chisel on the walls. Sometimes she saw it as a tomb. Her eyes traced the mottled white and gray veins in the blocks, and she thought of Papa's hair and beard. The teaching of Papa was like Adonai's granite mountain looming up in this distant outpost of Judaism.

But what was she? Zahav lived in a shadow, never fully feeling the sun upon her face. It was as though her existence was spent waiting in a corridor of unopened doors. Life was unfolding behind the doors, but not for Zahav. Except for the loss of her mother, no emotion but self-pity had ever seriously touched her. Neither had the joy of love burst onto her heart like a sunrise. Her acquaintance with both tragedy and ecstasy had been gleaned from the stories of her mother and father. They were not her own.

From Zahav's earliest memories Papa was always white-haired. Tragedy had transformed him. Mama had told her once that the color had changed overnight when he returned to Beth-lehem from a journey and found his young son murdered and his pregnant wife out of her head with grief.

They had survived all that.

Now Papa was in his sixties, and his hair was sparse above the wrinkles that marched across the high dome of his forehead. But below eye level, brows, earlocks, mustache, and beard mingled to flow down his chest without a gap. His drooping nose and perpetually amused eyes appeared in the midst of the wiry mass whenever he lifted his head from the Torah portion he studied. But even that action was more difficult of late because of failing eyesight and the permanent stoop of his shoulders.

It was good Zahav was with him, Papa said. Each evening when night fell and the light was not good enough to read by, such a comfort she was.

It was good that, one day, when his eyesight failed entirely, he would have one daughter who could read aloud for him. Yes, Zahav could read as cleverly as any Torah scholar in the academy! For Papa's sake Adonai had known what He was doing when He marked Zahav as one who could never marry. Zahav was his treasure! His gold! Such a keen mind she had for study! Useful. Yes. A comfort.

Such praise from a father toward his daughter should have given her pleasure. Zahav was his treasure, but she felt more like ore imprisoned in the granite of his life.

Nothing, nothing was her own self. No longing ever fulfilled. No dream ever ripened into reality. She waited always in the corridor. No door opened for her.

When her sisters came to visit and nephews and nieces clambered up and down the steps or piled onto one another or sat on Papa's knee, Zahav should have recalled Papa's praise and been content. But she did not. Could not. She fought against envy. Her younger sisters had grown beyond her now. Conversation revolved around their husbands, their children, the ordinary concerns of life. Another pregnancy. Little worries about this and that. They talked to one another as if she were not there. They whispered about things she could not fully understand.

And that was the way it had always been.

Today was no different. Papa needed her to cook a leg of lamb like Mama would have done. Expected her to give up her room to an uncle she had never met.

Because . . . well, why not? What else did she have to do with herself?

Veil in place, wicker basket over her arm, Zahav descended the steps of the crooked lane that led from the Jewish Quarter. She would go first to the cloth merchant. Purchase a bolt of Egyptian linen and the azure yarn required to make the fringes of her prayer shawls. On the way home she would pick up the leg of lamb for tonight's supper.

Ahead the Jewish alley emptied onto a broad thoroughfare of the Gentile souks.

Light streamed down on a large crowd milling expectantly in front of the shop of Alexander bar Dan, the flute maker. Alexander, the apostate Jew. His lifestyle dishonored the memory of his forefathers, her father said. Alexander had married outside the faith and thus had broken his family's last ties with the Jewish community.

Voices cackled like a flock of geese. How many were there? She guessed one hundred blocked the street outside the door. So many musicians! And there among the people was an effigy of their evil god to be carried in some vile procession. What was this? A pagan celebration so early in the morning?

Careful not to proceed beyond the boundaries of the Jewish Quarter and perhaps be defiled by some idolatrous ritual, Zahav paused in curiosity.

Music began. A dirge. A woman shrieked and tore her clothes. The red door of the house opened. The crowd formed a rank on either side. From the dark interior a bier holding a shrouded body floated out into daylight on the shoulders of six men. Following behind, haggard, exhausted, eyes red from weeping, came a man carrying a fragile golden-haired boy in his arms.

Alexander. Zahav had passed his stall in the market a hundred times as the apostate played his instruments to draw in customers. But she had never spoken to him. Such a thing would make her unclean.

She had heard that his wife was ill, but had not heard that she had died.

From a shadowed alcove Zahav watched in fascination as the funeral procession formed around the body. The husband and son followed.

Poor man. Poor, befuddled man. How he must have loved her! His haunted face told the story of the dying, the loss, the denial. His longing and unrelieved grief.

Could this really be happening to them? his eyes seemed to ask.

Though Alexander was despised by the Jewish community, a traitor to everything they honored, Zahav winced with compassion at his expression. Only a truly hardened heart would not feel pity at such a spectacle! What would become of the little boy who clung to his father in terror?

The clamor increased as the procession moved slowly in the same direction Zahav had intended to take. She shuddered and turned away. She would not venture out of the Jewish Quarter. Never mind Egyptian linen. Not today.

Why should Zahav feel sorrow? She barely knew the couple by sight. Why should she waste even a minute of sympathy for the apostate musician and his son?

She told herself, *Enough!* Papa's guests were coming. There was leg of lamb to buy. Supper to prepare. No time to contemplate a husband's grief over the death of a pagan woman who never should have been his wife.

Zahav would not let herself think about the little boy crying for his mother in the night! She would put it out of her mind. Out of her thoughts. It had nothing to do with her. There was supper to fix, after all.

As the funeral procession left the house of Alexander, the day grew muggy and oppressive. Hero was dressed in the white toga Diana had embroidered with bright green leaves for him during the celebration of the vernal equinox.

Hero buried his face against his father as Alexander scooped him up. The troop of mourners whispered at the sight of the boy's blue eyes and blond hair.

"Handsome little boy."

"A pity though."

"Yes. Fine-looking child."

"Yes. A pity though, about him."

"Grief over the child is what killed her, they say. Surely."

"And her other babies. But better they were born dead than like this one."

"Looks a lot like her, doesn't he?"

"There's something of his father's jawline."

"The boy's eyes, though. The gold flecks in them. Like hers."

"She was a very pretty girl. I knew her well."

"To look at the child you'd never guess."

"No, never."

"I saw him have a seizure once in the marketplace."

"She was the only one who could control him."

"A burden for poor Alexander."

"Yes. A burden."

Perhaps Hero felt their open stares or sensed they were discussing him. The boy struggled in Alexander's arms, then fell limp, mouth open, eyes wide and staring at nothing. It seemed as though he was mimicking death, assuming the grotesque posture of his mother's corpse.

Blasts of wind off Mount Hermon collided with moisture from the

Great Sea. Thunder boomed down the hills. Plump drops of warm rain fell, producing puffs of dust with each impact, but never enough landed to cool either air or earth. The breeze died away. Oppressive stickiness enhanced the discomfort Alexander felt between his skin and the goat-hair mourner's shirt he wore, heaping misery onto misery.

The city of Caesarea Philippi was built high on a hill. The pool of Pan was at its base. Between the two locations was a plateau used for public gatherings like political orations or funerals.

The procession wound down the switchbacks of the slope, Alexander and Hero in the lead. The priest of Pan came next, musicians behind him. The bier was on the shoulders of pallbearers in the center. Professional mourners carried her image, and friends brought up the rear.

The discordant braying of five sets of double flutes contrasted sharply with the plaintive melody carried by panpipes and lyres. Dirge succeeded dirge, played in doleful, minor keys.

Alexander was grateful for his membership in the musicians' and instrument-makers' guild. His business had suffered during his wife's long illness. Because of her medical needs, and because of his exhaustive care of her and Hero, his savings were nearly gone. The guild paid for the painting of her funeral mask. It was an effigy worthy of her beauty. The music that surrounded the cortege created the illusion that someone rich and powerful was being honored.

There was a tenuous comfort for Alexander in this. People would go away and say, "*A very fine memorial. Alexander the flute maker did well for his wife.*"

Hero moaned softly and began to wriggle again. Straining to touch the bier, fighting Alexander in an attempt to reach his mother, the child called out. Only Alexander could interpret Hero's pitiful cries. He wanted his mother to come back to him, or he wanted to go to her!

The child's gyrations caused the coarse animal-hide shirt to dig into the bloodied places on Alexander's back. The knotted leather whip employed in the self-mutilation associated with grief had torn into his flesh. Alexander shook the boy harder than he intended, and Hero cried out even louder.

Struck with remorse, Alexander tried to soothe his son. He cradled Hero as if he were a baby. With one finger Hero traced the freshly shaved and deliberately gashed cheeks of his father. Unexpected tenderness in the child's gesture made Alexander cloud with emotion. If his son could speak, what would he say? "I miss her too, Papa."

Their beautiful child. The blending of their love.

Hero's mouth is exactly hers! Rosebud lips. The slight gap between the two front teeth. Her eyes. Yes, pity in his eyes. Ears so much like hers. Perfect like a seashell. Not at all the way mine stand out from my head. And his face is all I'll ever see of Diana.

Alexander determined he would not cry. But Hero sobbed and snuffled as if he would never regain his breath.

They reached the square. Like a boat rocking on the waves, the plank holding Diana's linen-wrapped body was passed hand to hand and placed on the timber pyre. Dried cedar boughs heaped beneath the frame protruded from both ends of the structure.

So pitifully small beneath the shroud. Like a child! Alexander wanted to cry aloud. *Diana! How will I ever live without you?*

There was no money left to pay a professional orator to deliver a eulogy. But the music! The music! Diana would have liked it very much.

The priest intoned a prayer, asking that the horned god of Paneas kindly accept the wife of the maker of flutes and pipes.

At Alexander's request one special honor was performed. A choir of ten priestesses from the grotto shrine sang a hymn.

Sensing that his mother was leaving him forever, Hero poured out his grief. He howled, then stiffened. His jaw clenched. His eyes became glassy.

Alexander placed his cheek against Hero's cheek and held him close. *Diana! I will love him even better than I have before.*

Then it was time.

The spasm passed. Hero's body relaxed. Alexander set the boy on his feet.

"Will you hold his hand?" Alexander put Hero in the care of the old widow who cleaned their house and cooked their meals.

A blazing pine knot was thrust into Alexander's fist by the priest of Pan. *Let's get this over with,* the priest's impatient glare demanded.

There was no money for frankincense to perfume the cremation, but there were hyacinths to throw onto the body.

Walking slowly three times around the pyre, Alexander stopped near Diana's head. He felt faint. He prayed that he would wake to find this all a dream. It had to be. Had to be a dream. He gazed at the crowd. Indistinct faces floated above a pool of colored robes and tunics. He saw sorrow there, pity . . . but no hope, no comfort. Alexander vainly searched for Diana among the throng. At the opposite end of the platform stood little Hero beside the old woman. Lost! Lost without Diana! This could not be happening! That could not be Diana lying on the platform! The torch was not in Alexander's hand!

But it was not a dream.

Alexander tried to form some words of praise. So much to say. Too much. Had he left anything unsaid to her? Had she died knowing how much . . . how much . . . ? He could not—could not—utter a syllable. Why hadn't he brought his flute? At least he could have played for her one last time.

Too late. Bowing his head and gritting his teeth, Alexander thrust the torch among the bristling branches.

The needles, sprinkled with pitch, burst into roaring life. Alexander stepped back as heat, like a blast from an oven, rolled out of the flame. Fire licked the tar that coated the platform and snarled in fondness at the taste of human flesh.

Instruments blared, unsuccessfully competing with the crackle of the conflagration.

Then through the shimmering heat of the inferno, past the oily fumes, Alexander saw a horrifying struggle begin. Hero, suddenly awake and aware, yanked violently at the matron's hand. With a strangled yelp of anguish the boy tore free from her and sprinted wildly toward the blaze.

"*The boy!*"

"*Her son!*"

"*Catch him!*"

"*What's he doing?*"

"*By the gods! Somebody stop him!*"

With incoherent cries of protest Hero reached the pyre. Frantically he clawed at the wood in a frenzied attempt to rescue his mother from the burning.

"Hero! No! Get back! Get back! You can't! Can't save her! Hero!"

Stumbling, shouting, Alexander pushed through the crowd of stunned onlookers. Why did no one help him? Why? They all stood back and watched while smoke from his mother enveloped Hero in one last macabre embrace!

Alexander tripped over a chunk of wood, grasped Hero's ankle, and pulled him out of the blaze! The hem of Hero's tunic was on fire. Dashing the child to the ground, Alexander fell across him, hammering out the flames and burning his own hands in the process.

Hero grew rigid again in a rictus of seizure that arched his spine backward toward his heels. Alexander sat on the ground, holding him tightly, rocking him frantically.

Now, finally, the tears came. Alexander raised his blistered fist, threw back his head, and wept. "You! You! Gods of torture! You gods of darkness! Aren't you satisfied yet with taking her life? Will you have even this child served up at your banquet of human suffering! I defy you! *I defy you!*"

In his father's arms Hero remained inflexible, transfixed by the sight of black, stinking smoke spiraling into orange clouds. At last Diana's body fell from its supports, disappearing into the cauldron. Hero sagged and drooped, lapsing into unconsciousness.

Alexander heard the priest of Pan mutter to one of the harpists, "A shame, really. He shouldn't have drawn the child out. It would have been better to let the boy go to the gods with his mother."

7

The tavern in Dothan, over the Samaritan border from Galilee, was squalid. Hundreds of flies droned lazily. It was rank with the stink of unwashed Samaritan mercenaries taking a break on the march toward their barracks in Tiberias. The wine was sour. Eglon was not happy with the accommodations, but in his reduced circumstances he had little choice.

Besides, once in the dungeons at Machaerus, even as a guard there, conditions would be much worse than this. Best to enjoy light and air while he had the chance.

Since he was out of the Galil Eglon had time to reconsider. Perhaps he'd been too hasty confessing his fears to Antipas. There was no going back to the tetrarch, but Eglon was a tough, seasoned, ruthless man. The legions of Rome should have a place for him if it weren't for the fact that Centurion Marcus Longinus hated him.

Still, Longinus was not the only Roman commander in Judea. Rome was always interested in inside information on their puppet rulers. Herod Antipas had been involved in many more plots than the killing of Yochanan the Baptizer and the attempted killing of his cousin Yeshua. The scheming between the tetrarch and High Priest Caiaphas should be worth something as well.

Surely Governor Pilate would find a place for him in exchange for a few juicy bits to hold over Antipas' head.

That was the plan, then. Eglon would not have to serve in the dungeons at Machaerus after all.

Slapping a handful of copper coins on the greasy table, Eglon called for more wine.

"Do you mind if I join you? Name's Shamen." The speaker was narrow-framed, stoop-shouldered, balding, and potbellied. He had more Adam's apple than chin and more hair in his eyebrows than in his patchy beard, but his clothes appeared costly.

Probably afraid he'd be robbed by the legionaries and looking for a protective companion, Eglon thought. If opportunity served, he might just rob the man himself.

Eglon waved a calloused hand at the bench opposite, then laid his palm across his coins. "Suit yourself . . . if you're buying."

The newcomer sniffed at the empty pitcher on Eglon's table. "Surely even a cesspit like this can do better for two gentlemen like us." Displaying a silver coin got the landlord's immediate attention and a flask of wine considerably better than the last.

The decurion in charge of the Samaritan mercenaries bawled out an order for them to assemble outside.

Shamen noted, "Little better than brigands."

Eglon turned his head to study the Samaritan recruits. As he did so, he failed to notice a slight trickle of white powder that floated out of Shamen's right sleeve into Eglon's wine goblet.

"Your health." Shamen saluted.

Eglon grunted and drained the cup.

Shamen passed him a scrap of parchment. "This may interest you."

Unfolding the note Eglon parsed out the Hebrew with difficulty.

This man is in the pay of Rome.
He murdered Yochanan the Baptizer.
He tried to kill Yeshua of Nazareth.
Death to traitors.

Eglon's vision blurred and his head hurt. It surprised him how strong the new wine was. His throat constricted and he had trouble breathing. There was a stabbing pain in his chest.

Eglon half rose from the bench, grabbed at his throat, then slumped without a word across the table.

Shamen rejoined Ona outside. "My dear, you are amazing. It'll be hours before they know he's not dead drunk . . . he's dead."

Three days after tasting the year's almond crop in his drying barn, Manaen felt overwhelmed by the bustle and chatter of Bethsaida. From the quiet and solitude of his estate he was plunged into the teeming population of market day, when the already substantial population tripled. The clamor was amplified by the hammering and shouting accompanying the building of a new temple. Tetrarch Philip intended honoring the Empress Julia, deceased mother of Tiberius Caesar.

Susanna left Manaen, old Hashim, and three servants at the entry to the Bethsaida produce-seller's bazaar. "I have other matters to see to. And anyway, you don't want me around, interfering with your business. You and Hashim stop by the fabric stalls when your dealing is done."

Manaen experienced a moment's panic. Since being reunited with Susanna, she had seldom been far from his side. Her eyes were his eyes, she said—all he'd ever need.

Now she was deliberately leaving him alone!

Unreasonable dread swept over him. Manaen recognized and appreciated that his wife wanted him to regain a measure of his self-esteem. But now that the time had arrived, he longed for the quiet of the estate.

Resisting the urge to call her back, Manaen remained rooted in place. At last Hashim's familiar squeaky voice remarked, "Shall we go in, Lord Manaen?"

His hand on Hashim's bony shoulder, Manaen allowed himself to be led into the cul-de-sac where those with substantial specialty crops to sell met those seeking to buy. The heady aroma of summer fruit mingled with other sharper scents: mint, garlic, and cinnamon. Manaen waved his hand in front of his face to clear a path through the swarming gnats and flies.

Hashim directed one of his grandsons who trundled the creaking cart after them: "Set up over there."

The bar Talmai estate not only produced the finest almonds in the

Galil. Where hillsides were too steep for nut trees to flourish the land had been terraced into vineyards. The bar Talmai clan had never dealt with wine. Instead they grew table grapes to be turned into raisins, gathered at the peak of sweetness and laid between the rows to dry. The fruit was expertly tended until perfectly cured. Bar Talmai raisins were pressed into cakes that kept well and were a staple treat of travelers on long journeys.

These were the sources of the wealth from his father's estate for which Manaen had long contested with his brother, Demos. Now Manaen was an affluent landowner . . . so why did he feel so hollow inside?

Manaen diverted himself from his melancholy by attempting to recognize the merchants around him by their voices. Heavily accented, deep-voiced Aramaic emanating from the back of the stalls confirmed the person of a spice dealer who had been in the business before Manaen was born. The nasal drone of the trader in melons was likewise familiar to his ears.

To his instant regret Manaen also identified other voices. He singled out the high-pitched whine of Demos' plaything, Gadot. Manaen heard the gruffer tone of Demos' former gambling companion, Acteon, accompanying the eunuch.

Hashim wheezed, drawing Manaen's attention back to business. "Lord Manaen, Kuza, steward of Herod Antipas, has entered the souk. There, he sees you. He raises his hand in greeting to us. From the weight of the purse dangling at his side, I'd say he is here to make a substantial purchase."

Manaen judged the steward's approach. As the steps neared the table he said, "Shalom and welcome, Kuza. Is it nuts or raisins you're in the market for today?"

Kuza sounded surprised at this accurate greeting from a blind man but recovered quickly enough. "Shalom, lord Manaen. The Almighty be praised you're doing so well. My Joanna asks after you and your wife. She asked me to deliver her greetings and best wishes to you both." Then, as if he had been too forward, Kuza turned awkwardly to commerce. "Almonds. Sailed over from Tiberias expressly for them. Ten hundredweight, delivered to Antipas' villa in one week. What's your best price?"

While he had nothing against Kuza, Manaen would have loved to tell Antipas he would never sell to that bloated toad ever again. But Manaen resigned himself to doing business. "What figure did you have in mind?"

Suddenly Gadot exclaimed with mock excitement, "Oh, look! A blind monkey! Quick, Acteon, play him a tune. See if he dances."

Manaen felt himself flush. He turned his back on Gadot's voice and addressed Kuza. "I'm sorry. Would you repeat that?"

"I said fifty denarii."

Manaen's thoughts swirled. The amount was twenty denarii more than he'd expected to settle for. "Fifty?"

"Do you suppose he's deaf as well as blind?" Gadot simpered.

Manaen heard the scrape of chair legs on the pavement, indicating that Gadot and Acteon were settling in to heckle.

Manaen's clenched fists rose. He lunged forward but collided with the edge of the table. Kuza's restraining hand touched his arm, and he heard a whisper in his ear: "Manaen, old friend, you are the descendant of kings. Don't let the insults of worthless rabble annoy you."

"Yes. Thank you . . . for reminding me. Yes, Kuza, my thanks." The laughter of Demos' former companions still ringing in his ears, Manaen forced his attention back to business. "Fifty. Your master pays well."

There was a repeated snapping noise, followed by a light patter on the flagstones: Gadot and Acteon cracking and eating nuts.

Kuza asked, "Isn't it enough?"

Something more substantial than one of the myriad fruit flies bounced off Manaen's forehead. Another struck his ear, then two stuck in his beard. Almond shells, thrown by the eunuch or his companion.

Stooping quickly toward the open fifty-pound sack of nuts that Manaen's servants had brought to display their wares, Manaen hefted it by the neck with one hand and swung it onto the table. "The house of bar Talmai has a reputation for quality and for giving good measure."

Perhaps the small demonstration of his wrestler's strength, coupled with the bravado of a threatening pun, deterred the hecklers. The rain of shells stopped.

"Your offer is generous, Kuza. But no. It isn't enough."

"What . . . what then . . . is your price?" Tension's brittle edge was obvious.

"There is no sum large enough for Herod Antipas to pay for my produce."

Kuza lowered his voice. "Don't do this, Manaen. Even here in Bethsaida, across the Jordan, Antipas has eyes."

"With so many eyes to spare, Herod Antipas might have left me with my two to see with. But he took them. Much good may they do him."

The palace official swallowed hard. "I'm sorry. No changing that. It's best—best for all, Manaen—if you try to get along."

"Kuza, you're not a bad sort. I pity you. I do. But my answer is what it is. I will not sell to him at any price."

Kuza clasped Manaen's wrist and hissed a warning in his ear. "I balance on the edge of a dagger here! And so do you. If ever you or Susanna want to cross into Galilee and live! Manaen! If you intend to return even once to Yerushalayim, he is not a man to be insulted."

"He is not a man at all." Manaen shook off the restraining grip.

"I beg you, don't . . . do . . . this."

The chatter in the souk died away as merchants paused in astonishment to listen to the exchange.

Manaen raised his voice so everyone could hear. "Kuza, remind your master that the ancient house of bar Talmai is directly descended from King David. David, who was a true son of Abraham. Though old Herod the butcher, father of your master, destroyed the records of Jewish genealogy, my ancestors are recorded in the *Book of the Kings*. Tell Herod Antipas the house of bar Talmai will not sell to any Samaritan son-of-a-butcher, no matter how much he offers. There are other farmers here in Bethsaida who are not Jews. And in Gadara I hear they grow raisins and almonds, which they feed to their swine. No doubt they're willing to satisfy the appetite of Herod Antipas. But, Kuza, you have traveled to the bar Talmai stall in the market of Bethsaida to no purpose."

The threatened thunderstorm did not materialize, and yet a storm raged in Zahav's heart. She completed the embroidery on Messiah's prayer shawl.

Yahweh-Shalom, God of Peace.

How could she believe such a name had anything to do with her hectic life? She pressed the shawl against her cheek and closed her eyes.

Yahweh-Shalom, God of Peace, there is no peace in my heart. No peace in my life. I'm fooling everyone, aren't I? So capable, so willing. My moments of tranquility are disrupted by the needs of everyone else. If you are Yahweh-Shalom, then where are you in my storm?

There was no heavenly reply as she put away needle and thread. She had not believed there would be an answer. Too much to do. No one to do it but herself.

Supper would be served in the courtyard of the rabbi's house.

Perhaps only Zahav considered the visit of her uncle, after thirty years' absence, unusual. Why had Zadok come so far, after so long, to visit the family of his dead sister?

Zahav wondered about the meaning of it throughout the day. And now he had arrived.

Mama's elder brother, Zadok, towered over Papa. Formerly Chief Shepherd of Beth-lehem, Zadok's face was weathered from years of living outdoors. He had a visage like iron covered by leather. His thick white beard was plaited in two braids. A patch covered his left eye and a scar split his forehead down to his jawline. He was fierce, grim, and formidable at first sight. He seemed stern and implacable.

And then he saw Zahav's veiled face. He clasped her shoulders and gazed into her eyes. "It's the vision of my sister herself! Look at her! Will y'? Look! The eyes of her! Aye! Can y' see the resemblance, Eliyahu? You and I have grown old these thirty years since we parted that black night. But my sister still lives youthful in the eyes of this daughter. And not just the lovely eyes. Strong as an ox was my sister, your wife! The shoulders of a shepherdess she had! Built for carrying lambs and bearing children. Now my eyes have seen the daughter my sister bore y' in your grief! Zahav! Rightly named." He kissed Zahav's forehead. "Stately and lovely as your dear mother!"

Surely Zadok knew of the Samaritan's handprint emblazoned on his niece's cheek. And yet he did not mention the memory concealed behind her veil.

Papa embraced Zadok. "And can she cook! Come in! Come in! The whole family is here to greet you! Such a meal Zahav has made! Like her mama would cook for you if she were alive!"

Supper like Mama? Food enough for only two guests? That was what Papa ordered this morning.

Zahav had known all along what Papa meant. A feast! A banquet under the summer stars! Enough extra so Papa could wander to the fire, gaze at the meat, raise his nose to inhale with pleasure, smack his lips, and ask, "Such an aroma! What was I thinking? That's more than a leg of lamb. Your brothers! Their wives. Your sisters! Rebecca! Ishah! The husbands. The children! So many! Twelve grandchildren! Like the tribes! How could I have forgotten them? Tonight how I would love for your uncle Zadok to meet my whole family. Daughter? Might we have enough?"

Zahav had thought ahead to this eventuality. She had conquered the challenge before Papa asked. Before noon she had called at the homes of her sisters, Rebecca and Ishah. Then she visited the sisters-in-law. All four women had been recruited to assist Zahav with preparation.

An entire lamb, seasoned with garlic cloves and stuffed with sweet onions, had roasted all afternoon over an open fire in the courtyard, driving the Torah schoolboys mad with the tantalizing aroma.

Platters of succulent meat accompanied a heaping dish of couscous, peaches, and raisins—Mama's own recipe. There was baked eggplant. Cucumber salad. Bread and hummus. Stuffed grape leaves. Honey wafers. Bowls of fruit. Clusters of grapes for the children. Gallons of wine and cider to drink. It was almost like Passover. Meal enough to make up for thirty years of missed seders. All for the long-lost Uncle Zadok and his very quiet son-in-law, Simon!

Tonight Rabbi Eliyahu's family converged on the courtyard like a horde of field mice lured into a box by a wheel of cheese.

By flickering torchlight Papa presided at the head of a long low table set up outdoors beneath the stars. Old Zadok reclined like an aged lion on cushions at Papa's right. The handsome Simon, in his late thirties, reclined at Papa's left.

The rabbi's sons and sons-in-law were arranged in descending order of age and Torah education. Daughters and daughters-in-law sat at the opposite end. Each of the four women tended one of their youngest offspring.

At a separate table beneath the oak tree the older children ate, laughed, and wrangled with one another. This allowed the men to discuss the politics of Rome and Jerusalem and Nabatea without interruption.

"*Maybe there will be a war.*"

"*If King Aretas has his way . . .*"

"*They're crazy, these Arabs.*"

"*It won't affect us here in the North.*"

"*King Philip is no warrior, but other armies have fought here.*"

The four mothers philosophized about other things.

"*Teething! He will not sleep the night through. If I would have had him first, I would never have wanted another!*"

"*Rub a little wine on his gums. He'll sleep all night.*"

"*I could use a little wine on my gums!*"

"*Tell me this? How can a child outgrow sandals in one month?*"

"*And so I said to her, she'd better use a little discipline, I said. I was honest. You know I'm honest.*"

Toasts were drunk to life. The cups were filled again. Everyone was having a good time.

And then there was Zahav. So much like Mama, everyone said. She did not sit down at the table, not once. There was too much to do. She shuttled back and forth, carrying this and that, scooping out second helpings of couscous for the older children, pouring for Papa and for Zadok and the men.

"*Pass the hummus.*"

"*A little more of that!*"

"*Fine!*"

"*Very good!*"

"*Yes, I would like a bit more, thank you!*"

"*Send the cucumbers round again, if you please. . . .*"

At last the platters were empty and little ones trundled home to bed.

It was quiet in the neighborhood. Peaceful and pleasantly cool. Torches in the courtyard sputtered and died in the breeze that swept down from the direction of Lebanon. Zahav lit a single oil lamp for Papa, Zadok, and Simon, who remained in the courtyard. Now the visitors could talk openly to Papa. They would give the real reason Zadok had come to visit Papa after thirty years.

Inside the dark interior of her workroom Zahav sank down on a cushion beneath the open window to listen. She busied her hands plaiting the knots of tallith fringes, encoding the sacred name of Yahweh and His commands within the pattern.

Papa began. "So, we're old men now, Zadok. We share a common hope, a mutual sorrow. I have never stopped looking for Messiah. Never. But I'm getting old. The world is past ripe and into rotten. I'm going blind, I fear. I had hoped to see the face of the child grown to manhood."

Zadok replied, "Do you remember the words of Jeremiah we sang over the graves of our sons the day we buried them?"

"Who could forget such a thing?" Papa cleared his throat and then, with quaking voice, began to sing the song:

"O my Comforter in sorrow,
my heart is faint within me.
Listen to the cry of my people
from a land far away."

Zadok and Simon joined Papa in the melancholy tune:

"Is Yahweh not in Zion?
Is her King no longer there? . . .
The harvest is past and summer has ended
And yet we are not saved.
Since my people are crushed, I am crushed;
I mourn, and horror grips me.
Is there no balm in Gilead?
Is there no physician there?
Why then is there no healing
For the wounds of my people?"[9]

Zahav knew the mourning song of Jeremiah by heart. And yet she had not realized this had been sung at the burial of her brother and the other little boys of Beth-lehem.

Papa said, "Thirty years and more the Jordan has descended from this mountain and still we wait. We wait. Will he ever come?"

Zadok's voice was soothing. "Eliyahu, brother, the wait is over. The true Balm of Gilead, who can heal our wounds, has come at last. He will heal his people!"

Papa whispered, "The child?"

"Aye. Aye, Eliyahu! Think of it! I've seen him. Grown to manhood."

There was silence as Papa took in Zadok's words.

Then Simon spoke. "And I've come here with Zadok to bear witness. I am living proof that he who is both physician and healing balm can heal our wounds."

"Tell him, Simon," Zadok urged the younger man.

Simon's words tumbled from him as though he had been waiting for this opportunity. "It's like a distant nightmare, but true. I was . . . *tsara* . . . stricken with leprosy."

Papa gasped. "You? *Tsara?* But how can such a thing be true?"

Simon continued eagerly, "My hands were consumed. I hid my disease from everyone but my wife. Tried to heal myself with every earthly cure. Nothing worked. I was discovered. Cast out. At last, when I had no place else to turn, I made my way to the one Jeremiah wrote of, the true Healing Balm, the *Tsori* of Gilead. Yeshua—"God is Salvation"— is his name. And Yeshua, the Tsori, healed the wounds of this *tsara*. Nor does he only heal bodies! He is true balm for corruption of the soul." There was a significant pause as Simon allowed Papa to understand that it was a confession. "Yes, he healed not only my wounds but those of many others."

Papa whispered, "Then he lives. Zadok, is it the same little fellow? The same we knew in Beth-lehem?"

"Aye, Eliyahu. Yeshua. Salvation. Grown up like an oak into manhood. I've come to know him well."

Papa cried, "Blessed are you O Adonai, Lord of the Universe, that I have lived to hear such news! How long have we been waiting for you! Every day we pray that the Anointed will come! Now, Zadok, brother, you bring such good news!"

Simon added to the tale, "He's hated by the rulers in Yerushalayim."

"Good. Yes. As it should be," Papa said. "Darkness cannot survive in the presence of light. So it has been since the beginning. If he is the Anointed One, then he will be hated. Despised and rejected. It is written."[10]

Zadok took over. "In the Temple he drove out the merchants. Aye! He plaited a whip and drove them out with the cry of Jeremiah on his lips: *'You have made my Father's house a den of thieves!'*"[11]

Papa was exultant. "He did this, did he? Fulfilled the prophecy of Jeremiah? *'Has this house, which bears my name, become a den of thieves to you? But I have been watching! declares Yahweh.'*"[12]

Zadok growled his approval. "Aye. Yahweh has indeed been watching. Now Yeshua has made fierce enemies of Herod Antipas, Caiaphas, and most of the Sanhedrin. Have y' heard the edict of Herod Antipas and the Sanhedrin here in the North? The people of Judah and the Galil are forbidden even to speak to him. Yet still they seek him in spite of the danger."

Papa mused, "There were rumors through the years. We hear them but seldom believe. But from your mouth, Zadok, to my ears, proof enough."

"Herod Antipas is trying to kill Yeshua," Simon interjected.

Papa acknowledged, "So should the Samaritan son of Herod the butcher be different than his father?"

Zadok added, "Everything is happening exactly as it is written in Torah and Tanakh, Eliyahu. The little Prince we held in our arms! Immanu'el! God-is-with-us indeed!"

Papa's voice quaked with emotion. "Zadok! For thirty years I have not made pilgrimage to Yerushalayim because of those beasts who killed the hereditary high priests and took power! The families of Caiaphas and Annas are an abomination to Yahweh! So I wait here, eh? I wait where the tribe of Dan settled in the northernmost boundaries of David's kingdom. I shepherd the lost lambs in this place and I wait. It has not been easy, let me tell you! So many are fallen from the truth."

Zadok confided, "Yerushalayim remains in the iron grip of Caiaphas. Few righteous men are left on the council. When I dared to speak the truth about Yeshua, the Sanhedrin stripped my office from me. Now a son of Caiaphas is Chief Shepherd of the Temple flocks."

Papa considered this sad news. "So. This is as close to Yerushalayim as I will go until Messiah calls me to return. I built my little sukkah here at the source of the Jordan! Every day I wash my hands in water that descends from the mountain to quench the thirst of Israel! You know? Zadok! Every day as I wash I pray for the Anointed One who descended from heaven! Pray for the baby whose birth was announced by angels! How I've longed for that child to grow to manhood and come find us! To purify the source of the river! Will he come to the North, Zadok? He has reason to come. Herod Antipas has no power here. Philip cares nothing for religion. Yeshua could prepare his army here. Will he lead us home and reclaim Yerushalayim? restore righteousness? comfort those of us who mourn? remind us that our sons did not die in vain?"

"He will come, Eliyahu. From Dan in the North to Beersheba in the South! Yes. Prepare your congregation. He will come."

The evening of Diana's funeral procession Castor, the youthful Greek physician, completed bandaging Alexander's hands. "A few weeks and you'll be good as new. You were lucky this time, Alexander." Castor washed in the basin and glanced toward the bed where Hero lay sleeping.

Alexander waved his fists in frustration. "Lucky? I have an order of fifteen panpipes to be sent to Damascus next week. I was already behind. Now this. How will I work, Castor?"

"I wasn't talking about your work."

"Hero?"

The doctor snapped his fingers. "A few seconds more—and you would have lost him to the fire."

Alexander nodded soberly. "Lost. Yes. Yes." It had been a near thing. "Diana could always calm him. I . . . I don't know what to do."

Reaching into his satchel, the physician produced a blue glass vial the size of an egg. He held it up to the light for a second, then placed it on the table beside Alexander. "Hero's hands are burned, yet he feels no pain. One drop, you see? And he's fast asleep."

"Only one drop?"

"Two and he will sleep for days. Three, and . . ." The doctor did not finish the thought.

"Dangerous then."

"For those who no longer want to live in pain, it is passage to Elysium. Stronger than my other remedies. I offered this to Diana weeks ago when her pain began to be unbearable. She wouldn't have it."

"You didn't tell me."

"Be comforted, my friend. That's proof of how much she loved you and the boy. She could've put an end to her suffering, but she chose to stay with you and Hero to the very end. Quite a sacrifice on her part. To go on living when life wasn't worth it."

Alexander stared at the light shining on Hero's hair. Diana had stayed alive for his sake. "He's so beautiful when he sleeps. She always said so."

The doctor silently rolled a linen bandage, replacing it in his bag. "Yes. When he's asleep." He looked again at the vial, then stared pointedly at Alexander. "He's tormented when he's awake. And when he sleeps, he has nightmares we can't imagine. There are other ways a human creature may suffer unbearable pain."

Alexander drew himself erect. He had not thought of Hero's suffering, only of his own. "Unbearable?"

"We can't know what demon tortures him, Alexander. To throw him into the fire! He didn't fear the flames. How deep is the boy's anguish if he'll leap into a fire?"

Alexander shook his head. "Truth is . . . oh, the truth. The truth? Castor! You don't know how badly I wanted to become smoke. To drift away with her! I know! I know what he's feeling."

"You're a grown man. Time will heal your grief. You've got a full life ahead of you. But what does Hero face? If living becomes too much for him?"

"We'll manage, him and me. What choice do we have? We'll go on without her."

"You have a choice. It's my duty to give you the options. I tell you about this because . . . Hero's pain may be too much for a father to bear."

Alexander blinked at him dumbly. His voice shook with emotion. "Don't talk about this tonight, Castor! Not tonight! How many drops would it take to kill a grown man? Tell me so I won't drink too few! Not tonight! Don't tell me Hero might be better off . . . because if I think about going on without Diana . . . ? Tomorrow you may come and both Hero and I will be dead!"

With a shrug the doctor closed his bag. "I'm telling you the truth. You have a life ahead of you. Hero has nothing. If he died he would be with his mother. Where he longs to be."

"You don't know that! You can't know something like that!"

"Then at least he'd no longer exist in misery."

"Castor, you've known me my whole life! You brought Hero into the world. How can you think I'd help him leave it?"

"You're still a young man. You'll marry again. But what woman would marry a man with such a child?"

"Hero is . . . the priests say . . . Hero is touched by the gods."

Castor laughed. "Oh, yes! The Romans teach that those who have the 'falling sickness' are somehow holy. Romans create their own reality for a Caesar who collapses in the Forum and froths at the mouth. They say it is the sickness of a god!"

"And if the lie helps me cope, then why take the lie from me?"

"We Greeks face reality when it must be faced. Pragmatism, not sentiment, is true mercy. If there's no hope, then what would be best for Hero?"

"Best? You ask me what would be best for him? It would be best if I keep my promise to Diana! If I love him and—"

"Your child is in anguish. It will be worse for him since his mother is dead."

"I can't hear this, Castor. Don't talk about this. I can't bear it."

"There's much more to Hero's infirmity. When the spells are not on him, can he think? Can he reason? A child who throws himself into the cremation fires at his mother's funeral? His grief is greater than physical pain. Is that human?"

Alexander mumbled fiercely, "I promised Diana I'd take care of him. I . . . offer . . . sacrifices to the gods of my fathers. I beg daily for his healing."

Castor scoffed. "As you begged for Diana to be healed? There is no god of mercy to hear your prayers."

"There must be hope for my son!"

"He's incurable. A deaf mute in the house of a musician. The gods, if they exist, have played a cruel joke on you, my friend."

"Should I end the life of my son because Pan and Hermes made him a thing to be laughed at?"

Castor put a consoling hand on Alexander's shoulder. "The seizures may kill him, and then it's out of your hands. But if the sickness doesn't kill him—his mind will be more damaged with every seizure. And burning to death is torment beyond imagination."

Alexander shrugged off his touch. "Enough! You won't speak of this again under my roof."

"You'll know if the time is right."

"You can find your way out?" Angry, Alexander turned away.

The physician saluted in farewell. "I wouldn't be a friend if I didn't tell you."

The fire on the hearth had long since died, yet the intense heat of the emotional furnace was palpable. Manaen felt it on his face, his ears, his neck.

"How could you do this to us! How?" Susanna stormed. "Are you crazy as well as blind?"

She had remained silent on the journey from the Bethsaida market back to the estate. But once they were inside and the servants dismissed, Susanna held nothing back.

"First you tell me Gadot and Acteon are there, and then in the next breath you admit you insulted Tetrarch Antipas in front of them! Herodias is already sharpening her dagger!"

He gritted his teeth. "I won't sell to that Idumean pig. No one can force me to!" Manaen's despair over the loss of his eyes expressed itself in blazing anger, scorching all nearby.

She paced the floor. "Right! When you're dead—stabbed or poisoned or thrown from a cliff—you won't sell to anyone!"

Manaen stiffened as she passed near him. "Would you have me be less than a man?"

"I'd have you be alive! Oh, Manaen, can't you just live? Can't we?"

"Antipas stole my eyes. But you'd let him turn me into Gadot."

Susanna knocked over a chair in response. "We could've been safe here across the border. We *would* be safe! All we have to do is leave things alone. But no! You insult Antipas and make sure everyone hears it! Doesn't matter if Philip and Antipas hate each other. Philip can't let that sort of insult stand. He'll never protect you now."

"His protection! Who wants it?"

"You're not thinking of me! You never think of me! When you're found guilty of treason, executed, and our land seized, what will happen to me?"

"If we starve, it's better than toadying to Antipas."

"I left you to manage the business on your own, so you'd feel better, better about yourself. I felt sorry for you because—"

"The truth. At last. Pity the poor blind man."

"You've got enough self-pity to go around."

"Let him think he's useful."

"You might be useful if you'd act like a man!"

"Antipas put out my eyes. He didn't make me a eunuch!" Manaen attempted to storm from the room but tripped over a stool. Brandishing the stool by one of its legs, Manaen roared, "Get out of here! Get out!"

"Gladly," Susanna's shaky voice called as she retreated down the stairs.

Kuza did not have to carry Manaen bar Talmai's insults back to Herod Antipas. Herodian spies in Bethsaida—or the wind, or a chirping bird, or a demon whispering to Antipas in the night—had already repeated the tale of defiance.

Antipas was drunk and in no mood for excuses by the time Kuza returned the following day to the villa at Tiberias with a cargo of almonds purchased from a farmer in Chorazin.

Antipas raged to Herodias. "After everything I did for him! Manaen! He's a dead man! A dead man! Who does he think he is? He won't sell to a . . . what was it he called me? What?"

Kuza, hands clasped, eyes to the ground, did not reply.

Antipas shrieked and struck out with his staff, knocking the steward to one knee. "Did you hear my question, Kuza? What did Manaen call me?"

Blood dripped on the pavement from a gash near Kuza's eye. He stammered, "A . . . a . . . Samaritan, my lord. And an Idumean."

Herodias, not nearly as drunk as Antipas, slurred, "How can you be insulted, Antipas? You *are* a Samaritan *and* an Idumean!"

The monarch whirled as though he would strike her as well. "Don't you hear what it means? Don't you understand anything? He was announcing to everyone, to everyone in my brother Philip's territory, that I am not fit to reign! That I am not a Jew! Not a descendant of David!"

"Half the population of Eretz-Israel claims to be descended from David, my darling. You are unique. A king over the Jews who has not one drop of Jewish blood."

"Well, I am not happy!" Antipas struck Kuza again, sending him sprawling to the floor.

Herodias restrained Antipas. "Don't kill Kuza over it. Where will you find such competent help? Not a Jew? Does it matter, Antipas? That's why you married me, remember? I'm descended from the Hasmonean princes. I'm one of the Maccabees, if you go back far enough! Maccabees . . . the family your dear old father murdered one by one until I am one of a handful who remain. Manaen's wife, Susanna, is another through another line. But surely you'll kill her along with that arrogant husband of hers, and I'll be the only one left."

Antipas sputtered, "I'm surrounded! Surrounded by treachery! Manaen bar Talmai. Why isn't he dead? Wolf assured me he killed him. Cut out his heart. But Manaen is alive and Wolf escapes into the desert! Escapes to King Aretas! I hear them laughing! And now that magician from Nazareth! Is Yeshua a descendant of David as well? Will he fancy himself a . . . a . . . a king? take my crown?"

Herodias lifted a mirror from a side table and examined her reflection. "That's the nature of politics, is it not? The winner is the one left breathing when the dust clears. Listen to me and you'll live a long and prosperous life, Antipas. Yeshua and Manaen are destined for early graves. We've made sure of it. But you'll still need a good steward to be happy. So let Kuza crawl back to his accounting. He brought you your almonds, didn't he?"

Antipas inhaled, regaining control of his emotions. He nudged Kuza with his toe. "All right. All right. Not your fault, I suppose. Get out. Just . . . go."

Herodias laughed as the steward left the room on all fours. "And now, my great Samaritan king! Here is the surprise I promised you! It will lift your spirits. I swear."

Herod Antipas allowed Herodias to lean on his arm as the royal couple descended a flight of stone steps into a basement room beneath the palace.

An hour earlier a note had been passed to the tetrarch's wife by one of her attendants. It read simply: *Have something of interest.* It was signed *Shamen.*

By the glow of a trio of oil lamps, Antipas discerned the husband and wife assassins. A third figure was present, huddled in a corner. As Antipas' eyes adjusted to the dim scene, he studied the unknown man.

Elderly, thin, poorly dressed, and casting anxious glances around the room in plainly fearful anticipation, the subject appeared eager to be anywhere else. His chest and legs were tied to the wooden chair on which he sat. His wrists were bound to the arms of the chair so that his hands extended, palms downward, in front of him.

Antipas demanded scornfully, "What's this? I have plenty of beggars outside my gates already. Do I need more?"

Shamen bowed deeply. "My lord expressed interest in the deeds of the Galilean prophet? This man claims to have been healed by him. In fact, lord Antipas, we take small credit for locating him. At an inn just off the Magdala road, no more than five stadia from here, this fellow was getting free drinks for telling and retelling his story."

Antipas moved closer, leaning in. "A tavern braggart? He doesn't look as if he's ever been ill. He's certainly not blind or crippled. What does he say was his trouble?"

"Leprosy," Shamen replied laconically.

Antipas bolted upright and backed away several paces. "Impossible!"

Ona raised a rounded, grandmotherly chin. "Others at the inn confirm this *is* the same man who begged outside the old cemetery near Tiberias, Ebyon by name. He had no nose, no ears, and no fingers on either hand."

With peremptory gestures, Antipas ordered that the man's chin be jerked upward toward the light so his features were free of shadow. "Still impossible. No one can make ears and noses grow back. You, Ebyon. What do you say?"

Ebyon stammered, "All I know is that he healed me, sir. And that's the truth. My face is mine again. My hands likewise. He told me to show myself to the priests, but what good are they? They never healed me. They never even tried."

Antipas nodded. "Quite right. And your family? Aren't they excited to have you restored?"

Emboldened by the sympathetic tone, the beggar replied, "Bless you, sir. I've got none. No one a'tall. I know no trade but begging. How was I to live, I ask you?"

Antipas raised one eyebrow and cocked his head at Shamen. "A test is in order."

"Exactly my thought, my lord."

In a single fluid movement, adroit for one so seemingly awkward, Shamen produced a hatchet from beneath his robe. Moving faster than Ebyon could protest, the hand ax flickered up and down, severing the four fingers of Ebyon's left hand.

Blood and screams gushed out of the man. After the initial ear-piercing outburst, Ebyon's anguished gasps took on a mechanical, repetitive quality. His hoarse cries kept time with the pulsing jets of gore.

The onlookers studied the mutilated hand in dispassionate silence. The tetrarch sounded disappointed, like a child at a magician's failed trick. "They're not growing back. The blood is still pumping. Whatever healing was done wasn't permanent."

Ebyon's cries subsided to dull grunts. He rocked back and forth against his bonds.

"Away with him." Antipas turned toward the stairs.

Shamen wiped the hatchet on a silk scarf. "A moment more, if I may, Majesty."

At Antipas' permissive gesture, Shamen waved his hands over Ebyon's face and stump. "In the name of Yeshua of Nazareth, be healed!"

Nothing changed.

Nothing.

"By the power of the man called the prophet of the Galil, be healed!"

Spreading his hands to indicate the trial was ended, Shamen stepped back.

Antipas waggled one finger impatiently.

Ebyon's moans ceased abruptly when Ona flicked a silk scarf over his head and jerked the garrote tight around his throat. "Better than other means when speed is called for," she offered cheerfully.

Zadok and his son-in-law stayed only one night and left just after noon the following day. After they departed, Papa closed himself off in his little room to study the prophecies and didn't come out the rest of that day.

Zahav was worried. Even the news Zadok and Simon had brought him that the infant king of Beth-lehem was alive and well hadn't taken away her papa's anxiety. It was as though, prior to Zadok's visit, Papa's mysterious vision of the linen-wrapped Torah scroll had somehow sapped his strength. Whatever he had seen in addition to the baby wrapped in swaddling clothes had somehow broken his heart. And he could not be consoled.

The very next morning, when Zahav knocked on Papa's door, he did not reply. Upon opening the door, she found him asleep across the open text of the scroll of Zechariah. The candle had burned out. He was still dressed. He had never gone to bed.

"Papa?" She tapped the old man lightly on his shoulder.

He stirred and opened his eyes. The opacity of his cataracts seemed more pronounced today than yesterday. "Daughter? I've fallen asleep. So late. What are you doing up?"

"It's morning, Papa." Could he not see the light streaming through the high window?

"Ah. Yes." He frowned down at the scroll. "Sun will be up soon, then."

"Come on. Sleep awhile. You've been up all night again, Papa." She chided him and helped him to lie on his bed.

"I was . . . I was . . . this passage in Zechariah. I was trying to . . . I know it's there, eh? In the left column? It begins with, *'And I will pour out . . .'* Would you read it?" He remembered the position of the writing, though he could not see it.

Zahav scanned the page and began to read:

"'I will pour out upon the house of David and upon the inhabitants of Jerusalem, a spirit of grace and supplication. They shall look on me, the

one they have pierced, and they will mourn for him as one mourns for
an only son, and grieve bitterly for him as one grieves for a firstborn
son.'"[13]

"Yes. Yes." He turned his face to the wall. "I see."

But Papa did not see. Could not. Zahav frowned. "Papa, you have to rest your eyes. Must. Did you remember to put on the salve?"

"No. It's all gone. Days ago."

"Papa! You didn't tell me."

He was drowsy. "I forgot, Daughter. So much going on. So much. So many secrets to ponder."

"Rest. I'll be back. Just rest awhile."

Every time Zahav exited the narrow lane of the Jewish Quarter opening onto the Cardo, the north-south axis of Caesarea Philippi, she shivered.

The Jewish Quarter of Philip's capital city was, in many ways, a self-contained world. Besides the synagogue, which literally and spiritually formed its center, the Quarter possessed its own commercial district. Jewish tinsmiths, cobblers, carpenters, and produce sellers existed side by side, never having to deal with Gentiles from one Shabbat to the next.

But it was not possible for the Quarter to meet all its needs internally.

At the corner where the Quarter intersected with the Cardo Zahav passed Ari bar Pehter's goldsmith shop. Jewish artisans were widely sought after for their skill in hammered gold and filigree work. Ari's honesty in assaying the quality of gold was also highly regarded. Gentiles in dispute over the value of ore from mines in the Golan often brought samples to his shop for analysis.

Ari's workmanship brought silver coins bearing the faces of Tiberius Caesar and Tetrarch Philip into the Quarter. Ari bought his kosher lamb from Haran, the butcher, who spent the same coin at the shop of Josiah, the baker, whose wife went to Zahav to obtain a prayer shawl for their boy's bar mitzvah.

And so it went.

Eventually those and similar transactions within the settlement allowed Zahav to venture out to buy the fabric, thread, dye, and cord she needed for her talliths.

Once on the Cardo Zahav was in a different world. Men with shaved heads and wearing earrings were trailed by strings of wives. Philip's uniformed guardsmen tramped the streets, as did Roman legionaries. Curly-haired Greeks in short tunics conversed with Scythians in conical hats and trousers.

This morning Gentile men eyed Zahav as she passed, made lewd comments. Veiled Jewish women were mysterious and therefore desirable.

Zahav hurried her pace.

She came to the Street of the Unguent Makers. The sticky sweet aroma of balsam, the famous "balm of Gilead," announced the row of perfume and lotion shops without having to pass down its length. Obtained from the bark of a bushy evergreen tree, the ocher-colored resin was burnt as incense or mixed with olive oil as a pleasant-smelling lotion that could supposedly heal cataracts. The oil extracted from the leaves and berries, dissolved in water, was also used to cure headaches. Papa had cataracts; Zahav had a headache. Today the cure was much needed.

The odor of balm wafted around her as Zahav entered the apothecary shop of Meshek, an assimilated Jew who sold to both Greeks and Jews. He kept his beard and spoke Hebrew fluently. But in dress and ability to get along in the world outside the Quarter he seemed indistinguishable from a Gentile. All the same, he was trusted by the Jews of the Quarter.

Shelves were lined with mysterious bottles behind the table where he measured out the remedy for a middle-aged Greek woman who was saying, "I can't sleep from remembering it! A horrible sight, I can tell you, Meshek! The child! Poor thing! Throwing himself upon the flames of his mother's pyre!"

Meshek clucked his tongue as he ground the concoction. "This will help you sleep. A pinch in a glass of wine. You'll sleep."

The woman lowered her voice conspiratorially. "His father pulling him out of the flames! A nightmare! Bad enough Diana is dead, leaving the little boy without a keeper. Everyone thinks the child would be better off dead. How will Alexander find another wife with a burden like that on his back? How will he manage his business?"

More clucking of the tongue from Meshek. "A tragedy. Truly. One cannot help but think it. A tragedy." Meshek glanced up at Zahav and smiled broadly. He addressed her in Hebrew. "Shalom, Zahav! Finished here in a minute! How's the rabbi?"

Zahav pretended to study the labels on the jars. "His eyes. You know. A little more of the salve. It seems to help."

Meshek nodded and poured the potion into a bottle for his customer. The conversation was spoken effortlessly in Greek. "Here you are. Three nights and you'll be on schedule again."

"I do hope so. It's not easily forgotten, such a pitiful sight." The woman paid and left the shop without once looking at Zahav or acknowledging her presence.

Meshek shook his head as the woman bustled out into the street. In Hebrew again: "Such a yenta, that one. Everything there is to know, she knows."

"I saw the funeral procession the other day," Zahav said. "On my way to market. The wife of the flute maker? Is that it?"

Meshek ran his finger along the row of salves, finally choosing the correct medicine. "The little boy, Hero. Possessed. He tried to follow his mother's body into the flames of her burning. A terrible thing. The whole city is talking about it."

"He's hurt badly? The boy?"

"No. I made the salve. Not serious, the burns. His father pulled him clear. No one else even tried to help from what I hear. A sad case. Very sad."

Zahav raised her chin in scorn. "Those Greeks. That's compassion, eh?"

Meshek wagged a finger in disagreement. "Yes? The kosher wife of your kosher butcher was in this morning. She heard about it. Said the whole thing was a punishment from God against Alexander and his ancestors. 'God threw the boy into the fire,' she said. I reminded her that Yahweh was not Molech and preferred his children alive—happy and raw, not roasted. She was insulted." He passed the jar of ointment to Zahav. "Enough for a month. Half shekel, please."

Zahav left the apothecary and hurried to the entry to the Street of the Cloth Merchants. She told herself she needed more wool fabric for her prayer shawls, but most particularly the sky blue woolen cord that would be twisted and knotted into the fringes. Dyed from a shellfish extraction, no one knew exactly when that particular shade of yarn first became associated with Jewish talliths, but for centuries white and blue had been the colors of the Jewish nation.

She found herself browsing distractedly as she passed the various stalls. At last she reached the far perimeter of the souk. A few doors beyond was the shuttered shop and home of the instrument maker. A placard hung across the red door where Zahav had seen the body on the bier.

The place appeared deserted. Had Alexander taken his child and gone away? A sad case. So sad. Shoppers surged past her as she stared at the house with morbid fascination.

As she was about to turn away, the red door swung back. Alexander emerged, blinking up at the too-bright sun. Hair uncombed. Clothes dirty and disheveled. A couple days' growth of beard. He was gaunt, half starved. Like someone who had stumbled out of the desert after weeks of wandering. There was no sign of the little boy.

In bandaged hands Alexander carried a chamber pot to the center gutter in the street and dumped it. *A sort of metaphor for his life*, Zahav thought.

Glancing up the street, he then retreated into his house, slamming the red door behind him.

Zahav put a hand to her forehead and closed her eyes, as if she could see what was behind the door.

"O Adonai! O merciful One. Oh. Oh."

❦

Alexander sat with his face buried in his bandaged hands. He had not slept for the past two nights. Whenever he closed his eyes he revisited Diana's funeral pyre. He saw Hero's rush toward the flames. He saw the blaze reach out to embrace the child.

Shuddering, Alexander turned his head to look at his sleeping son. Exhausted from the ordeal and the pain of his burns, Hero at least could rest.

It was not untroubled slumber. Even after Castor's sedative the boy whimpered and fidgeted. What would happen when he awoke? Would Alexander be able to comfort him? to control him?

Tearing his eyes away from the boy, Alexander stared somberly around the room where Diana had last been alive. Clothes were heaped in a corner. Makeup and perfume bottles were strewn carelessly across the dressing table. The roses he'd bought to cheer her last week drooped brown and lifeless.

It distressed Alexander to see everything so chaotic. In health Diana would never have allowed such mess. "One temperamental, absentminded artist in the family is bad enough," she said. She always scolded, then picked up after him anyway.

She was never impatient. Not with Alexander. Not with Hero.

With a burst of motion he scooped up an armload of clothes and set them on a chair. Bending over the dressing table Alexander tried to restore it to order, but the second alabaster vial of scent he touched froze him in place.

Her clothes! Her perfume!

But not her!

Never again.

As much as it pained him to see their home so muddled, Alexander could muster no more energy to do anything about it. How could he, when every sight, every smell, every touch reminded him that she was not returning?

How could he manage without her? How? Alexander felt the icy waters of hopelessness closing over him.

A groan drew his attention back to his son, who wrestled with his own inner torment. Alexander fingered the medicine bottle in the pocket of his robe. What if one drop was not enough?

The thought brought a new wave of anxiety.

Usually Alexander could rely on music to come to his aid. He always counted on melody when he needed to think things through. It was never a match for Diana's comfort, but it provided solace of sorts.

The musician stared ruefully at his wrapped fingers. Not tonight. There was no relief to be found in flute playing tonight.

Nevertheless the notion drew his attention toward the shelf where his special flute, the one he'd carved for their wedding day, was kept. Ebony wood, inlaid with ivory, it was unmatched in both appearance and tone. Its pitch was so true and its sound so lingering, Diana said, that Alexander could charm lions with its haunting refrain.

It was missing!

The rosewood rack was empty, tipped over on the ledge. Could the flute have been stolen? taken while the funeral was in progress? And he had not noticed until now?

Alexander ranged around the space, throwing aside blankets and tunics, digging under a stack of parchment. Where was it?

After ransacking the bedroom, the workshop, the display counters, and the kitchen, Alexander returned wearily to Hero's side.

The boy had been writhing in his father's absence. The bedclothes were knotted around the child in a fat cocoon. Cautiously, so as not to wake him, Alexander untangled Hero. The lumps and twists in the fabric were a mirror of the contortions in the child's body.

And in his mind? Were Hero's thoughts as disordered as Castor said? And was he going to get worse?

With a last awkward tug, Alexander straightened the top blanket. Something dropped softly on his toe with a light tap.

It was the flute. It had been trapped within the tangle of boy and bedding all along.

But how had it come to be there? Had Alexander bumped the shelf and the instrument fallen unnoticed? Or had the boy stood and reached up for it?

It was the riddle Alexander finally fell asleep puzzling over, holding the flute in his lap.

PART II

The devil took Him to the holy city and had Him stand on the highest point of the temple. "If You are the Son of God," he said, "throw Yourself down. For it is written:

*"'He will command His angels concerning You,
and they will lift You up in their hands,
so that You will not strike Your foot against a stone.'"*

Jesus answered him, "It is also written: 'Do not put the Lord your God to the test.'"

MATTHEW 4:5-7

The required days of mourning passed. Hands had healed, but hearts remained a mass of gaping wounds.

Friends from the musicians' guild did not bring food for Alexander and Hero this morning. The absence of visitors was a reminder that life moved on. Father and son were on their own.

It was market day. Once a week peasant farmers from the outlying districts brought their produce into Caesarea Philippi for the city dwellers to buy.

Alexander had resisted going out to purchase food. That had been Diana's job. What did he know about running a household?

He and Hero stood together, staring into the empty larder. Only a handful of beans remained on the shelf. And half a loaf of moldy bread.

Alexander summed it up: "I was hoping if we left them alone they would mate and have babies. Clearly it doesn't work that way." He glanced at Hero and noticed for the first time how gaunt and pale the boy was. When had he last eaten? "She would know. She would make sure you were fed."

Silence. Hero's stomach growled. That was the sole complaint Alexander heard from the boy.

"Then it's up to us."

They washed and dressed and left for the souk. Each was the prisoner of the other. A cord tied to Hero's wrist was attached to Alexander's belt for safety. The dark curse that held the boy hostage also held the knife of fear to Alexander's heart.

They passed the synagogue where the wealthiest class of Jews, the Sadducees, gathered for their Sabbath. Hero's head pivoted in curiosity toward the group of bearded, strangely clad Hebrews arguing in Greek about the meaning of some passage in their holy book. Blue-trimmed prayer shawls, like sails, billowed in the morning breeze.

Hero stretched his fingers wide in an attempt to brush the glistening fringe of a silk garment as they passed.

The Sadducee drew back with a scowl. "You! Boy! Stop!"

Hero mimicked the men's gestures and expressions.

"Does this creature mock me? To touch a Jew is to defile him! Does he have no respect? King Philip has declared by law we may not be harassed. Keep him on a tighter leash or I'll report you."

Alexander felt color rise in his cheeks. Yes. King Philip was partial to these merchant Jews. Persecution of their race was not tolerated. But surely such an innocent gesture of delight from a child could not be construed a civil offense. Alexander restrained his anger and tugged Hero's cord, pulling him close. "He's a deaf-mute. A good boy. He meant no harm."

"The cost of my tallith is half a year's wages for a Greek laborer. If a Gentile touches the garment, it is defiled. You understand? Ruined."

"He meant no harm."

"What he meant is not my concern. By Philip's edict we are not to be harassed. If the boy destroys the property of a Jew, you will be liable for damages."

Alexander gathered Hero in his arms and nodded, understanding the threat. A claim filed in civil court would be devastating. He backed up, then turned and hurried away, lest the incident be reported to the officials.

Hostile glares pursued man and boy from the scene.

Hero glanced back over his shoulder. Chin sank to his chest. He hid his face against Alexander in shame.

Around the corner and out of their vision, Alexander set him down and stooped in an attempt to cheer him. "Look at my face, Hero. Look.

It's nothing. Nothing. See? They're religious Jews. Everything about us—everyone not like them—offends them and offends the vengeful god they call One God."

Hero's brows knit together in consternation as he studied his father's face. A long moment passed before the boy patted Alexander's cheek in a gesture meant to comfort him.

The two pressed on. As they approached the stone well of Paneas at the heart of the city, Hero halted, refusing to budge. He began to tremble and pointed. His gaze was riveted on the back of a woman about Diana's size as she pulled up a waterskin from the depths.

Alexander understood at once. "No, Son. No. It isn't her." He led Hero to the rim of the well so he could see the stranger's face. "You see. See? Not Mama. No."

Hero's shoulders sagged. And then, in exhaustion, he rested his hands on the rim and stood tiptoe to peer into the depths of the well.

Suddenly Hero pointed and shouted. The shrill cry echoed back. Pedestrians turned to gape in alarm.

Hero screamed again and struggled to jump into the well. The cord broke and he was free from Alexander! It was as if the waters were a door opening into a familiar room where his mother was waiting for him.

One leg up and over the wall!

Women screamed in alarm.

"No!" Alexander shouted, lunging to grasp his arm as the boy slipped over the side.

Hero fought fiercely to break free. Alexander fell backwards to the pavement as he pulled his son out. But the fight was far from over. Alexander strained to hold on to him.

So strong! Too strong for a four-year-old child! No woman could control such superhuman strength!

Alexander pinned Hero's arms to his sides. The boy's eyes rolled back as he stiffened in a convulsion. Frothing at the mouth, his teeth clamped on his tongue until blood mingled with spittle. Alexander tried to pry the boy's mouth open. No use. Hero would bite off his tongue or swallow it and strangle!

"O spirits of the well! Release him! He is my only son!"

The spasm gripped Hero more savagely. He urinated, soaking himself and Alexander.

Then Alexander felt a firm hand on his shoulder. A woman knelt beside him. "Quickly now," she ordered, taking charge. Rolling a scrap of leather around a stick, she pressed hard on the hinge of Hero's jaw. His bite loosened for an instant. Slipping the wedge between his teeth, she laid her hand on the child's brow and muttered quietly in a foreign language. At last, with a moan, Hero fell limp.

"He's still alive." Alexander wept.

She stood. In heavily accented Greek she asked, "He's breathing?"

By speech and dress Alexander recognized she was Jewish. Had she not broken some Hebrew law by touching Hero? Her aid was a surprising contrast to the Sadducees, who had threatened a lawsuit if Hero so much as brushed the fringe of their garments.

"He's breathing! Yes. He's breathing."

The sun was a halo at her back, concealing her features. "Take him now. Home. Away from the crowds. Feed him. Broth and bread. He's skin and bones. Then he'll need to sleep. A quiet place."

Not until then did Alexander look around him. When he turned to thank her, the woman had vanished through the wall of spectators.

Whispers.

"I saw it all. It's the instrument maker, the widower. The little boy saw something in the well. A spirit. He pointed and screamed."

"The well! A bad omen."

"Trying to throw himself in."

"The convulsion. He's possessed by a spirit."

"So strong! If the man had not stopped him, he would have drowned!"

"The Jewess. Did you see what she did? Spoke some Hebrew incantation and the spell was lifted. Where is she?"

"Gone."

"What about the boy? The gods call to him."

"My son. He is my . . . only son." Tenderly Alexander smoothed Hero's perspiration-soaked locks back from his face.

The circle of onlookers parted as Alexander rose to his feet and carried Hero home.

Food and a quiet place to rest, the Jewess had instructed. Soup? What did Alexander know about soup? And rest? There was no quiet place for Hero's mind to rest. Even slumber was populated by demons.

One drop? Two drops?

How many drops of opium would it take to obliterate the nightmares?

Alexander closed the door behind them and laid the boy on his cot. Retrieving the vial, Alexander knew he could never trust anyone but himself with Hero's safety.

Zahav hurried back from the market. She nodded to an elderly friend of her father, unconsciously crimping the tightly folded corner of her scarf more firmly against her cheek. She remained flushed with adrenaline as she replayed the incident with Alexander and his little boy.

Had anyone from the congregation spotted her? she wondered. There would be accusations that she had defiled herself, no doubt. But what would the outcome have been for the child if she had not stopped to help?

Now that she had held the featherlight form of the boy in her arms, she was certain he was literally starving. Possibly he was refusing nourishment because of grief. But what could she do? Today she had crossed the line of propriety. No respectable Jewish woman would speak one word to a man like Alexander, let alone kneel in the dust and attend to the child of a pagan. And yet Zahav felt so sorry for the man and his son. How could she help again without drawing criticism down on herself and on her father? She tried to put it out of her thoughts.

Zahav was late for the Torah schoolboys' choral rehearsal, but that fact did not stop her from appreciating the beauty of the Jewish Quarter and the synagogue.

An arch hung at the center of the six-columned colonnade marking the front portico of the building. The graceful curve mimicking Adonai's rainbow of promise was repeated in the window over the main entry and again two stories higher, under the sharp angle of the steeply inclined roof. Red roof tiles defined the boundary between honey-tinted stone walls and sapphire sky.

Zahav passed beside the carved frieze of palm trees and pomegranates and turned in at the Torah school annex adjoining the synagogue. Though her house was around the back of the structure and out of sight from this courtyard, Zahav was relieved to be back in her own world.

Closing her eyes, she sniffed the air. The Caesarea Philippi Torah school had a unique aroma, comprised of lilac growing on the wall out-side and the musty odor of old parchment.

The sounds of the place were distinctive as well: pen nibs scratched, unison readings droned, individual recitations alternated between high-pitched nervousness and deep-voiced correction.

In the center of the terrace, where the light was best, young boys with ink-smeared sleeves and faces copied Hebrew letters onto scraps of parchment. Their fourteen-year-old tutor, conscious of his respon-sibility, nodded gravely to Zahav. Until a year ago he had been one of Zahav's best sopranos. Now his face was blotchy with a scraggly beard and pimples, and his screechy voice bobbled worse than the quills of his charges.

The double-height court was surrounded on three sides by class-rooms. Boys beyond bar mitzvah age studied inside with Rabbi Eliyahu, but the younger ages were out here. The *bet hasefer*, the "house of the book," trained male children above the age of five every day except Sabbath, from daybreak until noon. After the midday meal the boys learned a trade from their fathers, or were apprenticed to other craftsmen, or helped in the shops . . . but each day began with school.

Singsong rhythm of unison recital floated down from the upstairs classrooms. Since Hebrew was written without vowels, the way to learn it properly was to hear it spoken aloud.

Under the balcony at the rear of the courtyard, the hazzan of the synagogue directed the older boys of the *bet Talmud*, the "house of learning." Here the advanced class listened and discussed the Law and the oral traditions.

"How do we know the Almighty has a plan for our lives?" Zahav heard the hazzan ask his charges.

It was a good question, not one Zahav had succeeded in answering for herself. She hurried into the synagogue where the waiting boys choir squirmed with noisy impatience. Mothers glanced up resentfully as Zahav entered.

"Shalom! Shalom!"

Her sister Ishah chided from a bench as she passed, "You're late. In the market, were you?"

Zahav ignored Ishah and addressed the mothers who glared at her from around the hall. She met their hostility with false cheerfulness. "Sorry I'm late. Couldn't be helped. Have you practiced, boys?"

"It's past noon. You'll make us late for Shabbat preparation," came the muttered reply of the mothers.

Zahav pretended not to hear.

Youngest sister Rebecca, little Aaron on her hip, approached as Zahav fumbled through her music. She leaned close enough to whisper, "Watch yourself, Zahav. The butcher's wife saw everything."

"Gossip travels fast."

"The fellow, the instrument maker? You spoke to him. Touched his son. He's apostate. Unclean. His boy is mad. They are cursed of Adonai. Dead to us."

Zahav bit her lip and stared at her music parchments without seeing. She nodded, thanking Rebecca. There was nothing to do but get on with the practice. Act as though nothing had happened. But she would have to tell Papa what she had done before someone else did.

Seated on the knoll behind his house, Manaen lifted his chin and sniffed the air. A breeze stirred, its direction veering into the west as it often did in the late afternoons of good summer weather. The sun, well past the heat of the day, was still warm on his cheeks as he faced it, but not on his back or neck.

A wineskin beneath Manaen's bench lay collapsed into flaccid lifelessness.

The rhythmic chinking of hand ax and adze, the scraping of the cooper's draw knife, ceased to resonate from inside the barn. In place of those noises Manaen heard the clatter of metal on metal as tools were loaded into carry crates.

Laborers' voices grew louder and more bantering as the remaining casks of nuts were filled, their lids hammered home. The workers grunted as they muscled the last of the day's produce into racks.

The tinkling sound of chimes around the neck of a bellwether came to Manaen from the path descending the hillside. A minute later the muted commands of a goatherd driving his flock in from pasture confirmed Manaen's surmise.

The aroma of roasting lamb wafted toward him. Preparations for the evening meal were already under way.

By these and a thousand other subtle yet recognizable signs,

Manaen realized the end of another day had come. Toil came to a halt. Productive useful workers, whether goatherd or barrel maker, common laborer or craftsman, each reached temporary fulfillment. The war between man and the thorns and thistles of the cursed earth came to a transitory truce during the night watches.

It was a time to be satisfied with accomplishments, however slight, and enjoy well-earned rest. Yes, a time for every man to be satisfied and feel a degree of pride . . . except for Manaen.

What use was it to be able to tell the time of day from breeze and temperature and sounds? A parlor trick anyone could do? Information anyone could, with closed eyes, possess?

Bitterness burned his thoughts like flame consumed straw. The dregs of too much wine were bitter in his mouth. He had done nothing all day. Nothing! Hashim had tactfully come to him with a range of insignificant problems, none of which required any talent or intellect to solve. "I need your opinion, sir. Shall I seal the contract with red or blue wax?"

Kindly meant, but each needless inquiry underscored Manaen's uselessness. All important questions were presented to him in predigested form: "The nuts in the fourth and fifth dryin' racks will be ready for roastin' tomorrow. Shall we prepare the fires?"

Manaen wanted to scream, *Don't bother asking me! I'm blind; don't you understand? I'm useless! I never learned my father's business when I had eyes, and now it's too late!*

Nor had the hostility between him and Susanna over his rebuff of Kuza been resolved; it had been ignored, buried, avoided, but not resolved.

Manaen forced his thoughts away from the present gloom and into the realms of memory. What had life been like before he was blind?

There had been other summers, other breezes. A place came to mind. A place and a time associated with the strength of young manhood when anything—everything—was possible. An afternoon like this one, judging by the touch of the air.

The patter of small bare feet scurrying at a great rate of speed along the cobblestone path toward the cookhouse caught Manaen's attention. He called out, "Samu'el! Samu'el, is that you?"

The footsteps skidded to a halt. "Uh-huh" was the boy's terse reply.

Samu'el was the cook's boy—seven or eight years old. Manaen

couldn't remember exactly what she'd said. She was new, hired since Manaen and Susanna had moved into the house. Cook was from Paneas at the northern end of Philip's country, but she'd grown up near Bethsaida and was pleased to be near the rest of her kin again. Manaen had spoken to her no more than ten or so times, leaving household management to Susanna.

He'd given orders to the boy but had conversed with him only once. No great conversation either—all "uh-huh" and "huh-uh."

"Samu'el, tell your mother to fill this wineskin again and then you bring it to me."

Samu'el skittered away, returning minutes later. Without speaking, the boy thrust the turgid leather bag into Manaen's grasp, then jerked his hands back as if eager to be away.

"Not so fast." Recollections of wine and other summer evenings again attracted Manaen's thoughts. "Boy, do you know a place called The Pinnacle?"

Of course Samu'el did. Everyone who traveled the river road along the Upper Jordan from Bethsaida north to Paneas knew the spot. On the east bank of the stream, sheer cliffs towered over deep pools upriver of a patch of turbulent, boulder-strewn rapids.

Manaen had challenged his courage there in his youth. He and his friends had dared each other: Leap from the heights into the swirling water. Fight free of the river's grasp before the current sucks you under and onto the rocks.

While all bragged of their courage, no one wanted to go first. But Manaen the wrestler did, emerging with a victorious, scornful shout. It had been an evening much in feel like this one. "Take me there," he ordered.

The boy made a noise of protest.

"You don't have to stay long. Just take me there and you can race right back for your supper."

His hand on Samu'el's shoulder, the pair started for the river. From Manaen's manor it was no more than a mile away, upstream.

Outside the gate, the cobbles of the walk gave way to the uneven footing of a dirt path: ruts made by oxcart wheels. The furrows were deepened by the amount of wine Manaen had consumed.

Manaen stumbled, pitching forward against the boy. "You idiot! Warn me next time!"

A remorseful murmur came from Samu'el, but nothing further.

When they reached the embankment of the Roman road, Samu'el alerted Manaen with a tap on the man's arm. They advanced up and over the curb stones without incident but also without conversation.

Manaen thought, *I've cowed this child with my crossness.* "It's all right, boy. It's not you. I'm not fit company is what."

The thin shoulder under Manaen's palm shrugged.

"Are there any travelers on the high road tonight, boy?"

"Huh-uh," came the curt reply.

The scent of the air changed as they drew near the river. Cooler, fresher updrafts, flung aloft from the stream, cascaded upward, whistling among the rocks. Carefully, slowly, they approached the brink.

"There's a flat spot, wide enough to lie on. A ledge behind a boulder. Do you know it, boy?"

Samu'el led the way to the desired location, and Manaen folded his legs beneath him, placed the wineskin near, and sat down. His sightless face turned left and right at the sound of the rushing water.

Manaen said with a degree of satisfaction, "I remember this place. This is the place I jumped from. And later I brought Susanna here. You can see all the way down to the lake from here. At least I think you can. Did I imagine it? Can you see it, boy?"

A negative noise replied.

"The lights should be coming on in Chorazin. Set on its hill, it's impossible to hide, even from this distance. Am I right, Samu'el?"

Nothing.

Manaen cut the air impatiently with his right hand. "Or the bridge on the road to Chorazin? It's upstream there. I remember it well. Great arches spanning the canyon. Do you see it?"

"Uh-huh."

His face toward the recollection, Manaen requested urgently, "Tell me about it. Remind me. Are there four arches, or is it five? I need you to help me remember!"

No response.

Manaen exploded. "Dolt! Are you a complete idiot? Can't you speak?"

Wordlessly Samu'el took Manaen's hand and pressed it to his mouth.

Manaen's fingers touched, then jerked away in consternation and guilt. The space beneath Samu'el's nose was split, like a dog's snout. He had a gap, a cleft palate. The boy could not speak, would never be able to make himself understood beyond grunts and obscure, inarticulate noises.

Manaen stammered, "I . . . I didn't know. I couldn't . . . go home, boy. Go on home. But don't tell anyone I'm here. I want to be left alone."

Nearly suppertime.

The aroma of fresh-baked bread drifted up to Susanna as she worked to finish the embroidery on Manaen's new cloak. Heavy gold thread accented sheaves of wheat stitched on the broad border. Though Manaen would never see the intricate detail of her needle-work, Susanna hoped when he touched the raised pattern he would know how beautiful it was, understand the care she poured into its creation. Then he would wear it and remember how much she loved him.

But was her love enough to make him happy? she wondered.

The light was fading. Susanna set aside the needle reluctantly and raised her head to listen to the sounds of servants finishing the last tasks before night fell.

Where was Manaen?

Folding the cloak and laying it in a basket, Susanna stepped onto the balcony. Twilight. The first star gleamed in the eastern sky.

The bench beneath the oak tree was empty. It was too late for him to be in the drying barn, so he must have returned to the house. Probably was tapping his foot, waiting for her to come to the supper table beside the fountain. How she dreaded his inevitable irritation. How would she break through to find the man she had fallen in love with?

"Manaen?" She called over the banister.

No reply.

"Manaen? Is supper ready? Are you waiting? Sorry. I was . . ." She hurried downstairs to the courtyard. Torches flickered. The table was set near the cool water as usual. But Manaen was not there.

At Susanna's voice, Cook appeared at the door. Scowling, the portly woman wiped her hands on her dress and snapped, "He asked for lamb roasted in wine and mushrooms. Said it was your favorite. Said for me to tell you it was proof he thought of you often. Whatever that means. All day it took to prepare. Now it's perfect and he's nowhere. Will you eat alone?"

"Nowhere?" Susanna stared at the table. It was heaped with bread, lentils, fresh fruit, wine. Everything there except the main course and the master of the house.

"As I said, if he doesn't come to table soon, the lamb won't be worth eatin'."

"But . . . how could he . . . go . . . anywhere?"

Cook shrugged. "All the same, your husband, the lord Manaen, is gone. He ordered lamb and mushrooms baked special for you and he's gone. He's not here."

"The barn maybe?" Susanna peered out the door at the dark structure. Oil lamps glimmered in the servants' cottages.

Cook sucked her teeth and muttered, "Sent my oldest down to the barn to look for him a while back. Day's work done. Field servants are at supper. Everyone fed but myself and my boys. Cook's last to eat. We can't eat until lord Manaen eats. There you are, bent over your embroidery all day and him sittin' like a blind stone idol under that oak. Sayin' nothin'. Doin' nothin'. Snappin' his fingers now and then for my little Samu'el to fetch him this and that."

Susanna's stomach knotted with dread. How could a blind man wander off alone? The gale of despair surged around her. She loved him and yet couldn't help him. The howling storm of despondency threatened to shatter their lives completely.

"Broodin'. Broodin'. Has to have lamb for you roasted in wine and mushrooms. Well, now he's vanished and the food'll be wasted."

"Manaen wouldn't just . . . leave. Think! Who saw him last? Where was he?"

Cook ruminated, staring at the fountain for a time. At last she raised a finger in recollection, turned on her heel, and retreated into the back of the house toward the room she shared with her two sons. She bellowed the name of her youngest boy. "Samu'el! Saaamuuu'el! Where are you, child?"

Susanna's heart drummed as she hurried after the portly woman. She thought of how Manaen ate in silence every night, refusing to be drawn into conversation. How Susanna resented his bitterness! She replayed the harsh words they had exchanged that morning, how she had reproached him for wallowing in self-pity. Did he ever think of what she must be feeling, she had asked?

He had not replied, had not spoken to her for the rest of the day. And he had left orders for her favorite meal to be cooked before he had gone away. But gone where? And how? How could he leave without someone knowing?

"Samuuu'el! Come out here, boy! Where are you? Lady Susanna and me have a question for you!"

The child peeked around the doorway. He hid the cleft behind a grimy hand. "Uh-huh?"

"There you are!" Then to Susanna, "Here he is! My little Samu'el. Wouldn't do to lose more than one per day, now would it?" As Cook halted in front of Samu'el, her gruffness melted. She stooped until her round ruddy face was level with his. Smoothing back dark hair, she whispered, "My darlin' boy. My helper. You're a good boy. Make any mother proud. Come out from there, Samu'el. Don't be timid. See here. The lady Susanna is worried about lord Manaen. He's gone missin' from his perch beneath the oak. Let's see. You took him wine. Yes?"

"Uh-huh." The child nodded.

Was he merely painfully shy or was that fear in his eyes? Susanna wondered.

Cook continued the gentle interrogation. "And did he like it well enough?"

"Uh-huh."

"Did he ask for more?"

Samu'el held up three fingers to signify the order for wine was made and filled three times. "Uh-huh."

"And then did Master Manaen ask anythin' more of you?"

The child glanced at his mother and then gawked at Susanna.

Yes. That was fear in his eyes!

"What was it, my darlin' son? What was it Master Manaen wanted?"

"Uhhhh. Uhhhh."

"He's gone missin' from the grounds, you see."

"Uh-huh."

Susanna put her hand on his shoulder. "If you know where he is, Samu'el, if you know, you must tell us!"

He shook his head in a negative. "Naw. Hay naw."

Cook interpreted. "He means Master Manaen ordered Samu'el not to tell."

"But you must show me where he is," Susanna begged. "Please, Samu'el! Master Manaen could stumble and fall if he's on his own. It's dangerous for him."

At this Samu'el's eyes widened. "Uh-huh!" He grasped Susanna's hand in a gesture that begged mercy. "Uh-huh!"

"There," Cook cooed. "You see, lady Susanna? There's my good son. It's dark. We'll need a torch, will we, Samu'el?"

The boy nodded vigorously. Tears of desperation brimmed in his eyes. "Uh-huh!"

With Susanna and his mother following close behind, Samu'el set out along the narrow path.

10

The instrument shop remained closed the rest of the day after Hero's wild attempt to throw himself in the well. The breeze from Mount Hermon stirred the hollow wind chimes outside the window.

Hero lay sleeping. Alexander, chin in hands, had not moved from his bedside since the boy slipped into the opiate-induced slumber.

How beautiful his son was. Eyes closed in peace. Long lashes curved like a smile. Blond hair mussed. Fair skin like hers. Hand beneath his cheek. How peaceful. How happy he seemed in dreamless sleep.

Alexander tried not to think of what might have been. If Hero had not been born flawed. If Diana had lived. And yet what-ifs and might-have-beens taunted him, breaking his heart over and over again throughout the long day.

What have I done to you, boy? Willing you to stay alive? How I've made you suffer. Holding on to your life like it was my life. Telling myself I couldn't breathe if you stopped breathing. I've hurt you every day. I'm sorry, Hero. My Hero. My son. I would let you go to her. I would. I know you want to go to her. So do I. But what if there's nothing to go to? What if I let go of your hand and you slip away from me and everything is darkness on the other side? Ending like the day. A night without stars. Nothing at all. Or worse: an eternity of terror searching for her. I don't know what's there. So I can't. You see? I can't let you go, Hero. My Hero. My son. My only son.

Rapping on the shop door interrupted his melancholy. Alexander was tempted not to answer. Hero did not stir as the knocking grew more insistent.

With a heavy sigh Alexander rose. He made his way through the dark shop to the door. Leaning his forehead against the wood panel, he called, "Closed for the night. Come back in the morning."

A woman's voice replied, "No. No, thank you. I haven't come to buy. I . . . I brought you and your boy supper."

Food. There was a thought. Alexander had forgotten why he and Hero had ventured out this morning.

But who was this? Not anyone he recognized from the guild. He opened the door. Cool air revived him. It was dark outside. Dark inside. No lamp or candle shone.

The dim shape of a woman waited at the threshold. "I brought you soup," she said in a soothing voice.

He remembered. "You . . . today. You helped me." He threw the portal wide. "Come in. And welcome."

"Oh. No, I couldn't. But here's a meal for you and the boy."

He tried to make out her features. The Jewess. He remembered clearly. Of course she would not enter his dwelling.

"I meant no offense asking you in. I mean—"

"No offense taken," she said quickly. "Today I told you he needed to eat. But then I realized that you might have been on your way to market."

"Yes, but we didn't make it."

"Oh . . . I'm sorry. So I brought soup and bread. Oxtail soup. Simmering all day, yes? It's good. A few things to get you through another day or two." It was a youthful voice. Gentle. Full of concern. "Our Sabbath. I couldn't get away till now. And I wanted to check on him. Wanted to bring you both nourishment."

"Without his mother, you see, I don't know how to manage myself."

"An awful thing."

"He's been sleeping since we got back. He has medicine. It makes him sleep."

"Has he eaten?"

"Nothing. Nothing at all and I . . . he just sleeps and sleeps. He can't bear life without his mother."

"You are his father. You must help him bear it, yes?"

"Who will help me?"

"Oxtail soup, bread, and stewed apples will be a start." She thrust the basket into his arms.

The aroma of hot food was intoxicating. "Smell it! But . . . you . . . don't know us. How did you find us?"

"Someone in the crowd recognized you, yes? There was talk. I heard them. They said things had been . . . very difficult for you. Alexander and Hero. Difficult, yes? For some time. Your shop wasn't hard to locate. Alexander the flute maker."

"But why? You're not . . . I'm not . . . like you."

"You didn't look like a fellow who knew anything about making soup."

"You're right on that score." A weak cry drifted from the back room. "He's waking up. I have to tend to him. Have to light a candle. He's afraid of the dark. Will you wait? I'll come back."

"No, I can't. I must get back."

Hero's squeak became a shout.

"Please wait. Wait? Back where? I want to thank you."

"He's telling you he's hungry, yes? Go feed him. That's the cry of a hungry boy if ever I've heard one."

"Will you come back then? Tomorrow? The shop will be open. So I can thank you properly?"

She had already stepped into the lane. "Today El Olam brought our paths together. No need to thank me. Good Shabbat, Alexander. Shalom tov. May the One God bless you and your son and give you peace."

Then she receded into the night.

Zahav, nauseous from her sense of guilt, glanced back at the house of Alexander as she hurried through the dark towards home. Her thoughts were a tangle of conflicting emotions. When had she ever violated Papa's teachings?

By carrying food to the house of the apostate after sunset she had broken the command against work on the Shabbat for the first time in her life.

Not to mention the ordinance forbidding aid to a transgressor!

How many commandments had she broken? Her head throbbed. *Remember the Sabbath day by keeping it holy.*[14]

Vayikra, Parashah 31: *"Work is to be done on six days; but the seventh is a Shabbat of complete rest, a holy convocation; you are not to do any kind of work; it is a Shabbat for Adonai, even in your homes."*[15]

Didn't B'Midbar, Parashah 37, tell the story of a man caught gathering sticks on Shabbat who was stoned . . . to death?[16]

And what about B'Midbar, Parashah 39: *"This is the law: when a person dies in a tent, everyone who enters the tent and everything in the tent will be unclean for seven days."*[17]

Everyone knew that apostate Jews were the same as dead! Worse, even!

And the fifth commandment, to honor her father, was shattered into a million pieces![18] What would Papa say if he knew what she had done? She had waited until after he went to bed before she sneaked out of the house with provisions in hand.

But what if Papa found out?

Today Papa had listened patiently when she explained what had happened to the child in the marketplace. She told him she had acted instinctively. It was as though the boy was Dori or one of her nephews in trouble. Even now she was concerned for the child. He would surely die of starvation if he did not eat.

Papa had replied, "Zahav, you are a dove. That man is a snake. His son is a snake. Doves and snakes must live in the world together, Daughter. But the dove must not go near the snake or she will surely die. Stay far from those people. They are not your people."

Yet all afternoon, as she cooked in preparation for tonight's Shabbat meal and for tomorrow, the feel of the child's bone through his tunic and the look of helplessness in the eyes of the father had been vivid in her mind. Her heart felt as though it would crack if she did not do something. Something . . .

And so she broke the Shabbat command.

The all-seeing Yahweh knew what Zahav had done, carrying food to those who were defiled. The Shabbat prohibitions lay desecrated in the dust! Surely Yahweh condemned her.

But the thought of Papa's disapproval seemed even harder for Zahav to bear. Tears of shame streamed down her cheeks.

She tucked her head and quickened her pace, praying no one had seen her leave—or return to—the Quarter.

The evening deepened.

Manaen's fingers fumbled with the wineskin, brought the spout to his lips, and upended the bag. Red warmth sprayed across his face, then into his mouth. It coursed down his throat and heated his stomach, while also numbing fingers, cheeks, and toes. He struggled to keep his thoughts moving forward. His interior dialogue felt as impeded as a man swimming in the swamps of the Huleh marshes.

He should be able to see Chorazin on the height across the gorge. Would be able to if he could see at all! And behind him the homes on the hill of Bethsaida.

His recollections were fuddled. Things he'd seen a hundred—a thousand—times in childhood were no longer clear to his inner vision. It was as if he'd lost part of his memory when he lost his eyes.

It was unfair! Shouldn't his memories be sharper? Wasn't he entitled to carry something into the perpetual darkness?

He raged against the cruelty that had brought him to this pass.

Manaen's legs were stiff. Awkwardly turning to the right, he dislodged a rock, heard it plummet over the edge, then strike the water.

Manaen stopped and regarded that image: The stone, plunging into the river, never to emerge, left no trace it had once rested here on this height. It was as if it had never existed.

He faced upstream. From here the peak of Mount Hermon was visible, towering over the landscape although it was more than thirty miles away. The melting snow of The Mountain Set Apart fed the springs of Caesarea Philippi and created the pool of Paneas. It pushed the Jordan out of its cradle and sent it hurrying down the gorge. Water from the heavens landed nine thousand feet above the surface of the earth but sank to six hundred feet below it by the time it entered the Sea of Galilee. And it dropped another thousand before it disappeared into the stinking oblivion of the Dead Sea.

The Jordan, also called the River Descender, left the heights of Hermon, watered the whole length of Eretz-Israel, and gave its life in the process.

The Dead Sea never overflowed its banks, the rabbis said, because from there the Jordan went up into the clouds again.

Manaen leaned forward and listened to the rushing current. The snows of Mount Hermon were passing beneath his perch. Sixty feet below, to be sure, but only the breadth of the four-foot-wide ledge truly separated him from its embrace. Down to the Dead Sea but then up into the clouds, he mused.

Manaen heard the river speak.

Upstream children played in calm pools. Manaen had once been one of them.

Upstream, lovers caressed in secluded glades while the water presented a strand of silver to their view. It recited their poetry, endearments, and promises. Manaen and Susanna had once dripped verses and pledges into the stream.

Upstream was Caesarea Philippi, where men of ambition and talent—and vision—sought the patronage of Tetrarch Philip. Builders of families, businesses, reputations, and empires, they poured libations into the pool of Paneas . . . thank offerings to the god Pan for favors rendered.

The river echoed their prayers.

And then the murmurs were inside Manaen's head—growing until they joined together and overwhelmed him.

How could he sit there and dwell on memories of things that would never come again? Was he so easily deluded? He'd never play in a rockbound pool again. He stumbled going up his own stairs! He'd never see his wife's face or look into her eyes . . . ever again. How would he know what was in her eyes?

Manaen fought against the doubts. He knew Susanna loved him. She had been true to him and would always be so. He'd not expected her to wed a blind man, and yet she'd risked coming to him in prison and had still married him after.

But what if she didn't love him? What if she only felt sorry for him?

Perhaps she felt guilty. If Manaen had not fought Demos for her, he'd still have his sight, wouldn't he?

But pity and guilt aren't the same as love, are they?

Manaen argued that he could feel love in her embrace, in her soothing touch on his forehead, hear it in her words.

But he couldn't see it in her eyes, could he? How could he judge what was in her heart unless he could see it in her eyes?

Leave me alone! Manaen wanted to shout to the voices, the doubts.

He'd never play with his own children. Even if he did, he pictured the contempt, the ridicule on their faces. Poor, blind, pathetic Papa! And how would he know they were truly his? Living jokes for him to be mocked with in the marketplace?

"Get away from me," Manaen slurred aloud. He rose to his knees, batting the air with the wineskin.

He knew where this would end. Why fight against something he could never change? Why prolong the agony? Had he lost his courage when he lost his sight? Wretched, pitiable shadow of Manaen the wrestler! What reason did he have for living?

Awkwardly he clambered to his feet. He could feel the uprush of air from the chasm.

Manaen stood swaying on the brink.

Susanna's feet stumbled on the jagged rocks. It was hard to keep to the faint path in the increasing darkness.

"This way?" she demanded of Samu'el.

The boy nodded vigorously.

Susanna's breath burned in her lungs as she ran; horrifying images seared her thoughts.

A cluster of boulders. A screen of oleanders. A gnarled acacia tree pointed its thorn-covered branch toward the precipice like an accusing finger.

The last turn before the ledge. What would she find? It was too dark to see into the gorge. *What if . . . ? What if . . . ?*

Susanna pitched around the last turn to find . . . Manaen sitting cross-legged on the ground, his head bowed in his hands.

He raised his face at the sound of her approach. "Susanna? Knew you'd come," he muttered.

Her heart pounding in her ears, Susanna struggled for calm. "Supper is ready, Manaen. Will you come home?"

Manaen nodded.

The following morning Alexander ignored comments overheard in Caesarea's streets:

"See! There they go."

"Twice the god tried to take the child and twice the father interfered."

"And look at them: both starving to death."

"The child will always be a burden."

"No woman will marry a man with such a wild beast around!"

Alexander was glad Hero could not hear their words.

The boy knew people were staring at him, but he didn't seem to mind. Mostly he studied the faces of passersby with disconcerting frankness, searching for someone only he could recognize.

Utticus, the physician in the Street of the Wine Merchants, was reportedly the best in the city. Surely he would have answers.

Alexander identified the correct shop by what looked like a pair of bells hanging above the door. Closer inspection revealed them to be cups used for the medical practice of bleeding.

The door squealed on its hinge post as Alexander pushed it open.

Utticus advanced to meet them from behind a screen shielding a back room. Somewhat taller than Alexander's medium height, the doctor's bald head gleamed. Bushy gray eyebrows curled upward. A silver beard hung down on his chest.

Hero buried his face in his father's tunic.

"My name—," Alexander began.

"I know who you are. Alexander the instrument maker. My wife's brother owns one of your teak-and-ivory pipes. Says it's the finest he's ever seen. And I know why you've come."

Alexander spread his hands. "My son. He was always . . . difficult. But since my wife's death . . ."

"Let me examine him." The doctor drew aside a leather curtain over a window, allowing sunlight into the dark room. With an abrupt swing he swept Hero up onto a table.

Hero fought back. Rolling into a ball he lashed out with his feet, trying to kick the doctor in the chin. When this maneuver failed, he swiveled his head from side to side, attempting to bite.

"Help me hold him," Utticus commanded.

Alexander pressed on Hero's shoulders. The doctor quickly tied the child's feet together and lashed them with padded leather cords to the table legs.

Alexander could not bear the reproach he saw on Hero's face. The boy panted like a cornered creature.

Utticus poked and prodded Hero's stomach and rib cage. Lighting an oil lamp he waved it in front of the boy's face and watched Hero's fearful eyes follow the flame. "I don't find anything physically wrong with him. He seems frightened, but so do many children who have lost a mother or father. You say he does not speak?"

"Sometimes he makes sounds that I recognize—or think I do—when he's hungry or thirsty. But nothing like words."

Utticus pulled his beard and frowned. "You had him to the priest at the shrine of course?"

Alexander nodded. "It did no good."

The physician grunted. "Not surprised. I myself trained at Memphis. Know all the incantations to Apis, Isis, and Imhotep. But we've come a long way from offering powdered deer antler mixed with the yolk of an owl egg. Bleeding's the thing. Too much pressure on the brain, you see. Need to relieve the pressure."

"If you really think . . ."

"Nothing better. Won't take a moment and I charge only five pennies. Of course he'll need more than one treatment."

"I want my son to get well. I've nearly finished four new sets of pipes. I can pay you when they sell. Next week?"

Utticus nodded. From a shelf beneath the table he produced a tray covered by a cloth. With a flourish he flipped aside the fabric to reveal a gleaming array of scalpels, lancets, probes, hoods, and whetstones. A pear-shaped brass cup, stained with the dried blood of the last patient, rested there also.

At the sight of the instruments Hero squirmed.

"Can you hold him?" Utticus inquired.

"He's stronger than he looks. I . . . I don't think so. Perhaps . . . tie his hands down too?"

Hero's arms were trussed at his sides. Alexander thought of Aunt Flavia. He avoided the desperate pleading in Hero's eyes.

"This won't hurt, boy. Be over before you know it," Utticus uttered perfunctorily.

The doctor slipped a loop of sinew, like a thick bowstring, around Hero's upper arm and twisted it tight with a wooden peg.

"Good veins," he observed as a blood vessel popped up inside the bend of Hero's elbow.

The boy's struggles intensified. He made frantic grunting sounds.

Selecting a lancet, Utticus bent forward with the cup in his other hand.

Alexander took a step back. The father was so in tune to changes in his son that he spotted the tremor when it was merely a twitch in Hero's eyelid. "Watch out," Alexander cautioned.

"Patience . . . ," Utticus replied.

But before he finished the thought, a full-blown seizure erupted down the entire length of Hero's body. Hands and feet jerked toward each other. Leather cords snapped.

Hero's fist flashed past the doctor's startled face, collided with the doctor's hand, and dashed the knife away. Utticus jumped back. The razor-sharp lancet barely missed his eye. It twanged as it struck the ceiling over his head and stuck there.

The boy clawed at the remaining straps until he was free. He sat on the table, clutching his knees to his chest, rocking.

The doctor panted like a wounded animal. "Worse than I thought," he said, regaining his composure. "Too much pressure for mere bleeding to help." With a trembling index finger he pointed to the instruments, to a sawtooth disc mounted on a handle. "Need to go straight to the problem. Cut a hole in his skull. That will fix him."

"I-I can't let you do that," Alexander stuttered. He moved between Utticus and the boy. Hero accepted his father's arm around his shoulders. "What if he died?"

Utticus sniffed. "Would dying be more regrettable than his life? Go, then. But you'll soon be back here begging for my help. And bring your cash next time!"

11

CHAPTER

No one could count the thousands who had come that morning to hear Yeshua. Too many sick for Him to heal them all. They could not reach Him. Not in a day or a week or a month.

Peniel's friend, Amos, squinted into the silver glare reflected on the surface of the Sea of Galilee. Yeshua perched on the bow of a fishing vessel moored just off the beach, out of harm from the jostling multitude.

Amos had been a beggar, a twisted dwarf living beneath the viaduct in Jerusalem before Yeshua healed him. Now a big brawny man with large feet and hands like hammers, he leaned close to Peniel and jerked his thumb toward two wealthy-looking women inching through the crowd toward them.

Amos attempted to whisper and failed. "Peniel. Look there, will you? Joanna. Wife of Kuza. You know? Kuza? He's steward to Herod Antipas."

Peniel nodded once, not wishing to gossip when the woman was so near. And then he noticed a rough-looking, thick-necked Samaritan following close behind her. The hilt of a sword protruded from beneath his cloak. Arms crossed over his chest, the man stared pointedly at the wife of Kuza.

Peniel nudged Amos and inclined his head toward the fellow. He put a finger to his lips. "Shut up, will you, Amos?"

Amos, whose voice had grown large with his body, did not grasp Peniel's meaning. "Kuza, her husband, fears Herod more than he fears God himself. I heard Joanna secretly supports Yeshua. But Kuza? To keep his job he'll pay Herod all his life, eh?" Amos feigned a trembling hand to demonstrate Kuza's fear of his master.

Kuza's auburn-haired wife sat with her companion a mere arm's length from Peniel and Amos, at the edge of the crowd lining the wall of a vineyard on a nearby hillside.

In a stone trough beside the vineyard five men holding on to ropes strung overhead trod on clumps of grapes. Other vineyard workers emptied wicker baskets brimming with fruit into the pit. The bright juice flowed through a channel into waiting stone jars, the production unceasing.

On the shore was a large boulder.

Around this backdrop swirled groups of Yeshua's closest followers. Peniel noted Judas, Philip, Thomas, and Levi. Each of the twelve apostles wore expressions of self-satisfaction today. So many people, so many needy—all coming to Yeshua for an answer. Celebrities by association, the Twelve were being pointed out as members of Yeshua's inner circle. They basked in the reflected light of their Teacher's notoriety.

Peniel remarked to no one in particular, "It's the bait that lures, not the fishermen or the tackle."

Amos, who loved a new proverb more than wisdom itself, beamed. "Well spoken, Peniel, old friend! Old fool! What's it mean?"

"I mean they love honor more than they love the Rabbi."

Amos screwed up his face in an intense effort to think of a retort. "True. I've heard them talking in the camp. They're growing impatient. And who isn't? So are we all, eh? Wouldn't it be fine if today he stood up and declared himself king of Israel!"

"A bloody day it would be. I've seen mercenaries in the crowd. Big ugly fellows with daggers."

"Well, well. But wouldn't it be fine? I'd be happy just grooming horses in a king's stable. I'll ask him if I can tend the horses. Don't need some exalted position like the others."

"That's good, because you're not likely to have one. What do you know about horses?"

Amos boasted, "I was nearly stepped on by several in bygone days. Noble creatures. And I can look 'em in the eye now. Sure, I'd love to be a groom."

"Not likely. Nor are any of the rest of them going to be ambassadors or whatever they're after. They'd be better friends if they'd shut up and listen to him."

Amos clucked his tongue and raised a meaty finger. "Better a good enemy than a bad friend, I always say. I suppose Yeshua has his talmidim figured out. Wouldn't worry your tiny brain about it, Peniel. However! If Yeshua has any ambition for politics, we could soon be dining regularly in the old Hasmonean Palace in Yerushalayim. We'll see. We'll see which way the wind blows. You know what they say, 'The crow flies high but often lands on the back of a hog.' Yes. We'll see where our crow lands."

Amos had a proverb to fit every occasion. But today Peniel was in no mood.

Yeshua stood up in the boat, took a drink of water, and mopped His brow. His talmidim signaled for silence. The throng complied. The buzz of conversation subsided to a muted hum.

On the opposite side of the audience from Peniel and Amos was an official delegation from Jerusalem. A band of Pharisees, recognizable by their broad sashes and phylacteries, kept uneasy company with high-ranking Sadducees, Temple officials.

Joanna's nearly inaudible murmur carried to Peniel's keen ears. "Yeshua knows the danger, but it doesn't stop him. The rest of us who love and believe in him are threatened too."

Her friend replied, "You can understand Kuza's thinking. He works for Herod Antipas."

"Yes," Joanna acknowledged with a quiver in her voice. "And there is the monster Antipas with my husband now."

Peniel followed her gaze to the top of the slope leading to the lake. Kuza, a swarthy, harried-looking fellow wearing the gold chain of Herodian office, stood in the middle of a knot of grim, burly-framed men . . . clearly guards of some kind. And beside Kuza, dressed in a plain woolen cloak, was another man.

Who was he? Peniel wondered. Fleshy features were half concealed beneath the cowl of his cloak. The retinue seemed intent on him, shoving spectators roughly aside as they advanced.

The newcomers approached till they reached the edge of the crowd. The light shone full on their faces.

Amos took a deep breath. "By all the Pantheon in Greece! Herod Antipas himself! Hide yourself, Peniel! The woods are no doubt thick with assassins who'd love to take your eyes and hack off my long legs." He covered his mouth with the hem of his keffiyeh and slouched down in an attempt to appear small.

A hum of recognition and amazement rippled through the crowd.

Peniel studied the dissipated countenance of the Herodian prince. Beneath the cloak of his disguise, Tetrarch Herod Antipas stared sullenly out at the scene through hooded eyelids. He appeared as evil in the flesh as his reputation painted him.

And what was that? Peniel turned as he heard a hissing like steam escaping from a boiling pot. It was a distinct voice and yet not human!

All the world I can give you if . . . ! We'll share power! Unimaginable wealth! You! If you will! If you show me a sign! Prove it! If you are the Son of God, prove it! A sign!

Peniel squinted as, for an instant, a faceless shadow—contorted yet shaped like a human—reared up over Antipas' head and shoulders as if to embrace him. As Peniel watched, it descended on the tetrarch like water being poured into a jug, merging with *Antipas' body!*

Peniel shuddered, looked away, and then back again!

Nothing. It was nothing.

Joanna's friend said urgently, "Antipas? Here? Shouldn't we warn Yeshua? They'll arrest him . . . or worse!"

Joanna's reply was shaky. "No. The crowd's too big. There'd be rioting. No, Kuza told me this might happen, warned me to keep out of the way. Herod Antipas wants to meet Yeshua for himself. See? He wants to see a sign. Kuza's making his way down to Yeshua now to ask."

Was the world turned upside down? Peniel wondered. The bloated tetrarch coming to see the man many claimed to be the Messiah of Israel? But surely Herod Antipas only did things for his own motives, not because he'd had any heart change. What if the ruler of the Galil proposed a truce with Yeshua? or a bribe? What if he offered the Preacher money and acceptance into the higher rank of society?

Though Antipas appeared without his trappings of authority and wealth, his disguise had barely lasted long enough for the first of the multitude to be jostled by the guards. Each onlooker in turn recognized the tetrarch. He was like a fat toad appearing from beneath an upturned rock. The mob parted around him, edging away.

Peniel searched the multitude. Was the audience salted with Herodian guards?

Kuza approached the boulder where Levi stood. Levi nodded once in greeting of his old friend. He listened to Kuza's request, then waded into the water until he was waist deep beside Yeshua's boat. Yeshua bent to hear Levi's message as Levi spoke briefly to Yeshua. Yeshua's reply was an amused smile. Levi retreated back to shore and relayed the reply to Kuza.

Kuza blanched and rubbed his forehead as if he had a splitting headache.

Yeshua addressed the spectators in a thunderous voice. But it was clear to Peniel His words were directed at Herod Antipas: "There was a landowner who planted a vineyard. He built a wall around it, dug a winepress in it, and built a watchtower."

As Yeshua offered this description He pointed to the elements of His parable visible on the hillside behind Herod Antipas. Obligingly the crowd regarded each of the items in turn. The vineyard. The wall. The winepress. The watchtower.

A sense of anticipation gripped the audience. Would this be the time when Yeshua would confront the Herodian usurper and reclaim the throne of David?

Yeshua continued, "After this the landowner rented his vineyard to some farmers and went away on a journey."

Herod Antipas remained rooted in place beside the winepress, seemingly as transfixed by the parable as the rest.

Yeshua gestured toward the vines. "At the time of the grape harvest the landowner sent his servants to the tenants to collect his fruit."

At this point in Yeshua's story the men treading out the grapes stopped to listen. Porters balanced baskets on shoulders. Laborers in the rows paused from wielding bronze sickles.

"But the tenants seized his servants! They beat one . . . killed one . . . and stoned another."

Peniel watched the expression of Antipas change to defiance. Was the tetrarch thinking of the night he executed Yochanan the Baptizer?

"Then he sent other servants to them, more than the first time, and the tenants treated them the same way."

The Pharisees from Jerusalem stirred uneasily. This was as close to preaching revolution as Yeshua had ever come. And in the presence of Herod Antipas, no less.

"Last of all, the landowner sent his son to them. 'Surely they'll respect my son,' he said. But when the tenants saw the son they said to one another, 'This is the heir. Come on, let's kill him and take his inheritance.' So they took him and threw him out of the vineyard, and killed him."

The crowd held its breath as Yeshua turned toward the outraged religious rulers.

Yeshua shouted the question, "When the owner of the vineyard returns, what will he do to those tenants?"

Amos cupped his hands around his mouth and bellowed, "He'll put the wicked men to a horrible death!"

There rose a thunderous cheer from the crowd.

Were revolt and civil war proclaimed in Yeshua's parable?

Totally swept up, another young man called out, "He'll rent the vineyard to other tenants who will give him his share of the crop after each harvest."[19]

From throughout the crowd the evil voices swelled in antiphonal fury:

Drive out the usurpers! Kill them!

Give us a sign!

Put them to death!

Show us a sign!

Take back the land!

If you are the Elijah we have been waiting for, call down fire from heaven on them!

Show us! Fire from heaven!

Had anyone missed the meaning of the story? Yeshua was not speaking about profit and loss, about buying and selling, about tenants and landlords. This story was plainly meant for Herod Antipas and the religious rulers who governed the people without hereditary right or scriptural authority. The high priest and his family had paid Rome for their positions. Herod the Great, appointed by Rome, had been the first non-Jewish monarch to rule Israel. These were the tenants of Yeshua's story and they knew it well.

At that instant a sight line opened, connecting Yeshua with Herod Antipas. Peniel watched with fascination as the eyes of the two men, Rabbi and ruler, locked.

A shadow rose like smoke from within Antipas. Long sinewy arms stretched wide. A high shriek pierced the air!

Peniel covered his ears and ducked his head. Yet no one else seemed to notice!

Yeshua raised His right hand, commanding silence. The unearthly wail abruptly ceased, along with the chatter of the crowd.

Yeshua spoke again. "Haven't you read in the Scriptures: 'The stone the builders rejected has become the capstone; Adonai has done this and it is marvelous in our eyes'? Therefore, I tell you that the kingdom of Yahweh will be taken away from you and given to a people who will produce its fruit! He who falls on this stone will be broken to pieces, but he on whom it falls will be utterly crushed."[20]

Heads tilted back as thousands searched the sky for a sign. Seconds passed.

No fire fell from heaven to devour Herod Antipas and his henchmen.

No longed-for heavenly judgment stone slammed down to crush the ones who had so long crushed the spirits of the *am ha aretz!*

Nothing. Merely an empty blue sky. Cloudless. Unremarkable.

Peniel observed the fear in Herod Antipas' visage change to rage. The shadowy creature at the tetrarch's back folded in on itself and merged again into the body of its host.

And there on the hill, renewed hatred burned in the eyes of the Pharisees and Sadducees.

Then this new hope arose among the spectators: Perhaps Yeshua did not mean to conquer by conjuring brimstone to destroy Israel's enemies. Perhaps freedom could be won by the people! One call to revolution from Yeshua's lips, and Herod Antipas was a dead man. The reign of false religious rulers in Jerusalem would come to an end! The crowd would turn on the corrupt authorities with the same fury as in the days of the Maccabees. Yes! So many now stood ready to overpower the Herodian guards! In an instant the people would rally, pick up stones, and . . . Israel would be free! The revolution against Rome, the Herodian dynasty, and false priests would begin here! *Now! Today!*

If only Yeshua would give the order!

Amos scooped up two fist-sized stones and placed one in Peniel's hand. Under his breath he urged Yeshua on, "Come on. Come on! We're for you, man! Do it!"

But Yeshua did not issue the order.

"Why does he wait?" Amos asked.

What now? Peniel considered every detail of Yeshua's parable. If Yahweh was the landlord, and Herod Antipas and the priests were tenants . . . if Yochanan the Baptizer was the murdered servant, who then was the murdered son? Who? Who was heir to the vineyard? Who was the one dragged outside the vineyard and killed by the tenant farmers?

Peniel saw Kuza's spine stiffen. He was strained and pale. The steward turned away from Levi.

The hillside was planted thick with listeners. The path through the forest of people was not the same as Kuza's approach. Halfway back to Herod Antipas, he spotted Joanna and directed his steps toward her.

Without seeming to acknowledge her, Kuza covered his mouth as if to cough. Peniel heard each terrified word Kuza whispered to his wife in passing: "No compromise. Yeshua won't see him. Get Boaz! Leave home. Leave Galilee. Go to Susanna! I'll send word when I can."

Peniel understood. Kuza feared for his family, and who could blame him? Yeshua had no intention of calling down fire on the heads of the usurpers! Nor would He ride into Jerusalem as a conquering king at the head of a Galilean army!

In an instant opportunity for action had vanished. A ripple of fear coursed through the multitude.

Who among them were in the pay of Herod Antipas? How many were Herodian spies? Had a comment made against Antipas or the chief priest or Rome been overheard? Which of the spectators had come to gather names of possible insurgents? Who noted those young men who were eager to go to battle against the authorities and overthrow the government?

Would open approval of Yeshua's parable result in arrests? torture? death? As if the same thought entered every mind at once, the crowd turned away from Yeshua and began to leave.

None doubted Herod Antipas' reaction to Yeshua's rejection. After today Antipas would declare open war on anyone who claimed to follow Yeshua!

And Yeshua of Nazareth had not raised one finger to prevent it.

Though the afternoon crossing of the Sea of Galilee was calm, the tetrarch's bellows were almost enough to propel the ship. Herod Antipas was so infuriated his jowls quivered, his hands shook, and he stuttered as he expressed his outrage.

Pacing up and down the center planking, he stopped to aim another backhanded blow at Kuza's head. The steward's scalp was already streaked with blood where Antipas' heavy rings had scored it. "Me! He called me a usurper! A tenant farmer, stealing from the true king!"

He cuffed Kuza again, this time tearing a gash in the corner of the steward's eyelid.

The oarsmen kept their heads down and their attention fully fixed on their rowing.

Kuza had no way to either duck or escape; he was manacled to the mast, forced to remain on his knees.

"Don't think I didn't hear them . . . the dirty, sniveling *am ha aretz.* 'Like King Ahab,' they said. 'Yeshua's another Elijah,' they said. 'Call down fire on the head of Antipas!' I'll have their heads . . . every last one of them."

Argument, explanation, excuses—nothing would serve to deflect the tetrarch's wrath. If it came into his mind he could have Kuza's throat slit and his body tossed over the side, and no one would dare protest. All Kuza could do was shut his eyes, hope that Antipas' fury would spend itself before it rose to the level of execution . . . and be silently grateful he'd warned Joanna to take their son, five-year-old Boaz, and flee!

Few words were spoken by the small band returning to Yeshua's camp that evening.

The moods of the Twelve, especially John, Ya'acov, and Shim'on, were contemplative at best. It was plain enough to Peniel that Yeshua's failure to put an end to the oppressors by summoning brimstone down on their heads was a grave disappointment to them. As for the others in Yeshua's camp, thoughts and recriminations remained unspoken as fires were built and the evening meal was prepared.

Peniel felt the same despondence that clouded the minds of those who remained.

Why hadn't Yeshua acted when He had the chance? Was a tiny sign too much to ask? A bolt of lightning shattering a tree? Maybe a little earthquake to knock over the watchtower? Some miniscule proof of Yahweh's wrath would have been sufficient to send Herod Antipas scampering away like a frightened dog. But Yeshua only used words to disarm His enemies. What use were words? And what did Yeshua's story really mean?

Why had Yeshua not called down fire as Elijah had done? If Yeshua possessed such power, if He was truly equal to the prophets of old who served Yahweh, why did He not use this power to silence those who intended to harm Him and His talmidim?

The sun set. Peniel shared a seat on a log beside Amos.

Amos' eyes were downcast and his lips pressed together as he broiled a fish over the open fire. At last he spoke. "Ah, Peniel. Our high-flying crow landed on the back of a hog today, if you know what I mean."

Peniel did not respond at first. He gazed into the flames and wished the day had turned out differently. "You're leaving?"

"I'm no Torah scholar. I don't understand half of what he says."

"But you can see for yourself what he does! The people he helps. So many."

Amos shrugged. "Today he did nothing at all. And I think if he could've given us all the sign we're looking for, he should have done it."

Peniel countered, "Maybe he has a moment—a particular moment ahead—fixed in his mind. And then he'll declare himself! Yes. That's it. It's just not now."

"Only in our dreams are cabbages as big as bears."

"True. Well spoken. Point taken. But Amos! Will you turn your back on him after what he's done for you?"

Amos tested the cooking fish with a forefinger, yelping when it burned him. "The world has a saying: 'Better to lose with a wise man than to win with a fool.' This is a saying I don't agree with. Better to win with a fool, I say. And I don't think this wise fellow Yeshua really wants to win. He insults the leaders and then, assuming he could burn them up with a single fierce look, he decides to let them go home where they can plot and scheme how to kill him. And how to kill us. No. I don't think he'll win and I, for one, don't want to be here when the end comes. Don't fancy drawing my last breath nailed to a Roman cross." He offered Peniel a chunk of broiled fish.

Peniel refused. "It won't come to that," he argued, though he wasn't sure he believed his own words.

Amos countered. "No? Then who was the murdered son in his story? I ask you, Peniel. Answer me that! Who was the murdered son? Does Yeshua fancy himself a martyr? Peniel, when people say someone's crazy, believe it. Come with me. This can't end well for anyone."

Peniel looked up at the first three stars in the evening sky. "No. No. I can't leave him. Not after what he's given me."

"Then I wish you luck. I hope I'm wrong. He's a very good fellow. A righteous man with a talent for healing. But . . . well . . . I hope I'm wrong."

"What will you do?"

Amos poked the embers with a stick. "I'm going west. To the ocean. I've always wanted to see the Great Sea with my own eyes. I hear it's an amazing sight. Yes. And I fancy seeing it myself."

"But what if Yeshua . . . is? I believe he is. I do . . . I hope."

"Don't sell the hide of a bear when it's still in the woods, eh? When Yeshua sits on David's throne and rules in Yerushalayim, maybe I'll come see him. I'll cheer and throw flowers when he passes out free bread to the poor. And then you can tell me how wrong I was. I would have liked to be a groom in a king's stable. Meanwhile, hoping and waiting makes fools of clever people. Yes. While we're all hoping and waiting, I'll go down to Joppa. Maybe take a boat to a far country. Have an adventure. Meet a girl and marry, maybe. Have children. I'll name a son after my old friend Peniel."

Peniel nodded, barely able to speak. He blurted, "I'll miss you, Amos."

Amos scoffed at Peniel's sentiment. "You won't! You know me! I'm a fool. You can't make a hat out of a pig's tail. I'm no scholar. Not meant for this sort of life. You, on the other hand, know the Book by heart! Backwards and forwards! You were meant to study Torah. But your Rabbi's doomed, I'm afraid." He placed his big paw on Peniel's arm. "Watch yourself, my friend. You think you're safe with him to protect you but . . . watch yourself, will you?"

And so, the next morning before dawn, Amos slipped quietly from the company of Yeshua's talmidim.

And he was not the only one to leave.

12

CHAPTER

Before noon Yeshua's mother entered the camp in the company of five other women. They led three donkeys laden with food. Seated on a rock, Peniel watched the arrival.

Judas cracked a nut and popped it into his mouth. "Where's your friend? Where's Amos the fool?"

Peniel looked up sharply. "Gone. But he's no fool."

"Well if he's gone, I suppose he's not a fool. Maybe we're the fools, eh, Peniel? Doorkeeper? Yes. We're fools for staying."

"Why are you talking like this?" Peniel was angry. He dug in the earth with the point of a stick.

"Time was, not so long ago, the roads were never empty. People were always moving towards him. You know what will happen now? Since he came face-to-face with Antipas and did nothing?"

Peniel thought of the lepers of Mak'ob. "Them as have need of him still come. So many sometimes I can't make out their faces. All one weary face. All needing him."

Judas flipped the leather money pouch at his belt. "Less and less. Less and less. If Yeshua had declared himself king when he had the chance, I'd be treasurer over a kingdom. The people would have

— 141 —

followed him to Yerushalayim, killed every guard, overrun every out-post. But now fewer and fewer will come every day."

Peniel resented being sucked into this unpleasant discussion. "They're afraid of the Herodian edict. Maybe that's why."

"They weren't afraid before. He says such odd things. That his body is bread and unless we eat his body we have no part of him."

Peniel brandished the stick. "Torah calls the words of God our bread of life. Yeshua's teaching feeds men's souls. Only a Herodian, a Roman, or a member of the Sanhedrin would turn the meaning of that upside down."

Judas smirked. "These ignorant sheep can't be expected to under-stand what he's talking about."

Peniel was defensive. "If you ask me, to my way of looking at it, the simple folk are the ones who *do* understand."

"They would have made him king, but he refused. So? Who is he? Who is he? Not Elijah. A healer, yes. A magician, maybe. But one sign. That's all they needed. Is he incapable?"

Peniel frowned. The campfires of Mak'ob returned to his mind. He remembered the Valley of Lepers had first been discovered by King David while he searched for a lost lamb. First the king of Israel must be a shepherd; later He would be the king. "Yeshua's not finished search-ing. You heard him. Searching for the lost sheep of Israel."

"If he was in Yerushalayim right now in the palace, the sheep would know where to find him. Now they're all running from him."

Peniel scratched his head. "Well, take myself as example. Yeshua heals me. Gives me eyes. And the same day I'm turned out of the syna-gogue. My parents won't have anything to do with me. And who can blame them? The Sanhedrin would cut them off from their customers. No buying or selling."

"People are afraid of the things Yeshua says. Nobody understands what he's talking about half the time. Who can stay when he says such wild things?"

Angry at this fellow's criticism, Peniel broke the tree limb with a snap. He stood abruptly. "I can. I will. I'm staying."

Judas scoffed. "You have no place else to go."

"Point taken. You're right. Well spoken. No place. Nothing left to lose. All the same, even if I did, even if I had someplace to go, I'd stay."

With those final words from Peniel, Judas stalked off.

Peniel crossed his arms defiantly and fixed his gaze on Yeshua. He thought about the Valley of Mak'ob and the lepers, the captives who were now free to return to homes and families.

And there was Yeshua. Ordinary looking. Who would know what He had done? There He was, unloading baskets from a donkey while His mother rested on a tree stump and talked with Him the way any mother talks to a son. Concerned, yes. Worried even. But such love radiated from her face. It was a lovely thing for the heart of the blind man to witness. Peniel had so often wished his mama could have looked at him even once in such a way. He would have felt it if Mama had ever looked kindly on him. But she had not.

Peniel whispered, "Mary. Kind lady. You'll stay with him till the end, won't you? Yes, I know it. You'll still be here when everyone else is gone. Do you see what's happening all around your boy? Do you feel the storm clouds gathering? The wind is up. I feel it. It's up, dear lady. And I'm sorry for you."

Surely Yeshua was aware the opposition was growing even among His own followers. He seemed to know everything. Could He shield His mother from the forces marshalling against Him?

Mary saw Peniel looking at her. She gave him a cheerful wave. He blushed and waved back. He thought what a fine thing it was to see into someone's eyes and glimpse the quietness of a good soul in an instant!

Kind heart. Gentle lady. Thanks for seeing me. You give your son to everyone. What's to become of you? They're turning now. Turning on him. I'll stand by you, good lady, if ever you need my help. I have nowhere else to go, you see.

Shim'on roared toward him. "You! Peniel! That's the trouble with you. Don't you know anything? Gawking at the Teacher like you have a right! No respect! No respect!"

Yeshua glanced toward them. Shim'on's tirade created the very interruption the big fisherman had wanted to forestall. Extending His hands, Yeshua assisted Mary to her feet.

Yeshua addressed the talmidim, and called for Shim'on, Ya'acov, and John to gather close around Him. He surveyed the group, then instructed, "You three come with me. We'll be gone a few days. While I'm gone, Nathaniel will be in charge. If you have questions, see him."

Zahav consoled herself that the story she told Papa was not a complete lie. Carrying a basket of food, she left Papa and made her way through the dark streets to Rebecca's. Concealing the basket on top of a stone fence, she knocked on the door.

Rebecca's husband, Heli, let her in.

Children clambered over her as she and Rebecca discussed Papa's failing eyesight. It was time, the sisters confided to one another, that the elders of the synagogue hire an assistant rabbi to relieve some of Papa's burdens. There followed the usual gossip about other women in the congregation or boys in the chorus who showed a streak of rebellion.

Thus passed a pleasant hour. It was just long enough.

No one would guess Zahav's visit with her sister was a ruse to hide her true intention. Tomorrow, if Papa asked Rebecca what she and Zahav had talked about, Rebecca would have an answer.

"Yes, Zahav and I are very concerned about your eyes, Papa. You must rest, Papa. Zahav and I talked it over. You work too hard. . . ."

He would never know that all along Zahav had in mind another destination outside the Quarter.

Zahav kissed Rebecca good-bye and touched the mezuzah on the doorpost. *May the Lord bless my going out and coming in.*

Retrieving the food basket from the wall, she set out down the lane. The red door of Alexander and Hero was a short five-minute walk away.

It had been a good day for business. Browsers and shoppers from all over the eastern provinces had come and gone. Whenever a woman entered the instrument shop, Alexander had hoped it was the one who had brought him and Hero supper almost a week earlier. Not that he would recognize her.

Every day since then he had hung her basket on a hook beside the door, thinking she would see it and make herself known to him. In gratitude for her kindness he had carved a fine ivory whistle and engraved it with the Star of David. It was there, wrapped in red linen, in her basket. But she had not returned.

Just the same, four sets of Alexander's most expensive panpipes had sold today. Three double flutes. Alexander swept the pavement in front of the door then scanned the deserted street. No one was coming. He closed the shop and latched the door. The sun set behind the western hills, drenching Caesarea Philippi in deep shadow.

Alexander lit the lamp and played his flute as Hero sat at his feet. Alexander's breath mussed Hero's hair. The boy smiled and cupped his hands as if to catch puffs of air like butterflies.

Hero was doing much better. Alexander was certain the oxtail soup, apples, and fresh bread had pulled him back from the brink. Eyes were clearer. He seemed interested in playing with toys again. Pebbles painted as people. Blocks of wood. Miniature chariots and carved horses were spread out before him.

A knock sounded on the shop door. Alexander paused to listen. Had she come back after all?

At the sight of his father's pleased expression, Hero's eyes grew wide, as if waiting for a surprise.

Three knocks. Silence. Three more. Exactly like the other night.

"Ah, Hero, my boy! We have a visitor!" He took up the lamp and clasped the boy's hand. "Come on, then. Let's see who's here." Hurrying through the shop he called, "A minute!" Then to Hero, "She'll be glad to see you're better."

He threw the door back. Yes. Outside the circle of his light was the woman.

"Shalom. I was passing by on my way home and—"

"I was hoping you'd come back!"

As before, her features were hidden. She wore a veil as the Hebrew women of the city often did when they were outside their Quarter.

She spotted Hero. Dark eyes crinkled at the corners with pleasure. "You! Handsome fellow! You're looking well. Yes! Very well!"

Hero tucked his face against Alexander's leg.

Alexander patted him. "He's shy. But if he could speak, he would tell you how much he enjoyed the apples."

"And I would tell him it was a little thing. He looks much better, yes?"

"Thanks to you. He ate every bit of the apples. The soup lasted two days. Yes, I was hoping you'd come back. I have your basket here. A little gift inside for you from Hero. We kept the shop open late, he and I. Looked for you each day. We wanted to thank you."

"Please. It's not more than anyone would do." She extended a fabric-wrapped parcel containing a clay dish. "We had a little extra left from our table tonight."

"And you remembered us." Alexander accepted the gift. The dish was warm. He passed the woman her basket in exchange.

"I wanted to see if Hero was thriving, yes?"

"And you see . . . we are still alive. Please. What's your name, kind lady?"

She did not reply but stepped back from the lamplight.

He asked again, "I told Hero you were perhaps not real. I'll believe you're a spirit unless you tell me your name. Please."

"I am Zahav."

Alexander shook his head. "My Hebrew is not good. What does it mean?"

"Golden."

"Golden." He tried the Hebrew pronunciation. "Zahav. Beautiful. Yes, I would have guessed you had a name like that. Yes. It suits you."

She said quickly, "Zahav is not . . . I mean . . . Zahav is another way we have to call our Holy Books, yes? Our treasure. Our gold. My father named me Zahav because he is a Torah scholar and . . . and when he speaks my name it reminds him that children are all treasures. Created and beloved by The Eternal One."

"You're a good cook too. Zahav suits you well. I thank you. Hero thanks you."

"I have to go."

"Where do you live? Shall we bring back the dish? Tomorrow?"

"No!" Her tone contained an edge of alarm. "I mean . . . no, thank you. I wouldn't be . . . allowed, you see. I am Jewish. You are . . . not."

He remembered the Jews outside the synagogue. Their warning that if Hero so much as touched the hem of their shawls they would be unclean. So, what was true for them was also true for Zahav. He would not press the matter.

"Well then. Thank you, Zahav. Hero and I are more grateful for your kindness than we can say."

"Shalom."

He stood in the doorway, listening as her footsteps retreated down the lane.

Then she stopped. From the darkness he heard her gentle explanation. "I confess. When I helped you and your son the other day, I knew who you were, yes? I have heard you play your flute before. Yes, I confess. Many times. I often come here on market day and stand for hours. Over there, across the road . . . I stand there, you see? To listen to the music of angels. I want you to know how beautiful . . . how beautiful . . . and how many times you have nourished a hungry soul. I'm very sorry for your loss. Very sorry. She was a lovely person, your wife, and I am sorry."

"Zahav! Will you come again?" Alexander called.

There was no reply. She was gone.

Hero tugged his arm and inhaled the aroma of lamb stew.

On the southwest shore of the Sea of Galilee, halfway between Tiberias and Philoteria, was the Galilee country villa of the Jewish high priest Caiaphas. It was airy, spacious, set on a hill to take advantage of the breezes . . . and Herod Antipas hated having to go there to meet with the Temple official.

Just because Tiberias, where Antipas' palace sat, existed on land where an ancient cemetery had been unearthed, pious Jews would not set foot there. Privately, High Priest Caiaphas didn't give the weight of a sneeze for such religious quibbles, but appearances had to be preserved. Caiaphas would not attend a meeting with the tetrarch unless it were held somewhere away from Tiberias. The *cohen hagadol* had suggested his own compound as being the most comfortable alternative.

Antipas disliked leaving his own estates. Because of rebel threats against his life, the tetrarch never moved without his own phalanx of soldiers and an honor guard of Roman legionaries. Even with their protection, he did not feel entirely secure until he returned home.

It also grated on Antipas' sensibilities that he, a hereditary prince of the House of Herod, had to call on this puppet priest who retained his position solely at Rome's discretion. It did not matter, in Antipas' view, that his own title was also the property of Tiberius Caesar. His was the higher authority and that was that.

But today's conference was important enough to make Antipas swallow his pride and make the journey. Yeshua of Nazareth no longer appealed simply to the masses. Several high-ranking and wealthy men had declared their allegiance to Him. Whispers circulated about what a powerful prophet He was. Even though He'd wisely refused to allow His followers to call Him king, the notion that He might become a rebel leader would not die.

And if that idea would not die, it was past time for the object of that impulse to do so.

Or at least to be discredited in some permanent way.

That evening, as the litter of Antipas and Herodias approached the curving marble walkway toward the villa, the tetrarch stuck out his lower lip in thought. The story of this journey would make the rounds of the *am ha aretz*. The dirty commoners would repeat the tale of how Antipas respected their high priest. Amid the griping over taxes and the still-simmering scandal about the murder of Yochanan the Baptizer, a little perceived humility hurt nothing.

Antipas grunted and shrugged. The gesture was slight but sufficient to turn his red-haired wife's attention away from the oiled back muscles of the broad-shouldered slave she'd been eyeing. As if she read his thoughts she suggested, "It never hurts to know what Caiaphas is thinking. He's so pompous and slow-witted that even without trying he provides opportunities to blame him for things. Let him think you value his opinion; flattery works well with men of great ambition and little real ability. And no one is better at the game than you."

When Antipas and Herodias had been conducted into a central hall, seated in state, and guards posted outside each door, the other attendants were dismissed. The consultation would take place in private. This was not only important to prevent the spies of Rome, of which there were many, from listening in, but it also made any rash commitments later regretted that much easier to disavow.

Caiaphas—head and shoulders taller than Antipas, thinner of face and body, with features as chiselled as Antipas' were squat—swept into the room. "My lord tetrarch and my lady! You do my humble home such honor."

When pleasantries to which neither side paid attention had been exchanged, Caiaphas asked, "The matter of Yeshua of Nazareth continues to be a problem for both of us; isn't that so? Clearly he is a charlatan and a blasphemer, and I simply need a little more material to have him up on charges before the Sanhedrin. One of your subjects—a man named Simon of Capernaum, and a Pharisee of all things—wrote to me, offering his services in such a connection. But after some initial unsatisfactory reports, I've had nothing else from him."

Herodias laughed once in derision, not mirth. "As difficult as it is to believe, he's been seduced away from you," she reported. Herodias proceeded to supply the details of how Simon had supposedly contracted leprosy, been pronounced *chadel*, "rejected," and then was miraculously healed by Yeshua.

"Preposterous," Caiaphas blustered.

"Of course," Herodias said in a nasal tone. "But it's Yeshua's reputation we're fighting here, not his reality."

Antipas waved away a servant offering a jug of wine. "Nor is he the only one of his family to give us both grief. Zadok, Simon's father-in-law, who used to be your Chief Shepherd of the Temple, follows Yeshua too."

Caiaphas nodded slowly. The corners of his mouth turned down and his nostrils pinched. He looked as if he'd bitten into an uncured olive. "Grief enough to go around. It was Zadok who, in front of the whole council, brought up that old myth of the star of Beth-lehem announcing the birth of a Messiah. Said Yeshua was born there, fulfilling the prediction of the prophet Micah.[21] You know the tale . . . which ends with your father accused of murdering all the boy babies."

Antipas' jaundiced face reddened. "Exactly the kind of gossipmongering we don't want!"

Herodias looked from one frowning face to another. "So who is this Yeshua, anyway? What do we really know about him?"

Forefinger raised, Caiaphas announced, "He's from Nazareth. Supposedly the son of a carpenter."

Herodias offered scornfully, "From making table legs to healing crippled legs? So he was born in Beth-lehem. I'm not familiar with all the myths of the coming Messiah. What are the other requirements?"

Caiaphas, like his fellow Sadducees who occupied most of the seats on the Sanhedrin, had no belief in an afterlife. There was no room in their religion for angels, no heaven, and no miracles. In short, when they thought of the Almighty at all, it was in terms of how to keep Him happy—much as the Romans courted the god of fortune with the proper ceremonies so their earthly life would be prosperous. Their religion was closely linked to their politics, which centered on maintaining the status quo. Caiaphas liked his powerful position, even if it meant being subservient to Roman governors and half-breed tetrarchs.

Keeping the present power structure intact and unshaken was precisely the point at which his interests and those of Herod Antipas met.

As high priest, Caiaphas knew the list of prophecies about the Promised Deliverer of Israel, but he never expected a literal fulfillment.

Caiaphas clasped his hands and raised them to his chin. "It's been said that more than a magic star was connected with Yeshua's birth."

Herodias manifested eagerness. "Do tell us. Who better to hear it from than the high priest himself?"

Caiaphas, flattered despite his political savvy, unconsciously adopted a lecturing mode. The volume of his voice increased and his index finger pointed upward, demanding attention to every word. "In the scroll of Isaiah it is predicted that Messiah will be born of a virgin."[22]

Herodias' eyes narrowed, and her perpetually crafty eyes took on a conspiratorial gleam. "How droll. Go on."

"Miraculous-birth stories are connected with several of our patriarchs and prophets." Caiaphas ticked the examples off on his carefully manicured fingers. "Isaac, Samson, Samu'el . . . this is one more like those."

Antipas groaned. "Useless. We know he's the son of a carpenter, but that doesn't stop the *am ha aretz* from following him anyway. Besides, there's nothing there that can be challenged. He's what? Thirty? I could make the same claim about my mother, and who could prove otherwise?"

Caiaphas nodded. "I merely report it as one more requirement Yeshua is said to fulfill."

Herodias said with exasperation, "Men! You always look at things the wrong way around! Didn't I say we don't care about the man but about the reputation? Here's the perfect opportunity—and neither of you see it!"

"Explain," Antipas urged.

"He's not a carpenter's son."

"He's not?" Caiaphas repeated stupidly.

"No! His mother was raped—no, this is better—seduced! Seduced by a Roman soldier! That's it! Yeshua of Nazareth is the illegitimate son of a Jewish harlot and a Roman soldier."

Caiaphas arched both his interlaced fingers and his eyebrows.

Antipas' heavy lids drooped in thought. A smile crawled across his face. "This is good. Very good."

Herodias mused, "And his name . . . what is it they say about the Messiah? He'll be the lord of the earth or some nonsense like that?"

Caiaphas nodded, spellbound.

Herodias' rings jingled when she clapped her hands together. "His father's name was . . . Panterra. Yeshua of Nazareth is actually Yeshua ha'Panterra. That will send a ripple through his followers. Named for the god of the earth: Pan . . . Terra. Good, eh? And it's a common enough name among Roman soldiers from . . . I forget where. Sidonia? Macedon?" She waved dismissively. "Doesn't matter. Common enough to be believed."

Antipas grabbed her hand and planted a kiss on the palm. "Excellent! That'll even play well over the border in my brother's territory. Loads of Pan worshippers there. Can hardly walk without tripping over a Pan shrine or idol or something."

"So we spread the word that Yeshua is an illegitimate half-breed." Caiaphas looked as smug as if he'd thought of the plan himself.

"Until we come up with a more permanent solution," Antipas said approvingly. "An excellent beginning."

The gentle sounds of night in the countryside should have lulled Susanna to sleep. Instead she lay awake into the third watch of the night. She had lost Manaen. She knew that now and yet she could not fully accept it. Had he not loved her when he could see? Why then had love died when he lost his eyes?

She told herself that she knew the answer, but it did not make the truth easy to accept: Like weeds in a garden, bitterness and self-pity had taken root in his heart. There was no room for anything or anyone else to grow there.

No hope that he would ever see a sunrise or sunset again. The joys of vision were gone forever. Why could he not accept what was irrevocable and move on to other joys?

What was lost had become the god of his idolatry, everything he longed for. The one thing in life forever unattainable was the one thing he longed to possess.

Not Susanna. Not children. Not life.

Misery was his daily bread.

And what about Susanna? She wondered if she had not also become blind. She could not have Manaen as he had been. And yet she could not accept him as he was. The very thing she could not have was the thing she most wanted.

Finding some way to make him whole again was all she dreamed of these days. Restoring his happiness had become her goal, her one desire, the god of her idolatry.

His misery was her daily bread.

Her heart was a leaf tossed by the wind of his mood. Tonight sorrow ripened with her bitter thoughts, and yet there was no answer. She began at the beginning and retraced every step again and again, always arriving at the same dead end.

Hours passed.

Urgent knocking at the door finally disrupted the cycle.

"Susanna? Oh! Susanna! Wake up! Wake up! It's me! It's Joanna! Let me in!"

Susanna recognized the voice! It was her dearest friend from the days when she had lived in the court of Herod Antipas.

Clothed only in her shift, Susanna hurried downstairs to the atrium. Then, cautiously, Susanna pressed her forehead against the thick wood door. "Is it really you, Joanna?" She listened for the sound of other voices.

"Please. Let me in!" the voice begged.

"Are you alone?"

"Only Boaz and I!"

Susanna still hesitated, imagining the armed guard of Herod Antipas holding a knife to the throat of Joanna's son and forcing her to betray Susanna. "Where do you come from?"

"Capernaum."

"But are you alone now?" Susanna pictured a phalanx of Herodian guards standing on the steps of the villa.

"Yes! Only Boaz and I. We could think of nowhere else to go!"

Manaen called down to Susanna from their bedchamber, "Who's there?"

Susanna pretended she did not hear him. Screwing up her courage, she pulled back the bolt and opened the door a crack to peer out.

Joanna's ashen face blinked back at her. Young Boaz was in her arms. Joanna cried, "I didn't know where else to go!"

"Joanna!" Susanna grabbed her wrist and pulled her in. Not taking a second look, she slammed the portal closed.

Panting, Joanna and little Boaz collapsed into Susanna's arms. "I came as far as Bethsaida in the boat of a fisherman." Explanation surged from Susanna's auburn-haired friend; fear lurked in her light blue eyes. "Kuza insisted I leave Galilee!"

"You're safe. No one will bother you in King Philip's district."

Manaen called from the banister, "Who's there with you, Susanna?"

Susanna attempted to sound lighthearted. "Good news, Manaen! It's dear Joanna. Kuza's sent her to visit us! Yes, come to visit. Brought little Boaz too."

Manaen muttered, "Shalom, Joanna. You would wake the dead, the two of you."

Susanna replied, "Go back to bed, Manaen." And then she added cheerily, for the sake of illusion, "I'll be up in a bit."

Joanna leaned against the wall. "Manaen isn't glad to see us."

"He's awakened out of a sound sleep. He'll be more polite in daylight. Come on then." Susanna checked the bolt one more time and led Joanna into the atrium, lit by torchlight.

Joanna whispered, "The fellows at the quay in Bethsaida said you and Manaen lived only a short walk from the city. It was still daylight when we started out! These people of Bethsaida! A short walk, indeed! Boaz and I walked and walked into the countryside, and it became darker and darker until I couldn't see anything! Boaz sat down and refused to go one step more. He fell asleep, so I've carried him the whole long way."

Susanna took the sleeping child from his mother. "But why didn't you send word you were coming? I'd have come myself to meet you!"

"No time. I . . . I've left the Galil without anyone knowing. For Kuza's sake."

"Trouble?"

"When is there not trouble with Antipas since he married Herodias? Jezebel and Ahab all over again!"

Susanna brushed the boy's hair back from his forehead. "Well, I'm glad to see you. Very glad. You and Boaz must stay as long as you like. Forever is fine with me! I've missed you, Joanna. It's been lonely here. Such a big house. Only Manaen and I and the servants rattling around. So far from the town and people. Lonely."

"Not a day passed that I didn't wonder about you and Manaen.

How I wished you could have been with me in the Galil to see the things going on there!"

"Not safe for Manaen and me anymore in Herod's territory. We decided to leave right away. The day we married. We'll never go back to Galilee or Yerushalayim so long as Antipas is in power."

Joanna embraced her. "I wish you could, even for a day! Oh, Susanna! So many things happening there! It'll take a week of talking for me to tell you!"

Susanna clasped her friend's hand, cheerful for the first time in weeks. "And now you're here. What's the news? You must tell me! I want to hear every scrap of news! Come on! Are you hungry?"

The cold roast chicken was nearly gone. Susanna sat across the table from Joanna and listened until dawn ripened red in the sky. Little Boaz slept on cushions in the corner of the room.

"Red sky at morning," Susanna said absently.

"I didn't want to leave Capernaum. But it's better for Kuza if he doesn't have to worry about Boaz or me. There's danger for everyone within reach of Antipas and Herodias. If Antipas suspects for an instant that Kuza is a follower . . ."

"Storm coming, I think."

"I can't think about it now. Can't." Joanna's eyes brimmed with worry as she gazed at her sleeping son. "When you meet Yeshua, you'll see. Even the winds are at his command, they say."

"They say that, do they?"

"Even the winds."

"But can the storm of a soul be calmed by him?"

"His voice is oil on troubled waters for some. Peace. Yes. Hope. I feel it, although I'm afraid. We're hoping for something, but we don't know what. Oh, yes. Those who have nothing to fear do not fear Yeshua."

"As for the others? The guilty ones?"

"Herod Antipas fears Yeshua as he never feared a man. When Antipas struck off the head of Yochanan the Baptizer for denouncing the divorce of his Nabatean wife? Susanna! That was a small thing compared to what might happen in Yerushalayim and the Galil!"

"Will they kill Yeshua too?"

"They're trying even now. Especially since Yeshua refused to meet with Antipas. Kuza says there are assassins and spies at every gathering. But I can't believe that any son of Herod the Great will ever cut off the head of Yeshua! No. No one can take anything from Yeshua by force. Unless Yeshua wishes to give a thing, it won't be taken from him. Especially not his life! The Herodians, the Romans, and the religious leaders demand he tell them straight-out who he is! He won't speak to them. They demand he give them a sign of his power to prove he is . . . whoever he is . . . and Yeshua shows them nothing. Nothing! He refuses to perform tricks like some sort of court magician!"

She waved her hand to make a point. "Then when they're gone, Yeshua raises a dead child or heals lepers! And he says to those he heals, *'Tell no man!'* If there is any true justice in heaven, it will be the heads of Antipas and the high priest and a Roman governor on a platter, I think. But until that moment the lives of all who seek Yeshua are in danger. All suspected."

Joanna told story after story about Yeshua. She repeated the same theme over and over with countless variations. "You must see him yourself! Hear Yeshua's words with your own ears! Take Manaen to him! There's no one else in heaven or on earth who can restore to Manaen what Herod Antipas stole."

"Antipas took more than Manaen's eyes. Much more."

At last, replete and exhausted, Joanna and Boaz were shown to a guest room in the villa.

Though she had been up most of the night, Susanna was no longer tired. She left the kitchen and stood barefoot in the wet grass to watch light break on the snowy peak of Mount Hermon, forty miles to the north.

Behind her in the house, servants were stirring. Old Hashim, stretching and yawning, hobbled stiffly to the drying barns. Birds flew up from the orchards and wheeled slowly overhead.

Susanna considered the hope Joanna had carried with her from Galilee:

"The roads are never empty anymore. Those coming to Yeshua are like a tide never turning. The people are all asking, 'Who is he?' Some say he is even more than we dreamed Messiah would be. This may be why many can't believe him. Some say he's more than a prophet. More than a priest. More than a king! You must go to him secretly in Capernaum! See for yourself!

Bring your beloved to him and then all darkness will be dispelled from his life and yours."

There was much more to Yeshua of Nazareth than it was possible for Susanna to believe! She could not dare to hope unless she saw for herself!

Susanna whispered aloud as dawn broke, "Yeshua of Nazareth. Carpenter. Rabbi. Healer. Prophet? Messiah? Who are you? What are you?" She gazed at the shuttered window of their bedchamber and wondered if her only hope—*their* only hope—could be found in the man some were calling the Messiah.

A meeting between Herod Antipas and his two new assassins was held in the marble-and-onyx-paneled drawing room at the old Sepphoris Palace. The ceiling was too low, bouncing dry heat back onto Antipas' sweating neck and forehead.

Before Herod Antipas developed the lakeside town of Tiberias, Sepphoris had been the most important city in the Galil. In the Galilean hill country, it was both the heart of the flax-growing region and a center of linen weaving. Sepphoris was significant enough for Herod the Great to have built a palace there.

Antipas hated Sepphoris. He hated it for being hot, dry, and dusty. He missed the marble baths, lavish gardens, cooling fountains, and Greek statuary with which he had decorated Tiberias.

Most of all, Antipas hated Sepphoris because of its associations. After the death of Herod the Great, during the time Antipas' older brother Archelaus had been ruler of Judea, a rebellion had broken out. A sicarius named Judas the Galilean had seized Sepphoris, arming his followers from the arsenal in the royal palace. From there the insurrection had spread, until crushed by the might of Rome.

It was evident that Archelaus could not manage the ironfisted rule like his father, so eventually the inept Archelaus was deposed and exiled. Judea had become a province under direct Roman governorship. Antipas had narrowly avoided suffering exile with Archelaus, till his glib tongue managed to put the blame for the unrest on his brother.

Antipas wasted no sympathy on his bungling sibling. The bad memories in Sepphoris had to do with Antipas' ambition. After Archelaus' departure, Antipas should have been made ruler of all Israel, as his father had been. He still could be, at the rate Governor Pilate was making mistakes and enemies. But only if Antipas kept rebellion out of his territory for a while longer.

Antipas made himself appear in Sepphoris with a legion of soldiers, asserting his power, emphasizing his control. But always, in the back of his mind, was the nagging reminder: Rome was slow to forgive error and often quick to punish it.

Antipas could not afford any mistakes.

That was the context of the present meeting. Antipas was anxious to conclude this conference but not so hasty as to encourage a misstep that might come back to haunt him.

Eglon's missed assassination attempt of Yeshua had nearly been a disaster, uniting opposition to the tetrarch and renewing interest in Yeshua as a king.

Rome was watching.

Antipas knew Yeshua was a threat but removing Him had to be done carefully, so as not to make a martyr of Him. If only Yeshua could be caught in some crime against the state and arrested. If only there was some way to make the Romans do the dirty work.

So far none of the plots had succeeded.

Shamen, the assassin, prodded the tetrarch again: "We have perfectly clear, tasteless, odorless poisons, lord Antipas, which can easily be introduced into a glass of wine. Yeshua would simply go to sleep and never awaken."

"Not good enough!" Antipas protested.

Shamen's wife, Ona, fluttered an Oriental paper fan painted with nightingales next to her flushed cheek. "Perhaps lord Antipas thinks the subject may have enough magic to survive it? Wouldn't that be an interesting experiment to make?"

Shamen stroked his scraggly beard. "Suppose it was obvious that poison *was* the cause of his death . . . and just as obvious someone else was to blame."

Antipas sat up a little straighter in his low-backed chair. "Better. But we need to plan it carefully. We need to know who he trusts, who's close to him that might betray him. Give us places and times."

Ona grinned a gap-toothed smile.

Shamen bowed, saying, "We already know of such a one, lord

Antipas. He is dissatisfied, ambitious, and eager to be on the winning side. Such a one is easily led. We'll be meeting with him again soon."

It was warm. Sunlight sparkled on the snow atop Mount Hermon. A patch of sky through the window of Alexander's workshop proclaimed a beautiful day. The air smelled like flowers from the gardens of King Philip.

Hero, holding his box of toys, stood at the door of the shop until Alexander noticed him. Perhaps the medicine—and Zahav's cooking—was working after all.

"Yes, Hero. Too nice to stay indoors, eh? Is that what you're saying?"

Alexander moved his workbench, tools, and materials from the shop so he could work beneath the oak tree.

Hero played happily in the dirt beside him, digging roads for his prize toy chariot and horseman to travel. Scraps of wood Alexander had carved were houses along the way. Smooth pebbles painted by Diana were Hero's imaginary friends. There were merchants and soldiers and a king. A mother, a father, a little boy.

To look at Hero on such a day, playing at his father's feet, who would guess the truth about him? Customers always said:

"Your son plays so nicely."

"A sweet child."

"Wish my boys could be that quiet. Rowdy ones, they are. Never stop talking for an instant."

Alexander's thoughts ranted at him as he worked. If only the what-ifs and whys that shouted at him every waking hour would fall silent and let his spirit rest!

What a gift it would be to have a child's voice interrupt the assault of memories and regrets in Alexander's brain. To know what Hero was thinking and feeling. What a miracle that would be!

Hero tugged Alexander's tunic for attention.

Alexander glanced down at the pretend town. "Very nice, Hero. Yes. There's our shop. Our house. Yes. Me, you, and Mama."

The boy scrutinized the family of three smooth pebbles in his palm. He kissed the mother. Then the father. Then he gently tapped child and mother together in an embrace.

"So this is what you're thinking of. Yes. Me too. Every hour I think of her. Wish it could be like it was," Alexander said aloud. "I miss her too."

Hero presented the mother pebble to Alexander's lips. A kiss. Hero smiled. His eyes were clear today. Flecks of gold glinted against the blue. Like her eyes.

Alexander picked up the little boy pebble and kissed it as well. "I love you, Hero. My boy."

Understanding, Hero opened his mouth and laughed a silent laugh.

Who would know by looking at the child? At that instant who could tell?

"Yes, yes, I remember. Yes, I know. I miss her too, Son."

Zahav found an excuse to walk past Alexander's house. On her way to the butcher's she strolled along the Cardo in hopes of seeing him and Hero.

Since delivering the lamb stew, twice she had stood across the street and listened to Alexander play his flute to draw in customers. Hero's color had returned, his sad eyes had brightened, and he played quietly. Zahav smiled to see him smile.

Caesarea Philippi was clogged with travelers escaping the heat of the lowlands. Many of the wealthy from Damascus owned summer homes here.

At over a thousand feet above sea level and perched on a shoulder of snow-topped Mount Hermon, the city was uniquely placed to enjoy an excellent climate and beautiful scenery. The breezes out of the north cooled the land for much of the year, making the place a sought-after refuge for those who would escape the desert heat.

It was also fertile and well watered. In springtime waterfalls jetted out from the cliffs of the higher peaks like garlands of white flowers and cascaded toward the newly birthed river Jordan.

The runoff from the mountain fed countless streams, springs, and creeks. Rain and snowmelt made mulberries flourish on the lower slopes and plane trees higher up. By midsummer canyons were turned into sheltered archways by the overhanging oleanders. Those tunnels of trees were perfumed with fragrant honeysuckle vines.

Paneas had always been a desirable place to live, from earliest times.

It had been so attractive that the Canaanite populace had been driven out by the Hebrew tribe of Dan during the conquest of the Promised Land. Their original settlement lay no more than four miles northwest of Caesarea, on the road to Tyre.

Travelers from Jerusalem came to Caesarea Philippi, exchanging the summer dreariness of Judea for the refreshing foothills. Once there, many expressed the wish to remain and never go back to the drier world south.

This wish for separation from Jerusalem had led to serious consequences in the past. To satisfy the people who did not want to go to Jerusalem to worship at the Temple of the One God—and to satisfy his own political aims—Jeroboam, king of the northern half of the divided Jewish empire, set up a golden calf in Dan.

What had once been part of Eretz-Israel and dedicated to the service of Adonai ELoHiYM sank rapidly into an easy acceptance of whatever new god came their way. The cities under the sway of Caesarea Philippi bowed down to Jeroboam's golden calf, the lightning-wielding Hadad-rimmon of the Syrians, the Ba'als of the Canaanites, the ruler worship of the Greek successors of Alexander the Great, and now to Rome's cult of emperor devotion.

Zahav remained apart from the unclean men and women who flocked to hear the flute maker play. But she envied the goyim in a way. They could, without fear of violating a religious edict, speak to Alexander, ask him how he was feeling now that time had passed since the death of his wife.

But who would ask him such a thing? No one. Still, Zahav imagined herself marching up to his booth, taking his hand, asking, "How is Hero these days? Is he eating well? sleeping better?"

She wished she could tell this prodigal son of Abraham, "I prayed for you in synagogue this morning. I thought about you both last night. I hope you are well."

Shabbat afternoon. The day of rest. Yeshua had been absent from them for two days.

Embers of yesterday's cook fires had gone cold. They would not be relit until the end of Shabbat at twilight.

The larger group was divided into seven circles of ten men. Each circle represented the Ten Commandments and comprised a minyan. Each minyan prayed together at dawn before sharing a simple breakfast of challah, the Shabbat bread.

Throughout the morning they read the Torah portion and discussed Yeshua's teachings until after a midday meal. It was the in-between time of day when some slept and others turned their conversations to personal matters.

Peniel sat beside the cold campfire with Levi, the leader of his minyan. The other members of their group dozed beneath the trees or near the stream at the foot of the hill. Their absence left the usually lively circle of comrades a dull and too-quiet threesome.

Peniel was silent as Judas discussed the dwindling treasury with Levi. Such a worldly concern was a forbidden topic on Shabbat. "Fewer willing to contribute these days."

Levi shrugged. "Herod Antipas has raised taxes again."

"There's more reason than that. It's the strange things Yeshua's saying. The old faithful are falling away. The people aren't coming anymore. Not like they used to. I'll say it again: When he taught that his body was bread to be eaten, who could understand such a thing?"

This was something from Torah that Peniel could address. He was grateful to get off the theme of money and contributions. He raised his hand timidly, like a schoolboy who knows the answer to a question.

Judas gave him a dubious glare. "You have something to add, blind man?"

Levi defended, "Leave him alone. Let the boy have his say."

"All right then." Judas looked away, elaborately disinterested.

Levi extended his hand, palm up, indicating that Peniel should speak.

Peniel shifted uneasily. Perhaps he should not have interrupted, but they were supposed to talk Torah today, of all days. And he had learned a lot as a beggar at the Temple gates.

"Well, what Yeshua said about the bread being his body, it's from Torah, you know. Manna, bread from heaven, given to our fathers every day for forty years by the hand of Yahweh."

"You don't say." Judas rolled his eyes.

Levi tossed a pebble into the ashes. "Go ahead."

"It's a prophecy about our Messiah. The word *manna* means

'What?' or 'Who is it?' Every morning for five days the Israelites would gather enough manna for only one day. They would eat the question Who? But on the sixth day, just before Shabbat, the Lord provided a double portion of manna. They would not have to gather their bread on the seventh day.[23] That's why we Jews bless two loaves of bread at table on Shabbat. Remembering the double provision of the Lord's Word for his people. Each loaf represents the answer to the question Who? Mosheh the lawgiver is one; the other, Messiah yet to come. The Shabbat loaves are blessed and anointed with oil and covered by a cloth. The covering is because Mosheh's face was veiled. After he met with the Lord, as a man meets with another man, Mosheh's skin shone so brightly from the Lord's glory![24]

"And the other bread is covered because when Messiah first comes to us, we won't recognize him for who he is! But then he'll remove the veil and we will see the Lord as he is, face-to-face. Man-to-man! Like Mosheh saw him. We will know the answer asked by the word *manna*. The Messiah, see? 'Who is this?' Yeshua was saying he is the bread, the word, sent by God to nourish us."

Judas studied his fingernails. "Is that it? So, Peniel, the blind Torah scholar, you believe Yeshua is equal to Mosheh the lawgiver. Then why doesn't he prove it? Give us a sign. It's not too late! He could rally the crowds if he'd do something—something important! Not these healings of . . . nobodies! Show us the face of Yahweh." He snorted in consternation that his advice was so ignored. "You're quite a learned man. You think this up on your own?"

Peniel blushed. "Oh. It's not original. I heard it from a very old rabbi who took shelter in my sukkah once. I mean, aren't we supposed to discuss Torah today?"

"How do you know these things?" Levi asked, one eyebrow lifted in surprise.

"People talk. When you're a beggar in the Temple of Yerushalayim, you pick things up."

Judas scowled. "Newcomers with us now. Know-it-alls. The important men hardly ever come. Look at this. A beggar discussing Torah like he knows something."

Peniel did not like this conversation much. He was not a beggar anymore. He was not an invisible blind man to be stumbled over and talked about. He was a man of Israel. A member of the seventy talmidim in Yeshua's Torah academy.

"Yeshua welcomes those to his academy who are most worthy." Levi seemed genuinely impressed.

"I suppose the most ignorant men in Israel are the most worthy," Judas mocked.

"Peniel studied Torah with his ears as he sat at Nicanor Gate in the Temple, Judas. That's clear, isn't it? He listened and learned from your old teacher, Rabbi Gamaliel. And the rest of them too. Isn't that right, Peniel?"

It was true enough, but Peniel did not dare reply. Levi was using him to needle Judas. Peniel did not want to get in the middle of the growing resentment between these two men.

To make a point, Judas passed a fragment of parchment to Peniel. "Well, Torah scholar, can you read this?"

Peniel stared at the meaningless scratches, then shook his head. "You know me—I'm Peniel. Can't read."

Judas snatched it away. "So these are the quality of talmidim Yeshua invites to study in his academy. And those other pack mules who share our meals? The former scum who make up our distinguished minyan of outcasts are just ignorant! What a relief it is not to have to listen to their jabbering this morning!"

Ire rose in Peniel at the barb. He could not resist. "Point taken. I can't read . . . yet. But I love a good story. Sat in darkness for seventeen years in the Temple of Yerushalayim listening to you important fellows talk about storming the Antonia Fortress and killing Romans and driving out the oppressors like your relative, Judas the Maccabee."

Judas glared at Peniel in surprise.

Levi howled with laughter. "Aye! Judas! Wasn't that your old great-grandfather or something, Judas? Ran the Greeks out of Yerushalayim, he did! And then, in a stroke of genius, your Maccabee relatives invited the Romans into Yerushalayim to protect Israel from invasion. Using wolves as stock dogs to guard the sheep. And now the high priest is bought and paid for by Rome. Bright fellows, your ancestors!"

Furious at the insult, Judas jumped to his feet and stormed away from Levi's camp.

Levi and Peniel were left alone. They munched Shabbat bread

without speaking for several minutes. Then Levi tossed a crust to a bird and slapped Peniel on the back. "Well done, lad. Well spoken. I didn't think you had more than two words in you for anyone. Most pleasant Shabbat I've had since last time Judas was insulted."

"I remember Judas. Sure. Recognized his voice from Yerushalayim. He and a few others of Gamaliel's talmidim sat on the steps of Nicanor where I used to beg. Don't think he remembers me, though. He talked a lot about rebellion. Argued with his rabbi about it and left the city."

"But the sword of Judas Iscariot has never been out of its sheath except to peel an apple or swat a fly." Levi shifted his weight and studied his bread. He muttered under his breath. "Don't know why he's assigned to our minyan. According to himself, he's better than all of us."

Peniel did not mention to Levi that Judas had never once dropped even the smallest coin into Peniel's begging bowl. Nor in the bowl of any other beggar in Yerushalayim as far as he knew. Why had Yeshua placed such a tightfisted, ungenerous fellow in charge of the treasury? And why was a well-educated fellow like Judas assigned to eat with Levi's group of former beggars and outcasts? There were other groups that would have suited Judas better.

Levi warned, "You've made a true enemy today—you know that, don't you?"

Peniel wished it was not so. "I'm sorry for it."

"Don't be. You know a good man more by his enemies than his friends, my old father used to say. You've gone up some in my estimation, Peniel ben Yahtzar."

"I'm glad of that, Levi. Indeed."

"Would you like to learn to read? Then you wouldn't have to pack so much information around in your head. I'll teach you if you like."

"Would you? You know me. I'm Peniel! I've always wanted to read. I know Torah by heart. Most of it anyway. But oh! To see the letters just like the finger of God painted them! Lovely things! A garden on parchment! And to study the order of them and see how they're placed and what they mean!"

"Won't take a lad like yourself long at all."

Peniel followed Levi's gaze to Judas. Judas sauntered slowly through the camp, stopping to say a word, to listen in for a minute. At last Thomas invited him to join their group.

Levi lowered his voice in warning to Peniel. "You'll have to watch your back, Peniel. Judas is a bad one. You've hurt his pride and he's a proud man. You'll have to be careful now."

14

A pair of magpies scolded one another from adjacent oak trees. The racket matched Peniel's thoughts. The *cack-cack, squabble-squabble* was an unpleasantly accurate rendition of how relationships had deteriorated in the camp of the talmidim under the stewardship of Nathaniel after only two days of Yeshua's absence.

Peniel made his way down to a secluded pool of the brook. Sheltered from view by a large boulder, he hoped to find a little peace and quiet. Wash his clothes. Dangle his feet in the water.

It was like this every time Yeshua was not around, he reflected. Personalities clashed, egos rose, tempers flared. The woman everyone called Honey, because she and her husband, Clopas, kept bees, was anything but sweet. Three of her sons were among Yeshua's inner circle: Simon the Zealot, Thaddeus, and Little James. Honey was related to Yeshua by marriage and called the Rabbi "Nephew" in a way that made her sons cringe and other women roll their eyes. She constantly pushed her sons forward. She was jealous of John and Ya'acov, whose mother, Salome, was sister to Yeshua's mother. A mild mutiny was taking place among the crew designated by John to scavenge firewood.

Honey insisted, under her breath, that if Thaddeus, Simon, and

Little James were given the chance to prove themselves in leadership roles, there would be peace.

Peniel kicked off his sandals and soaked his feet.

Above his head a magpie stole a bit of string; the other bird claimed it. In the ensuing wrangle the twine dropped, falling into the water and washing away downstream. The birds proceeded to squawk louder than ever, gabbling accusations at each other.

Honey's and Clopas' nagging would have been bad enough, but the situation was made worse by other contenders: Yeshua's aunt, Salome, was equally vocal on behalf of her sons, John and Ya'acov. Why shouldn't everyone acknowledge them? she wanted to know. After all, they were kin. *Near* kin, she emphasized. If Yeshua was truly going to be king someday, then clearly her boys should be prime minister and treasurer of the new government.

The sets of brothers were alternately embarrassed by their mothers and prodded into being more aggressive. The rest of the band hated the wrangling, kept their mouths shut about it in front of Yeshua, then verbally tore the contestants to shreds behind their backs.

On and on it went. Who had the stronger claim? Who was smarter? more polished? more educated? more diplomatic? The competing assertions were endlessly, ceaselessly argued.

Peniel dipped his tallith in the stream, scrubbed it with soap, then squeezed the water out. Peniel's mother had thought him useless. She repeatedly told him so. Never once had she expressed any belief that he'd amount to anything, never thought he was worth fighting for. Who could have guessed Peniel would feel relief at *not* being fought for?

Peniel strangled the tunic into agreeing with him about how obnoxious the situation was, then slapped it harder than needed on the boulder to dry.

The quarreling magpies found something else to bicker about. It was shiny and its gleam attracted another pair of the black-and-white birds. Soon a half score were chasing each other in and out of the branches, making Peniel reconsider the serenity of his choice of location.

Between the bubble of the stream and the avian argument overhead, Peniel did not notice the approach of other people at first. How long had they been on the opposite side of the rock?

"And I tell you again, I don't *know* where he is!"

Peniel recognized the speaker as Judas Iscariot. He peered over the boulder. Judas stood before two strangers, a middle-aged man and his portly female companion.

Judas spread his hands in a gesture of innocence. "He goes off by himself for days at a time. Sometimes he takes two or three of his cousins with him. Sometimes he goes alone, telling no one. But he'll be back. Tell your master that: He'll be back."

The stranger glared at Judas. "Cousins? Who can say who his relations are? Who can say?" His accent was Egyptian, Peniel recognized.

His female companion dusted off a tree stump and sat down. "He claims to be the son of a god, does he not? Are all his relatives also divine?" Her accent was clearly Alexandrian.

Judas crossed his arms defensively. "The people want to believe it. They ask him for a sign. I thought for a time, perhaps, that the circumstances of his birth were a sign. The prophecy in Jewish writings. The book of Isaiah. A ruler from the royal line of David. Born of a virgin in Beth-lehem."

The woman's shrill laugh echoed across the water. "Born of a virgin? You Jews! Gossip from Jerusalem says Yeshua's illegitimate. His mother seduced by a Roman soldier."

The man spit. "A Roman soldier by the name of Panterra."

Judas raised his chin in challenge. "Yeshua? Half Roman? Who invented such a lie? Who chose the name? Lord Herod? Or Caiaphas? Pan Terra? Pan, god of the earth? Can't they do better? Their slander mocks him, but what if he was the king all of Israel has been waiting for? Well, tell the tetrarch it would take more than slander to stop Yeshua if he truly was—"

Peniel heard the woman's disdain. "So the truth of it. You defend his honor! First you tell us Yeshua is a fool. You say you hate him because he is a weakling! But here's the truth! You love him!"

The warning note in Judas' voice was evident. "I confided in you my hate. Hate for his weakness! I never opened my heart to you!"

The man wiped his mouth with the back of his hand, half-concealing his smile. "Your heart . . . holding a place for that rebellious, illegitimate impostor? What a joke!"

Judas lunged at the man, grasping the front of his tunic. "What do you know about anything! What do you know about him! The whole world would go to its knees if only he would—"

In a flash the woman threw her silk kerchief around Judas' neck. A twist brought him to his knees. He clawed helplessly at his throat, unable to break free. Face reddened. Eyes bulged.

She leaned down and spoke into his ear. "So. You're on your knees. But you forget who holds the real power here. It isn't Yeshua. Hate him or love him. It's nothing to us. Nothing!" She released her grip of the scarf, sending Judas sprawling and gasping for breath.

The man smoothed the front of his tunic. "Remember who we serve. The rumor is already taking root. The people are laughing behind their hands at him."

The woman stepped back, coiling like a snake ready to strike. She glanced toward Peniel's hiding place as though she sensed his presence. He ducked down. "Yes! The people are beginning to believe that this fellow they hoped was their Messiah is nothing more than an illegitimate son of a Roman soldier. Yeshua ha'Panterra, they call him. That is what they say in the Temple courts. If Yeshua claims he is the son of a god, why not call him son of Pan? And as for his mother—an uneducated peasant, I hear. She says she saw an angel? Perhaps her angel wore hobnailed shoes and carried a Roman sword?"

At this slander of the gentle lady and her good son, Peniel's ire rose. Of course the Herodians and the Sadducees would promote such a lie! What better way to discredit Yeshua than to invent a story that Yeshua was the son of a Roman soldier whose name meant "All Earth"!

Judas dully croaked, "Maybe it doesn't matter. The excitement has almost run its course. Unless he does something spectacular again or moves to a new location, like back to Yerushalayim, eventually he'll fade away. The people are tired of him. They wanted a king, not a preacher."

Peniel drew himself up. What was Judas saying? What! Peniel's blood pounded in his ears. It was one thing for the talmidim to fret amongst themselves and something entirely different—disloyal—to gossip with strangers.

The woman's voice demanded, "Where will he go next? Where? Can you tell us when he'll be near a city?"

Judas responded, "Do you think he tells me what his plans are? That big dumb fisherman, perhaps, or one of his imbecile cousins, but me, no. He knows my advice is too sensible. He'd just ignore it. But I'll know more soon. Tell your master that."

A few more sentences were exchanged, most of which Peniel could not hear; then Judas' visitors took their leave. By the crunching of the foliage under their feet, Peniel judged their progress away from the stream.

When he knew they were out of earshot, he leapt up and jogged to where Judas sat brooding on a rock ledge, digging at his fingernails with a dagger.

Peniel shouted, "You! Who were they? What was that about? I don't like the way you talk about the Teacher. Or the good lady, his mother! Or the way you talk about people like you know what they're thinking! Who's tired of him? Who? Nobody. Except you maybe."

Judas, startled, hopped up quickly. The knife disappeared beneath his robe so fast Peniel wondered where it had gone.

"So the blind beggar is also a sneaking spy; is that it?"

Peniel clenched his fists. "I was here first. And, anyway, you were talking loud."

Judas closed the gap between them, edging around Peniel so that the younger man's back was to the boulder. "Listen, sneak. You'll keep out of other people's business if you know what's good for you."

"I could say the same—"

Before Peniel could finish his sentence, Judas' hand flashed forward and his fist slammed into Peniel's stomach. The blow knocked the wind out of Peniel. He gasped for breath. No air. No air. He bent over, putting a hand on the boulder to steady himself. The world turned yellow. It was not something Peniel had experienced before. For an instant he wondered if he'd been stabbed. Prying his fingers away from his gut, he stared at them with apprehension.

No blood.

"A little instruction from me to you, see?" Judas next brought his fists together on either side of Peniel's head. The pain in both ears was intense. "Who are you, anyway? You sold out the Teacher already once, didn't you? You'd save your own miserable, worthless life at any cost. Who are you to make any charges against anyone else?"

Peniel sank to his knees. The world spun around and Peniel's eyes would not focus properly. "You! Traitor! You—"

"Herod Antipas is rounding up beggars who claim Yeshua healed them. Some of them were faking before, eh? Like we know you were?"

Peniel shook his head, ducking quickly at the slightest movement of Judas' hands. "No! Never!"

"There aren't many willing to risk tongue or ears—" Judas' index fingers darted out like spikes, stopping close in front of Peniel's eyes— "or eyes, eh? Something's got to give soon. You don't want to be . . . trampled . . . when it does."

Judas kicked Peniel in the ribs, driving all the air from Peniel's lungs with a tormented exclamation. Peniel toppled over and lay curled in a ball. "Traitor . . ." Peniel managed to spit out.

"Schoolboy. Out of my business, eh? School's out, but you won't like it if I have to give you another lesson. Now clear off."

Sometime later, when he was finally able to breathe without stabbing pains, Peniel rose. Abandoning his laundry by the creek, he wandered away up the slope and into the apple orchard.

Alexander clamped the olivewood in the padded jaws of his vise. With the golden block secured on his workbench the artisan operated the bow drill with his right hand. The bit cut evenly into the hard surface, punching out the third in a series of holes of increasing diameters.

It was an experiment the instrument maker had thought of in his sleep. He crafted a multivoiced panpipe from a single piece of wood instead of binding hollow reeds together. The differing pitches would be achieved by changing the size of the holes rather than varying the lengths of the tubes.

Hero sat quietly at his father's feet. The boy had a length of leather cord. From a box of discarded bits of drilled bone, wood, and antler, Hero strung necklaces. Sometimes he played for hours this way, arranging and rearranging the makeshift beads.

Presently Hero pushed the strand away and got up. Alexander was too absorbed in his work to pay attention as Hero padded silently out of the room.

Must be hungry, Alexander thought. *That's good.* The craftsman's stomach growled. *So am I*, he noted.

The boy returned, but instead of bread or dried fruit in his hands he carried the wedding flute. Patiently he waited beside his father until Alexander looked down. Then the boy extended the instrument. The message was clear: *Play for me.*

It seemed an odd request, since Hero was deaf. Perhaps he remembered the times Alexander performed for Diana. Perhaps it was a way of recalling the contentment he'd known when all three of them were together.

Laying aside his tools, Alexander obliged. "What'll you hear?" he asked with a smile. A Jewish melody came to his mind. It was a poem set to a tune called "The Lilies."

"The bride, a princess, waits within her chamber,
Dressed in a gown woven with gold.
In her beautiful robes, she is led to the king,
Accompanied by her bridesmaids."

A love song, it moved Alexander twice over: First because he missed Diana so, and again because Hero could not hear the sweet refrain.

Reaching up his tiny hand, Hero placed his palm near the opening of the flute. As the warmth of his father's breath tickled his fingers, he grinned.

Alexander stopped abruptly. *Hero can feel the rhythm. He cannot listen to the tune, but he can* feel *it.*

With mounting excitement, Alexander switched to a more lively rhyme:

"Shout with joy to God, all the earth!
Sing the glory of his name;
And make his praise glorious!"[25]

Hero clapped his hands with the pulsing beat of the phrase. The boy hurriedly replaced his palm as if afraid to miss a single note.

An inspiration drove all thought of his other projects from Alexander's mind. He motioned for the child not to be upset but to wait a moment.

Rummaging through a chest of completed instruments, Alexander found what he sought. At the bottom of the heap was a child's set of pan flutes made of bone. One-third normal size, the pipes were designed to train young musicians.

Because of Hero's disability, Alexander had never considered teaching him to play, never believed it possible. Resuming the same tune, he guided Hero's fingertips to the ends of the tubes. Now Alexander's breath not only varied in intensity but came from different locations as well.

Hero's grin grew till it encompassed his eyes. His tiny frame shivered with pleasure—not the tremor warning of an imminent convulsion, but the trembling of real enthusiasm.

Reversing the pipe, Alexander handed it to his son. Patiently he guided Hero in holding it just so, showed the boy how to place his lips and blow across the opening. Carefully, anxious not to destroy the concentration, Alexander brought Hero's free palm up to the tubes.

Hero sensed his own breath coming from the openings!

The boy played a note—a single, quavering sound, but a perfect whistle, all the same.

He feels the vibration in the tube! Alexander exulted. *He can learn to play.*

The musician's son took to the lesson like a duckling learns to swim! Eye to eye with his boy, Alexander tapped each pipe in turn to indicate the order and duration of each note. Haltingly at first, then with increasing confidence, Hero worked out the musical phrase *Say to God, "How awesome are your deeds!"*

Father and son fell into each other's arms!

Alexander reached for his own set of panpipes. Mimicking lips and hands, Hero did his best to copy his teacher's actions. And when the tune was done and hunger drove them to stop at last, both man and boy laughed with joy, new freedom, and hope.

Twilight filtered through the branches of the apple tree. Breathless, Peniel dropped on all fours to the ground and covered his head with his hands, drawing himself into a ball. He was a stump. A stone. An abandoned sack of rotting apples lying on the orchard floor! The betrayer would not see him. Would not find him!

Would he?

What if the betrayer followed him? discovered him cowering? turned him over to spies from Herod's court? Or what if he slit Peniel's throat while Yeshua was away? hid his body and explained Peniel's disappearance as if he had grown disillusioned lately and turned back?

How long had Yeshua been gone with John, Ya'acov, and Shim'on? A few days only and yet everyone and everything in the camp of Yeshua's talmidim was chaos!

Fear of the edict of the Sanhedrin! Fear of Herod Antipas! Rumors of arrests, torture, and death of many healed by Yeshua! Speculation! Doubts! Arguments! Possible mutiny. And Peniel could add his own terror to the list of faithlessness. Judas was right. Peniel was not worth much. The first sign that things were not going well and Peniel's faith disintegrated and blew away like dust in the wind!

He was grateful for encroaching night. The voices of the talmidim carried to him on the breeze. Suppertime. But even the aroma of fried fish and roasting apples could not draw Peniel out of the orchard. He would not come out unless Yeshua was back to protect him!

He did not move or speak until, at last, total darkness surrounded him. Crickets chirped. The scent of woodsmoke wafted through the orchard. Voices from the encampment fell away to a few murmurs.

At last, the stump, the stone, the sack of apples, stirred and raised his head.

Blessed night! Black and moonless night!

Peniel sat up. With his bare hands he scraped away last year's fallen leaves and debris, clearing a place to sit in the moist earth. He glimpsed stars through the branches, then whispered, "I'm afraid again, Lord. Judas will kill me. Or hand me over. Maybe give you to them too." Then Peniel again recited his own unfaithfulness. How near Peniel had been to betraying Yeshua Himself when Eglon had threatened to put out his eyes and kill his friends! Peniel was no better than the rest of them. His doubts were just as dreadful. What right did he have to accuse anyone?

"Have they already arrested you, Lord? Where are you? Where are you, Lord? I'm a sniveling weakling without you close. All of us are! Do you hear the grumbling in our camp? We won't last long if you don't come back soon!"

His empty stomach growled. Peniel had grown accustomed to sitting around the fire with the others. Eating at a regular time. Listening to stories. Thinking high and lofty thoughts. Talking about what each Torah portion really meant. Compared to begging, being among Yeshua's scholars had been a very fine way to live. Peniel had grown comfortable, satisfied that following the Rabbi would always be easy.

But no longer.

Peniel crept to the edge of the camp. Like a timid rabbit he observed the nine comrades of the inner circle sitting apart from the others, engaged in fierce conversation by firelight.

It was not only Judas. *Everything* had spun out of control. Most of the ordinary followers were fast asleep. The nine chosen argued once again about civil posts they would hold in Yeshua's government. Then which of the Twelve would be chosen prime minister and who would be judge. Carping against Shim'on, John, and Ya'acov circled once and then again. Finally opinions of what Yeshua should do to prove Himself popped and hissed and crackled and flew up like sparks and embers!

Philip: "When we followed Yochanan? Even he was uncertain who Yeshua was. Do you remember? He sent us from his prison cell to ask Yeshua if he was the one."

Andrew: "And even then Yeshua didn't give a straight answer."

Nathaniel: "Remember the prophecy of Malachi about Elijah? *'Look, I am sending you the prophet Elijah before the great and dreadful day of the Lord.'*"[26]

Philip: "Didn't we believe that Yochanan was the prophet?"

Thaddeus: "Some believed Yochanan was the Anointed."

The light of the flames glinted in the eyes of Judas. "We saw no fire fall from heaven from either man."

At this thought the circle fell silent for a time, each lost in his own evaluation. And then it began again.

Nathaniel: "In my opinion he ought to . . ."

Thomas: "But who is he really? I won't believe it until he proves it."

Levi: "We've seen so many miracles. It makes sense that if he wanted to he would."

Little James: "If he can . . . why not now?"

Thaddeus: "If only he would. Who is he? What if he is the Elijah to come before Messiah? Or one of the prophets? All the prophets performed signs."

Simon the Zealot: "Ten thousand swords will be at Messiah's command! If he is—"

Judas: "If he is the coming king? If he is who he claims to be, then why doesn't he? A simple question, that. Are we wasting our time? The people are fewer and fewer. Soon they won't come at all. Soon."

Peniel determined he would not return to the encampment unless Yeshua was present. Peniel was too small and unimportant to be missed. And yet surely his disapproval of such talk would be noticed. He could not conceal it.

He considered the conversation among Yeshua's favored apostles and consoled himself. Endless speculation was not treason. Opinion was not mutiny.

Peniel retreated deep into the shadows of the orchard. Exhaustion overtook him. The sickening scent of rotten fruit surrounded him. He covered nose and mouth with his cloak to filter out the stink. "Oh, Yeshua! Lord! Am I the last one left? Amos gone. So many others leaving. Unsure. Herod Antipas would catch me like a bug in a jar. Put out my eyes. I'd be better off dead! There's nothing I can do! Nothing!" he muttered as despair and sleep pressed down on him.

15

C H A P T E R

he aroma of lavender awakened Peniel. It was still night. Un-
covering his face, he inhaled deeply. Yes. Lavender! Here in the
heart of the apple orchard, where decaying fruit littered the
ground! Lavender! Where was it coming from?

In Jerusalem Peniel had often sat across the lane from the herb
seller's stall just to smell the open baskets of lavender. And when the
cart had been trundled away for the night, Peniel had knelt on the cobbles to drink in the sweet scent. By his nose he located each tiny bud
spilled from the scoop. One by one he had retrieved them, cupped the
spoonful in his hand, held them close to his nose, and breathed in a garden, a field, the fragrant bank of a river!

But here? In the orchard? How? Where had it come from? In the
wind that stirred the branches above him?

He heard the snap of a twig beneath someone's foot. But he wasn't
afraid. Peniel reckoned he was dreaming. He was glad. A dream with
the aroma of lavender was a fine dream to have in such a place.

"Who's there?"

A friendly, amused voice whispered, *Peniel. Peniel. I was sent to ask,
why are you hiding here?*

This was a voice Peniel did not recognize from his dreams. He opened his eyes. Framed by starlight, the figure of a powerful, fierce-looking man towered over him. He was clothed in leather. Hair and beard were grizzled and unbraided, windblown like a thousand-year-old tamarisk tree clinging to the side of a mountain. Though he had no sword, Peniel suspected that this was the assassin sent by Antipas to kill him.

"Have you come to kill me?"

Why are you hiding? the man asked.

"Because I'm afraid. I'm the one left in the camp who would die for the sake of my Master."

This evoked a laugh from the visitor. *Ah, Peniel! A man of such courage. And yet you're hiding in an orchard of rotten fruit.*

Peniel, aware that he had been insulted in his own dream, sat up and challenged the imaginary visitor. "I'm waiting, that's all. Waiting for Yeshua to return. He's gone, you see. And I'm just trying to sort it out while he's away. Trying to sort out his story about the vineyard. Who is the son? Who was he talking about? What is to come?"

Good questions.

Peniel flared. "But who are you to mock me? What do you know about it?"

My name is Elijah.

Peniel strained to see the fellow's features more closely, but darkness concealed the details. "Elijah. They've been talking about Elijah the prophet in the camp. They were . . . wondering . . ."

Yes. They were heard.

"But . . . Elijah? Common enough name. Where do you come from?"

I was born in a village called Gilead.

Now this was something! "But . . . Gilead? Like the prophet Elijah? Elijah of old? The one we've been wondering about?"

Yes. I was born in Gilead.

"I suppose everyone in Gilead nowadays names their boy babies after the prophet Elijah. In Yerushalayim I knew a cutpurse named Elijah who was from Gilead. He didn't live up to his name."

Often the case, Peniel. Most could not live up to such a name. Elijah means "Yahweh is God." Speak such a word and believe its meaning. Say it aloud, and in the world unseen by the eyes of mortal men, dark spirits flee in terror at the truth.

Peniel whispered, "Elijah . . . Elijah . . . *Yahweh is God.*" Again the scent of lavender wafted through the decay of the orchard. Peniel blinked at the shadowy figure. "But . . . how do you know what goes on beyond the eyes of mortal men?"

Yahweh is God.

A chill coursed through Peniel. "But . . . who . . . are you?"

Yahweh is God.

Peniel drew his breath in sharply. He covered his face with his hands. "Elijah of Gilead! Elijah the Tishbite! The prophet who didn't die. The one who called down fire from heaven to consume the soldiers of Ahab! The one who defeated four hundred and fifty prophets of Ba'al on Mount Carmel and raised a boy back to life and gave endless bread to the widow of Zarephath!"[27] He paused for a breath, then welcomed his distinguished visitor. "*Ulu Ush-pi-zin!* Be seated, exalted guest! You are the prophet who never died."

Elijah sat across from Peniel. *You know your Scriptures.*

"I love a good story. And so I listened, listened every day to the teachings in the Temple."

And yet you're afraid. Hiding here.

"You ran away too. Ran from King Ahab and his wife, Jezebel. I remember. Though you were the fellow who called down fire from heaven, still you were afraid. You ran away into the wilderness and you lay down beneath a broom tree and waited to die."[28]

That I did. Aye . . . aye. Despair. My greatest enemy. And yet the Lord sent ravens to feed me and bade me rest before the long journey ahead of me.[29]

Peniel clutched his knees. "Will you tell me about it? Your forty days in the wilderness? The cave. The still, small voice of the Almighty when he spoke to you? [30] What it was like to be taken up in a heavenly chariot in the whirlwind?[31] Will you tell me all of it?"

Another time, Peniel. Tonight we were talking about names, remember?

"Yes. Yes. Mosheh the lawgiver told me once in a dream that everything means something."

A strong, approving hand patted Peniel on his arm. Very solid. *Almost real,* Peniel thought.

Elijah said, *Well spoken. Aye, lad! Everything in Torah and Tanakh means something. Points the way to Messiah.*

"Back in the camp, everyone is wondering about you, Elijah. They're confused these days. Wondering if Yeshua is you."

Yahweh is God, Elijah replied quietly. He did not speak for a very long time, and yet he was still there in the orchard, sitting across from Peniel. At last the prophet sighed. *Everything means something. Aye! As it was in my day, so it is now. Once again Eretz-Israel is divided as it was in my time. When I was prophet, King Ahab was king of the northern kingdom. He was not a descendant of King David. He came to power as a result of four rebellions.*

"Point taken. As Herod Antipas is ruler in the north now." Peniel made the connection.

Ahab. Scripture says no one had ever done such evil in the sight of the Lord as Ahab. Until this present age. Ahab. Here is where the irony of Scripture is seen clearly. Ahab's name means "Friend of His Father." And yet Ahab was no friend of father Abraham. He broke every covenant. Desecrated Torah. Profaned the Living God.[32]

Peniel added what he knew. "Ahab offered living children for sacrifice in the fires of Molech. Built pagan temples everywhere, polluting the land. Married Jezebel, daughter of a powerful pagan priest-king in Sidon."

Elijah's great head swung to and fro in the memory of her. *Jezebel. A woman, yet a dwelling for evil. How she hated the Lord, the God of Israel!*

"She hated you as well."

Her religion called for ritual prostitution in the temples of her gods. And her name means "Chaste." Elijah tapped his finger on Peniel's temple. *Think, lad. Now. Now then. I want you to consider the meaning of the name of the one who now rules the* am ha aretz *of Israel here in the Galil!*

"Herod! Herod Antipas!"

Aye. Think of it! Antipas is not a descendant of King David. He is not even a son of Abraham! Antipas is half Samaritan, half Idumean. His name in Greek proclaims every plan Satan intends to bring about to destroy the Almighty's promises to Israel! Think of the meaning of the name Antipas!

"Sorry. My Greek. It's not half good."

The name Anti-pas—Anti, *"Against" or "Instead of"* pas; *"The Father"! Antipas has been granted the powers of great evil for a time in an effort to destroy the true King sent to redeem Israel. His plan is set against the Father. Like Satan in the first rebellion in heaven, Antipas longs to rule "Instead of the Father." But one day the Anointed One, Prophet, Priest, and*

King, the promised Son of our Father in Heaven, will reign over the earth and sit on the throne of David in Yerushalayim. His name means "Salvation"! He is Immanu'el, "God-with-us." But for now, Antipas, the false shepherd, rules over the lost sheep of Israel "Instead of the Father." Like Ahab, Antipas has married a woman infused with darkness and ambition. As I preached against Ahab and Jezebel of old, so did Yochanan the Baptizer preach against these serpents, Antipas and Herodias, in your day.

Peniel considered the parallels between the time of Elijah and the present. How had he not understood them before? One question arose again in his mind. "All right, then, I can see it. It makes sense to me. But Yeshua told a story about a vineyard. Tenant farmers who killed the son and heir of the landowner. Antipas and Herodias are the tenant farmers. Who is the son in the story?"

Peniel sensed the enigmatic smile of the prophet, although he couldn't see Elijah's face.

Have you not heard the story of Naboth's vineyard, Peniel? How Ahab and Jezebel desired to possess the vineyard of Naboth with the intention that they would rip out the ancient vines to plant . . . vegetables! Think of it! Remember how Ahab and Jezebel stole the vineyard of Naboth, this righteous man, by bribing false witnesses to testify against him? Remember how they lied and claimed that Naboth had cursed God and the king and so must die? Have you not heard how Naboth was dragged outside his own vineyard and murdered?[33] *Everything means something. The name* Naboth *means "Bountiful." It is one of the names of the Messiah. And so that event from my time pointed to a future day when the true heir of the vineyard of Israel will be arrested, slandered, and condemned to die. He will be scourged and ridiculed and humiliated. He will be taken outside the wall, and there he will be murdered. Then Antipas, "The one Against the Father," will claim the vineyard as his own. Ah, Peniel! That day is nearly upon us.*

"But. But when? How can this be? Who is to die? Was it Yochanan? I don't understand, Elijah! Who then in our day is the son to be murdered like Naboth was?"

Yahweh is God! Elijah stood abruptly. He raised his hand in farewell. *Everything means something. There's so much more I can't tell you now. But listen. Study and show yourself approved by El Olam! Everything written in Torah and Tanakh means . . ."*

". . . something! Yes! Yes!" Suddenly unable to think another thought or consider another question, Peniel leaned his head against the trunk of a tree. He sighed and slept deeply as the footsteps of the prophet retreated from the orchard.

There was no doubt Zahav was closest to her youngest sister, Rebecca.

Ishah, middle-born of the three daughters of Rabbi Eliyahu bar Mosheh, was jealous of Zahav.

Zahav could read and discuss Torah like a man. Zahav had no children to wake her in the night. Zahav was Papa's favorite. Zahav had kissed the fringes of the tallith at the hour of her birth and thus had become famous, part of the legend of Herod the Great and the Exiles.

If only Ishah had known the truth. Zahav would have changed places with her in an instant. Children. Husband. Sharing a life with someone. What was anything compared to those blessings?

But Rebecca, docile and pleasant as a cow chewing her cud in the sun. Her children pulled her skirts and hung from her hips and kissed her round, smiling face a thousand times a day. Rebecca was a rock in the middle of a bubbling stream. The sky was blue above her—even when it was not. Rebecca could not read one word, but the words she spoke were spoken kindly. She knew the twenty-two letters of the *alefbet* but had no interest in study or advancement.

And so it was to Rebecca that Zahav revealed her confusion. No, it was more than that—her *feelings* for Alexander and his wounded son, Hero.

Brown doe eyes studied Zahav as she confessed the bringing of meals to the widower. "It's only that I feel so sorry for him. For the boy."

Rebecca sighed as she considered Zahav's deception. "You think you can fix everything."

"I know. I know."

"What would Papa say?"

"I know."

"And on Shabbat too."

"I can barely raise my head. I'm ashamed."

"I know how you must feel, Zahav. I'm blessed. Heli and the kids. Who am I to tell you anything?"

"I don't know why I'm drawn to him. I'm afraid, Rebecca."

"Afraid? You? You who were in Mother's womb when she hid in the well? You who were born in a cave? You who kissed the fringes? Afraid? Then you must be done with it. With them. With Alexander."

"I need to tell him. Face-to-face. Poor man. So alone."

"Then go. Tell him. And then don't go back to him, Zahav."

It was good advice. Loving. Offered with compassion.

Zahav disguised herself in a Roman dress but retained the veil. She left Rebecca's house and entered the world of the Gentiles, the great capital of King Philip. Today she moved through the streets beyond the Quarter without evoking comment from the goyim. She forced herself to look at the city as Alexander might have viewed it.

Everything about Caesarea Philippi reflected the ambition and the beliefs of its ruler.

It was the intention of Tetrarch Philip to build his capital into a truly cosmopolitan city. Combining the two things the Greek-thinking world most admired—university, or "cosmic," appeal with the vaunted status of citizenship—Philip was well on his way to achieving his dream. Just as he wanted to be thought of as a citizen of the wider world, and not simply the local chieftain of a backwater province, so too he desired his capital to achieve widespread renown.

Every noonday the scope of his ambitions was displayed by the interplay of sunlight on white marble. The priests of the temple of Augustus advanced out to the terrace of their edifice. There they made sacrifices and poured out libations to honor the dead emperor and to pray for the living one. Sacrifices of thanksgiving by citizens anxious to pay their respects were received. Augurs read the livers of goats and foretold the success or failure of business ventures.

Not many of the worldly merchants of Syria or Trachonitis fully trusted the oracles' advice. However, it was widely reported that Tiberius himself had his fortune told every single noon, and so it was fashionable to follow suit.

Herod the Great, Philip's father, had founded the temple to Augustus Caesar some four decades earlier. But in the thirty-four years of his own reign over Gaulinitis, Philip had enlarged and enriched both the temple's size and appearance.

The expansive plaza fronting the temple contained a fountain crowned with a figure of Pan dancing with woodland nymphs. Beyond this rose the half-formed walls of the temple of Julia, wife of Augustus and mother of Tiberius Caesar. Since her recent death there had been a race amongst Rome's vassal states to honor her memory. What better way to curry favor with the present emperor than to venerate his mother? After all, hadn't she been named Augusta at the same time her husband had been designated Augustus?

Though it would be but half the size of her husband's structure, the rising columns of Julia's sanctuary glistened in the light. The four columns erected to support the ceremonial front porch were in place and behind these the walls were rising. Philip wanted it finished in no more than another year, so that it, the similar temple in Bethsaida, and the renaming of Bethsaida as Julias could occur simultaneously.

Zahav did not fit in this world. She would never fit. She was resigned—buried in the only life she'd ever have. Guilt at ever wanting more pushed hope far, far down.

She stood across the street from Alexander's shop and gazed at the red door until she was certain it must be near closing. His world could never be her world. He and his family had forsaken the One True God for the world of Philip and the shrines to Caesar. Not even putting on a Roman dress could change what Zahav was on the inside.

Though Alexander had been born a Jew, descended from Abraham, there was no mezuzah containing the Name of Yahweh to mark his doorpost.

Rebecca was right. Zahav mustered her courage. She would tell him why she could never come to his door again.

Hero practiced chuffing on his new panpipes. One note. Two together in a chord. An accidental scale played quite well.

The feel of focused breath emerging from the cylinders fascinated the boy. He endlessly drummed his fingers in rhythm with his playing. For hours deaf Hero played, never imagining the fullness of sound. In the days when Diana was well such monotonous droning would have driven Alexander mad.

That was before.

As Alexander worked, he would encourage his son with an occasional touch on the shoulder. A nod. A smile.

Yes, yes. You're doing it right. Very fine, Hero. Yes.

Alexander could not shake off the ache of loneliness as he bored the finger holes in an ornate double flute destined for Pan's temple. Throughout the day he had caught himself a dozen times almost calling out to Diana.

Almost.

Customers came and went, leaving seeds of conversation to germinate and sprout a crop of memories. Her voice, going on about a thousand ordinary things.

Would he help her reach the cups on the top shelf? Did he think it would rain? Had he noticed that Hero seemed to be happier since she had been giving him that tea from Crete? Would he stop work to lunch with her and Hero beneath the oak? or play with Hero while she hurried to the baker's shop before closing?

How irritated he had been then at trivial interruptions. But now! Now? What would he give to answer her slightest request? to hear her voice call his name again? What would he give?

Unbidden, the thought of the Jewish woman came to his mind. Kind. A good soul. Someone he could talk to. How could he let her know that he needed someone to talk to more than he needed food?

Maybe he would just say it. Next time she came. *If* she came back. He would be honest and tell her how lonely he was. How good it would be if they could talk together. Spend time somehow.

The bell above the shop door jingled at closing time, announcing the entrance of the last customer of the day. Alexander tapped Hero, indicating he should stop playing. Leaning back from his workbench Alexander peered through the curtained doorway into the music shop.

It was a woman. A foreigner. Tall, slender, veiled, and richly dressed in a blue cotton tunic and yellow palla shawl of Roman fashion. She turned slowly in the center of the small space, as if she was looking for some specific instrument. She examined an Egyptian-style double flute inlaid with ivory and mother-of-pearl.

He greeted her in Latin. "Welcome, visitor, to the shop of Alexander the flute maker. Each pipe and flute has a fine voice to cheer you."

Startled at his words, she stared at him above the veil with large luminous eyes. Beautiful eyes. Rich brown, matching the wisp of hair that escaped the veil.

"Shalom," she replied.

He knew her voice instantly. "Zahav?"

And then he saw the ivory whistle with the Star of David he had carved for her. It hung around her neck from a gold chain.

"Yes. Shalom."

He stood abruptly, half stumbling into the display room. "But . . ." Questions crowded his mind. What was she doing here? Why had she entered the shop of a pagan? And why was she dressed as a Roman?

He could see she was embarrassed by his curious gaze. She pretended to study the inlaid instrument. "Dressed like this, I could walk everywhere in the city."

"But . . ."

In the workshop Hero began to puff on the pipes again. One note only.

She inclined her head. "Unlike me, Hero remains true to the song ordained for him to play, yes?"

"He doesn't know what tune he plays." Alexander rubbed his cheek nervously.

"Nor do I."

"I was hoping you'd come back. So I could thank you."

"I wanted to come here in the daylight. To tell you myself why I can never come back."

"What?" He took a step toward her.

She backed away. "That is why I came today. I didn't want you to misunderstand."

"You're married then? Surely you are . . . must be . . . married, I mean."

"No."

"A widow?"

"Never married."

"Then what?"

"I am the daughter of my father. Only that, but it is everything. Everything."

"Who is your father if he's everything?"

"Eliyahu bar Mosheh, chief rabbi of the synagogue of Caesarea Philippi."

"I don't understand." He forced himself to remain still, lest she bolt and run from the shop like a frightened doe.

"I have a responsibility to my family and my faith."

"Your father and your family would be dishonored if they knew you helped me and my boy? Is that it? Because my family left the faith . . . worse than ordinary Gentiles . . . is that it?"

"No! That's not my reason."

"Then what, Zahav? Why can't you come back? You're betrothed then? Is that it? Promised to someone?"

"I will never marry, Alexander."

"Not even one of your own people?"

"It is ordained that I live alone. Settled the hour I was born."

He searched her eyes. Deep pools of sorrow. He wanted to pull back the veil. "Alone. Who could make such a judgment on a baby? Live life alone?"

"It is what it is." With her fingertip she traced the vine leaf on the ivory flute. "Like this which you have engraved and inlaid, I am what I have been created to be. I cannot change what my Creator has made. And so I cannot come back here."

"We are different creatures then? You and me? Or is your family so great that you can't be seen with a lowly flute maker?"

"My father is descended from a revered rabbi, yes. Many years ago his father taught in the courts of the Temple in Yerushalayim. In the days of Herod the Great, a sign appeared in the heavens proclaiming to the world the birth of the new king over Israel. Foreign royalty traveled to Herod's court and inquired about this star. King Herod consulted my grandfather, who was respected for his interpretation of prophecies about the birth of our Messiah."

"Ancient tales?"

"The One we Jews have been waiting for, Alexander. Descendant of our King David. Deliverer. Healer of all our diseases. Savior. Redeemer. King of heaven and earth. Son of the One True God of Israel."

Alexander imagined the world governed by such a king. Could He heal Hero? "Herod Antipas rules Galilee. His half brother, Philip, rules here. Rome governs us. Who is he? Who is this Messiah of yours?"

"We don't know. Herod the butcher king burned the genealogy records in the Temple. They say the fires could be seen as far as the sea, yes? My grandfather was executed. And with him many other righteous men who taught that the years of Messiah's coming had been fulfilled as written in Dani'el's prophecies. After that, the king slaughtered every male child under two years of age in Beth-lehem.[34] This was foretold as the town of Messiah's birth. It was the home of my grandfather. No babies escaped. My brother perished in the massacre. So Father and Mother fled to this place."

"And they never went back? Why? What if your king comes to Jerusalem after all?"

"He will come one day. But until that day Yerushalayim and the Temple are controlled by men who are puppets of Rome. Here and in Alexandria there are Jews who watch and wait. My father carries on the traditions and teachings of his father. We hope. We wait. We believe."

"But is this healer, this son of the gods, alive?"

"He is the only Son of the One God."

"Everyone but a Jew believes there are many gods. And that many gods have had sons who have come to earth."

"That belief is what separates your people and mine."

"But Zahav, you can teach me. I'd like to know more about this Healer-King, Son of the Hebrew God."

"I can't. I must not. There is much more that you will never know or understand."

He blurted, "I am . . . I have so little hope. My son. My only son."

"I know. Yes, I know." She turned to go. "I'm sorry."

"Please! Zahav! Meet me! Day after tomorrow! Noon. I'll be in the meadow above the sacred pool! We can talk."

She did not reply as she left. The latch clicked solidly shut behind her.

16

I t was early morning. Peniel had slept for two nights alone in the apple orchard. Shafts of light pierced the canopy of leaves like pillars holding up a dome. Peniel heard a twig break beneath a footstep. He looked up. Yeshua, the sun behind Him, stood over him. "Shalom, Peniel."

"Shalom."

Yeshua plucked an apple and tossed it into the air. He caught it and took a bite, then found another and tossed it to Peniel. "Why are you here, Peniel?"

Peniel did not want to admit the truth. "Wanted to breathe a bit. Think. You know. I slept a little. I dreamed dreams."

"You're hiding in an orchard full of bad fruit."

"Sorry about the smell. First I thought of hiding in the boulders beside the stream, but so many come and go there, you know? The stream is a pleasant place. I thought it would be better to hide somewhere no one wanted to come."

"Yes. I see what you mean. Rotten apples. Such a stink. Who would think to find you here?"

"Only you." Peniel sat up and gazed into Yeshua's sad eyes.

"Apples. Left here by the harvesters for the poor. As Torah commands. To be gleaned by the poor, I suppose. But no one wanted them."

Yeshua took another bite. "A good law, that. Adonai's law to provide for the poor of Israel, for the stranger and the outcast. The best of the harvest was meant to be left for the hungry. For widows and orphans to gather so they wouldn't starve. Somehow over time the meaning of it got turned around. The landowners and the foremen of the harvesters take the best for themselves. Leave the wormy fruit behind. Leave what nobody else wants. Let the poor survive without dignity on what is cast off, worthless."

"Point taken. Well spoken. Yes. No one wants to eat wormy fruit. . . . But you've found two good apples. A miracle. Anyway, I thought this was the safest place to hide. Sit down if you like. But I can't guarantee what you're sitting on."

"I'll take my chances." Yeshua sat an arm's length from Peniel.

"I'm glad you've come. The air smells fine since you're here."

"Peniel, put out your hand. I brought a gift for you, from my mother's garden." Yeshua placed a single bud of lavender in Peniel's palm.

"A gift for me?"

"One of many. There is always a gift to meet every need."

Peniel raised it to his nose and breathed in. "Very fine. Very, very . . . *extraordinary*. There's a word. Never smelled anything quite like it! Better than the herb seller's in Yerushalayim. One grain. More potent than his entire bushel basket. His whole cartload!"

"Ah well, Peniel. That fellow used to mix colored sand in with the buds and cheat his customers."

"Sand! Who would think it!"

"Each grain in a man's heart is weighed and counted and known by Adonai."

"But he seemed like such an honest and friendly sort."

"Liars and thieves usually do. Often they appear to be the most honest, most friendly, and sometimes the most religious. At least they are religious about pointing out what is wrong with everyone else."

"Point taken. I'm finding that out. It's a hard lesson. No one is what they appear to be."

"Where I come from a bud of lavender is lavender."

"Where is that? I mean, where are you from, really? I didn't know flowers grew in such a place."

"No flowers?" Yeshua said in an amused tone. "There's a lot you don't know, Peniel. But I'm not talking about gardens. Not entirely. You know that, eh?"

"Point taken. Well spoken. I suppose we're talking about what's true and what's not true."

"That's it. Yes. Truth. The Word, the Promise of Adonai."

"I'm listening. All right, here I am. Lavender bud in my hand. I won't lose it."

"Well then, Peniel. Place this one bud of truth, this gift, given to you by Adonai onto the scale. On the other side heap up a bushel basket of some-truth, half-truth, near-truth, and lies. Which has more weight?"

"Judging from the lavender bud you brought, I'd say truth."

"And which would you say is worth more?"

"Well, it depends. I reckon in the market all the people would look at the colored sand and say the larger heap was worth more, if you know what I mean."

"But you, Peniel. What do you say? You, as you are. Which would you rather receive and hold on to? One true grain of lavender or a basket of colored sand?"

"Me? You know me. I'm Peniel. I travel light. Take only what I need. I'll take one bud that's real, potent! One bud that'll drive out the stink of everything rotten around me and in me! Carry it with me for the rest of my life. It'll last forever, won't it? I'm for the one true grain of lavender over the whole big basket of colored sand."

"Well reasoned. I thought you'd say that."

Peniel grinned and sniffed the bud again. "Hard to miss the metaphor when it smells so good. I'd be a fool if I didn't get it, wouldn't I?"

"Peniel, what sort of fool would you be if, after you had the truth in your grasp, you forgot it was there?"

"Can't forget something as nice as this. Fills the air with the reminders, doesn't it? Always right under my nose, if you know what I mean."

"An easy answer. But I ask you a hard question."

"Ask me. Anything. I'll tell you the truth. Wouldn't do any good to lie because you'd know the truth. Lavender is lavender."

"Point taken. And so this is the question Adonai sent me to ask every heart."

The ground quaked. Peniel put his hand out to test the trembling trunk of the tree.

A deeper voice, a whisper, spoke. But it was not entirely like a voice.

Why are you anxious about lies the world believes? Grains of colored sand on the scale, or an orchard of bad fruit that no one can live on. Peniel! You have seen the face! Why tremble because of half-truths and lies when you have seen . . . yes! You have seen . . . with your own eyes . . . your eyes, Peniel! You have seen the face! You have seen . . . the Truth. Why do you cringe when they speak? Are not my Word and my Truth and my Light more powerful?

Peniel buried his head in his arms. He waited until the echo died away. Did he dare reply? He peeked up. Yeshua was still there, sitting across from him.

Yeshua urged, "Peniel! Go on. Tell me anything!"

Peniel swallowed hard. "I . . . I'm afraid. Not that your promise isn't true. But just afraid! That's all. I'm a coward to my core. And that's the truth."

Silence. Yeshua reached out to touch Peniel lightly on his shoulder. Peniel was suddenly very tired.

"Tell me, Peniel, what are the others saying about me?" Yeshua knew already. Peniel saw it clearly in His expression.

Peniel exhaled loudly in exasperation. "Lord, you know everything before I answer. What can I say that you don't know already?"

"It's good to hear from your mouth. You're an honest fellow. One of the few honest fellows walking the earth, I would say."

"I do my best. But you know, they mean no harm. They just think you should think like they think. Do what they want you to do, in the way they want you to do it. Prove yourself."

Yeshua laughed. "Tell me about this."

"Some . . . some of your talmidim are afraid the people won't come to hear you teach anymore."

"Why?"

"Some say—O Lord, not that I agree, mind you—but they say the people want a sign."

"Are eyes created for a man born blind not sign enough?"

Peniel thumped his chest to emphasize his agreement. "Point

taken! Well spoken, Lord! Yes! Seeing is sign enough for me because they're my eyes you've made. But for the others? They want something else from you. Want you to match the description of what they want in a Messiah. Do what they want. Everybody wants a miracle of their own, Lord."

"That's why I was sent. A miracle for everyone. One miracle at a time."

"They want bigger proof. Proof you are. Proof you can. Proof you will do . . . what they want and when they want it."

"That would prove I AM who I AM?"

"If you are truly the Son of God, they say . . . you'll . . . do something to prove it."

Yeshua sighed and whispered, "I've heard those words before. He never gives up. He's beaten and he knows it, but he never gives up."

Yeshua stood and Peniel followed suit.

Peniel did not know who "he" was. Did Yeshua mean Judas? or Herod Antipas? or the high priest? All of them wanted a sign, a miracle, a conjuring trick as proof that Yeshua was . . . was . . . Who *was* he?

Peniel cleared his throat. "And everyone has a different idea what the sign should be. There's the trouble."

"But if there was only one sign I gave them all. All of them at once. What sign should I give the people to prove I AM who I AM?"

"Some say you should storm Yerushalayim at the head of an army and be Israel's king. They're unhappy because taxes are high and Rome is unjust and Herod Antipas is not even a Jew. And you won't lead them in a battle against Rome, they say. If you won't overthrow Rome and Herod Antipas, who is not even a Jew, and set up a kingdom in Yerushalayim, how can you be the Anointed One? That's what some are saying."

Yeshua remarked, "Herod and Rome and the high priest wouldn't like such a sign."

"Well, no. They'll want you to prove it some other way. I haven't figured that one out."

Yeshua persisted. "Anyone with a sword and a horse and a few hundred men can lead a charge and capture a tower. Many have done it. Governments and kingdoms ripen and fall like apples from these trees. Look at the ground here. What do you see?"

"Last year's apples lying in the mud. Never gathered. Left to rot."

"So history is littered like an orchard floor with the overthrow of princes. And with the establishment of new earthly kings and kingdoms which, in turn, grow old, fall, and decay."

"Well spoken. Point taken."

"And what do you say, Peniel, about a sign? If I were to give the rulers and the rebels and the people one sign? What should it be?"

Peniel considered the question. "The *am ha aretz* want you to give them bread. Free bread. Lots of it every morning. They're poor. That's the sign they want. Like Mosheh gave the children of Israel manna in the wilderness. Yes. That's a sign they'd like. They'd follow you anywhere if they knew there was breakfast, lunch, and dinner to be eaten along the way."

Yeshua walked alongside Peniel in silence for a while. "What about you, Peniel? What sign would you require of me as proof that I AM who I AM?"

Peniel laughed. "Oh, Lord. I have it. You gave it. I was blind before I met you, wasn't I? But I was looking for you every day. With my heart I was looking for the Light. Longing for the Light. And when you did come, it was like your Word promised. Quietly. When I was in my solitude, there you were. That you saw me sitting in the dust and cared enough to stoop and speak to a beggar like me? That was my miracle."

"Seems simple enough." Yeshua stroked his beard.

"Yes! It seems simple enough for me. If you never do another thing. Well then . . . what's left for you to do for me?"

Yeshua hesitated before he answered. "One thing I must do for you, Peniel. One sign I must give you. You'll understand when you see it."

"I don't need another thing, Lord. I'm a happy fellow. Content. I love learning Torah, being one of the talmidim in your academy. I love light and colors. Birds. People. Faces. I suppose I'll have to learn not to stare, though."

"And would you trade your personal miracle to have a new king, the Son of David, sit on a throne and rule in Yerushalayim? Tomorrow?"

The question startled Peniel. He was not so unselfish as all that. A Jewish king, the son of David, instead of the Idumean swine, Herod Antipas, would be very good, yes. Lower taxes and all that. But Peniel had grown attached to his eyes. He enjoyed talking face-to-face with Yeshua.

"It's a lovely thing to be able to see. Maybe I shouldn't say it, but I'm quite happy with you just the way you are. Studying Torah—and life. Discussing the true meaning of true things, like now. Us walking and you explaining to me about things and talking about things here in this apple orchard. A very nice day for it. The sky is blue. I'm content.

"If you were in Yerushalayim fighting Herod Antipas, and busy overthrowing the Roman Empire and all that, we wouldn't be here now, would we? And if crushing Rome was the sign required to prove you are the Anointed One—if that's what you are, whatever you are—well, all I can say is that from the beginning of the world there have been a lot of generals who captured Yerushalayim.

"And more kings and potentates ruled in Israel than I can count. But since the world began, not one of them ever made eyes for a blind man and made him see. If the sign you were meant to give the world was to capture a city and rule a nation? Then I might still be sitting in darkness at Nicanor Gate with an alms bowl in my hands."

Yeshua clapped him on the back. "Well spoken, Peniel. The Son of David wasn't sent to capture a city but to set captive souls free."

"No one but you, Lord. No one ever noticed my heart was a prisoner, chained up by worry. Sad over the way Mama and Papa never wanted me to be their son. But I'm free now."

"The ancient war between the Prince of Darkness and Yahweh is fought to redeem one soul at a time. I wasn't sent at this time to rule an earthly kingdom. First I must establish my kingdom in men's hearts."

"The heart. There's a dark land to conquer."

"Guarded by a fierce, unseen enemy. The Father of Lies. He claims all mankind for himself. He rules by fear. By making people doubt the love of the Father for his children. Many choose to believe his lies rather than trust in Adonai's love for them."

Peniel shuddered. "I've felt evil come near me at times. Heard a sort of whisper, calling me. A feeling like everything is falling apart. My whole life, useless. Falling like rotten apples. Of no use to anybody. Might as well give up and die. Well, you know all about that, Lord."

"Yes. I know the lies the devil shouts in men's hearts to drive them from Adonai's love. When you hear it, speak the promises of Torah out loud. Answer the devil's accusations with the living words of the Living God. When darkness is confronted by light it flees."

"It's just my own mind. Feelings. My own thoughts. Nothing, really."

"It's more than that, Peniel. The Prince of Darkness, the Prince of this world, is as real as this apple tree. The rotten fruit is his doing, not mine."

They came to the edge of the orchard. Crowds had already begun to gather. "What can I do to thank you, Lord?"

Yeshua clasped Peniel's arm and searched Peniel's face with his deep brown eyes. "For now, today, see them with my eyes, Peniel."

"Your words were the true light I was waiting for, Lord. I longed to meet you face-to-face."

"Would you have followed me even if you hadn't received your miracle?"

"You know me. I'm Peniel. I would have come along just to hear your stories! I didn't know then how wonderful light was, so I didn't miss it. I never expected you would do what you did for me. Not ever. But I'm very glad you did. And if you can make eyes for me, I believe somehow your inner light will beam into the darkest corners of men's hearts."

"Giving sight to one born blind is easier for God to accomplish than convincing a man with two good eyes that he's blind. The first blindness is obvious."

"But you taught me, Lord, that nothing is too hard for God."

"Ah, Peniel! Nothing is too hard for God . . . except man's will. Man's desire to choose a lie over the truth."

"But why? Why do we choose the lie?"

"Easier to blame everyone else, even God, than accept that you can't change—won't be changed—until you humble yourself before your Creator."

"Pride. Is that what you mean? You mean, that's what keeps us from seeing ourselves? from seeing you? from knowing you as you are? from being like you?"

"Pride. All evil springs from it. All . . . every sin! Pride is the soil. Pride is the seed. Pride is the sun. Pride is the water. Pride is the second blindness. Incurable unless . . . until . . ." Yeshua's words trailed away. He inhaled, as if the answer was too difficult for Him to speak aloud.

Peniel asked, "Unless what, Lord? How can such a thing be healed?"

"My friend, watch and listen. I have work for you yet to do. Pray with me. The wind is up. I hear thunder. The storm is near."

Rumor of the coming King swept through the great city of Caesarea Philippi like a wind. It touched the beggars crouching in doorways. It swirled through the vegetable gardens of the poor. It stirred the trees of vast orchards and whipped the vines in the vineyards of the mighty.

Zahav added names onto Messiah's prayer shawl:

Yahweh-Rohi: "Jehovah Shepherd"
Yahweh-Ropheka: "Jehovah Healer"
Yahweh-Tsidkenu: "Jehovah our Righteousness"
Yahweh-M'Kaddesh: "Jehovah Who Sanctifies"

But Zahav's heart did not feel shepherded, healed, righteous, or sanctified.

Papa taught The Coming from the Torah scrolls in the synagogue, and the people listened. Drawn by the possibility of hope, they came even when not required. They sat spellbound as the old rabbi cracked open secrets embedded in every word of Torah and poured out revelation like fine perfume.

From the gallery Zahav watched Papa's lips move as he preached, but she did not hear his words. Her thoughts returned again and again to the lonely man in the music shop. *Apostate.* To the fragile child held prisoner of evil through no fault of his own soul.

She could not banish Alexander and Hero from her mind. She told herself that she was just being kind. Would she not have fed a stray dog at the back door if it happened her way?

But she knew there was more to it than kindness. Much more.

In broad daylight the secret weighed heavily on her. She felt as though, simply by looking, the people of the Quarter would know her heart had moved beyond the boundaries of their world.

At night she thought of Alexander. Desire surprised her. Shame almost smothered her. How long had it been since she had longed to be held in the arms of a man? How many years since the vague yearning of loneliness had taken the substance of a face, a form, a name?

Alexander.

So her kindness was not without motive. She could not excuse herself.

His words echoed in her heart: *"Come to the meadow . . ."*

And she added in her mind one more name for Messiah:

Yahweh-Knower of Secrets.

It was noon. Two evenings and a morning had passed since Zahav had last seen Alexander and Hero. Now she lingered on the parapet lining the cliffside road between the town and Tetrarch Philip's citadel. The breeze from Mount Hermon cooled and cleared the air. She hoped it would do the same for her thoughts and emotions.

From this high vantage point she could see Alexander and Hero on the edge of the meadow, just as he had promised they would be. There was a basket on the blanket. The child chuffed on his panpipe. Alexander played his flute. Snatches of melody drifted up to Zahav.

They would share a meal together. Talk a bit. She would tell him he could turn away from his useless gods. He could come back to the God of his fathers. They could be friends and . . . maybe more than that if only . . .

What was wrong with that?

She was dressed in her finest Shabbat clothes. Azure linen dress tied at the waist with a gold embroidered belt. Her veil was blue silk. Would she remove it today? Tell him the story of the Samaritan's slap? Surely he would hear and understand. It would not matter to him that she was marred. He would see her kindness, hear her heart. Know that she could be good for Hero.

She shook her head, denying the possibility that he would laugh at her, reject her. Her hands trembled. She could not go to him while her hands trembled.

Perhaps turning off her thoughts for a time was the answer. *Study what you see*, Zahav told herself. *Be here, now.*

South, far below the meadow and the mount on which Caesarea Philippi perched was a broad, flat plain. On the benchland was a score of caravansaries, each built roughly to the same plan. Each walled enclosure contained wells and watering troughs, and fodder for camels and donkeys. Two sides of each secure half-acre site were built up into double-height stone structures. Single rooms on the second floor accommodated families, while goods, servants, and pack animals were quartered in arched alcoves beneath.

Here commercial travelers from Babylon rested on their journeys to Athens and Rome, where they hoped to make their fortunes selling magnificently woven carpets.

Camel trains from Jericho were laden with the precious unguent known as the balm of Gilead, reputed to cure headaches and relieve cataracts. The very unguent Zahav had often purchased for her father's eyes.

Merchants from the seacoast, their animals burdened with amphoras of the dark red dye known as Syrian purple, crossed paths with dealers in silk. The Syrian silk merchants, it was said, dealt illegally with the Parthians, who in turn had connections to India and beyond.

Whenever an updraft reversed the direction of the breeze, the air was tinged with exotic odors. Lebanese cedar, Indian peppercorns and cinnamon, Arabian frankincense and myrrh combined to perfume the air.

Also unmistakable were the aromas of ambition and greed. There was profit to be made, business empires to be conquered.

And there was fear. Outside the barricades were thieves and bandits, ready to pounce on the unwary. Each caravansary had but a single gate, barred at night and guarded against robbers and rebels.

The plain itself was no stranger to desperate struggle even before the present inns were built. It was there, some two centuries earlier, that the descendants of Alexander the Great's generals fought to see who would possess Judea. King Ptolemy of Egypt brought armored elephants to the battle. These so frightened the horses of Antiochus the Third that his cavalry and chariots bolted and fled the field.

But from behind the cover of boulders on the unassailable heights Antiochus' Seleucid archers rained iron-tipped arrows on the great beasts. The hail of darts killed their mahouts and drove the elephants mad with pain. When elephants stampede, they do so without regard to friend or foe, so Ptolemy's victory turned into defeat.

From that day until the rise of Judah Maccabee, the borders of

Syria extended all the way past Jerusalem to the Wadi of Egypt, ushering in the age of Antiochus Epiphanes and the Abomination of Desolation.

And so Zahav's thoughts turned to the others who shared the protection of the caravansaries with the merchants: Jewish pilgrims bound for the Holy City.

Zahav had never taken the pilgrim road to Jerusalem. She had lived her life in exile. Papa had vowed he would never return to the great city until the true and righteous King, the Son of David, sat upon His throne.

Zahav would tell Alexander about that too. Why not?

Suddenly she felt calm, eager to go down to the meadow. Yes.

And then the familiar voice of Heli, Rebecca's husband, called, "Zahav? Is that you, Zahav? Dressed like Shabbat? What are you doing on the road? Dressed for a wedding? Rebecca told me you were . . ." His befuddled grin faded as he followed her guilty glance down to the man and child in the meadow. His eyes narrowed. "So, Zahav, you have come to this. You disgrace your good father, the rabbi."

Tears brimmed in her eyes. "It was nothing. Nothing!" She turned away.

"Nothing? Look at you. Look at you. And look at him and that demon child waiting down there for you. 'Nothing,' she says. This meeting was arranged by a bird chirping the invitation?" Heli grasped her arm. "For the sake of your father I will not uncover your shame to all the world. But you will come back with me. You will leave this folly forever. You will come . . . *now!*"

17

CHAPTER

Zahav did not come to the meadow that day. Alexander waited for her as long as he could while Hero dug contentedly in the dirt at the foot of an enormous oak.

Alexander had often thought of the Jewish Healer-King since Zahav had told him the story. Had the Messiah escaped the massacre of babies in Beth-lehem? If He was alive, who was He? Could this great one, this King of Heaven and Earth, the only Son of the Hebrew One God, heal Hero of his sickness?

Zahav had left him with so many unanswered questions.

Better not to hope, he decided. Better not to risk offending his patron deity by thinking about the Hebrew One God. And yet, what had Pan ever done to help Alexander? Had not he and Diana offered their only son to Pan? What had Pan given them in return? Sickness, sorrow, and death.

It was twilight. Shadows lengthened over the valley below, marking the start of the Jewish Sabbath. Zahav would not come now.

Alexander knew she would not ever return.

With the ache of disappointment, Alexander hefted Hero onto his shoulder and climbed the steep path toward home. Hero clasped his

— 205 —

fingers on Alexander's forehead. As they entered the city gate Alexander heard melancholy singing drifting down from the Jewish Quarter.

He understood only fragments of the Hebrew lyrics,

"Answer . . . call . . . righteous God . . .
Relief . . . merciful . . . hear my prayer . . ."

It was almost dark.

Impulsively he turned onto the crooked alleyway leading to the synagogue. The music pulled him inexorably on.

"How long, O men, will you turn
My glory into shame?
How long will you love delusions
And seek false gods?"[35]

Light beamed from the windows of the white stone building where this strange race of people worshipped their One God. Alexander was not one of them, and yet the question that resounded in their song seemed to be directed at him.

Was Zahav inside? Did she sing with them?

"Know that the Lord has set apart
The godly for Himself.
The Lord will hear when I call
To Him."[36]

Alexander halted at the top of the lane. He asked, "How can I call you when I don't know your name?"

Hero rested his cheek on Alexander's head and fell asleep.

"Many are asking, 'Who can show us any good?'
Let the light of Your face shine upon us, O Lord."[37]

Light! How long had Alexander been searching for a glimmer of hope? What would the face of this Hebrew Messiah, this merciful Healer-King, look like? How would men recognize Him? Would the face radiate mercy for those who looked upon Him?

Where was He? Was He alive somewhere? Could Alexander somehow find Him? bring Hero to Him? What was His name? Who was He? Would He come for all men? or only the people of Israel?

Alexander crept forward slowly until he reached a pool of luminescence gleaming on the cobblestones. Afraid of being spotted by some tardy worshipper, he did not step into the beam.

He thought about Zahav. No doubt she knew the lyrics to every song. What would it be like to stand among the Jews in this place? he wondered. To lift his voice and sing to their One God?

"I will lie down and sleep in peace,
For You alone, O Lord, make me dwell in safety." [38]

To sleep in peace and live in safety?

Alexander reached up and gently stroked Hero's back. "If only I could give you peace and safety, Hero," he whispered. "If only I had the power to offer you such a gift as this Messiah, Son of the One God, will bring to his people when he comes!" The music faded away. Alexander remembered the stern faces of the Jewish worshippers the day Hero had reached out to touch the fringes of a prayer shawl. "My son. Hero! My little son! My only son. Their song isn't meant for us. Home, then. We aren't welcome here."

With a doubly aching heart Alexander retraced his steps to the shop.

The children had been sent outside to play when Heli arrived home with Zahav in tow. But they knew something was desperately wrong with their Aunt Zahav. Her complexion was ashen, a stark contrast to the bright red birthmark on her face. Eyes downcast, she could not manage a smile for them when they had circled around her in greeting.

She collapsed in Rebecca's arms.

Heli, glowering and scowling, towered over both women. "So, this is your sister! She shames us! Look at her! Dressed as if she is going to synagogue! But she was going to meet that apostate!"

Zahav sobbed with shame. "Oh, Rebecca! Oh!"

Rebecca crooned to Zahav, "What? What? What, flower? What is this? Your heart is breaking! What?" Then with steely eyes she snapped at her triumphant husband, "What have you done to my sister?"

Heli crossed his arms in defiance. "Ask her! She would have gone to meet that Alexander and his growling creature of a son! Ask her!"

Rebecca snapped at Heli, "Get out, you snarling, gloating hyena! What do you know about Zahav? What could you know about love? Look what you've done to my sweet sister! Leave us alone, Heli! Go outside! Watch the children and keep your big mouth shut about this to everyone! To everyone, you hear me? Silence or you'll be sleeping in Dori's bed for the rest of your life!"

Insulted, Heli stalked out of the house, slamming the door behind him.

Rebecca patted Zahav. Stroked her hair. Led her to a chair. "Sit. Sit. Oh, your best dress."

Zahav could not make words come. She nodded. How could she confess even to Rebecca what she felt? what she had imagined when she thought of Alexander?

Rebecca gazed solemnly into her face and wiped her tears with a gentle finger. "So, you love him?"

Zahav swallowed her emotion. She shook her head slowly from side to side. "Love him?"

"You are in love with him, Sister?"

"I . . . don't know. I know I wish I could be loved. Wish I could be in love. Like you and Heli. You know. Children. A life. Oh, Rebecca, have I caused you and your husband unhappiness?"

"He'll get over it. Men are brutes sometimes. Can't understand a woman's heart. Because they're men, I suppose. Did he humiliate you, Sister?" Rebecca shook her fist. Very unlike Rebecca.

"No. No. I did that myself. He simply saw me on the road above the meadow. Saw me look at Alexander and Hero in the meadow and he knew."

"Well, he'll keep it to himself. Don't worry."

"But he was right. I was going to meet with Alexander."

Rebecca sighed. "Then perhaps you do love him?"

Zahav touched the birthmark. "I can't . . . love. Not permitted. You know that. Can't love . . . any man."

"Can't? But you do, I think."

"I pity him. I . . . grieve for him. He's so lost, Rebecca. And my heart cracks whenever I think of Hero. His eyes. So sad. Like the eyes of a dog waiting in a cage for someone to turn him loose. There's nothing I can do. Nothing. How can I help them without my life becoming a tangle? There's no hope that my life will ever be anything other than what it is."

"And what do you think your life is?"

"My life. My life. It isn't mine to live at all."

"We love you."

Zahav hung her head. It wasn't enough to be loved by sisters and nephews and father and brothers. But how could she speak such ingratitude to Rebecca, whose eyes reflected her pain? "It should be enough."

Rebecca hugged her, held on to her. "But it isn't. Oh, Sister! You are the bravest woman I have ever met."

The two women wept together awhile. Nothing was solved, but Rebecca heard Zahav's heart. For today that was just what was needed.

After a time, Zahav returned home. She closed her door, and when Papa called she told him she was not well.

Now she once again picked up the unfinished prayer shawl. So many names inscribed upon it. Each name meant to meet every human need. But what about the needs she did not know she had before now?

She threaded the needle with gold thread. Gold because her name meant gold. Zahav began to embroider the name as though it had been spoken to her.

Yahweh-Yireh: "The Lord Will Provide"

So much unfulfilled in my life. O Lord, I am lonely! Longing for something. I don't know what it is, but I ache inside! I ache. My heart lies buried. Can you, Yahweh-Yireh, provide for me? Speak hope to me, Messiah! I long to hear your voice!

So now Papa knew everything. He extended his hand, palm up, to receive the ivory whistle from Zahav. He examined it first with his fingers, then held it inches from his face.

"The Mogen David he has carved on it. And the shape of the whistle is in the shape of a shofar, eh? Very fine. From the tooth of a whale. A valuable gift."

"Alexander is an artisan, Papa."

"Yes, he would be. As were his fathers before him. They always were. They were the makers of the shofar for every tribe and clan in days of old. They were men of honor before they came to this place."

"I see nobility in his eyes—and haunted sorrow. He is lost, Papa, wandering in the wilderness."

Papa tapped his hand on the table for emphasis. "Then he must look up to the mountain and see the pillar of Zion. Instead he follows the ways of the fallen angels who our legends say descended to Mount Hermon and took for themselves the daughters of men."

Zahav defended Alexander. "How can he know what it means unless he's taught? The meaning is forgotten, Papa."

"Alexander's fathers knew well the ancient writings of the prophet Enoch about Mount Hermon. The books of Enoch still exist in the Temple library to this day."

Zahav shifted uneasily in her chair. Papa would not be swayed by the defense of ignorance. "He wouldn't know of such writings."

Papa recounted the lessons of Jewish literature and Scripture about the importance of Mount Hermon. "Seth, son of Adam, was born after his murdered brother, Abel. Seth, like Abel, was righteous. He offered his sacrifices to Yahweh on Mount Hermon. One day Lucifer appeared to him as an angel of light as he stood on the highest of the three peaks of Hermon, on the peak called Zion. Satan offered Seth all the power of the world if only he would worship him. But Seth did not yield. This is a picture for us of Messiah, righteous son of Adam, who will conquer all temptation when he comes."

Nodding, Zahav acknowledged the story she had known since childhood. "If Alexander could come here to synagogue, Papa. Hear you teach."

The old rabbi raised a finger to command silence. "Alexander belongs to the other side. The prophet Enoch recorded the story of two hundred fallen angels who made an oath to destroy all mankind. These two hundred Watchers descended to Mount Hermon. They made an oath to band against the Living God. They took the daughters of men for wives and taught them sorcery, dark magic, and incantations. They begat a race of giants called Nephilim. Mount Hermon became the gateway of all evil knowledge. Demonic power entered into the world of mankind first in that place. This is so well known to Jews that only one sentence is dedicated to this subject.[39] From Mount Hermon all the myths of divine giants and the pantheon of pagan gods spring forth. Mount Hermon is a place of destruction for those who follow evil. Or for those who resist temptation like the son of Adam, it will become a place of divine revelation."

Zahav defended, "The origins of this can't be part of his history and education, Papa. I see a man who loves his son when I look at him. He isn't altogether bad."

Papa recited from the writings of Enoch. "Enoch wrote about the coming Messiah: 'I will not speak for this generation but for a future generation. The Great Holy One will leave his dwelling and the eternal God will descend upon the earth. All the Watchers will shake and be punished in secret places.' Messiah will come here, Daughter. Look for him. Prepare for him."

She touched her heart as if to show Papa her yearning. "But how can I help Alexander and Hero, Papa? What can I say to prepare them?"

The old rabbi was unmoved. "Oh, I know Alexander's history. It was indeed a noble history until his father's father drifted from the truth. He sold his heritage for the sake of doing business with the world. Give way on a little here. Give way on a little there. What did it matter, the grandfather asked, if he played his flute in the grotto of Pan? He asked, 'What is Pan but a thing carved of wood? A Nebech! A nothing. A no-god.' But he forgot that the carving represents a real and evil creature. Pan, the god of all demons."

Zahav pleaded, "I know that, Papa. But I don't think Alexander knows what it means. He plays his flute for Pan, and to him it's a shepherd's song. He says his god is a gentle god of shepherds, flocks, fields, and forests."

Papa flared at such nonsense. "Pan. Satan. Ever the deceiver. Ever the mocker of truth. The image of Pan—goat's horns, beard, and feet, half man, half beast—is a demonic counterfeit image of the Messiah of Holy Scripture, the good shepherd who cares for flocks of Isra'el. The Lamb of God who will take away the sin of the world. There are a hundred ways this pagan god raises his fist to mock and defy the Living God.

"But here it is entirely: Pan is Lucifer; the angel who led the heavenly rebellion against Yahweh before the creation of man. Lucifer. He fought against the Lord and the angel armies, and was cast out of heaven down to rule this earth. Since Lucifer could not ascend the Holy Mountain of El'Elyon in heaven, he claimed Mount Hermon for his temple on earth. The Greeks have now named it Mount Paneum, 'the mountain of all gods.' But you, Zahav, know the significance of this place in Torah and the Tanakh."

Yes, she knew. Did she not think of the meaning every time she looked at the three snowcapped peaks of the mountain?

Mount Hermon. In Hebrew, *Kharmon*. The root meaning was "korban," the holy sacrifice, a thing set aside only for the Lord's use.

The highest peak of three which made up the summit was Zion. The holy city of Jerusalem was often identified with this majestic peak.

Zion meant "exalted one," a monumental guiding pillar. It was the sign on the horizon, lifted up to guide those lost or wandering or traveling across the wilderness.

Zion was mentioned countless times in messianic psalms and prophecies. Each of the three peaks of Mount Kharmon represented one of the three aspects of ELoHiYM, the One God. Zion was not simply a place. It was a symbol of the Messiah.

From childhood Zahav had memorized each reference to Messiah and the peak of Zion at the summit of Mount Hermon. She taught her choir to sing from the psalms:

You rule over the surging sea;
When its waves mount up,
You still them.
You created the north and south;
Tabor and Hermon sing for joy at your name.[40]

Isaias wrote that the promise was made that the Redeemer would come to Zion, to those in Jacob who repent of their sins.[41]

The pagans called Mount Hermon and the highest peak of Zion *Paneum*, as if it were a temple to Pan. The tribe of Dan had settled at the foot of the mountain and was absorbed and eventually destroyed by the idolatry and evil that pervaded the land.

Papa instructed her, "The mountain of evil in whose shadow we Jews live is a dangerous place for us until Messiah is revealed in his glory. Messiah will come to Mount Hermon one day soon, I pray. He will ascend to the third peak. On Zion, by mercy and truth he will be revealed as the Holy One, Savior and Redeemer. This will happen on the very mountain where the Father of Lies and his army of Watchers lured the souls of mankind to destruction with empty promises and sorcery."

"If Alexander knew this! Papa! Something hideous has possessed his little son. A spirit of destruction! It overpowers the innocence of the child until he neither hears nor speaks nor behaves like a human child."

"Lucifer. Pan. Ever the liar. Ever the counterfeit! It is true. The Watchers are powerful in the unseen world. Enemies of the Living God and of all men. Lucifer and his demons may inhabit a human body, control a human soul. Lucifer by this imitates the *Ruach HaKodesh*, the Holy Spirit that indwells the hearts of Yahweh's beloved."

Zahav rubbed the mark on her face. "But Hero is a child. Descended from Avraham, Yitzchak, and Ya'acov, as we are."

"Hero is an innocent child offered up to the evil one who presides on the mountain of Paneum. The blood of innocent victims has defiled the springs of the Jordan for centuries. Yahweh detests any evil done to a child. Yahweh will destroy those who by word or deed harm a little one."

"What can be done for Hero, Papa? How is it his fault if his father offered his life to a false god?"

"It is not his fault. But still it is reality. I have no answer, Daughter. I look for Messiah to come. It is written that one day Messiah must come to purify the northernmost territory of Eretz-Israel. Jeremiah wrote that Messiah will first cleanse the Temple of Yerushalayim and, it is written, he will cleanse the hearts of men! He will bring forth the pure water of salvation from the rock. He will descend to earth and establish his Name forever over the springs of the Jordan that pour forth the water of life to Eretz-Israel. And living water will flow from the hearts of his people.[42]

"When Messiah, the son of Adam, the Son of God, comes to reclaim Mount Hermon on the peak of Zion, as Zadok says he will, then perhaps there's hope. If the child survives until then. Only Yahweh's strength can break the bonds of darkness that hold this innocent child prisoner. Like all the children of Israel who are led by the false shepherds in Yerushalayim . . . like every Israelite prevented by false teachers from seeing the plain truth written about Messiah in Torah!

"Hero is marked by Lucifer for destruction. Lucifer hates every Jew, every child of the covenant! He would destroy us, the children of Israel, first. He has a thousand different lies to lure us from the truth of the Scripture! As if that wasn't enough, he whispers in the ear of Gentiles, urging them to hate and destroy all Jews because we are the proof that God is faithful and merciful! Until the day Messiah comes, the House of Alexander and his son is like the house of the dead. As unclean as any tomb. Zahav, you must not go near them."

She contemplated his command in silence. How could she help them if Papa forbade her to go near? How could she tell them the good news that perhaps Messiah was coming, as Uncle Zadok had promised? "Papa. My heart breaks for them."

"As does the heart of the Living God break for all who are bound. But you will obey me, Daughter." Zahav glimpsed a flash of anger in his old eyes. It was nothing she had seen in him before. "This is a powerful force, beyond your understanding. You do not have the strength to overcome it or to withstand it. Evil will seduce you, draw you into the snare, destroy your life through misplaced compassion. Only the protection and authority granted by the Name of Yahweh can drive demons from human beings. When Messiah comes, take them to him."

She shuddered. "Yes, Papa."

He slid the ivory whistle toward her. "The Star of David. Wear it, then. And pray the mourner's *kaddish* for Alexander and his son. Pray for them as though even the dead in spirit can be born anew and live again. Perhaps we will see it come to pass."

They were coming! The *am ha aretz*, the people of the land of Israel! They were on the move, searching, asking for Yeshua!

Triumphant, Peniel glared at Judas. He had been wrong. It was not to be fewer and fewer today. No. Today those who crowded the roads and deserted their villages were more than ever! Today the whole world seemed to be on the move, drawn toward Yeshua!

The houses of Chorazin were empty. The market stalls shuttered. Shops closed. They came, these hungry men and women of Israel, moving like a tide. So many faces, so many feet, so many cloaks that the breeze seemed to stir at their approach.

A half smile on his face, Peniel spread his cloak on the boulder and invited others from Yeshua's inner circle to join him there for the lesson. Shim'on. John. Levi.

Yeshua's Aunt Salome sat near the Rabbi as He took His place beneath the old oak and motioned for the crowds to sit. He looked directly at Peniel. Raising His hand, Yeshua put a finger to His ear and gave Peniel a nod, as if instructing him to pay special attention. He must listen closely to what Yeshua was about to say!

You know me, Lord. I'm Peniel. I love a good story!

It was at that instant Peniel first felt the hum of something . . . a shadow rising from a broken pagan shrine on a far hillside. It swept down the slope where the crowds had gathered.

But what was it?

The growl of thunder stalking among the peaks?

But the sky was clear.

The hinges of the earth turning over beneath his feet?

But no one else appeared to notice.

The tramp of a hostile army approaching?

The hair on the back of Peniel's neck prickled. A shiver worked its way up his spine and down again.

Sunlight shone on the brown hair of Yeshua. Did He not hear this . . . this . . . thing? Coming toward Him?

Yeshua's dark eyes were filled with compassion. Unconcerned, He stood and began to speak. "I know you've come to this place to find me because you heard I gave bread to feed four thousand. . . ."

Suddenly there was a roar from the heap of boulders behind Yeshua. Peniel flinched. He heard a distinct challenge!

If you are the Son of God, tell these stones to become bread.[43]

The words were intelligible, but it was more a chorus than a single voice—a discordant ripping of sounds. The noise was at once hollow, like a tomb; achingly lonely, like a prison cell; strangled, like a drowning man!

Peniel's eyes darted left and right. Why was no one else perturbed by the unearthly utterance?

Yeshua shook His head. "I've told you before, you'll have no sign from me except the sign of Jonah!"

Once again Peniel heard sinister rumbling.

If you are the son of God, prove it . . . perform some miracle for these people! Yes! Prove yourself!

If you are . . . different voices emphasized different parts of the challenge; a tumbling cascade of accusation.

If, one said sneeringly. *If . . . if . . . if . . .*

You? another queried. *Where's the proof?*

Peniel, startled at the connection, realized that the voices made the same demands he'd heard the talmidim make!

Another whining, irritating tone cajoled, *Why not show them once and for all? That's it! Call down fire! Split the rock with a single word! Blot out the sun! If you're able . . .*

Peniel's skin tingled as he sensed a growing darkness. A great storm was approaching Yeshua, though the sky remained bright blue.

Peniel hugged his knees, ducked his face, and rocked for a moment. *Close my ears, Lord! I've heard enough!*

But Yeshua did not close Peniel's ears. Peniel heard scrabbling, hissing, like locusts in the grass.

Again Yeshua did not act concerned.

He smiled and spread His arms in an embracing gesture. "Dear friends, it is written, man shall not live by bread alone, but by every word which comes from the mouth of the One Eternal God![44] And so listen! Dear friends! Listen to the word of the Almighty, El Olam, Adonai, and be comforted by his love for you."

Then Yeshua began to explain the meaning of Torah as no one had ever taught Torah before. And the hideous voice was silent, cowed before the power of this Living Word!

In all his years as beggar at Nicanor Gate in the Great Temple of Jerusalem Peniel had never heard such truth, such authority, as he heard in the teaching of Yeshua!

Then Peniel looked up and saw grim-faced members of Herod Antipas' guards sitting on a stone wall. Not far from these, Peniel recognized the man and woman he'd seen speaking with Judas by the stream.

Shadows flickered over and around their benign features, like candle flames dancing above a wick.

Pharisees from Jerusalem crossed their arms in defiance and leaned heads close to discuss what they were witnessing.

And again Peniel somehow, unwittingly, heard their hatred!

Beneath the click of insects a new sound emerged!

Peniel covered his ears with his hands.

Whispers. Whispers. Inaudible sneers reverberated in the minds of those common folk who came to Yeshua!

And Peniel knew he was hearing the shouts of a dark army marshalled to defeat the Holy One.

The people watched as Yeshua's lips moved, creating sounds that spun away, out of their grasp, like dry leaves in a whirlwind.

Peniel could not block murmurs from polluting his own mind. A thousand evil voices. A legion of doubts assaulting every hope.

But what about . . . ?

My children?

My crops?

My husband?

Yes, the other voices prompted. *That's it. Go on. What does any of this matter to you?*

My wife?

My knee? My back? My stomach?

My business?

My past?

My future?

Did he really say someone cares about you? the unseen accusers shrilled. *Anyone at all?*

Yeshua answered every question! His words rang out like the steel clash of sword meeting sword!

Each time the invisible challengers reeled back, cowed, stunned.

His promises, like five loaves in His hands, could have fed the grieving multitude and left them content.

Peniel heard the ebb and flow of the argument, like the crash of waves on rock, like the hiss of an oncoming tide on sand, surging and retreating.

But the people . . . *they* only half heard Yeshua.

"Doesn't your Father in heaven see your needs? If your son asks you for bread, do you give him a stone? If you, who are evil, know how to give good gifts to your children, then how much more will your Father in heaven meet your needs?"[45]

Coming from the mouth of Yeshua, such assurance should have been bread enough to nourish the soul of anyone. Yes. *Yes!* It should have been enough. But unbelief turned the living bread Yeshua offered into stone!

Peniel's keen inner vision sensed a silence, a momentary peace, among the teeming ranks of humanity. But peace lasted merely for an instant.

Then it began again. Peniel heard it clearly, horribly. The clank of chains holding souls in bondage!

A sound like a death rattle in ten thousand throats began to argue:

Why doesn't he give us another sign?

Yes. We've come for a miracle. Where is my miracle?

If he's the Anointed, why doesn't he do more?

A shadow of fear came screaming down like a hawk out of the sun.

And Peniel recognized the tumult of the unseen battle taking place all around him. War was being waged for the souls of those who came seeking redemption!

Doubts—so many doubts challenging Yeshua's authority. Human thoughts drowned out the other voices, took over the accusations, grew strident in their defiance.

From the woman with two ragged children: *Did he really mean the Eternal God would care for you? Not you. What are his promises when you're hungry?*

From the publisher who sold religious souvenirs and scraps of Scripture on lambskin for twice their value: *Did God really say, "thou shalt not"?*

From the man with another man's wife at his side: *How can God call someone like you his child?*

From the adulteress: *God love you? After what you've done? Too late. No going back. Besides, how can you give up a man you love?*

The widow: *How can you trust him? If God is your father, then why would such a thing happen? Why are you left alone?*

The rebel: *Yeshua is a liar! He lies! He dishes up platitudes while your soul is starving to death! How can he know what you're going through?*

The religious leader: *Who does he think he is, anyway? Telling us . . .*

The banker: *Yes. Who is he? Who?*

The wife divorced by her husband: *What is he, that he dares tell you not to be anxious when you're suffering so much?*

The internal drama of each life made far too much racket for Yeshua's promises to be truly understood or trusted.

It was too much! Much too much for Peniel to bear. He could no longer stand the discord, the shriek of doubts and allegations. Covering his ears with his hands, he tried to shut out the tumult.

No use! Peniel still heard the reproach, the criticism, the challenges. Running, Peniel blundered away from the scene, away from the crowds, trying to escape the angry, reproachful chorus.

Thus ended the Torah lesson.

The tide of humanity ebbed at last, flowing toward home . . . and with them Peniel heard the voices retreat.

18

Why, why, had Yeshua opened the ears of Peniel's soul to the whisperers? The accusations of the unseen enemy had trampled the newborn truth in the meadow before it drew a single breath!

Peniel fled to the apple orchard. He closed his eyes in misery and leaned his back against the trunk of a tree. Clamping palms over his ears, he tried to shut out the memory of the voices he had heard.

But he could not shut out the despair that overwhelmed him.

"Why, Lord?" Peniel wept quietly as he prayed. "Why should I hear such things? I was happy here with you. Thought you were making a difference. Thought maybe I could make a difference too. Teach somebody something someday like you do. Tell somebody you love them. But no. No! They won't listen! How can they hear you with all that going on in their heads?"

Exhausted, Peniel finally fell asleep.

The afternoon sun was low when Peniel finally awakened. He was not refreshed. He smelled the cook fires in the camp, but he was not hungry.

The crowds had long since dispersed, returning to their dreary houses and unruly children and pitiful garden plots. Peniel was certain they had eagerly returned to reclaim every fear they had left behind. Walking through the door, tossing down their cloaks, they had scooped up each trouble. They had embraced old familiar anxieties as if worry were a beloved child in need of comforting.

Peniel knew no one had heard Yeshua. No one in that vast assembly had listened—really listened—to a promise from heaven that could revolutionize their life forever.

The *am ha aretz* had come, they had seen, and they had been entertained for a few hours. Was that all there was to the arrival of Israel's Anointed One? Was the teaching of Yeshua an empty bucket drawn from a waterless well? Were Torah and Tanakh merely a delusion meant to distract and preoccupy?

All the teaching. The healing. The studies. What were they for?

How could Yeshua compete against those hideous whispers?

Peniel clasped his legs and buried his face against his knees. Insects hummed around his head. He longed to be back home in Jerusalem, begging at Nicanor Gate. At least there he might have gone on believing that Messiah would descend from heaven with a shout and the world would be better somehow! It had been a happy dream, hadn't it? But the world was no different than it had been. Not really.

"Maybe I will go home then," Peniel said aloud.

A reply startled him. "And what will you do if you go back, Peniel?" It was Yeshua. He was watching Peniel from a distance. He stepped forward into a pool of dappled light. Yeshua seemed unperturbed by what had happened earlier that day.

"How long have you been there?" Peniel wiped his face with the back of his hand.

"Long enough," Yeshua said kindly.

"You might as well come sit down then, Lord. If you heard what I heard today rattling in the air, you must be very tired."

Yeshua joined him, leaning against the tree. "Peniel, why did you run away?"

Peniel bit his lip. "The voices."

"Yes. I hear them all the time. They are always working against us. They are the enemy."

"I'll be honest. It was a dirty trick, you opening my ears and letting my illusions be smashed like that."

"I thought you should know what you'll be up against if you're going to follow me. Discouragement is the Evil One's best weapon against those who do the work of my Father."

"Well spoken. Point taken. I'll tell you what I think. I think the people might as well have stayed home. And you might as well have saved your breath. And we might as well have not come all the way out here for the difference it's made." Peniel hung his head. "I heard everything. Everyone carrying on a full-blown conversation inside their head with some . . . some creature. And every person thinking it was just a thought *they* were thinking! But it was just a thought! I heard the voices plain as anything. All of them arguing with you. Arguing about you! Calling you a liar."

"That's the nature of the enemy," Yeshua said. His voice was calm. "He lies."

"He's strong. Too strong for me." Peniel shuddered.

"Did you notice the silence when I spoke the truth?"

"For a minute I thought you'd beat him. But then it started right up again. I was happier before I knew, Lord. Every human being in that field today was listening to some other . . . thing . . . talking, talking, while you taught. And all this time I've been staring dumbly into false faces of people and thinking they were true faces. You never know what a person is thinking until you get inside his head. I tell you, it's enough to scare me witless. Maybe nobody's true face ever shows itself! True selves are packed away and forgotten."

"There are some who fight self-delusion," Yeshua answered. "Some who fight the numbing grip of daily life. Truth. A handful in a thousand cling to it like to a life raft on a stormy sea. But it's a beginning. We're gaining a toehold here on earth. Yes, it's a beginning. Today there was a man near the back. I saw him come late. After everyone was already seated. He needed real hope today. And he drank The Word down like cool water. He chose to believe me."

"Chose? Can a person choose to believe?"

"Of course, Peniel. It's the only way your faith can grow. You choose to trust that I cannot lie. You act on the word I have spoken. Then you discover that what I told you really is the truth. Faith in the

Eternal One, in Adonai, isn't about what you feel. Feelings deceive. Trust in me and live out my words."

"Sounds more simple than it is. Especially with all the opposition."

"That fellow in the back of the crowd chose to believe that I would not lie to him. And in the instant he decided to trust me, I saw his personal lies, which had been hovering at his shoulder, scream in terror and spin away."

"Next time, Lord, if you don't mind, let me hear what's going on inside the ones who already trust you. Darkness is more than I can bear."

"Peniel. You are a candle. And when you call upon The Name of the God of Israel for help and guidance, the sun will shine down so brightly on you that not a shadow will remain! Now then. Do you choose to believe what I just told you?"

"Point taken. Yes. Yes! I want to hear only your voice, Lord."

Yeshua touched His finger to Peniel's ear. "I have known that about you from the beginning. Well spoken, scholar. Thus ends the lesson."

Alexander shouldered the sack containing two newly finished instruments and clasped Hero's hand as they set out for Pan's temple. He had not intended to turn aside into the Jewish Quarter, but the sound of singing tugged at him.

The melody of children emanated from their synagogue. Music drew Alexander to a banquet of praise as though he were a beggar outside a rich man's gate, sniffing the aroma of roasting meat.

The commerce and bustle of the Jewish Quarter surged around Alexander and Hero.

Alexander recognized the rhythm of a gittith, a joyful tune, easy to perform.

"O Adonai, our Lord,
How majestic is your name in all the earth!"[46]

Voices, high and pure, praised the Jewish One God.

Alexander cupped Hero's chin in his hand. "If only you could hear them, my son. If only!" He led the child toward the open door of the building. They peered in. Beams of sunlight shone on young children sitting rank on rank on long wooden benches. A woman of about thirty directed the chorus, her back to the entry.

"You have set your glory
above the heavens!
From the lips of children and infants
you have ordained praise!"[47]

What a startling thought. Was that true? Did the Jewish God delight in the company of children? If true, how different His worship was from the secret initiations demanded by other deities. Perhaps the God of the Jews was not solely the vengeful, wrath-filled divinity He was often portrayed to be.

Impulsively Alexander unwrapped his flute and began to play along. Hero entwined his arms around Alexander's legs as Jewish men and women stared at the intruders with curiosity.

"When I consider your heavens,
The work of your fingers,
The moon and the stars,
Which you have set in place,
What is man that you are mindful of him?"[48]

How Alexander longed for a compassionate god. One who would give Hero relief from his suffering. Did being "mindful of man" mean merely a detached, self-absorbed interest, as the Greek gods displayed? Or could it be that some greater power actually paid attention to individual needs?

In the shadowed hall the music director glanced toward Alexander. She tossed her head. Was that irritation? Was she angry at the distraction . . . or pleased? The line of her body flowed toward heaven. Her hands lifted the song, an offering to this One Lord she believed made heaven and earth and stars and moon! It was clear from her posture that the music was an act of worship to a god whom she was pleased to honor.

Suddenly Alexander remembered that he and Hero were outsiders.

He lowered his instrument and tucked his chin, embarrassed by his boldness.

An old Jew passing by remarked, "Quitting so soon, Greek? But that was very nice, eh? Sometimes music brings different worlds together. If just for a moment."

"They are fine musicians for such young ones," Alexander said.

The old man twirled his earlocks around his index finger. "They would be. Zahav would have it no other way. Music is her life."

Alexander blinked. "Zahav, you say?"

"Daughter of Rabbi Eliyahu. The Merciful One has given her the voice of an angel, eh? And he has trusted into her care the voices of many children since he ordained by the mark on her face that she will never marry or bear children of her own."

The song ended. Zahav remained still as the echo died away. Drawing a deep breath, she turned full on toward Alexander. Their eyes met. He attempted a smile, but his expression betrayed shock at seeing her secret unveiled: A dark red stain marred her face from throat to temple.

Her hand instinctively moved to cover it. Then, with a slight shrug, she looked away, an instant of pain replaced by resignation. As if she were thinking, *So now he knows why I cannot marry. And now he will return to his world without giving me another thought.*

As Alexander and Hero hurried away, he heard her praise her pupils. "Well done, Adam! Very fine! And my sopranos! Yes! Now let's try one more time, shall we?"

The fire on the grate had faded to dull angry eyes beneath lids of gray ash. Though he could not see the glowing hearth, Manaen sensed the loss as its warmth ebbed away from him.

He sat alone in the interior courtyard of the house. Above him, through the skylight, unseen stars wheeled overhead. They were more purposeful in their cold, endless journeying across the heavens than he in his life, he thought bitterly.

Susanna had given up and gone to bed hours before. She tried to conceal her sorrow at his refusal to adopt her suggestion. He recognized her soft weeping in the corridor stretching between the atrium and their bedroom; then it too faded away.

Even Manaen's heightened sense of hearing was more curse than blessing.

Susanna's claim was nonsense. No one could put back eyes that had been seared with a scorching blade.

Manaen's fingertips brushed his lids. Beneath them were useless globes that would never work again. Only pathetic fools believed such drivel. And Manaen knew himself to be pathetic, but he was no fool.

Susanna was not the only one to accept the tales about the Teacher, he reminded himself. Lepers had been healed, people said. Cripples walked again.

And there was that blind beggar from Jerusalem, Peniel. He had been born blind, they said . . . and now he saw. Had the young man faked his handicap all along? Manaen wondered. Peniel seemed so genuinely kindhearted. It was hard to reconcile such caring with such deceit.

What if miracles *were* possible?

Still, Manaen was right to refuse to humble himself before this healer from Nazareth. He had experienced enough of pity and scorn. He was not a man to be mocked; he still had a wrestler's strength and a wrestler's ego. But even his strength was a travesty. Like blind Samson, he was left with no recourse but to pull down the pagan temple on his tormentors . . . and on himself.

His refusal had been adamant, and yet Manaen wrestled with his conclusions. The notion nagged at him: What if the rumors were true? What if Yeshua *was* able to give him back his sight? Couldn't Manaen bear a little more shame if it meant having his eyes again?

The legends of the Greeks were stocked with heroes facing colossal tasks before receiving their rewards. If Manaen had been offered his vision in exchange for fighting a hundred armed foes, would he have refused the challenge?

If someone handed him a hammer and told him to chip away at Mount Hermon until it was gravel, if he truly believed the result would be his ability to see again, wouldn't he agree to try?

It would never happen for him, Manaen concluded. Even if a holy man had the power to heal, such a phenomenal gift was not for someone like Manaen.

Manaen had no illusions about deserving a divine benefit. True, he had been abused and cheated, but he had also caroused, drunken and unthinking. He had consorted more happily with sinners and the pagan Romans than with anyone remotely pious. Manaen had lived his life without regard to the religious scruples of his people. Yahweh, the One God, would want nothing to do with the likes of him.

What a saga had grown up around Yeshua. Supposedly He consorted with tax collectors and prostitutes. He forgave sin, Manaen heard. He healed souls as well as bodies. And He did it all just across the lake in Galilee.

But that was a problem. Herod Antipas was in the Galil. The viper and his venomous queen, who had ordered Manaen blinded and then approved his death, lurked there. Manaen would be risking his life to go there. He would be playing into the hands of his bitter enemies. How they would chuckle when he put himself into their grasp.

Manaen had no illusions on that score either. Once back in their power, he would not escape again.

Falling ash sighed downward in the grate.

Was his life so worth preserving? Manaen asked himself.

Another sigh joined the sifting powder.

"Who's there?" Manaen demanded. His heart pounded in his chest as he leapt to his feet. Spinning the chair around, he flourished it in front of him like a shield.

Had Antipas sent Eglon to finish the job? Had some other assassin been hired to avenge the tetrarch's wounded pride?

Manaen stabbed at the air with the chair legs. In his mind the apparition he presented was ludicrous. His back against the wall, Manaen ordered, "Speak quickly or I'll call the servants!"

"Uhhh," was the reply.

Manaen's shoulders sagged. Deliberately he replaced the stool on the floor.

"Samu'el. It's all right, boy. Come here to me. Lead me to bed. It's time to sleep."

Alexander bit his lip and scowled up at the stars. His eyebrows knit together. Rubbing the knots in his forehead he unconsciously imitated Diana. She'd always scolded him for frowning, told him he was making himself look older than his years.

The watchmen of Caesarea Philippi had passed some minutes earlier, but no one else was around. In a mulberry tree near the well a nightingale saluted the departing moon.

Hero was inside, sleeping, dosed with two drops of Castor's elixir. The boy was quiet, but he shuddered even in deepest slumber. When he drew breath, his shoulders quivered as if suffering unpleasant dreams.

Alexander looked down at his feet. How could he have been so stupid, so thoughtless? He, from aching for Hero, knew how painfully cruel looks and stares could be. Zahav must have seen the horror register on his face when he saw her birthmark.

Mentally he flogged himself again. She could not have missed seeing it! Alexander visualized anew the revulsion that had registered on his countenance. Zahav could not have looked more wounded if he had struck her!

Alexander longed to take it back, but how? He could apologize abjectly when next they met, but wouldn't that call even greater attention to what was obviously a very tender subject?

Even worse, what if he never saw her again? What if his insensitivity had driven her away forever? She was the kindest person he'd ever met. Zahav was practically the only one—other than himself—who cared about Hero's life. The rest wanted the inconvenience and discomfort the boy caused to simply go away.

Zahav's purple discoloration marred an otherwise perfect face. Alexander now better understood her compassionate heart for Hero. Her whole life had been spent being fearful of rejection.

For all that, it was fortunate she'd been born a Jewess. In many cultures, including the civilized, urbane environs of Rome, it was perfectly acceptable to abandon children with birth defects to death. Such unwanted little ones were exposed on the banks of the Tiber. If they did not starve to death or get eaten by wild animals, they could be claimed as slaves by whoever would bear the expense of feeding them.

But in Rome no one would claim a girl child with such a disfigurement. People would shun her wherever she went. The veil would be a necessity to shield her from curses or even blows. Any bad luck that befell a neighbor would automatically be her fault. Add only a little gossip and slander, and she would be taken up as a witch and stoned to death, simply because of the mark.

How much of that rejection had Zahav faced even in the land of the Jews? Their moral law, though at times as harsh as elsewhere, reverenced human life to a greater degree than any other nation's. But aversion could never be entirely hidden, nor the division it caused ever completely erased.

Alexander listened to the nightingale's song. Bringing his panpipe slowly to his lips, he blew a soft call in response. At the first notes of the flute the bird went mute, but when Alexander stopped playing it replied.

Unaccountably Alexander shivered. He made a sign to ward off evil before returning indoors.

Papa's command was absolute. Zahav would not speak openly of Alexander. She would not pass his house or leave the Jewish Quarter. When she ventured out, Rebecca went with her.

Zahav put a fence around herself, lest she stray from her father's will, lest she yield to her need to walk past Alexander's house or knock on his door. The longing to go to him was like a thirst. There was the water, and yet she could not drink it. And all the while her heart felt as though it had cracked open. Zahav no longer went into the streets of the Gentiles. Others shopped for her in the souk of the fabric merchants.

For several days, morning and night, Zahav wrapped herself in Messiah's prayer shawl, as if she were a man and had a right to. Caressing the sacred name of Yahweh woven into the fringes and tracing the names embroidered in the fabric, she prayed the mourner's *kaddish* for Alexander and Hero, and for the deadness in her own heart.

Two knots. Ten wraps.

"Magnified and exalted be his great name in all the world which he has created according to his will.

"May he establish his kingdom during your days, and during the life of all the house of Isra'el, even speedily and at a near time. Omaine."

Two knots. Five wraps.

"Let his great name be blessed forever and ever and to all eternity.

"Blessed, praised and glorified, exalted, extolled and honored, magnified and lauded be the name of the Holy One; blessed be he. Though he be high above all the blessings and hymns, praises and consolations, which are uttered in the world. Omaine."

Two knots. Six wraps.

"May there be abundant peace from heaven, and life for us and for all Israel. Omaine.

"He who makes peace in his high places, may he make peace for us and for all Israel. And you say, Omaine."

Two knots. Five wraps.

Two knots.

Each day she looked up to the third peak of Mount Hermon and wondered if the Holy One of Israel, Messiah, would descend to Zion in the clouds. Would He emerge from the Cloud of Unknowing to let Himself be known by men? When would Messiah's light split the darkness and shine out over all the world? When would He touch her heart and her face and remove the reproach of evil from her life?

She folded Messiah's prayer shawl and whispered a prayer, "When, Yahweh? Messiah? Why are you taking so long? Have you forgotten us, then? My heart is broken. Broken. But it isn't just my heart. We're all waiting here, in the shadow of the mountain. Once it was holy; now it is defiled. Once we were a holy people; now our hearts are dead, afraid to hope. Dead inside us. Will you come to Israel, Lord?"

She rubbed the Samaritan's slap on her cheek. "You see my reproach and yet you are silent. You see my loneliness too. And yet you haven't let me . . . love . . . them. Papa forbids it. Papa says, you know. My duty . . . my duty . . . I cannot . . . what's the use of wanting? No use. But Lord, from your high mountain look down on Alexander, Lord. And little Hero. Helpless child. They are lost. Wandering in the wilderness. The darkness. Have mercy on those whose hearts are aching even more than mine. Let your light . . . your light. Oh! Where is your light?"

PART III

Again, the devil took Him to a very high mountain and showed Him all the kingdoms of the world and their splendor. "All this I will give You," he said, "if You will bow down and worship me."

Jesus said to him, "Away from Me, Satan! For it is written: 'Worship the Lord your God, and serve Him only.'"

Then the devil left Him, and angels came and attended Him.

MATTHEW 4:8-11

19

nce a month was the province-wide artisan's day in Caesarea Philippi. Much more festive than the weekly markets, this day doubled the population in the city. Villagers from the Huleh district, from Gamala in the eastern Golan, and from as far away as Bethsaida came to barter, buy, and sell. It was a time for Alexander to promote inexpensive instruments to travelers and make business contacts for more lucrative orders.

Since Alexander's shop was on the main street ascending toward the fortress on the peak of the hill, business came to him. All he needed to do was spread an awning, set up a table, and display the wares.

Visitors easily parted with their pennies to take a set of genuine panpipes home to Tyre or Damascus. They paid even if the souvenir was formed of the cheapest reeds, because the blessing of Pan himself was said to rest on each one. For the more discriminating buyer or musician, there was a protected display case of ivory or polished bone flutes.

On market days Alexander performed on flute or pipes to attract attention. The evocative melodies called to shoppers who, moments before, had given no thought to purchasing music along with their dried chickpeas and woolen goods.

Today something new had been added. Seated at Alexander's side, looking solemn and dressed in his robe with the green embroidery, was Hero. Though he could not hear his contribution, the boy was trained to blow a simple chord on the miniature bone pipes.

Monotonous, true, but when produced in a regular rhythm, the bouncing note formed the basis of many compositions. Around this contrapuntal pulse Alexander wove marvelous flights of lyric trills. He varied the tempo by lightly tapping his own toe on the boy's foot. Everything from stirring ballads to heart-wrenching complaints of unrewarded love spun out across the summer air. Even master weavers need the simple threads of warp and woof for their most complex tapestries, and Hero's oft-repeated notes were the fabric supporting the musical creation.

When father and son first launched into "The Wayfarer's Psalm," passersby stopped and turned toward their stall. By the second stanza traffic was at a standstill and conversation dropped away. On the third verse nearby merchants, including the dour broom-and-brush maker two doors down, came away from their shops to listen.

Alexander sailed into the final line, finishing with a flourish. He gave Hero a double pat on the foot to signal the boy to stop. Hero dropped his hands to his chest and waited with a worried look.

The crowd broke into applause. Shouts of "Good man!" and "Well done!" repaid their efforts. A few shoppers laid coins on the display table. Twice as many lookers as usual crowded around to examine the instruments.

But the greatest reward for Alexander was on Hero's face: The boy smiled. He may not have understood what had been accomplished, but he recognized approval. He'd had little enough of that in his life.

Five times over the next two hours the performance was repeated. Each time the spectators demonstrated their appreciation. Even a troupe of Tetrarch Philip's horsemen reined up to listen.

Each time Hero smiled.

After the last rendition Alexander received a visit from a grizzled goatherd. The herdsman supplemented his meager income by collecting and selling antelope horns, deer antlers, and animal bones to craftsmen. "Got a nice bunch for y' this time, sir. Springy like. Not all dried up and brittle, do y' see?"

The afternoon business was almost done. There were no customers around the display at the moment. Hero had laid aside his pipes. The boy played in the dirt with the stone family and the wooden chariot. From the way the father and son stones leaned toward each other a little way apart from the Diana stone, Alexander gathered that the boy was reenacting their flute concert for this mother.

Bending close to Hero, Alexander pointed to himself and the goatherd, then pantomimed himself walking a short distance away. When he pointed to Hero and to the spot beside the table, Hero nodded his understanding.

Two minutes after Alexander rounded the corner the cobbler's son appeared. Ten years old and the local bully, he was accompanied by the tinsmith's boy and a pig herder's child.

The cobbler's son pointed at Hero. "Look at 'im there. My father says he ain't right in the head."

Both his friends agreed to this premise.

The tinsmith's brat, who could not carry a tune in a bucket, added, "Playin' music! What a laugh! No more'n a trained monkey."

The third comrade added, "Yeah. Shoulda been drowned, huh?"

Hero, who only just then noticed the trio, shrank back under their malevolent gazes. He pulled toys and panpipe closer to him, then looked anxiously around for his father.

"Going to go all floppy, are you?" cobbler's son demanded. Cruelly he mimicked one of Hero's seizures.

Tinsmith's boy laughed. "Hey! Maybe he *couldn't* drown, 'cause he's a fish. He flops like a fish. Are you a fish or a monkey?"

"That's it! Let's drop him in the well and see what happens," Cobbler's son suggested.

"You, fish!" Swineherd's child slapped his hands under Hero's nose. "He's so stupid. What's a stupid fish need toys for?" And he snatched up the wooden chariot.

Hero flung himself across the boy's arm but was thrown back to the ground.

"Fish can't play tunes neither," taunted tinsmith's monster. Grabbing the diminutive panpipes he snapped them in two between his fingers. "Sorry," he said mockingly.

Not to be left out, their leader noticed Hero clutching something to his chest. Prying open the smaller child's hands, he grabbed the three painted stones. "Fish don't need toys."

Hero made frantic noises, clawing at the cobbler's son. He was shoved down hard but jumped up quickly and grabbed the hand holding the mother figure. Before the fist could be pulled out of the way, Hero seized it and sank his teeth into the flesh as hard as he could.

The cobbler's son screamed. "Get 'im off me!"

The two accomplices grabbed Hero from either side and yanked him loose. In the process a wedge-shaped chunk was torn from their friend's hide.

Cobbler's son boxed Hero on one ear, then on the other.

Then, after displaying his continued possession of the three doll stones in his bloodied fist, he turned and threw them as hard as he could in the direction of the town well.

All bounced on the rim. The Diana stone plummeted into the depths.

A tremor began in Hero's arms and transferred to his chest and head.

"He's going floppy!"

Hero stiffened and froze in place. A second later a trickle of liquid pooled around his feet.

The cobbler's boy chortled, "He's peed himself! Look at him! Here, gimme some a'that horse dung. Make him eat it!"

From four houses away the returning Alexander spotted the attack and bellowed, "Get away from him! Now! Go!"

His arms laden with antlers, Alexander charged like a berserk bull elk. He would happily have impaled them all if he'd caught them.

The boys scattered and ran.

Alexander dropped the load and grabbed Hero by the shoulders. The eyes were vacant, staring at nothing.

It was the third watch of the night before Alexander heard Hero make any noise at all . . . and then it was a dismal whimper.

Manaen awoke.

It was day, he sensed. The morning air had the dusty quality he had come to associate with the warming of the land. The sun had already crept over the heights of the Golan.

Susanna's side of the bed was empty and cool to his touch. She had risen some time before him, no doubt still believing he would not ask the Rabbi's aid. But during the night Manaen had relented and decided, why not give it a try? At the least it would please Susanna.

Manaen groped for the sash to his tunic and belted it around his waist. He fumbled at the foot of the bed for his robe but couldn't locate it. This was frustrating. He always shrugged it off where he could find it again, but this morning it wasn't there.

Had he changed his routine last night, or had Samu'el done something with the outer garment?

Manaen bellowed, "Samu'el! Boy! Samu'el!"

There was no reply.

"Susanna!"

Nothing.

Where was everyone this morning?

Manaen's sandals should be beside the bedroom door. Searching for them by stabbing his feet at the slabs of stone, he grew increasingly frustrated. His shoes were absent from their proper place too.

Manaen's anger rose. Was someone making sport of him in his own home? This would not do. Had he not given instructions that everything must be in its place?

"Susanna!"

"Yes, yes, Manaen. I'm here." It was clear that Susanna was out of breath.

"Where were you? I can't find anything this morning. Where's my robe? Where are my sandals?"

Folds of cloth were thrust into Manaen's hands. "The hem of your robe was frayed. You were asleep. I thought I could repair it before you woke up."

Manaen cleared his throat uneasily. "All right then. Thanks."

She defended, "And the leather thongs of your sandals were cracked. I sent Samu'el to relace them. He's a good boy, Manaen. He tries so hard to be useful."

"Hemming my robe. Mending my shoe. Hoping I'll change my mind, are you? Go with you to find Yeshua?"

Her motive was transparent, Manaen thought, and he did not like being manipulated. Maybe he would not go with her after all.

"You're such good company when you're like this, Manaen. A man who can't even say thank you when someone has done something thoughtful."

How skilled she was at turning his moodiness around to bite him. "I said thank you. Don't change the subject."

"Good manners is the subject. Treating your wife with respect. Oh, you're a foul-tempered rooster when you want to be!"

"And you're a mother hen. Clucking! Hovering! Hovering over me!" He crossed his arms defiantly, now determined he would *not* go with her. No matter what she said, how she begged, he would not go! "You think you can turn me to your will like a horse with a bit in his mouth!"

Silence. Two people in the same room . . . worlds apart.

He was angry.

She pouted.

He heard her across the small space as she absently picked up bottles of perfume, plucked open the stoppers and inhaled. And then she found something that interested her.

He brooded, determined that she would speak first.

She did not.

"What are you doing?" he asked as the heady aroma of balsam drifted on the breeze. His favorite. "Susanna? What?"

He heard the rustle of her gown as she bolted the door and then approached him.

She lifted his palm to her lips, then took his index finger gently between her teeth. "I'm taking the bit. You hold the reins then. Ride me wherever you like."

Fire coursed through him. He resisted. "You don't fight fair, Susanna."

"Do you really want me to?"

"No. No. Just leave some illusion that I'm in control."

"But you are, aren't you? In control?"

"Another minute and I won't be."

"Shall I count? One . . . two . . ."

"A little pride. Can't you? Leave me a little . . . pride."

Guiding his hand to her throat, she whispered, "Good. And here. Kiss me here. Yes. And . . . feel my heart, Manaen. Yes. You break it every time you're angry. Still my heart beats for you. Feel it, Manaen?"

His mouth found hers. "You're cruel." He sighed at last, fury replaced by desperation. "Tell me what . . . you want."

Returning his kisses she pulled him onto the bed. "You. Only . . ."

With Rebecca at her side Zahav entered the apothecary shop on the Street of the Unguent Makers.

Meshek, the apothecary, spoke in guarded tones to a young Greek physician.

The doctor was subdued. "Of course they had it coming. They tormented him. Taunted him. He was defending himself. But the bite is . . . almost like that of an animal."

Meshek measured drops of a golden liquid into a small blue glass vial. "After what happened yesterday, Alexander will have difficulty taking the boy out in public. The gossip about this is butter on the bread of every mother in the district. They'll have Hero locked away if they can."

Zahav felt the color drain from her face. Hero. Alexander. What had happened to them? She covered her mouth with her hand to keep from speaking out. What right did she have to ask about it?

Rebecca squeezed her hand in sympathy and stared out the door, as if the news did not concern them. The sisters did not speak until the Greek doctor paid for the medicine and exited.

Meshek smiled brightly at them. "Shalom, shalom, Zahav. Rebecca. And how's your good father, the rabbi? Is he well? What can I do for you?"

Zahav could barely speak. Her voice quavered. "Shalom . . . Papa's eyes. You know."

"Is the salve helping?"

She nodded. "It keeps them moist. But his vision isn't improved." Zahav fought the urge to blurt out questions. After all, Meshek would know the details of what happened to Alexander and Hero. The apothecary shop was only a short distance from the instrument shop on the Cardo.

Rebecca clasped Zahav's sleeve. "But what is the gossip about the instrument maker and the little boy? You must tell us."

Meshek complied, offering up every morsel of hearsay about the demon-possessed little boy and his apostate father. "The only thing in such a case is to keep him sedated. Otherwise he'll be a danger to himself and to anyone near him."

Zahav turned away. "Sedated?"

"Poppy juice works wonders in such a case. It's the only remedy."

Rebecca chirped, "No remedy, that. It steals the senses."

Meshek defended, "It dulls the pain. Whatever pain he may have."

Zahav's eyes stung with fury at the solution for the child. "But it's no cure. It steals his life even as it calms him."

Meshek filled Papa's medicine jar with the salve and scraped off the spatula. "The boy is possessed. Driven to destroy himself in fire or water. There is no other solution but the opiate. And when he grows strong enough he will develop resistance to the efficacy of the medicine. Then he'll overpower the opiate. His end will be the same. Sooner or later Hero will die. One way or another. It is not a matter of if. It is a matter of when."

So Susanna had won the contest.

Momentarily mellow from their morning tryst, Manaen decided how best to apologize for his ill temper. "I've something to tell you. I've changed my mind. I *will* go to Capernaum to see that Yeshua fellow. Not that I expect it to do any good. But if it'll please you, I'll go."

"I hoped you would. Right away?"

Manaen confirmed it, mentally adding the unspoken supplement, *We better. Before I change my mind.*

During a quick breakfast of boiled eggs and barley bread, Samu'el returned with the sandals, strapping them on Manaen's feet. Manaen patted the boy's shoulder and thanked him.

It was while the final cross-braid of laces was going around Manaen's ankles that his steward Hashim arrived. "Good morning, sir. Lady. Bit of bad news, I'm afraid."

"What?" Manaen's good mood evaporated.

"Silas, the worker tending the roasting oven, fell asleep. He didn't turn the drum as he should. Whole batch is ruined."

This was part of an order for almonds placed by Tetrarch Philip for his palace in Caesarea Philippi. It was important to get it right.

Manaen exploded. "Idiot! Discharge him. How soon can we prepare a replacement lot?"

"That's just it, sir. The drum overheated and burst. It'll have to be repaired."

"Flog him, then! I'm sorry, Susanna, but I can't possibly leave today. Surely you can see that."

She did not reply, but the noisy clatter of dishes sent the signal that she was angry.

Hashim continued, "I've already ordered another drum brought from the old roasting shed. It'll be in place by this afternoon. No more than a six-hour delay at worst . . . and sir, about Silas. He's been here five years already. He's our most experienced hand, and our most reliable. He worked a full day yesterday and was only on duty again because . . . because you ordered the roasting to proceed all night."

It was true. Against Hashim's advice to the contrary, Manaen had commanded the process be speeded up by keeping the ovens going.

"You say it'll be working again by this afternoon?" Manaen questioned.

"Aye, sir."

"All right, then. Let it go. Warn Silas to be more cautious in future."

"Yes, sir." Hashim saluted as he left.

"If I were a Greek or a Roman I'd say the omens were against me going anywhere today," Manaen remarked to Susanna.

Susanna's chair scraped back from the table. Her voice had an edge. "You're not a Greek. Or a Roman. You keep your promises. Are you afraid to go back to the Galil? into Herod Antipas' territory?"

"Afraid? No, just . . . it's as if something's trying to keep me from going to Yeshua."

"Prevent you? A misplaced robe? A broken shoelace? Burned almonds? A burst roasting drum? In other days a legion of Herod's bodyguards with drawn swords couldn't prevent you from going where you wanted to go."

"I'm going for you, not myself."

She scoffed, "Omens! Stop making excuses! You promised me!"

He threw down his napkin in resentment. "Yes. Yes. A promise made when the bit was still between your teeth, Wife."

"A promise nonetheless, Husband."

"You're going to have your way or I'll hear about it the rest of my life."

"A wise insight for one married such a short time. Now here's another . . ." She slammed her fist on the table and stormed out of the room without finishing her threat.

After returning from the marketplace Zahav and Rebecca recited the story of Hero's thrashing to Papa.

"His heart is broken. Broken. Papa?" Zahav trembled as she spoke. Tears of anger flowed down her cheeks. Helpless. Helpless. No help to Hero or to anyone.

"I'm sorry for the boy. But you may not go to their aid, Zahav," Papa replied.

What good did it do to know about cruelty if there was no help to give to a victim? "How can we stand back and do nothing?" Zahav begged.

"You will obey me, Daughter." The old man did not raise his voice or his eyes. Fierceness was not required to ensure her obedience. She would not go against him. He was adamant. "There is nothing you can do in such a pitiful case, eh? Nothing. Say no more to me about it."

Zahav clung to her sister and wept in the corridor. To go against Papa's command would mean that Zahav would be declared anathema—and excommunicated. No one in the community would be allowed to speak to her or give her shelter. Papa's word was final.

Rebecca, looking miserable, stroked Zahav's hair and accompanied her up the steps to her bedchamber. "Take a little rest, eh? When you wake up maybe it won't seem so bad, Zahav. Maybe the answer will come. Maybe there is an answer."

Zahav lay down and tried to sleep. Her arms ached to hold Hero. To gather him in and stroke his head and somehow comfort him. But she could do nothing but grieve for him.

Hero sat by the edge of the cook fire, staring into the embers. Since the previous day's attack by the boys in the marketplace, he had remained unresponsive. Whatever wall Hero had erected to lock out the unpleasant world effectively locked him inside.

"Look, Hero," Alexander urged, "it's your favorite. Stewed apples. Smell that cinnamon?"

Nothing.

Alexander held out the Hero-sized panpipes. The replacement set was crafted with even greater care than the first. They were beautiful: polished antler cut to length and bound with expensive copper wire all the way from Damascus. Perfectly tuned and so finely wrought that the least puff of wind set them singing. Alexander had already turned down the offer of a whole denarius for them.

Hero ignored them. He would hold the instrument if Alexander insisted, but he would not play on them—not a single note.

No smile had crossed his face since the stone Diana doll had gone into the well.

Even worse, Hero's seizures came with greater frequency, severity, and duration. Now loud noises started the tremors. There seemed to be no heading them off either, even if they began from no more than a twitching eyelid.

"Look, Hero. You have to eat. Try this. You like it."

Obediently Hero opened his mouth for the wooden spoonful of spicy apple. He chewed placidly but without any sign of tasting or caring.

Alexander took up his own flute and placed the end against Hero's cheek. Consciously choosing a piece that always made Hero happy, his fingers and breath began the pattering rhythm of "The Shepherd's Bride."

Nothing.

Alexander surrendered himself to gloomy contemplation. There had been no benefit from the priest of Pan. Utticus, the specialist physician, wanted to chisel a hole in the boy's skull. Old friends stayed away after expressing their belief that Hero would be better off dead.

The only useful bit of help was Castor's elixir. And even its efficacy was failing. The single drop of medicine was still calming, but required longer than before to take effect.

Alexander hastily set that vision aside. He switched over to playing "The Pig and the Goat," but his thoughts remained morose.

There were noisy greetings in the street outside. From the loudness of their speech and the amount of cursing involved, Alexander guessed them to be donkey drovers. What was it about those who managed pack animals that made them so profane? All drover exchanges were carried out at the top of their lungs, as if across a canyon in the midst of a sandstorm.

One bellowed, "Demetrius! Haven't seen you since Methusaleh was a pup. Where you been keepin' yourself, you old sot?"

"Ha! Jehu! Still runnin' that same old string of fleabags outta Sidon? Alexandria, boy, that's the only place to make any real money. Cotton goods are what they crave up Damascus way. Load up in Egypt and off you go. Trip takes three months, but so what? And those Egyptian women, eh? Eh?" Ribald commentary ensued, then a question: "But say, you haven't been south at all, then?"

Alexander increased the volume of his playing and tried to ignore them.

Demetrius continued, "Big doin's down south. Lots of Jews killed in Jerusalem at their Passover. Some says Romans done it, others rebels, and some blames the brother of your tetrarch, eh?"

Jehu admitted he'd heard of the Passover massacre.

"And what of the famous sorceror, or what them Jews call a prophet? What of him? Plenty of talk about him up and down the country."

Once again Jehu loudly proclaimed his familiarity with the subject, adding, "Comin' through the Galil everyone tells me he's gonna raise an army of beggars and drive out the Romans. 'Course, in the next breath, they tell me he's gonna get hisself crucified, if Herod Antipas don't poison him first."

"What kind of fellow must he be to get 'em all mad at him at once, eh?" Demetrius pondered, bawling out his query. "Prophet or sorceror, either. People say he can heal lepers. Can you believe that? Lepers?"

It was Jehu's turn to contribute an even more astonishing bit of gossip. "Lepers, ha! In Capernaum they say he can raise the dead. Raise the dead, that Yeshua of Nazareth can!"

Alexander found himself engrossed in the tale against his will.

Demetrius repeated, "Yeshua of Nazareth? Not a proper start for a magician. Can anything worthwhile come out of Nazareth? Yeshua?"

"Like *you* wouldn't turn aside to see him? Yeshua of Nazareth?"

Hero jumped up so violently that Alexander's hair was spattered with stewed apples.

"Hero, what—"

The boy's face was contorted into a snarl. The vicious expression sent a shiver up his father's spine. In the next instant the boy leapt toward the cook fire, knocking the kettle of molten fruit hissing into the coals.

Alexander tackled his son by the legs and prevented him from getting seriously burned. The sickening stench of singed hair filled the room. Hero's eyebrows were scorched and the tops of his ears blistered.

During the ensuing wrestling match the child escaped his father's grip twice. Both times he tried to crawl back into the flames!

Finally Alexander pried open Hero's clenched jaws and dosed his son with two drops of the potion. It worked and Hero slept, but Alexander spent the night locked in despair.

20

CHAPTER

T wo middle-aged visitors from the east arrived shortly after noon in the camp. Philip and Nathaniel brought them to Yeshua.

Peniel surmised they were religious scholars by the look of them. They wore prayer shawls and phylacteries like every Pharisee in Eretz-Israel. But these were different. Peniel had often heard such accents during the festival days in Yerushalayim. The two men were Jews, yes, but spoke with the accents of Nabateans. They were from the kingdom of King Aretas, foreigners all the same.

Rumor circulated among the talmidim that these Nabatean Jews carried some warning to Yeshua with them. And also an invitation for Yeshua to leave the territory of Herod Antipas and set up a Jewish government in exile. Later, with the help of King Aretas, they would storm the palaces and forts of Herod Antipas. Take back the land from this Samaritan son of an Idumean! The line of Herod the Great would be brought into the dust!

It was a fine thought. A lofty goal. Liberate Eretz-Israel from the whelps of the non-Jewish butcher king!

Would Yeshua and His followers be breaking camp soon? moving across the border? Would the kingdom be established first outside the borders of ancient Israel?

Peniel pondered what it would be like to cross into another land. A nation "outside." He had never been outside Eretz-Israel before! He was both excited about the thought of a new adventure . . . and afraid.

The scholars were made welcome as Yeshua conferred with the Twelve.

Peniel had not intended to listen in, but he heard their voices plainly as he gathered fuel for the fire.

Yeshua, calm, reflective, remarked, "Haven't I chosen twelve of you? But one is a devil."

Judas, at his most submissive and flattering, replied, "Send him away. Once a man proves he can't be trusted, well . . . forgiving is one thing, true . . . but trust? Ever again?"

Philip remarked, "The news they bring isn't anything we didn't know already. Dangerous times, Rabbi. Spies are everywhere. The high priest sends them out. The Romans. Herod Antipas has them. . . ."

Peniel held his breath, not wanting to miss a single word. Who was Judas speaking of? What traitor was he referring to? There was plenty of complaining among the talmidim, but who was the secret enemy within their circle?

Judas interjected, "That was a narrow escape on the other occasion. I know . . . we all know . . . he says he was forced into it. But how can we be certain? What if Eglon failed to kill you, but Herod Antipas has still managed to plant a conspirator in our midst anyway?"

Peniel blinked rapidly. Judas was speaking of him! Peniel had been compelled to accompany Antipas' assassin into Yeshua's presence. Peniel had failed the Rabbi!

But Peniel had confessed his grief at that failure. Yeshua had forgiven him, embraced him, restored him . . . hadn't He?

"Now I don't say he *is* one," Judas hedged, urging restraint in judgment. "I just think it's better to err on the side of caution."

This was the moment Yeshua would set him straight, Peniel expected.

"There are many who can't follow where I'm going," Yeshua said.

There was a roaring in Peniel's ears. His eyes smarted and his throat constricted, as if a sudden change in the wind blew campfire ashes into his face. Yeshua didn't trust him!

Peniel fled back to the camp. Busied himself with chores.

The Master and the Twelve returned. Judas walked at Yeshua's left elbow. As soon as his eye lit on Peniel Judas smiled. It was a crooked, triumphant, mocking smile.

Peniel felt sick, too sick to eat the noon meal. He was hardly able to concentrate during the Torah portion. Was he too late? Was it possible even Yeshua listened to the lying whispers? How could the Teacher be so blind to Judas' deception?

After the teaching Peniel approached Yeshua and stood before Him.

Yeshua searched the once-blind man's face with kind yet sad eyes. "You're troubled, Peniel."

Peniel hung his head. He blurted out, "You know me, Lord. I say things straight out. Are you sending me away?"

Yeshua replied, "Are you afraid to go? afraid to stay in the territory of Herod Antipas? Even though Antipas would steal your eyes if he could?"

"Don't send me away! It's not true what Judas says about me! *He's* a liar! *He's* a deceiver. *He's* not to be trusted! *He—*"

Yeshua stopped the hemorrhage of wounded feelings with an upraised hand. "But, Peniel. Will *you* choose to trust *me?*"

Peniel gave a slow nod. "I do trust you, Lord, but—"

"Then trust me. You'll understand one day. But you must go."

"But Lord, where? Where will I go?"

The destination was a surprise. "To Beth Chesed, the 'House of Mercy,' the villa of Miryam of Magdala. My mother's there." Yeshua handed Peniel a parchment scroll bound with a bit of twine. "Take this to her."

"Then you're not just sending me away? You're not angry with me?" Peniel clutched the message to his heart, then added it to the contents of his leather pouch: half a loaf of bread, a packet of dried figs, and the linen-wrapped lavender bud perfuming the whole.

Yeshua cautioned him, "Listen to me, Peniel! Don't stop to speak to anyone you meet along the way. No one in the camp must know you're leaving. Or where you're going."

"Sure, Lord. I'll keep my mouth shut. If you say so, I will."

"Until the shepherd comes out to find you, don't answer any questions."

"What shepherd? What's his name?"

"When you hear your name called out, run to the voice and be saved! Later, after you're clothed and fed, tell the shepherd and the leper what you've seen and heard."

Peniel tried to comprehend the warning, but he could not. "Shepherd? Leper? What are you telling me, Lord? I don't understand. What's it mean?"

"The answers will be clear when you need them."

"But will you send for me? After that? After everything you're saying happens?" Peniel asked eagerly. "When can I come back again?"

Yeshua did not reply.

Peniel slipped away from the camp near Chorazin. No one noticed when he left.

Susanna's excitement grew as she and Manaen stepped from the boat onto the Capernaum dock. What if it was today? What if everything was put right in an instant?

The sun was high overhead. She scanned the shoreline, certain she could locate Yeshua's whereabouts just by the movements of the throngs of people. But the shoreline of the village seemed ordinary. So far no general direction, no clue as to Yeshua's location, was apparent.

"Keep to the alleyways." Manaen shuffled beside her, his chin high as though he was sniffing the air for danger.

Was he ashamed of his appearance? or afraid of returning to Antipas' domain?

Susanna felt the curious stares as they passed. Perhaps the villagers knew the reason Susanna and Manaen had come. How many thousands had entered the Galil in search of healing over the last months?

Susanna and Manaen passed through the city square.

Manaen gripped her arm hard. "Did you hear that?"

She shot back too quickly, too brightly, "No. Nothing."

"I thought I heard someone say our names."

"You're imagining."

"Get us out of here." His teeth were clenched.

She guided Manaen around the corner of the market square and into an unoccupied shaded passageway. "Wait here." Susanna lifted his hand from her forearm.

"What are you doing?"

"I'm going to ask. Ask about the Teacher."

Manaen grasped an upright pole supporting the awning of a baker's shop. "You leave me tethered like a dog."

She ignored his irritation. "I'll be right back."

Susanna entered a baker's shop where shelves were piled high with round flat loaves. The counter was buried beneath heaps of bread, enough to feed an army. The only vacant space was the view through a rear doorway opening onto a courtyard that shimmered with waves of heat from an outdoor oven.

"Shalom?" Susanna called.

"Be right there." A barrel-shaped man, black hair whitened with a dusting of flour, emerged from a doorway. "Shalom, madame. How many would you like?"

"I need information."

"You'll want it free, too, no doubt."

"My husband and I. We're looking for the Rabbi from Nazareth."

"You and everyone else in the Galil."

"But do you know where he is?"

"The Teacher? Gone."

"But we were told he was here. We've come a long way."

"Well, he's gone. Departed. Left. No known destination." The baker confided, "He had mercy on me. Stopped making free bread. Healed my ailing business."

"Gone," Susanna repeated dully.

He nodded curtly. "Gone. Want bread? Three for a penny."

Susanna paid a copper coin and mutely accepted a bundle of loaves.

What next? Manaen would demand they return home . . . back to his wine. Susanna had to have an answer.

Manaen grew increasingly impatient. He resisted the urge to bawl out Susanna's name like a calf bellowing for its mother. Sensing an intangible danger, he felt the urge to crouch, to disappear. He groped his way to a wall and slouched down against it. Where was Susanna? What was taking her so long?

Sharpened hearing aroused his caution before his conscious mind took note of voices: Gadot and Acteon! It was the two bullies who had taunted him in the Bethsaida market. Manaen turned his back to their conversation. He pressed his fingers against his forehead and hoped they would not spot him.

Gadot's simper asserted, "Lord Antipas will not be happy at this news. Now that he's made up his mind how to deal with Yeshua, he won't like it that the man's gone."

So they were looking for the Rabbi too.

Acteon's voice was unmistakable. "You're missing the point. We don't go back and say he's just gone. We find out where and *then* we go back. That way we get rewarded."

The pair moved off, leaving Manaen sweating and inwardly raging. What now? Manaen cursed his helplessness. Susanna was somewhere in the same streets with Antipas' bullies. And Manaen was unable to do anything about it.

Long minutes passed. At the sound of footsteps Manaen raised his head.

"Manaen?"

"Susanna."

"He's not far from here."

His face, gaunt, sweaty, and contorted with concentration, turned toward her. "But he's not here? Not in Capernaum?"

"Magdala. I asked a boy playing by the watering trough. Paid him a penny. He knew right away! Yeshua's in Magdala."

Alexander did not reopen the shop after Hero's desperate scramble toward the fire. Unmoving, Alexander sat beside Hero's cot and watched as the boy slumbered. The juice of bloodred poppies ran through Hero's veins.

Two drops.

Thick lashes fluttered as Hero dreamed. Lips curved in a smile as he lived out some secret vision.

Was he running to meet his mother? Did Diana hold him? caress him? rock him gently in her arms? Could he feel the beat of her heart beneath his cheek?

Alexander knew Hero would wake soon to a longing he would never shake off. The reality of loneliness united father and son. Diana's absence enclosed them both like a dark forest. Without her they had both lost their way—together.

With a reproachful glance at the impish idol in the niche, Alexander shuddered. "You grinning thing. You, piece of wood carved by my father. You're nothing there on the shelf. Wood and paint. The image of something we can't see. But the dark creature you represent is real enough."

Suddenly the hair on the back of his neck prickled. A presence had entered the room. The air became thick; Alexander found it hard to breathe.

Hero moaned and stirred. His brow creased with anxiety.

Dread came near. Panic. Alexander's heart beat faster. He addressed the dark force. "You! What do you want? Haven't you taken enough? Everything?"

It breathed in his ear.

Alexander resisted. "I feel the weight of your hand on my neck, pushing, pushing my soul to its knees! Breaking my heart. Breaking! You delight in our pain! Our wounded hearts are your bread! You! Lord of flies! You! False promises! You great lie! Always tomorrow! Always you promise tomorrow! What about today? We would have a son, you said! We would be happy!"

There was a low chuckle from deep within the throat of Hero.

"Give him back!" Alexander demanded.

A sneer on Hero's face was the only reply. It was too late, Alexander knew. Too late! The pact had been made!

Beads of perspiration dripped from Alexander's brow and soaked his clothing. He could barely speak. "We would . . . you said we would have everything we always wanted . . . you said . . . if only . . . if only . . . we would bow down and worship you! Oh, liar! Offer our baby to you . . . you said! So Diana and I? We believed you. We gave you our Hero. And you torment . . . him. Us! And now . . . we're lost. Lost! Stumbling on until the moment you devour us!"

Alexander could not breathe. He gasped and sank to the cold stone floor. Dread sat on his chest, squeezing his heart. A net of fire coursed through his left arm.

"Oh! Help . . . us . . . God of . . . Zahav! Nameless . . . One I don't know! One God! Help . . . me! Help us! Find . . . us! Save us!"

Then he lapsed into unconsciousness.

Magdala, located on the western shore of the Sea of Galilee, was a thriving commercial community. It was home to forty thousand people employed in industries as diverse as linen weaving, stone quarrying, and the spice trade. It was also a city full of tension.

The main public wharf was lined with armed men. Some wore the conical helmets and tan-and-green livery of Herod Antipas. Others were dressed in the short red tunics of Imperial Roman legionaries.

Susanna spotted the troops while she and Manaen were still a good way offshore. Casually she inquired of the fisherman hired to carry them across the lake, "The soldiers. Why so many?"

"Tetrarch Antipas is hosting some worthy Roman on an inspection of the province," the leathery-skinned boatman remarked, loading his response with sarcasm. Leaning away from the wind, he spat into the water to emphasize his loathing.

Susanna directed the boatman to make for a deserted pier at the far end of the man-made harbor. He grunted his compliance. If these two passengers had prices on their heads, he wanted no part of carrying them right into the arms of the authorities.

Paying the fare, Susanna led Manaen to an empty warehouse on the shore. Her eagerness to pursue Manaen's healing had driven her this far. Now she was hesitant and frightened.

A pair of washerwomen, wicker baskets of dirty clothes on their heads, passed by on their way to a communal laundry pool. Gossip, the sound of toddlers splashing, and an occasional smack on a child's bottom came from nearby. A good place to get news without alerting anyone official.

Susanna said urgently, "Manaen, there's a bench just here in the shade. I'll find out where he is and be right back."

Manaen asked resignedly, "Can anyone see me?"

Susanna scanned the area. "No one. There's a beggar leaning in a doorway across the street . . . a cripple, with his crutches and begging bowl lying beside him. No one else."

"Why not prop me up next to him? Maybe I can turn a copper or two so this day's not a total waste."

The laundry drudges looked up at Susanna's approach but showed little curiosity. They continued their labor, slapping tunics against the inclined stones of the pool's margin.

To pass the time, gossip made the rounds of the pool with greater energy than the scrubbing. One observed, "Guess it's right for that Mary of Nazareth to be staying at the home of the harlot Miryam, then."

"Home for lewd women and bastard children? Too right. And both of 'em havin' Roman lovers. Panterra, I hear the father's name was. Carpenter's son, indeed!"

"Did you want somethin', then?" a broad-faced, stout-shouldered redhead asked Susanna.

Susanna offered shyly, "Answers. The Teacher, Yeshua of Nazareth."

There was an exchange of looks among the five washerwomen. A wizened, stoop-backed worker replied, "We was just speakin' of him. You aren't the first to be askin', neither. Tetrarch's men're curious too."

The red-haired woman squinted up into the sun. "And that's not all. They're askin' for any as has been healed by him. Promised us a denarius for names, they did. Do you know him, dearie?"

"Just curious. I've only returned to the Galil from Yerushalayim. But even there we've heard such stories."

"Aye," the women chorused.

The ancient laundry woman commented, "Fewer stories now than a couple days ago."

The redhead looked over her shoulder. "Them as claimed healin' and boasted of it . . . they've either left Magdala . . . or up and disappeared."

Each of the laundresses contributed an identity:

"Elias the leper."

"That fellow with the terrible swollen legs who lay by the aqueduct."

"Blind Benjamin—got back his eyes and lost his head, most likely."

"None around now but old Eliakim there." The redhead jerked her sun-bleached locks toward the cripple sprawled in the doorway. "Oh, he got healed, right enough, but he daren't speak of it, see?" Tattered red curls wagged side to side. "Denied Yeshua done anythin' for him.

Pretendin' to be lame! More gloomy than when he really couldn't walk."

It took Susanna some time to digest all this. Those who were healed were afraid to say so?

"Them as claimed to be his followers—fishermen some was—they up and left in a boat. Maybe him they call the Prophet left too," one of the other workers added.

Susanna glanced toward the lake. "Where did they go?"

Slyly the crooked-backed woman inquired, "Just curious, are you, lady?"

Susanna's mind churned. Arrested for claiming to be healed? Talmidim frightened out of the territory? Yeshua Himself on the run or in hiding?

What had she done, bringing her husband to this place and then announcing who she sought?

Another pair of women carrying laundry hampers arrived. Susanna backed up into one, apologizing when she knocked a basket from her hands. Susanna and the laundress both stooped to retrieve a fallen shift. Foreheads almost touching, they rose eye to eye.

"Why, it's the lady Susanna."

It was Tobijah, serving woman of Herod Antipas. Susanna recognized her from the tetrarch's court in Jerusalem . . . and was recognized in her turn.

Tobijah said again, "Lady Susanna. What brings you to Magdala?"

"You're mistaken. Confusing me with someone else."

Tobijah shook her head. "Know you anywhere, I would. In trouble, are you, lady?"

Backing away, Susanna continued protesting, "Some mistake. Never saw you before. Good-bye, now."

The new subject of the Magdala gossip mill was grinding loudly before Susanna retreated around the corner and out of sight. She bundled Manaen hurriedly into a shabby inn, out of sight of curious, bribable eyes.

21

B eyond the fishing village of Capernaum, oppressive, late-afternoon heat summoned thunderheads, like flocks of birds, to gather and swirl above the hills.

Dark. Gloomy. Heavy. Like Peniel's thoughts.

No matter how hard he tried, Peniel could not place this journey to Magdala in a good light. Yeshua had sent him away. Yeshua had sent him away to avoid conflict and dissension in the camp. Peniel was the one *sent away*—not Judas. There could be no positive conclusions drawn about Peniel's position among the talmidim after such an outcome.

Peniel spotted the villa of a rich man ahead. Extensive grounds blocked the path closest to the lake and would require a detour inland, away from the cool relief of an occasional wisp of breeze. Beached fishing boats littered the shore.

The thick, torpid atmosphere exhausted Peniel. Sweat-soaked clothing chafed his skin. His eyes burned. He would stop here for the night, then travel on to Magdala come morning.

He smelled a storm approaching. Some time tonight high temperatures would rupture rain clouds the way a too-hot kiln cracked a bowl in his father's pottery shop.

Over Peniel's right shoulder the western horizon of the Galil took on a ruddy hue that intensified as afternoon slipped into dusk. Particles of dust diffused the last rays of sunlight into a myriad of colors. A roiling sky fire of red and orange glowed on the underbelly of clouds from west to east and reflected on the surface of the Sea of Galilee a hundred yards from the path Peniel traveled. All the world seemed ablaze with colors Peniel had never seen.

He exclaimed aloud, "The Red Sea!" Though he knew it was only the Sea of Galilee, the color nonetheless sparked his imagination, cheered him up a bit.

Crossing the Red Sea! Now that is a story I would like to hear!

Perhaps one day. But not today.

Meanwhile, a plunge in cool water was irresistible. He hung his precious bag of provisions on the bowsprit of a boat and stripped off his outer garments as he stumbled down to the bank. Carrying his bundle of clothes, he waded cautiously into the lake. He could not swim. From his near drowning experience in childhood, which had claimed the life of his brother, Peniel had always feared deep water. He ventured only waist deep along a breakwater of half-submerged boulders. At the end the stones hooked around to form a shallow pool. Behind this protective barrier, perhaps, the women of the village did their laundry or young children swam on scorching summer days. For now it was deserted. Peniel felt quite safe. He removed the rest of his clothes. The cool bath revived him, lifted his spirits another notch.

Rinsing his sweat-stained tunic and undergarments, he laid his laundry on the rocks to dry. Then he sat on a boulder, washed himself, and peered with fascination at tiny baitfish darting around his legs. He would stay and soak right where he was, he decided, until evening cooled the sunbaked land.

The colors in the atmosphere flared brighter, then began to darken into night. After so many years of being blind, Peniel was comfortable in the dark. He made no move to come out of the water.

Lamps began to glow from the window of the rich man's house.

Peniel raised his face to the first plump drops of rain. He would be as wet out of the lake as he was in the lake, so he was disinclined to leave the pool even when wind stirred the water on the opposite side of the barrier.

A flash of silver darted from the clouds and illuminated the land.

Light was followed by a distant boom. Then another. And another. Peniel stood up. He fixed his eyes on the place where the last three jagged spikes had split the evening sky. Lightning. Traveling rapidly his way. A blast erupted from a vineyard beyond the villa. In that instant of monochrome vision Peniel glimpsed the towering figure of a man, white-bearded, staff in hand, standing near the edge of the water. He beckoned Peniel to come out of the lake.

Peniel listened.

What? What did the man say?

Peniel! You fool! You fool! Peniel ben Yahtzar! Great fool! Get out of the w-water!

Was this rude fellow speaking to Peniel? Had he actually called Peniel's name? Peniel reckoned he had as much right as anyone to cool himself off all night in a pool of water at the lake.

The lightning! You fool! Peniel! Get out! Get out! Get out of the w-water!

How did this stranger know Peniel's name? Who knew Peniel well enough to call him fool and order him around?

The torrent of rain broke. Wind howled in behind it, stinging Peniel's face.

Another crackling flash slammed into the vineyard. Much closer. Very close indeed. The thunderclap after made Peniel's head ache! This time, when Peniel looked, the stranger was not on the shore.

Panic! Not stopping to retrieve his clothes, Peniel scrambled through the dark water toward dry ground before the next bolt exploded. But the liquid seemed to push him back, and he struggled against its resistance!

Tripping on a rock, he crawled the last few yards onto dry ground. As he drew himself up he smelled a pungent odor. Ducking his head, Peniel pressed himself flat on the sand. A shaft of fire roared behind him! The explosion shattered the stones just where his tranquil pool had been! The noise deafened him. He shoved his fingers into his ears. Too late.

Daring to raise his head, he crawled forward a few yards to the hull of the boat to retrieve his travel sack. The deluge sluiced water over him. His clothes were burned to ashes, no doubt. But the bag was waterproof. No fear that the parchment would be destroyed or the bud of lavender dissolved.

Naked, covered with sand, he scuttled into the craft. Crouching low in the bow, Peniel cowered beneath a tarp as the strength of the squall intensified.

Peniel's hearing was dull. The moan of the gale was a low whine and the craft's lines and cables hummed. The force of the tempest made the boat rock as though it was in water. Peniel leaned against a heap of fishing nets and closed his eyes. The boat smelled like old fish guts. Peniel opened the satchel and inhaled. The lavender was a comfort.

Peniel mourned the loss of his clothes. What would happen to him now? How could he go on since he was naked? Yes. He was a fool. A fool. The stranger who had warned him to leave the water should have also told him not to forget to gather his laundry!

Peniel, his nose in the bag, slept at last.

Papa had gone to Rebecca's house for supper. It was well past nightfall when Zahav heard voices in the courtyard below.

Pounding on her door roused her. It was Rebecca.

"Zahav! Sister! Come down! There's news! Something wonderful is happening, Zahav! Barakat, my husband's brother, came tonight from the Decapolis! Zahav! Wake up!"

Papa tapped his stick with excitement, urging Barakat to retell Zahav everything he had seen.

Zahav, Heli, Rebecca, and Papa sat silently as the story of present-day miracles unfolded.

Barakat, a brawny rug merchant with customers as far away as Persia, was known to be a skeptic's skeptic. He bought nothing without proof and certain provenance. Years in business had made him cautious to the point of being unpleasant. But here he was, babbling about strange wonders occurring daily in the Gentile territory of the Decapolis.

"Nefesh is his name. I myself was attacked by him some years back when I passed too near the graveyard where he lived. A madman. Possessed by demons who shrieked and wailed in a hundred voices all at once. Strong beyond human strength. Here's the story. I met him in

Hippus two weeks ago. I saw him cast out an evil spirit from an old woman in the souk of the rug merchants. I have known her for ten years. Her face was like stone. She wept bitterly, and her son, who runs the shop there, was in despair. Then Nefesh spoke an incantation and commanded the thing to be gone from her in the name of one called Yeshua, who Nefesh says is the Son of the Living God! And the woman was healed."

"You're sure this Nefesh is your madman?" Heli asked.

Barakat raised his glass of wine in salute. "Here's to Nefesh." He took a drink. "I spoke with him at length. He told me a story about meeting the Prophet on the shore of the lake. How this man of God commanded the demons to leave him and enter a herd of pigs, which then drowned themselves! So Nefesh was set free and commanded to speak freedom to others like himself. This incident with the stone woman was not an isolated case. Nefesh is casting out evil spirits all over Gadara in the name of the Prophet who healed him. People from throughout the Golan have heard of him. They bring hopeless cases to him and they are cured. He is not particular who he heals: Jew, half-breed, or Gentile. It makes no difference to Nefesh. He casts the demons out from them."

At this, Papa laid his hand on Zahav's arm. "So, Daughter, as I heard Barakat speak of this wonder, very strongly it came to my mind that perhaps this is news Alexander should hear. *Tonight.* Not one more hour should pass in hopelessness. So we will all go with you to the flute maker's house. You must tell him, Daughter, because the Eternal God has placed him on your heart. I know your burden for them. And now, perhaps, if there is help in the name of Yeshua for the little boy, then you must tell the father about Nefesh in Gadara."

Magdala overflowed with disappointed pilgrims who had come too late to find Yeshua.

Susanna had asked the innkeeper's wife to deliver a late supper in their room. Manaen lay on the cot as the old crone knocked softly on the door. Susanna opened it a crack. "My . . . husband's asleep." She put a finger to her lips in warning.

The woman nodded and tried to peer past Susanna into the room.

Her shriveled features were exaggerated in the light of the lamp she held. She whispered, "Is your man unwell then, dearie?"

"The heat. And the journey has been . . . difficult."

"Well, yes—" the woman hissed confidentially as she extended her hand for payment—"must be hard to travel when you have no eyes, eh? I told my husband when you two came in, 'Must be hard to travel,' I said. Will you be wantin' a lamp tonight? It's two lepta more for a lamp."

Susanna trembled as she dropped three coins into the greasy palm. "A little extra for your trouble."

The woman passed the lamp in to Susanna. "Bless you, lady! It's plain you're not one of the *am ha aretz*. Nay. Not one of the common folk. Nothin' common about either of the two of you. What I can't figure is how such a nice young woman as yourself come to be wed to a blind man. Was it an accident, then? Himself losin' his eyes? Come lookin' for the Prophet of Nazareth, did you? Come too late to find him?"

"We're here on business. Just like I said."

The woman shrugged. "Your business is none of my business. Magdala is crowded with folk full of infirmity. But if you care, the Nazarene's mother stays in Magdala, I hear. Mary's her name. She does laundry and cooks for outcast women and children at the villa where the rich prostitute of Magdala used to live. A mile south on the lake. Gossip's around that the mother of the Nazarene was once a woman of ill repute herself. Not that I believe such a rumor. I hear she's a kind soul. Maybe she'd know where you could find her son."

Susanna pushed the crone's arm out of the room, then closed the door and placed the lamp on the table.

From the corridor the innkeeper's wife called, "Shall I bring you breakfast in the morning, dearie?"

"Yes, thank you. But tonight we're not to be disturbed."

Beneath their window the tramp of hobnailed shoes echoed in the streets. Herodian soldiers.

Susanna waited until the steps of the old woman receded before she turned toward Manaen.

He sat up on the edge of the bed. His hands covered his face. Was he weeping? He muttered, "I need a drink. Is there wine?"

"Supper." Susanna made an attempt at cheerfulness. "Looks good too. Stew. She may be a witch, but the woman of the inn can cook, I think. Smell it. Hungry?"

"I need a drink." He rose slowly and groped toward the window. Closing the shutters he stood quietly listening. Listening. So many voices. The strain was evident in his countenance. "I thought I heard the voice of Eglon again. But no. Not Eglon. Others. Gadot and Acteon. Whispering. Outside. Near the gate. They're looking. Scouring the countryside for people the Prophet has healed. Or was I dreaming? Is it me they want?"

"I was recognized, remember? But they're looking for Yeshua. If they find him, Herod will have his head, I think. Just like the Baptizer. I'm afraid for him. Afraid for all of us if they arrest him."

"Yeshua's gone. Even if stories of his power were a rumor, they gave me some hope. Some . . . light in my soul that made me think I might not always have to live in darkness. But I've missed my chance. If he comes back? You're right. The Herodians will have him arrested. Or killed. By now Herod Antipas has got wind of the fact that I'm in his territory searching for a holy man to restore my sight. If I'm picked up on this side of the water I'm as good as dead."

"A day or two. They'll give up. We can go home. Home where we belong. We'll hire another fishing boat. Cross by night. Go home to Bethsaida."

"Home? What's the point?"

"Don't talk like that."

"We won't get to the quay. They'll spot me."

"I'll go alone. Find a boat that will take us. I'll come back for you."

"The spies of Antipas will be searching the fishing fleet. Asking questions of the fishermen."

"Then I'll wait. Wait until you think it's safe." She rushed to him, threw her arms around his waist. "Oh, Manaen! We shouldn't have come! I was trying to help you. Looking for an answer! Thinking if you met him he could give us back our life somehow. Hoping you'd love me again if only you could see me!"

Manaen was unresponsive. She sank to the floor.

"Doesn't matter," he said coldly. "Never mind, Susanna. Get up. Our dreams were just dreams. Everything in my life . . . is gone dark, numb. It's nobody's fault. Nobody. Just the way it is. Now. Get up. I need a drink. Is there wine?"

Susanna poured a cupful of wine. Manaen drained it and held it out for more. She resented his need to drink himself into oblivion again. Yet she acquiesced and watched sullenly as he drank down his second cup.

"It'll be dark soon." Her voice had an edge.

"What difference does it make to me?" Manaen countered bitterly.

"We'll go south. A mile, the old woman said. We'll find the place where Yeshua's mother is."

"Pointless."

"We'll ask her where he is."

"I need more wine."

"You've had enough."

He leapt to his feet and bellowed, "Did you hear what I said? Susanna! More wine!"

"No, Manaen. No more."

He lunged toward the sound of her voice, stumbled over a stool, and sprawled to the floor. The empty goblet clattered across the boards and came to rest against the wall. He groped for it. "Where is it? Where?"

Staring at Manaen with disgust, she stepped beyond his reach.

He groaned and struggled to rise. "Help me."

"You're drunk."

"What of it?"

"You've been drunk—on wine and bitterness—long enough."

"So what?"

"You've become your brother. I thought I was marrying the man I loved. Instead I find that Demos bar Talmai won the contest for my body after all."

"Susanna, don't—"

"What's the difference? What's the difference between you and him? I might as well have married Demos. Drunk. Cruel. The man I used to love isn't here. They put out your eyes, but I thought you could still see me. Thought my love would be light enough for you to live by."

"Not enough." He rolled over on his back and stretched his arms upward in a gesture of hopelessness. "God! Oh, God! Not enough!"

"Hating Demos wasn't enough. Revenge against him wasn't enough. Loving me isn't enough."

"My soul is blind. Sorry. Sorry. I don't know what to do anymore,

Susanna! Love? I . . . I feel nothing. Empty. Sorrow for what we can never have."

She sank down beside him. Stroked his hair. They wept quietly together as the clamor of the city grew still.

Alexander heard pounding. A drumbeat passing in the streets? Or was it in his head?

He was aware he was on the floor but could not rouse himself enough to get up. It hurt to open his eyes, so he kept them screwed tightly shut.

How long had he been here? he wondered. Was he dying . . . or dead? What would become of Hero?

The hammering continued. Alexander wished it would stop, tried to shout against the throbbing, but his tongue was wooden in his mouth. He was mute, waiting for something that never came. His life was like an unplayed melody.

Yes. He was as mute inside as Hero . . . and as paralyzed.

The drumming subsided. A breeze wafted across his face. Was wind blowing over the waters?

He sensed someone. Someone kneeling by his side. Tender, caring hands sponged his forehead with cool water. Murmured words caressed his soul.

He spoke a name. "Diana. Don't go, Diana."

It was only a dream of Diana, but it was a good dream. Pleasant and without grief. He saw a painted mask of her face across the water.

She waved to him and spoke, but her lips did not move. *Live your life, Alexander. Let me go. Since we were children you have disguised yourself from everyone. Even from yourself.*

"Not from you," he protested.

Even from me. Truth is a melody you never played. Your true self is hidden in a closet like an unused broom. Dust covers everything. Everything. Old fears and musty secrets are hidden away. Hidden. Seek truth or your life will end unlived, Alexander.

"What do you want me to do? Diana?"

A worried voice replied, "Alexander! I want you to open your eyes." The cool cloth patted his cheek, then one on the other side. Tentative at first, the taps grew progressively stronger and more insistent. "Alexander? Alexander! Stay with us."

Alexander groaned. He clung to the dream. Almost against his will his eyes flickered.

A face swam in and out of focus above him. Deep brown eyes filled with concern and brimming compassion. They belonged to Zahav.

"You." Alexander's words were slurred. At her shoulder was the face of a dark-bearded bear of a man.

"I am Barakat. I travel the world and have no fear of any man," the stranger explained.

Zahav stroked Alexander's forehead. "My father and sister are outside. We all came. We knocked, yes? I heard what happened to him. So we came. I knocked. No one answered. I looked through the window and was afraid you had . . ." She stared pointedly at the blue vial. "I let myself in."

"I . . . I'll be all right. But Hero's worse. Shows no interest in anything. I . . . sometimes I think I'm wrong to keep him suffering."

Alarm suffused Zahav's face. "Don't! You mustn't say that. Don't give up hope."

"There is no hope," Alexander returned, knowing he sounded beaten down. But he was unable to help himself. Even the sight of the ivory whistle hanging around Zahav's neck failed to cheer him.

"But there is. That's what we came to tell you." After peering around once more, she unfastened the veil on one side of her head covering and let it fall open. The small gesture was surprisingly intimate.

And then he saw it again—the bright birthmark etched into her face like a red country drawn on a map.

Alexander struggled to sit upright. Zahav and Barakat assisted him, but only until he leaned against the wall.

"You're very ill. Your color is . . ." She gestured toward the lime-washed wall.

Alexander glanced toward the niche. The figure of Pan stared insolently back at him. "Not sick. Something horrible. I don't know how to explain it."

Her voice trembled. "Get rid of that thing." She did not say what thing, but he knew she meant his god. "It is evil, this ancient god. The oldest of false gods, my father says. Very old. Very cruel."

"Yes. Yes. I felt it."

Zahav instructed, "Barakat, help him up. I'll see to Hero." She leaned her ear onto the boy's chest. Hero's breathing sighed through the room, but he could not be roused.

Barakat asked, "Should I fetch a doctor?"

Alexander explained. "No, it's the poppy juice. It keeps his seizures away."

Zahav's eyes sparkled with suppressed anger. "You drug him till he's like this?"

"I have no choice."

"You want him to be a lump, a mindless stone? Is that all you want him to be?"

"No, I . . . I don't know what to do. I don't know what he is."

At his confession of helplessness Zahav's irritation disappeared. "He is a little boy. Little. Living with something frightening that he cannot understand! There must be an answer!"

"I shouldn't have left him in the stall alone. Those boys. They took pleasure in hurting him."

"Yes. I heard what happened. Terrible. Terrible. I came to bring food. Bread and soup, eh? A little jar of honey." She gestured toward a covered wicker basket beside the door. "Hero must be fed, eh?"

Alexander labored to get to his feet. He put his hand to the wall to steady himself, then plopped down heavily in a chair. "I'm better now," he claimed, though the room spun around him.

Zahav gathered Hero into her arms and began to rock him. The child stirred at the back of her hand on his brow. Eyes fluttered open. He smiled weakly as his pale fingers raised to touch the mark on her face.

She said, "He feels love, yes? He misses his mama, you see? You mustn't keep him locked up, a prisoner of this drug. There is a soul held captive in this body, yes? Help him, Alexander."

"How?" He pressed his head in his hands.

"Let him live. Even if life hurts sometimes, let him live. And when it does hurt, comfort him. Hold him."

"Since Diana died . . . I don't know what to do."

"There. Barakat, fetch the basket. It's suppertime. Hero's hungry. Feed him."

Alexander said, "I . . . am no cook."

She scolded, "I brought food. Feed him. He's a shadow. A wisp. Like you. Look at you. Both of you. Skin and bones."

He peeked beneath the cloth. Fresh bread. Stewed apples. Soup. Honey. "You said you would not be back," he said softly.

"I heard what happened. Heard you and Hero are living like dry leaves on a wind."

"But you all . . . all of you . . . risk your reputation to help us."

"There are rumors from Galilee. Rumors that someone—a great healer and prophet—has come, yes? He performs great signs. My grandfather died because he believed the times were fulfilled when Messiah would deliver the children of Israel. I couldn't believe before. But what if it is true?"

"I'm not a true son of Israel," Alexander said sadly.

Zahav turned her scarred cheek to one side but continued to regard Alexander with a compassionate gaze. "You heard me speak of a man of my people who is a healer? Who may even be the Messiah?"

Alexander agreed he'd heard the tales but protested, "Not for me. How can that help with—" He jerked his thumb toward the unresponsive Hero.

Barakat spoke up. "There is another man, a Gentile, living in Gadara of the Decapolis. He was possessed by demons. Horribly afflicted, they say."

"And?" Alexander asked, his interest rising in spite of himself.

Barakat explained, "The Healer—Yeshua of Nazareth—cured him."

Hero's spine stiffened. The boy's head rose incrementally, like a coiled viper lifting to sniff the air.

In a rush Zahav delivered the rest of the story. "His name is Nefesh. He's going throughout the Ten Cities doing the same thing for others! He heals people of sicknesses and delivers them from evil spirits . . . all in the name of Yeshua of Nazareth." Zahav's hand went up to hide half her face as she turned. "Isn't it worth checking into? For his sake?"

Of course it was.

Zahav's voice was heavy with longing, "It is written that when Messiah comes, he will be a light also for the Gentiles. He will set captives free."

"Captives. Like Hero?"

"Perhaps. Yes. And when I heard the state you were in! What if I did nothing and you died? What if Hero died? And the next day Messiah came!"

"If only I had hope! But who is he? How will I know him?"

She cast an angry look at Pan. "Begin by getting rid of every idol that bars your way to the One True God! If you worship falsely, turn from your false god! Renounce all lies. Call on the El Shaddai of Israel, because he alone is Truth and is merciful to all men."

Could such a God even hear his prayers? The prayers of one so far outside the fold of Israel? Alexander glanced out the window. "It's dark."

"We should go now." She stood and placed Hero's frail form into Alexander's arms. Barakat waited at the door. She lifted her face and without embarrassment began to pray, "Blessed are you, O Adonai, who shows every creature mercy. Pour out your mercy and compassion on this helpless child, O Adonai! Come soon, Savior of Israel, and set this little one free. Bless this grieving father, El Shaddai! Embrace them both."

Alexander fought back emotion. Who had ever prayed for Hero before? No one. Never! He managed a reply. "May your great One God repay you."

"He created the hearts of all men to yearn for him. You are his child as well as I am." She admonished Alexander, "And you are this child's earthly father! Feed him. Embrace him! Love him always, yes? Wipe away his tears; don't run from them! As he sleeps, sit by his bed and pray to the Eternal One who hears every father's heart! Pray for Hero's sake, even if your own heart is bitter and wounded, yes? If you can't love yourself, you must love your only son! Hero must survive! He must! What if . . . what if . . . he did not survive! And the next day we found out the rumors of Messiah were true! I must go now. But I'll pray for you every day, Alexander!"

A boisterous crowd of Syrian soldiers passed by from the tavern by the city gates. From their rowdy, vulgar jests Alexander guessed they were full of potent barley wine.

Zahav's eyes took on a fearful, hunted quality, and she hastily reattached her veil. "I must go," she said abruptly. And then she hurried away with her companions in the direction of the Jewish Quarter.

22 CHAPTER

Who was calling Peniel's name?

It was an old man's voice. Strong enough to penetrate the storm and the hum in Peniel's ears.

"Peniel! Peniel ben Yahtzar! Where are y' hiding, lad?" A fist hammered on the side of the vessel.

"Mosheh?" Peniel sat up with a start. He felt the rough rope of the fishnets under his fingers and remembered where he was. *"Ulu Ush-pi-zin!"* he shouted. "Mosheh? I'm here. Mosheh?" The tarp was lifted. A light shone into Peniel's hiding place, blinding him. *"Ulu Ush-pi-zin!* Welcome, exalted guest."

There came a surprised snort from the other side. "So it *was* you! Peniel ben Yahtzar! Naked as the day you were born! Avel spotted y'. Swore it was you coming along the road. We waited at the house. Supper ready. When y' didn't pass, I came to find you, lad!"

"Zadok?" Peniel squinted into the glare of a lantern.

Zadok, one eye covered with a patch, appraised him with his good eye. A trim red dog trotted alongside. "You're a pathetic sight! Pathetic! But you're alive. Aye. Where's your clothes, lad?"

"I was washing my clothes while I soaked. Put them out on the rock to dry."

"Put them out to dry, eh? In the worst gale in ten years?"

"My clothes! They're burned up! Gone! The lightning! All I saved is this bag."

"Burned up, y' say, lad?" Zadok tugged his beard. "Burned up. Well then. Aye. You put 'em on the rock to dry in a storm and now they're burned up. The prophet Elijah himself couldn't do better. Can mean only one of two things. Either the Lord has accepted your offering, or your tunic was an offense to heaven and earth! I'd say the second choice is probably it, eh?"

"But you called me in. From the shore you called. Warned me."

"Well, well. 'Twasn't me, lad. Doesn't matter. Come on home with me. My grandson is near your size. He'll have a spare tunic on hand just for such an occasion. In the meanwhile, take my cloak. What brings y' down this way, boy?" Zadok asked in his customary booming voice.

The former Chief Shepherd of Israel had no difficulty making himself heard above the storm. Severe weather appeared to have no effect on a man who had spent a lifetime in open country, tending the flocks and herds destined for Temple sacrifice. His skin was as tough as the leather patch that covered his left eye. White beard and hair were braided and thus impervious to the fitful wind. A shepherd's staff, no longer needed as a tool for wayward sheep, was a formidable weapon in Zadok's large square hands. "Heard Yeshua was teaching up near Chorazin?"

"That he is."

"Coming south again, is he? Bringing the flock?"

Enveloped in Zadok's cloak, which flapped in the wind, Peniel shouted back, "Just me. Yeshua sent me . . . to carry a message for him."

Zadok seemed to expect more information. Peniel was not inclined to add detail, so the shepherd let the matter drop.

It was after midnight when Peniel and the old man reached the mansion Peniel had spotted on the shore. Over the howl of the gale Zadok explained it was the home of his son-in-law, Simon of Capernaum. "A Pharisee. Respected among the rulers of Israel before his illness. Before Yeshua. Now he calls himself Simon the Leper. Wants everyone to know Yeshua healed him."

Suddenly Yeshua's words made sense. "The shepherd and the leper!" Peniel blurted out.

"Eh?" Zadok returned.

"Something Yeshua told me," Peniel said.

Although the rest of the house appeared to be asleep, Simon waited beside the doorway, holding aloft a lamp. He shielded its flame from the blow. He was in his late thirties, handsome, and well groomed. Six inches shorter than Zadok, he had dark hair and a beard. His mouth curved in a curious smile as he stared at Peniel's eyes. "You found him."

Zadok shook the rain from his clothes. "It's him, just as the boy said it was. Come south from Yeshua's camp. Take a good look, y' two. Aye. Feast your eyes and know! Peniel the blind, this is Simon the Leper."

"Shalom and welcome Peniel," Simon exclaimed, ushering Peniel into his hallway. "It's a foul night! No time to be out! Here, sit down while my servant removes your sandals."

"I've lost my shoes, sir. And my clothes as well, I'm afraid." Peniel knew what a comic figure he appeared, wrapped in Zadok's cloak. Miles too long for him, the hem of the garment dragged on the ground and the shoulders slumped off Peniel's slender body.

Simon smiled. He asked the air, "Where to begin?"

Zadok growled, "Under my cloak he's naked as Adam. Found him hiding in a fishing boat. Don't ask where his things got off to. Swallowed into the abyss. He'll need clothes before food, I should think."

Simon called, "Jotham. Jotham, will you help me, please?"

A sleepy-looking youth just past bar mitzvah age appeared. Simon introduced his son. "Jotham, this is Peniel ben Yahtzar. Like your grandfather, he is a great friend of Yeshua. About your size, I'd say. Please lay out a fresh tunic and robe. Sandals too."

Minutes later an elderly servant led Peniel upstairs to an empty bedchamber. A lamp burned beside the bed. A basin of water, soap, and a towel were on a stand on the opposite wall. Clothes were laid out as if he had been expected.

Peniel washed away the sand and donned a fine linen tunic. The fabric was soft and cool against his skin. He was given a richly brocaded robe tied with a sash and new sandals.

Peniel found the dinner company gathered in a room just off the central terrace of the house. The wind had lessened, but in its place a steady downpour came through the opening in the roof into a pool beneath.

At table were Zadok and Simon, both clearly weary from the late hour but eager to hear news from the north.

Cold duck, bread, and lamb chops were heaped up before Peniel. He gave the latest news around mouthfuls of supper.

The offer of refuge made by the Nabatean king sparked interest in Zadok. "Aye. Old King Aretas liked the way Yochanan the Baptizer preached against Herod Antipas' divorcing Aretas' daughter and marrying Herodias. I do believe Aretas regretted that he couldn't save the Baptizer from the axe."

Peniel continued, "Many say Yeshua is the Baptizer raised from the dead. I thought perhaps the rumor has reached the Nabatean palace in Petra."

Simon the Leper leaned on the table. "But will Yeshua go? Will he cross over the Jordan until the danger's past? take refuge in Nabatea?"

Peniel wiped his chin. "I don't know. I keep my ears open. But I don't know. The other talmidim, the Twelve, thought it was a grand plan. But that doesn't mean Yeshua agrees."

Zadok selected a lamb chop and jabbed the air with it for emphasis as he spoke. "Aye. It's all written in the Book. Every detail. What was. What is. What will be."

Simon asked, "What's in it for Aretas? for Nabatea?"

Zadok considered the question. "I met King Aretas when he was still a young prince. Aye. That was some thirty-two years ago in Beth-lehem. A Persian astronomer served his father's court in Petra the year the great star appeared in Israel's constellation of the Two Fish. Aretas was a young man when he came to Beth-lehem to see the baby. He told me that when the star first appeared, the wise men of Nabatea studied the archives and discovered a prophecy about the coming King of Israel that had been given in ancient times by the prophet Balaam to King Balak near the River Arnon."

Simon whispered, "By River Arnon. In the land of Moab. The heart of the present-day kingdom of Nabatea."

"Aye. The very same. Israel had not yet entered the Promised Land. They camped beside Arnon. Balaam had been summoned by King Balak to curse Israel. Instead Balaam prophesied blessings upon them by the command of the Eternal." The old man closed his eye and lifted his chin as he rasped out the prophecy. *"This is the message of Balaam son of Beor, the prophecy of the man whose eyes see clearly, who hears the words of God, who has knowledge from the Most High, who sees a vision from the Almighty! I see him, but not in the present time! I perceive him, but far in the distant future. A star will rise from Ya'acov. A scepter will emerge from Israel."*[49]

Peniel had not heard that youthful Aretas, Prince of Nabatea, had also followed the star to a lambing cave in Beth-lehem and paid homage to the infant King of Israel! "But that same prophecy says the King of Israel will crush Moab! Wasn't Aretas afraid?"

Zadok continued the history. "Prince Aretas was an intelligent lad. Out to make alliances with the future king of Israel. Prince Aretas came with a delegation of many princes and wise men from the Eastern kingdoms. First they went to the palace of Herod the Great to inquire. But old Herod had no little sons to replace the ones he murdered. And not one of those four Herodian princes who remained, Antipas among them, had a drop of Hebrew blood in their veins. So the old butcher king knew well that the prophecy about the star and the scepter of Israel could not be about him or his sons. He inquired of the Torah scholars where the true King of Israel would be born.

"The writings of the prophet Micah foretold the place—Beth-lehem, city of our shepherd-king, David.[50] Thus the princes of the East were directed to Beth-lehem. They came to my home where the mother and child and her husband stayed. These princes and ambassadors from the east brought gifts for the true King of Israel. A way of forming a bond between nations, it was. Proper protocol. And those of us who witnessed such things had high hopes in those first days.

"But Herod the Great would not let it be. So that was the beginning of sorrows for many of my clan and my family."

Deep in thought, Simon rubbed his forehead. "I see it all clearly now. I remember my father speaking of the day Herod the Great destroyed the genealogy records in the Temple. And then the lie was circulated that Herod's son Antipas was also born in Beth-lehem years before Yeshua's birth."

Zadok explained, "Aretas believed the lie. For that very reason King Aretas gave his daughter in marriage to Herod Antipas. Aye. He knew Herod the Great had killed all the infant boys of Beth-lehem after the visit of the Eastern princes. Aretas reckoned Yeshua had died in the slaughter as well. When Aretas heard that Prince Herod Antipas had been born in Beth-lehem, he believed that Antipas could be the rising star in Balaam's prophecy. It was natural Aretas would want his house allied with that of Herod the Great."

"What a shock to Aretas when Herod Antipas divorced his daughter," Simon ventured.

"Aye." Zadok nodded. "Disgrace beyond measure." He stretched and glanced at the candle. He directed his next question to Peniel. "Now, there's the background of the present dispute. What word do y' bring of Yeshua's plans?"

"There is some . . . disagreement in camp," Peniel said at last. "Some think Yeshua should do more to keep the crowds of people coming. A great sign they're asking for. Others think he's afraid of Herod Antipas."

Zadok rumbled, "Afraid of that bag of guts? Not afraid, not ever, I'll wager. But right to be cautious. Antipas is a murderous scavenger like his father was, right enough, and his wife is worse."

"Some who have been healed by Yeshua are denying it now out of fear," Simon noted.

When Peniel acknowledged he'd already heard that report, Simon continued, "I'm ready to speak up—anxious to, in fact. But the Temple authorities—all Saduccees and cozy with Tetrarch Antipas—got in the way! They're spreading the story that what I had wasn't leprosy at all . . . got better all by itself, they claim!"

"False prophets, every one," Zadok muttered. "No better than in the days of old Israel when the priests of Ba'al were here. What we need is another Elijah to come and slaughter them all! Call down fire from heaven, eh?"

Peniel nodded. "It would simplify things."

Zadok said, "Comparison's exact, come to that. Antipas and Herodias couldn't be more like old King Ahab and Queen Jezebel, eh? Alike as peas in a pod. Jezebel gave Elijah grief in his day too."

"But never succeeded in cutting off his head," Simon remarked softly, referring to the executed prophet, Yochanan the Baptizer.

"No, you're right there. Thought the Baptizer might be Elijah, but—" Zadok shook his head sadly—"Antipas would still like to be king of all Israel. Guess he doesn't believe the prophecy about the Lion of the tribe of Judah any more than his father did."

Peniel looked eager for more of the tale. "More prophecy? Is there another story to go with it?"

Zadok smiled. "Aye. Simple enough. In the *Book of Beginnings*, next to last chapter, Father Ya'acov is getting ready to die. So he blesses all his sons. At a time like that . . . a man like that . . ."

Peniel pointed to himself, referring to the meaning of his name. "I know. He saw God face-to-face!"

Zadok agreed and continued, "Such a man has the gift to see into the future. Well, when Ya'acov comes to his boy Judah, he says, *'The scepter will not depart from Judah, nor the ruler's staff from his descendants, until the coming of him to whom it belongs, the one whom all nations will obey.'*"[51]

Peniel had heard this prophecy many times in his days as a beggar beside Nicanor Gate. The Messiah would be a descendant of Judah. "Yeshua is from the tribe of Judah," Peniel ventured.

"Aye, lad. That he is. And there's a promise that there'd be a whole line of kings from Judah, true enough. But right now I want y' to think on the small words within the prophecy. *'Until* the coming of him to whom it belongs.'"

"I think I see what you mean. The line of kings from the tribe of Judah would someday stop, and then a non-Jew would become king. That would be a signal that the greatest king of all Israel was soon to come."

Zadok slapped a heavy palm on the table, making the plates jump and rattle. "And do y' know when the first non-Jewish king actually ruled the land? I don't mean a foreign conqueror, for there have been many, but an actual king who ruled Israel from Yerushalayim and bore the title King of the Jews?"

It was silent around the table for a time; then Simon ventured, "When Herod the Great became king. *Until* Messiah comes every king will be descended from Judah. *Until . . . until.* I hadn't thought of it before now. Not ever."

Zadok nodded his approval. "Simon, your father knew what the prophecy meant. That's why Herod had him murdered. My brother Onias knew the truth of it. That's why Onias was tortured. Why he fled to Alexandria. Many of us knew when Herod the Great became king that our Messiah must be born in Herod's lifetime! Because Herod, being a non-Jew and not from the tribe of Judah, was the first exception to the prophecy made by Ya'acov to his son Judah.

"Why do y' think the old butcher king was in such an uproar when the wise men came to tell him the star of a new king of the Jews had appeared, eh? And in Beth-lehem! City of the ancient kings! Herod, that old Idumean fraud, knew he was no true king! No descendant of Judah! The scepter of Israel had not departed from the descendants of Judah *until* Herod! The prophecy says only descendants of Judah will hold the scepter . . . *until* . . . the one to whom the scepter truly belongs comes to claim it. Herod's reign fulfills the *until* in the prophecy!"

Simon whispered in astonishment, "And now the one to whom the scepter of Israel's kingship truly belongs is here! Yeshua! The star! He'll take it back again! Living among us!"

Zadok continued, "The vineyard of Israel is rightly Yeshua's, Son of David, Lion of the tribe of Judah! Herod Antipas will do all he can to keep possession of it. Failing that, Antipas'll try to kill Yeshua and steal his kingdom. And he'll be after killing any who are living proof of Yeshua's power. A blind man who can see. A leper who is clean."

The discussion continued long into the night. Deep into the third watch, the threesome finally climbed the stairs and went to bed.

Hearing the branches of trees scrape the house like daggers being drawn from their sheaths, it was a long time before Peniel fell asleep, clutching the linen-wrapped lavender bud.

It was a true council of evil. Antipas and Herodias, Gadot and Acteon, Ona and Shamen assembled in the dark chamber under the tetrarch's palace during the third watch of the night.

"Well?" Herod Antipas tapped jeweled fingers on the arm of his chair.

Ona crossed her arms over her ample chest in satisfaction. "Yeshua of Nazareth has been visited by emissaries from King Aretas. The Nabateans invited the healer to come to their kingdom, promising him safety and mentioning the death of the Baptizer as a strong reason to agree."

Antipas glared hatefully at Herodias. "I knew it! Yeshua is a traitor! Aretas will use him as a puppet. The Nabateans will claim they're supporting the rightful heir to the Jewish throne. Thousands of *am ha aretz* will join the rebels and the troops of King Aretas on the other side of the Jordan."

Herodias rubbed his bulbous nose. "Calm yourself, Antipas. If Aretas tries such a thing, Rome will crush him. Then you can add Nabatea to your holdings. But for now, do we even know if Yeshua agreed?"

Shamen took the lead in replying, "No, my lady. But after that visit he has . . . disappeared from the area around Capernaum. No one seems to know where he's gone."

Wringing his hands, Antipas fretted, "There, you see? He's crossed into my brother's territory. Philip has never liked me. Always been jealous. They're in league against me, like I said."

Herodias aimed a painted talon at Gadot. "You two were charged with locating Yeshua. Well?"

Gadot gulped several times and could not respond. Acteon blustered, "No one knows where he went. But we do have other news. We heard a rumor. Susanna and Manaen bar Talmai were seen in Capernaum. Seeking the Rabbi from Nazareth."

"That's not important now," Antipas said petulantly.

Herodias' sharp glance silenced her husband. "Perhaps it is. Where did Manaen go after that?"

"We heard . . . Magdala," Acteon answered.

Gadot finally found his voice. "But we checked there on our way back here. The healer's mother lives in Magdala. But Yeshua hasn't been seen there lately, nor did we see Manaen."

Shamen's head was turned to one side as though he was listening to something on the stairs. Ona tugged on her husband's sleeve, and he bent his ear next to her lips. She whispered to him for an instant, then said brightly, "My lord Antipas, this is excellent news. Perhaps we cannot, at this time, locate Yeshua. But he will come to you if you make his mother your . . . guest."

Shamen sniffed the air, then gestured for the others to continue their conversation, uninterrupted.

While Antipas chewed his lower lip thoughtfully, Herodias replied for him, "Well then, splendid. I should like to meet the woman who claims she became pregnant without a man's help. Bring his mother here . . . and do whatever you like with Manaen bar Talmai."

Padding silently toward the spiral staircase with a dagger in his hand, Shamen lingered at the bottom for a moment, then darted upward. A sudden cry of discovery was succeeded by a brief scuffle; then the assassin returned to the other conspirators.

He prodded Kuza ahead of him with the tip of the knife. "Found this one lurking on the landing, my lord. Listening to our plans."

Kuza protested, "No, I . . ." but his guilt was plain for all to see.

Blows fell like rain on Kuza's bloody back. Acteon on one side and Gadot on the other alternately slashed the steward with split cane rods.

While Herodias stood by looking on, Herod Antipas raged. Flecks of spittle flew from the tetrarch's chin. "Where did she go, Kuza? Your wife? Your house is deserted. Where has she gone?"

"I don't know," Kuza whispered wearily. The same question had been repeated as many times as the whips had fallen. The legal limit was thirty-nine stripes. But in the tetrarch's dungeon torture never stopped until he received the answer he sought, tired of the sport, or the victim died.

"I know she's gone across the Jordan!" Antipas' voice rose to a screech. "She's carrying tales about me to my brother, is that it? Telling him lies to use against me with Rome?"

Kuza shook his head.

Gadot took a step backward as drips of blood flew upward. The eunuch made a face at the gore. Acteon continued the beating, while Gadot rolled up the sleeves of his silk robe before resuming.

"Or has she gone all the way to Damascus? Did you send her to the governor there? How much did King Aretas pay you to spread lies about me?"

"Never . . . betrayed you," Kuza maintained.

"Then tell me where she is!"

Kuza fainted, slumping sideways. His body dangled by the wrists from leather straps.

Antipas wanted the beating to continue, but Herodias argued, "This is boring, Antipas. Kuza is a coward—always has been. If he knew anything he'd have talked before this. Nor can anything he knows hurt us. Throw him out and let's be done."

There was a ditch at the side of the palace where the tetrarch's garbage was dumped. Gadot and Acteon dragged Kuza's unresponsive body to the edge of the pit and rolled him into it.

23

Susanna slept sitting up. Her back was propped against the cool stone of their room at the inn. Manaen rested with his head in her lap. From the street she heard the steps of the watchman on patrol.

Susanna opened her eyes with a start. The lamp was guttering. Shadows danced on the walls. A narrow window framed a sky dusted with stars. There was no breeze to move the torpid air. For a moment she did not remember where they were.

Then, inhaling deeply, she caught the aroma of the Sea of the Galil, the strong scent of musty land and pickled fish, the soured wine on Manaen's ragged breath.

Magdala. Yes. They had come in search of a miracle, in search of Yeshua. But the miracle worker had fled the district of the Galil in fear for His life. No one knew where Yeshua had gone.

There was no hope left for Susanna. No signs. No wonders. No return of Manaen's vision nor restoration of their love for one another. It had all been for nothing.

The cry of an infant drifted up from a little house nearby. Manaen stirred and moaned softly.

Susanna ran her fingers through his hair. "Hush now, little one. Don't cry. Hush."

Surprisingly childlike, Manaen asked, "When will it be day?"

"Not for a while yet."

He rolled over, his face turned upwards. He had not remembered his blindness yet. The reality of loss had not penetrated his consciousness. "Susanna?"

"Yes, love?"

"The lamp is out."

She looked toward the feeble flame and did not tell him. "Yes. And the moon is down."

"A dream. I had a dream. Alone in an open boat. It was small, too small for the sea. There was a storm. Waves crashing over the side. I was sinking, going down. But there was . . . someone. Someone."

"I'm here."

"No. That's not what I mean. I was *looking for someone* . . . the lightning forked and struck the water. In the flash I thought I saw him . . . saw *him* . . . walking toward me. Arms out. In the light. An instant. So quick. He was there."

Susanna dared not ask who he had seen. His dead brother? His father? Who had been revealed in the instant of a bolt of lightning? "Just a dream," she soothed.

"Are there clouds in the sky tonight?"

She replied, "No. No clouds. Stars. Millions of stars."

"I remember. Yes. In the boat. Knowing I was blind. But the clouds parted and I saw the stars. I looked up, wondering. Wondering if anyone was looking back at me. And just for a second . . . someone."

"We fell asleep on the floor. We should get in bed."

He sat up suddenly and grasped her hand. "Susanna. Where did the old woman say she was?"

"Who?"

"His mother."

"Whose mother?"

"The Prophet's mother. Where is she? I thought I heard it. Was I dreaming? Or is she really here in Magdala?"

"You mean Yeshua's mother?"

"That's it. Yes, I remember now. I was drunk. But . . . did I hear right? His mother. Close by."

"A mile south. A charity. A house where women and children take refuge. A villa on the shore."

Manaen jumped to his feet. "Take me to the place, Susanna. If she's there I must . . . must see her. Speak with her. Maybe she can help us find her son."

The air was alive with the tingle of lightning-tickled sky. Peniel's hair stood out from his head. There was a metallic tang to each breath. He was thirsty. He reached for a jug on the bedside table, but it was empty. Had he drunk it all earlier? He could not remember. Somehow the absence of water made him even thirstier. But in that same minute he became aware of the presence of someone in the room with him. Someone watching him from the chair in the corner.

Shalom, Peniel, saluted a deep voice.

"Zadok? Is that you? I'm thirsty, Zadok."

No, not Zadok. But we've met before. Another night.

Peniel knew he must be dreaming again. "Who are you?"

And then again tonight, when you were in the sea.

"I thought you were Zadok."

Some have called me the great Zadiyk, one of the Righteous Ones. But I'm just . . . just a m-man. I warned you about the lightning, remember?

The figure in the room was white-bearded. The hood of his crimson mantle was back, revealing a stern visage. The slight stutter gave a hint to his identity.

"*Ulu Ush-pi-zin.* Welcome, exalted guest. I haven't even got water to offer you. But there's food downstairs if you're hungry."

Water and bread. Always provided by Yahweh. Yahweh-Yireh! Even when I was afraid we had reached the end of everything.

Peniel snapped his fingers. "You're Mosheh! Yahweh fed your people with water from the rock. Manna to eat in the morning and quail in the evening."

You haven't forgotten. Good. The details are as important today as they were in those forty years we wandered.

"Thank you for getting me out of the lake before the lightning bolt fell. You were right; I was a fool. Have you a story for me?"

A story. It's why I was sent. I will speak of events long past and yet how men's hearts are unchanged down to today. And even so, the meaning of the story won't be what you think.

"Are you going to talk in riddles?"

All life is a riddle. A tangle of riddles. Why men do or don't do what is right. Why men chose to believe a lie over the truth. All a riddle.

"Well spoken. Point taken. But when you led Israel out of slavery and through the sea, nothing was as bad then as it is now. People then could not have been as hard-hearted as they are now."

I didn't lead them. I'm just a m-man. We were protected and led by the pillar of fire, the great cloud in which the presence of Yahweh descended to earth! Messiah, the angel of the Lord's presence in whom His name lives! It was He who dwelt with the cloud! He who led us! He who parted the sea before us and closed it over the heads of our enemies. Here, Peniel, is an important truth, forgotten by nearly everyone. Listen! Mark well this lesson!

Written in the Book of Beginnings,
The Name of the Almighty and Eternal One God
Who created heaven and earth is
ELoHiYM.
The same letters of The Name form a command:
EL HaYaM! Which means "Into the Sea!"
The Lord had cast our enemies into the sea, yet still we doubted. Still we lived in bondage to our own fears.

Peniel thought about the stories of the crossing and after. Yes, he had to admit, the times had been bad indeed. "Point taken. Even with all the Lord did, the people still didn't trust him. No sign was enough. Is that it? People have always been blind, I suppose. Stupid. No miracle is enough to make anyone believe. But where's the lesson in that?"

It's here.

Lightning crackled outside the window. The features of Mosheh were clear only for an instant. He was smiling—smiling, as if he knew a secret.

The Hebrew word for thunder or rain cloud, anan, *also m-means "covering."*

"Like the protection given by the Almighty to his people?"

Well spoken. The protection of Adonai ELoHiYM was before us in the day. A pillar of fire revolving at our backs through the night. And yet the people did not trust that His presence was enough.

The cloud led us on and on for two months. Up a mile above the level of the sea, between two granite mountain ranges, we entered onto a vast high desert plain called El Rahah, "El's Provision." There were running streams to water our flocks. The tents of Israel dotted the land. At the head of the valley, jutting out like the prow of a great ship, loomed the mountain of Sinai. Its name means "Mountain of the Thorn."

Two months exactly after we left Egypt we arrived and I went up onto the mountain. And Yahweh called to me from the mountain and said—

Suddenly Peniel heard a voice in the distant thunder echoing in a canyon:

Mosheh! This is what you are to say to the house of Ya'acov and the sons of Isra'el:

Yahweh says this to his chosen ones,

You saw what I did to Egypt with your own eyes!

Remember!

The sea opened.

You and your children crossed on dry ground.

The enemy and all his horses and chariots pursued to bring you back into *bondage!*

Remember for the sake of my love for you what I commanded from heaven!

By the power and in the blessed name of

ELoHiYM!

Force of evil who seek to destroy my beloved children! They are free from bondage!

ELoHiYM commands! Darkness, pursue my children no farther! EL HaYaM! Be cast into the sea!

And with the roar of my judgment against those who had drowned the Hebrew babies, the sea closed over horse and rider, chariots and charioteers!

And I myself carried you on eagles' wings as a mother eagle lifts her fledgling young upon her wings lest they fall upon the rocks and perish! And brought you to myself! Now if you obey my voice and you keep my covenant then you will be to me a precious possession out of all the nations! Although the whole earth is mine, you will be for me a kingdom of priests and a holy nation![52]

Then Yahweh said to me:

I AM going to come to you in a thick cloud so the people themselves can hear me as I speak to you. Then they will always have confidence in you.[53]

This was not only a mark of Yahweh's approval of my leadership; it was also a kindness. You see, He would still have been the Almighty even if the cloud had not appeared, yet He gave the people that visible sign of His presence out of understanding of their weakness. That's what signs are for. Also the cloud was to protect them. If they saw the true appearance of I AM as He really is, no human could survive.

So the people agreed to do all the Lord asked.

I set up a boundary of twelve pillars, one for each tribe, at the base of the m-mountain, to prevent anyone from touching it lest they die. For two days all Israel purified themselves. On the morning of the third day there was a powerful thunder and lightning storm, followed by the blast on a ram's horn!

Listen!

Peniel heard it clearly, as though the mournful call of the shofar was right outside his window. One long blast. Three shorter. Nine rapid calls. One long note to end the cycle.

Tekiah _____
Shevarim _____ _____ _____
Teruah ___ ___ ___ ___ ___ ___ ___ ___ ___
Tekiah _____

Mosheh waited until the echo died away and then he spoke again.

So Sinai was covered with a pitch-black cloud, roiling like the smoke of a furnace! The mountain shook with a violent earthquake, and the trumpet blew even louder.

Each pattern of the ram's horn brought to our minds the memory of Avraham offering his son to the Lord on Mount Moriah! The knife lifted up! The Lord staying his hand, providing a ram caught in the thicket instead. And the Lord promising Avraham that through his line would come salvation for the world and the final atonement for all sin! Each blast of the ram's horn in our ear proclaimed a prophecy of the provision yet to come.

Tekiah! *One blast. The sealing of the covenant!*

Shevarim! *Three blasts. The covenant fractured, broken by our disobedience.*

Teruah! *Nine blasts. The Spirit of the Lord calling and shaking our hearts to* teshuvah, *to repent and return to Him!*

Tekiah! One blast. The final atonement for sin. The sacrificed Lamb of Yahweh lifted up on a pole. Driven into the ground as a sign and fixed in place eternally. By its blood canceling all guilt and sealing the covenant of mercy between God and man forever!

We heard and trembled at the trumpet blast.

And then, more terrifying than that, Yahweh came down upon the Mountain of Thorns. Then the Lord called to me to come up.

Yahweh said:

Come up here to me, and bring along Aaron, Nadab, Abihu, and seventy of Israel's leaders. All of them must worship at a distance. You alone, Mosheh, are allowed to come near to the Lord. The others must not come too close. And remember, none of the other people are allowed to climb on the mountain at all.[54]

So this was how the people were to show they agreed to the terms: Aaron, the very first high priest, and his two sons and the seventy elders went up to ratify the covenant with Yahweh on behalf of all the others.

A sacrifice of bulls was made at the foot of the mountain, and the bulls were presented as a peace offering to the Lord. Half the blood was splashed on the altar, and with the rest I sprinkled the people, confirming that this was now a binding blood covenant between Yahweh and His people.

Then the seventy elders, Aaron and his two sons, and I all went partway back up the mountain. There, in the very presence of the Lord, we shared a meal. The seventy elders, Aaron, his sons, and I all saw the Lord enthroned on a judgment pavement made of sparkling sapphire.

Now here is something important. Aaron—who was my brother and was to be chosen as Israel's first high priest—well, his name comes from a word that means "conception." Pay attention! The name is important! In Aaron were all the future hereditary high priests, all the sacrifices, all the ceremonies of cleansing and repentance and thanksgiving, all the Days of Atonement . . . for as long as his line lasted.

Peniel pondered that. "So at the exact moment of the giving of the Law, the Lord foresaw all the future generations . . . everything that would come after? And that the sons of Aaron would one day be replaced by false priests like Caiaphas and Annas?"

Exactly. And the Lord already knew that as good as His rules were, they would not be enough to restore humans to a complete relationship with Him. No generation . . . no individual . . . has ever kept all the Law. The covenant is broken to pieces. Priests rule in Yerushalayim who are not sons of Aaron.

A king not from David's line reigns over the people. And yet the true High Priest and King of Israel lives among men!

Peniel said, "Yeshua, you mean!"

What does the prophet Isaias say? "We are all infected and impure with sin. When we proudly display our righteous deeds, we find they are but filthy rags."[55]

"And that is why Yeshua teaches that a man has to be born again to enter the Kingdom of God."

Mosheh nodded. *Even after the cloud and the thunder and the lightning and the banquet in the presence of the Almighty, it wasn't long before the proof arrived of how bad at keeping covenants we humans are.*

"What do you mean?"

Mosheh's voice was full of old grief. *You remember Aaron's oldest sons, Nadab and Abihu? Fine young men, this pair of brothers. But full of ambition and eager to try on their new honor in front of the nation. Proud they had been called up the mountain, prouder still that they were next in line to their father as priests.*

Peniel was suspicious that all this preparation was not leading to a happy conclusion. "And . . . something went wrong?"

Mosheh agreed. *Book of Vayikra, Parashah 26: "Aaron's sons Nadab and Abihu put coals of fire in their incense burners and sprinkled incense over it. In this way they disobeyed the Lord by burning before Him a different kind of fire than He had commanded. So fire blazed forth from the Lord's presence and burned them up, and they died there before the Lord."*[56]

Peniel was stunned. "But . . . but . . . was it the wrong incense? the wrong coals? the wrong time? Did they say the wrong words? What was it?"

Mosheh spoke very carefully as if anxious for Peniel to understand. *It doesn't matter how they disobeyed. Get hold of this: They were bursting with pride and self-righteousness, thinking they could get to God their own way. They focused on themselves rather than on the Lord. So it is with those who now rule in Yerushalayim, and for every human who thinks he can reach God in his own way! "When we proudly display our righteous deeds, we find they are but filthy rags," remember? The cloud on the mountain was a sign of the absolute holiness of the Lord. What does King David ask in the psalms? "Who may climb the mountain of the Lord? Who may stand in his holy place? Only those whose hands and heart are pure, who do not worship idols and never tell lies."*[57]

Peniel shook his head. "Doesn't that rule out everyone? All of us have idols of one sort or another. All of us sin. We all have fallen short of the perfection of the Lord! All of us are guilty!"

Mosheh's voice grew fainter. *All but one. All . . . but . . . one. The Holy One from Israel! The Ram yet to be our atonement! The Provision of Yahweh! Listen to what Yahweh promised:*

I will raise up a prophet like you from among their fellow Israel-ites. I will tell that prophet what to say, and he will tell the people everything I command him. I will personally deal with anyone who will not listen to the messages the prophet proclaims on my behalf.[58]

And Adonai said:

See, I AM sending my angel before you to lead you safely to the land I have prepared for you. Pay attention to him and obey all his instructions. Do not rebel against him, for he will not forgive your sins. He is my representative—he bears my name.[59]

Don't despair, Peniel. The Prophet, the Priest, the Angel of the Name, The One Who Is and Who Was and Who Will Be, The True King of Israel, now lives among men, and you have seen His face!

24

he next day Peniel followed the shoreline and found the compound where Yeshua's mother lived. High white walls and the
red-tile roof of the Roman-style villa glistened clean and bright
in the morning sunlight. Once the residence of a wealthy courtesan, the
structure and grounds had been converted into a house of charity.

Its present purpose, the care of needy women and children, caused
as much consternation in the community as it had in the days when
men visited the former owner at all hours of the day and night.

Letters burned into the massive oak gate on the exterior proclaimed the name: Beth Chesed, "House of Mercy."

Peniel knocked on the gate and listened for the sound of voices
within. A sparrow fluttered onto an overhanging branch and cocked its
head, seeming to listen with him. No one answered. He knocked again.

Silence. The bird fluttered over the wall.

Peniel nervously reached into the leather bag to touch the message
Yeshua had sent with him. It was still there. And here he was. But where
was Yeshua's mother? Where were the residents of Beth Chesed?

He cleared his throat and gave a shout. "Shalom! Anyone there? It's
Peniel ben Yahtzar!"

Nothing. No sound.

Curious.

He scratched his chin. An old man with a basket of apricots on his shoulder walked toward him. Faded eyes relayed a furtive warning.

Behind him were two Herodian guards. They scowled at Peniel, walked to the end of the lane, turned, discussed something, and came back. Halting, they blocked Peniel's retreat.

"What do you want here, boy?"

Peniel glanced at the old man with the apricots. No help there. The fellow took one look at the confrontation and scuttled around the corner.

Peniel stammered. "I . . . I . . . was . . . looking for someone."

The bull-like Herodian crossed brawny arms. "He's looking for someone."

The short, potbellied soldier spat. "This is a house for women of ill reputation. Full of bastard children. Unmarried, pregnant-type women. Divorced women. Such like as that. What would the likes of you be looking for here, boy?"

"Came looking for . . . someone." Peniel swallowed hard, surprised at his stupidity.

"Someone? Well then. Well. Well."

The bull scrutinized Peniel. "How old are you, boy?"

Peniel stared at the cobblestones, not daring to raise his head. "Seventeen, sir." His heart pounded.

"You know that none but whores and bastard children live within, eh?"

Peniel jerked his head down once in acknowledgment. Shame colored his cheeks.

The bully stepped closer. "You know why we're here? Eh?"

Peniel shook his head from side to side. "No, sir."

"We're standing guard in case that bastard Nazarene stops by to visit his mother. We'll hustle him off to visit the tetrarch, who has some questions as to why an illegitimate fellow with no father is wandering the countryside claiming to be God's Son."

Peniel swiped sweat from his brow. "I don't know anything about that."

A finger poked into his shoulder hard. Pushing. Pushing. "Who would come to such a place, eh? Are you one of them? One of them disciples maybe? You a friend of the Nazarene?"

The rattle of a bolt on the opposite side of the gate disrupted the taunting.

The bar flew up and the gate swung wide, revealing a Roman centurion in full uniform. He called, "You there! Stop!"

The guards stumbled back as though they had been struck a blow.

Marcus Longinus! Peniel recognized the voice. The centurion was one among many Gentiles who quietly approved of Yeshua.

Peniel gaped at him. Why was Marcus Longinus at Beth Chesed?

The Roman scowled at the Herodian mercenaries. "What do you want here?"

"Here on orders, sir."

"On orders," the second mercenary echoed.

Marcus lowered his voice and raised his fist. "Half-wits! Get out of Magdala before I have you flayed alive! You'll ruin everything! Rome has this matter well in hand!"

The two Herodian soldiers blinked fearfully at the centurion. "Yes, sir. Yes, sir. Yes, beg your pardon. Of course. The tetrarch Antipas didn't . . . wasn't—"

Marcus' tone was threatening. "Then inform your master. Governor Pilate is conducting his own investigation, eh? You botch this up, who do you think will be blamed?" Marcus drew his finger slowly across his neck to make a point. "You."

Clapping his arm around Peniel's shoulders protectively, Marcus drew Peniel in. "Well, boy! You're back before I thought. Well done! Did you get it? Good. There's a good fellow." Marcus kicked the door shut in the faces of the troopers and bolted it.

Peniel stuttered. "What? What? What? Marcus?" Even the lavender fragrance of the garden did not calm him.

Marcus put a finger to his lips and listened for the retreating footsteps of Herod's soldiers. Then he asked urgently, "Who sent you?"

"Yeshua. A message for his mother."

At the mention of Yeshua, Mary emerged into the courtyard. "Shalom, Peniel! Shalom!"

Her face betrayed strain. She embraced him as he drew out the parchment.

He felt clumsy, inept. "Sorry. Sorry. Shalom. I've not done this at all well, I think. Those fellows were coming toward the gate when I arrived. Caught me."

Mary read the note, then passed it to Marcus.

The centurion studied the message in grim silence. He scowled. "So then, Yeshua knows as well. Yes, we all know what Antipas is up to. The question is, how do we protect you?"

Mary looked up at the silent balconies. "I've sent all my mothers and children away into the hills. One at a time. To my family. Trusted friends. Miryam's taken a dozen to Judea. Only Carta and me left. Every day the guards are outside. And in the night. I've been hoping it would die down. Hoping Antipas would turn his eyes away from us for a while."

Marcus was firm. "He won't. Lady Mary, you can't stay in the Galil. Your presence within the grasp of Herod Antipas makes Yeshua vulnerable. Just a matter of time. Yeshua's message is clear. It's safer in Philip's territory. He's right. Across the lake to Bethsaida. For a while. I can hire a boat. You and Peniel must sail tonight. I stopped by to fetch Carta. I have need of him. So few men can be trusted. And I have to warn you the Herodians have turned their filthy minds to the goal of tearing you apart."

Mary raised her chin in a gesture of defiance. "I'm not easily wounded. Not afraid of what they can do to me."

Marcus took her arm and led her indoors to where Carta, his young armor bearer, waited. "Common sense is not fear. Yeshua sent Peniel to bring you to him. Lady Mary, for the sake of your son's life, you must put aside your dreams and leave this place."

Mary smiled enigmatically. Then with a sigh she gazed up to where baby clothes, left behind, still hung on lines above their heads. "Will we ever be allowed back? So many broken hearts mended in this place."

The centurion did not offer hope. "There will be broken hearts to mend no matter where you are. And you'll find them. Carta and I must ride to Caesarea Maritima to meet with Governor Pilate and an emissary from Rome. There's a war brewing in the East. I'm certain of it. King Aretas will have the head of Herod Antipas if he can. I'll give my report. Rome may at last see Antipas and his lackeys for what they are."

Susanna heard the tramp of boots and the clank of armor around the corner of the deserted fish-drying sheds. She tugged Manaen down behind the rows of salting tables. A pair of the tetrarch's guards trudged up the street, not twenty yards from where she and Manaen took shelter.

Manaen was surprisingly calm. "We'll wait here until after dark."

Though no longer stationed in front of the garden wall, Antipas' soldiers constantly patrolled the streets of Magdala. This was Susanna's third attempt to take Manaen to Beth Chesed.

As with the two preceding efforts, they barely got back to concealment before being spotted. Susanna was uncertain why Antipas' men watched the inn. But if they had opportunity to seize Manaen bar Talmai, who had so heinously offended Herod Antipas, they would certainly do so.

Nor would Manaen escape this time at only the cost of his eyes.

Susanna despaired that they would ever reach Mary, ever find out where Yeshua was. Beth Chesed was there, beyond the highway and past the stone ring of an olive press, but it might as well have been across an ocean. Mercy just out of reach was no mercy at all.

"Maybe I can hire a boat to take us home," Susanna admitted at last.

"Not yet . . . behind the tamarack trees in the gully."

Two squads of soldiers arrived at the docks from opposite directions. They talked and laughed together, distracted from their purpose.

Susanna seized the opportunity to lead Manaen toward Beth Chesed. From the fish-drying sheds down to a lakeshore clump of willows; from the screen of willows, around behind a stone watchtower used as a lighthouse. From the lighthouse to the creek bed . . . so far without being spotted. Fifty yards farther were the walls of the villa.

Susanna watched the main road, peering up and down both directions. As she gauged the moment for their run toward the next bit of cover, she failed to notice someone approaching from behind them.

The wind sighing in the trees and the lapping of waves on the shore conspired to hide the sounds of a lone man walking up from the lake. A flash of red and the gleam of sunlight on bronze caught Susanna's eye. A Roman legionary! There was no time to act innocent, skulking here behind the bushes!

The Roman called, "Manaen! Manaen bar Talmai!"

Manaen's response betrayed a measure of relief. "I know that voice. It's Marcus!"

The centurion grasped each of the fugitives by an elbow. "Hurry! We'll talk inside."

And with that he hustled them across the stream course and into the garden gate of Beth Chesed.

Marcus and Manaen stood together by the fountain in the courtyard. Inside the house were Mary, Carta, Susanna, and Peniel. Marcus donned his helmet with its transverse plume of dark red feathers. Manaen heard the centurion cinch his helmet snug under his chin before continuing his instructions.

"Herod Antipas is showing the same madness as the creature who sired him. Rome won't stand for such mismanagement. If Aretas goes to war against Herod Antipas it'll cost Rome in soldiers and lost commerce. You need to lay low, Manaen, until Antipas is brought into line."

Manaen put out his hand and waited till Marcus took it. "The fishing boat. I'm sorry you won't be going with us."

Marcus clapped him on the shoulder. "All of you go down to the stone cottage at the end of the second watch. Place a signal lantern on the pillar. The boatman will come in close to the strand. You'll need to wade out twenty yards, he said. The lake will be full of fishing boats at that hour. Easy to slip across to Bethsaida unnoticed." Marcus sounded gruff, like a Roman officer merely doing his duty. "Mary says he'll be there. And when you see him—"

"See." Manaen held the word like a jewel.

"Yes. Do this for me: Warn Yeshua to stay out of the Galil. For his own sake. Even Bethsaida isn't far enough."

Manaen appreciated the warning but doubted whether a Jewish rabbi would accept Roman advice delivered by such an impious messenger as himself.

"And if I don't . . . see . . . Yeshua?"

"You will see him. Do for him what I can't. Tribune Felix always said you would've made a fine Roman officer if you hadn't been born a Jew. Strong as a mule."

Manaen laughed for the first time in weeks. "A mule with blinders on. Tie me to a mill wheel and I can tread the grain with the best of them."

Manaen heard Marcus buckle on his sword belt. "Carta and I must go. Believe this, Manaen. Yeshua can heal you. Look at Carta. His back was broken. And Peniel."

"I'm not even a religious Jew. Stubborn as a mule too. Why should he help the likes of me?"

"Why Peniel? Why Carta? What do I know about you? Stubborn, yes. You don't hold your liquor well. You're well liked by Romans because you frequently lose at dice. None of us are worthy, my friend. But would you bet your eyes that he won't help you? It's worth the roll of the dice to ask him."

For Manaen the long hours of waiting for the fishing boat that would carry them back to Bethsaida moved as ponderously as the seasons. In his world of eternal darkness sunset did not matter, moonrise was of no consequence, and the passing of unmarked minutes remained interminable.

He jumped at every noise. Sentences begun by him dangled in mid-air when a sudden sound transfixed him.

Manaen was not up to this challenge. Now he was responsible to get not only Susanna but also Yeshua's mother to safety? Why didn't Marcus summon a cohort of soldiers to take them across the border? Or couldn't the centurion have waited until the band of fugitives boarded the ship and left Magdala astern?

Peniel spoke encouragement to him, told him Yeshua would certainly heal his eyes. The boy who Manaen knew had been blind now had sight; there was no denying that fact. But how or whether Yeshua caused the change, Manaen was not certain.

There was another problem as well: Even if Yeshua was capable of such deeds, would He perform a wonder like that for Manaen?

In examining his past life, Manaen was brutally honest with himself. Before he was blind he had given no consideration to spiritual matters. He had lived for himself alone, for pleasure, and for the moment. The Almighty owed him no favors on that accounting.

And in the months since he became sightless? While it was true

Manaen had been innocent of the charges against him and viciously abused, was that enough for him to deserve special treatment? Hadn't he continued to live for himself alone, absorbed in his own inner struggle, without regard to needs of others?

Maybe Manaen had merely gotten what he deserved. Perhaps this was justice. His pride would not allow him to envision a future for himself that contained happiness. If that were the case, why not end his miserable life?

Somewhere a night bird called. Manaen directed his attention there. Was it real or a signal? Was the house surrounded by Antipas' killers?

Mary, in quiet conversation with Susanna, said, "It's so important you get somewhere safe. Out of reach of Herod Antipas altogether. You'll want to enjoy your baby without fear."

The bird stopped trilling. Manaen relaxed his vigilance. What was it Mary had said? A baby? Manaen wished there was a quiet moment to take the news in.

Someone banged on the door.

Manaen hissed, "Quiet! Peniel, come here. I'll boost you up to see how many there are."

From atop Manaen's shoulders Peniel reported, "Just one . . . and he's bloody from head to toe! He's falling!"

A minute later they dragged a barely conscious Kuza into the house.

The thin crescent of waning moon had not yet risen over Beth Chesed, the west Galilee estate of Miryam of Magdala. Wispy brushstrokes of clouds obscured the stars hanging over the sycamore fig trees. A stiff southerly breeze swept the plumes along, urging them toward the distant heights of Mount Hermon.

The single lantern at the garden gate painted a bare scrap of landscape a dismal orange. The door of a shed banged slowly with the wind.

Inside the stone cottage occupied by Mary of Nazareth, Kuza once more insisted. "Leave . . . me! Go . . . now."

Kuza lay facedown on a cot. Mary and Susanna tended his wounds by the light of a clay lamp.

Seated in the chair nearest the door, Manaen once more refused to rush away. He set aside anxiety for his wife and their coming child. "You risked everything to warn us, Kuza. We won't abandon you."

Peniel nodded in agreement. "As soon as you're bandaged, we're taking you with us."

Susanna applied lotion-covered strips of linen to Kuza's wounds. She whispered in Manaen's ear: "Moving him may kill him."

"If Acteon finds him here, he's dead for certain," Manaen muttered in reply. Then, louder, he asserted, "Peniel and I will carry him, cot and all. If we're lucky, by morning we'll be in Bethsaida."

From the window Peniel called, "The boat. It's here! There's a light on the water."

Manaen stiffened at a creaking noise from outside. Signaling for silence, he bent his head toward the door to listen. When nothing further was heard he said, "Quick as you can now. Let's go."

He surprised himself by taking charge. Blind or not, everyone looked to him to command; he had no choice. "Susanna, you're in front. Keep us on the path. Once out the door go straight into the lake. Wade in. Each hold on to the person in front. Follow the light into the water. Mary, you stay in front of Peniel."

As Manaen and Peniel lifted the cot, Kuza groaned. Manaen bit back a warning for the injured man to keep quiet.

Even before Manaen gave the order, he heard the door of the cottage creak open. Acteon drawled, "Look there! Blind monkey and traitor going somewhere? The centurion's long gone. No help to you now."

"Douse the light!" Manaen ordered, dropping the bed with a crash. Kuza cried out.

Peniel gave a triumphant shout as the lamp shattered. "Manaen! It's dark! The advantage is ours! Straight into them!"

Shoving Susanna aside, Manaen leapt for Acteon's throat.

If he could keep Acteon and Gadot busy, Manaen thought, the others might escape through the water and onto the boat.

The rush took Acteon by surprise. The gambler, while a big man, was quick in neither reflexes nor wits. Manaen's charge carried both men into a third and they tumbled together in a heap. An outraged squeak betrayed Gadot's presence underneath.

Manaen's forearm shot out. His elbow cracked Acteon across the mouth with a satisfying crunch. As part of the same move his hand snaked behind Acteon's head, binding it under his arm.

Acteon flailed, driving his fist into Manaen's side.

So far no sword had been thrust into him. They had not expected resistance.

Gadot's fingernails clawed at Manaen's eyes.

Manaen hammered his forehead downward onto the bridge of Gadot's nose. A fountain of warm blood gushed. The eunuch screamed once and went silent.

Manaen's fingers closed around Acteon's throat, held on until the man stopped flailing. It was over.

Manaen heard Peniel hurry Mary and Susanna to the water's edge. "Go! Go! Don't look back."

The two plunged in.

Then Susanna shouted a warning. More attackers erupted from the lilac bushes beside the lodge.

Peniel was flanked from both sides.

An old woman's voice implored, "We mean you no harm."

Peniel recognized the voice. It was the woman who had met with Judas.

Peniel put himself between Kuza's cot and the woman. "Then get out of the way."

The slightly built frame of her older male companion flanked the dumpy woman. "Tell your friend to stop fighting. We'll sort this out." A stray gleam from the lamp at the gate disclosed a gladius held low, barely visible among the folds of the man's oversized sleeve.

"Get him, Shamen!" the woman hissed.

Lunging forward, Peniel narrowly avoided being gutted on the point of the short stabbing sword. Grasping the man's wrist, he shouted, "I know you! I know you!"

Peniel battled to keep the weapon away from his ribs. He was winning the contest for possession of the weapon when a loop of silk flipped over his head.

Peniel ducked his head and the garrote tightened on his chin instead of around his windpipe. Behind him the woman assailant grunted with effort as she drove her knee into his back. He grasped a double handful of the woman's frizzy hair. She shrieked as Peniel bent at the waist and flipped her over his head. She hit the ground with a thud and lay still.

There was another crash, and Peniel saw Shamen go limp.

Susanna had returned. "That will keep him."

Panting, Peniel grasped her wrist. "Get back on the boat."

"I bashed him with a stool. Mary's on the boat. Manaen? Are you all right?"

Manaen staggered toward her voice. "Susanna? What are you doing here?"

"I came back. I came back and I bashed him."

"She bashed him good," Peniel said. He kicked Shamen, hard, in the stomach, to make certain he was no further threat.

In the instant of satisfied silence, Kuza groaned. "We've got to get out of here. They won't be the last."

Manaen added, "Grab their swords. We may need them."

25

Peniel stood in the prow of the fishing boat, peering into the early morning mist. The vapor obscured the Bethsaida shore. Not even Peniel's sharp eyes could pierce it.

After their escape from Magdala, Peniel had relaxed. But as they neared shore, Manaen dispelled that notion. "Keep watch. Might be soldiers at the docks."

The sun had not risen yet, but even so, Peniel heard workers on the docks unloading baskets of fish from the night's catch.

Dark pilings loomed up out of the fog like phantom trees. On the very end of the nearest pier stood a tall figure in a dark cloak, planted so stiffly he might have been one of the pilings himself. Was that a spear he brandished in his right hand? Should Peniel call out to the pilot to shear off?

Too late! The man on the dock had caught sight of them. "Shalom!" He waved his staff. "Is it Peniel ben Yahtzar?"

It was Zadok, the Chief Shepherd! Zadok, who knew Manaen too—he had helped Manaen once when he'd been left for dead!

The fishing vessel was secured. Zadok helped Peniel lift Kuza, then assisted Mary and Susanna.

"Yeshua sent me to meet you."

Susanna's voice trembled with excitement. "Yeshua? Here?"

Zadok rumbled, "Indeed. Sent a message to y' and lord Manaen there. 'Don't go home,' says he. Some trouble there, I imagine."

Zadok grasped Manaen by the forearm.

Manaen was solemn. "Found trouble enough on the far shore. Zadok, will you take us . . . me . . . to him?"

On the outskirts of Bethsaida was a home belonging to a winemaker. Though the sun barely topped the heights of Golan, a crowd was gathered around its entryway.

Manaen's blindness exaggerated every sound. Every wisp of breeze. The warmth of the sun on his face. The rough face of stone wall beneath his groping hand.

Yeshua was inside.

Inside. The incoherent hum of voices asking, asking, asking. The clatter of cups. The *shisk* of a knife slicing apples for the guests.

Outside. Chickens in the yard. Birds bobbing on the branches of a bush. The braying of a donkey. Children shouting as they played stickball beyond the house. Voices everywhere asking, asking, asking, "But who do you think he is really?"

Accompanied by Mary, Zadok and Peniel carried Kuza's stretcher inside.

The hum and clatter ceased, as if the world held its breath to see what Yeshua would do about whip-torn flesh hanging from the ribs and spine of a battered fellow like Kuza.

Manaen, exhausted, remained outside with Susanna, near a stack of empty amphoras. He did not speak, though she attempted to engage him in conversation.

She asked, "What do you think?"

He shrugged.

"I mean, we've come so far."

He nodded.

"What are you thinking about?"

He shrugged.

She gave up.

Manaen was thinking about a lot of things. About the brother he had killed. About the serving girl whose life he had ruined when he was old enough to know better. About lies too many to count. About the rage and curses he had hurled at Susanna as she wept and asked him why. All these things were on his mind.

Manaen winced. He remembered small Samu'el with his cleft lip and palate, who could not utter a word. And how he had cuffed the boy hard the morning he and Susanna left his estates. How he had called the boy an imbecile for spilling the wine.

Susanna asked quietly, "Are you hungry? I could go find us something."

He was hungry, but it didn't matter. He reached for her hand. "Last night. Susanna? Mary said you were . . . that there is . . . a baby."

"Yes."

"Susanna. I've been . . . what can I say?"

"Miserable?"

"Yes. That. And cruel."

"At times."

"I don't deserve . . . you know. I don't deserve anything."

She held his hand to her lips and kissed his fingers. "Do you know how much I love you?"

"I don't know why."

"I want you to be . . . well. It would be a fine thing if you could see again. Yes, a fine thing. But Manaen, I love you even if you can't. Last night you took charge of everything even when . . . you know. And no matter to me if you can see or if you can't see. As long as you are well, *inside* yourself. Well and whole in your soul. If you know what I mean."

He smiled sadly. "I've been sitting here thinking something like that. Would you forgive me?"

Susanna kissed his hand again. "Of course. Oh, with all my heart!" She kissed his mouth and threw her arms around his neck. "We needed to talk. Good. Yes. Now shall I go find some bread or something? I was queasy early this morning. Mary says it's normal the first three months. But now I'm hungry. I'll go."

"Sure."

She stood to leave. Stroked his cheek and then, a gasp!

Manaen jerked involuntarily. "What?"

"Kuza! He's walking."

Manaen heard a man's voice. Yeshua's? "Antioch. You'll find Joanna and Boaz. Don't look back."

Kuza answered quietly, "Yeshua, I won't! I won't look back."

"You're free now. The scars. They're an honor, not a shame."

Susanna's breathing quickened with excitement. She clasped Manaen's fingers tightly. She whispered. "It's him. Him."

Silence. Outside. As if the world was waiting to see what Yeshua would do about the burned-out eyes of a hot-tempered fool like Manaen.

Footsteps. Then suddenly Yeshua's form blocked the heat of the sun. Strong calloused carpenter's hands grasped Manaen's. "Shalom. Manaen? Susanna? My mother told me what you did for her. For the others."

Susanna's words tumbled down like rain. "We were looking for you! Searching! Capernaum. Then Magdala. Now here you are!"

Yeshua replied, "And so are you."

Manaen stood and extended his hands, palms up. "My hands are bloody. Have mercy on me, Lord."

Yeshua called for Peniel and Zadok. Then, "Come with me, Manaen and Susanna and Peniel. Zadok, keep everyone else here, please."

A winding path took the quartet around a knoll and behind a screen of vines trained across heaps of rocks. Manaen remembered the place. Yeshua was taking him out of sight of the house and the others gathered there. Was Yeshua afraid He might fail and so was hiding the attempt?

They stopped again. Birds fluttered overhead. In the distance a dog barked. A mother called for her child to come.

And Yeshua asked, "Manaen bar Talmai, does your life have value?"

It was exactly the issue with which Manaen had wrestled ever since he lost his eyes. How did Yeshua know? Manaen wondered.

At last he could answer truthfully, "I was angry, living for revenge, but that wasn't the answer. I listened to voices of despair. But now I know . . . I love my wife . . . and our child. I can't do all I wish I could, but I found out my uselessness is a lie."

"So again I ask, what is it you want me to do for you?"

"Make my heart whole. It has always been blind, I think."

Manaen heard Yeshua spit in the palm of His hand. Gentle fingertips massaged warm, sticky moisture into Manaen's eyes.

Yeshua turned Manaen back toward the house. "What do you . . . see?"

Orange and green flares blossomed inside Manaen's eyelids, as if he'd stared at the sun for too long and dazzled his vision. As if the glowing dagger tip in Antipas' dungeon was again searing the light from Manaen's world.

Gradually, from the edges first, the bright spots shrank in size. There seemed to be a film over his eyes, like looking through colored glass or through a dense cloud of greasy smoke. Black stick figures, unnaturally elongated, stretched crooked, skinny arms skyward. Colorless cloaks swayed in the breeze like the canopy of an almond grove.

"I see . . . men. Men like . . . trees . . . walking!"

Yeshua reached out His hands. He covered Manaen's eyes with His palms so that all was blackness again. "Manaen, do you believe that I can heal you?"

Manaen nodded.

"Do you believe that I want to heal you?"

Another nod.

"Inside and outside? Blindness of the heart is worse than blindness of the eyes, eh, Peniel?"

"Well spoken. Point taken," Peniel agreed fervently.

Yeshua spoke quietly. "And believing the lies of the Accuser blinds your soul to the true light of life."

He dropped His hands from Manaen's face.

Manaen blinked at the morning. The house. The clusters of people waiting. Chickens pecking at bugs in the yard. A sparrow bobbing on a branch above his head! His vision was clear! Perfectly restored. Yeshua's eyes smiled back at him. Brown eyes, flecked with gold.

Susanna tugged at Manaen's sleeve. Laid her head against his arm. Wiped tears from her face. Laughed.

He embraced her, kissed her. Beautiful Susanna. Her hair tousled from a night on the sea. Her clothes rumpled. Her eyes shining with tears. Beautiful!

Yeshua warned, "There isn't much time. Susanna, will you accompany my mother on a journey north?"

She managed to speak. "Anything! Anything!"

And then Yeshua asked, "Manaen, can you think of any unfinished business here?"

Manaen pondered the unexpected question; then light as great as that bathing his eyes flooded his understanding. "A boy. My cook's son! Samu'el! He can't speak."

"You and Peniel bring him. But don't go back through Bethsaida. Your home is being watched. Bring him to me. You'll find us near the pools of Caesarea Philippi."

Twilight was fast approaching. Fears like a thousand shadows inhabited Peniel's thoughts.

On a knoll overlooking Manaen's estate, Manaen and Peniel crouched at the angle of a corral. Within the pen eight black-and-brown, long-haired goats milled about, unalarmed by the presence of two strangers near their enclosure.

At Manaen's direction Peniel remained hidden, not even peeking around the corner toward the house below. Manaen left to reconnoiter.

Ten minutes passed. To Peniel it felt like hours.

At the sound of gravel scraping under a sandaled foot, Peniel stiffened, then relaxed when Manaen reappeared. "Good thing we were warned. Two of Antipas' guards are watching the front gate, two more between the house and barn. And one . . . Acteon! He must have come here directly from Magdala. He's sitting in my courtyard. Saw him through a window."

"Now what?"

"Work our way left. Keep this pen between us and the barn. We can make it as far as that acacia tree unseen."

"And then?"

"Then . . . then we'll see."

The lack of a better developed plan was not reassuring, but Peniel was still grateful for Manaen's leading.

Peniel had plenty of time to study the soldiers while he and Manaen slid on their bellies inch by agonizingly slow inch down the hillside toward the thorn tree. This was not Antipas' territory, yet the men were armed with swords and spears and dressed in Antipas' uniforms.

The tetrarch was so anxious to capture Manaen he had risked the political consequences of ignoring his brother's border.

And now that Manaen had his sight again, how much more eager would Antipas be to silence him? Manaen would never be allowed to speak openly of the miracle or of the one who healed him!

Once beneath the acacia tree Manaen put his mouth next to Peniel's ear. "I'll distract the sentries by the barn. Then I can make it across the open space to the cookhouse. You stay here and keep watch. Whistle if they start to come back."

Peniel had no time to mention he didn't know how to whistle. Manaen grabbed up a fist-sized rock and hurled it over the barn roof and into the gully beyond. The heads of the two guards standing nearby jerked upward. One muttered, "Let's go have a look."

As their backs disappeared around the corner of the almond-roasting compound, Manaen darted across the intervening yard and into the kitchen.

Peniel fingered the hilt of the short sword. What good would it do him if it came to a fight? He was probably more danger to himself with a blade than to anyone else!

The two sentries returned. If they entered the cookhouse Manaen would be trapped!

Peniel puckered up his lips and experimented with a low whistle. The sound was dismal. Instead of a warning it would be a dead giveaway of his presence!

"What's that?"

"Maybe something's after the goats." The soldier walked toward Peniel's hiding place.

Then, from the cookhouse doorway, Cook's voice called out to the Herodians, "Here, you two! Keepin' guard's thirsty work, isn't it? Come have some barley wine."

"So, woman, you've changed your tune, eh?" one of the soldiers challenged.

Cook replied, "I've taken pity on you. And let's just say I don't want you lootin' my pantry. Barley bread, apples, and beer. Can't offer fairer than that, can I?"

"Just give us the pitcher."

Peniel peered around the tree trunk. Both guards converged on Cook. She had drawn them away from Manaen.

"Can't just hand over the jug. Greedy swine, that's what you are. There's more than two of you, if you don't mind. You'll share with the others, by my word! Follow me around front, and you all can have a glass."

The clink of mugs echoed from the path in front of the house. A minute later Manaen returned with Samu'el in tow. In another fifteen seconds Manaen, Samu'el, and Peniel were over the hill and gone.

"Cook'll spread the word to Hashim and the other servants," Manaen reported when they were safely out of earshot. "She understood instantly what was needed . . . once she calmed down! Last time she saw me I was blind! Made it easy to convince her to let Samu'el come with us! She'll go out to market tomorrow and just not return to the house. Then she'll follow us north to Caesarea Philippi. The other servants will slip away to Antioch, to Susanna's estates."

Peniel, Manaen, and Samu'el traveled north toward Caesarea Philippi. Yeshua and His company would have reached the foot of Mount Hermon by now. Perhaps they were already settled in, cook fires kindled, supper broiling over the coals.

Manaen, his strength renewed again by receiving his sight, could have left Peniel and the boy in the dust. Instead he slowed his pace to match their less certain steps.

A confined valley of vineyards and olive orchards opened at last onto a range of boulder-strewn hills. Green-and-silver plane trees stood out against black basaltic cliffs. Creepers curling round a tree trunk made it resemble the mythical caduceus of Hermes, the snake-spiraled staff of healing.

Farther up the climb a plateau of rich soil and abundant water made for plentiful wheat harvests in season. For now the land rested, awaiting the early fall rains to settle the dust. It would be a month or more before the plowing and the planting were possible.

The path paralleled the Jordan, a ribbon of bright blue within the canyon's embrace. The gorge's sheer walls teemed with flowers: towering sheaves of pink and white oleanders, patches of spine-covered, cherry-colored wild roses, and tangled thickets of fragrant sunrise-hued honeysuckle. And the path continued to climb, winding in and out of the hills, but with its end ever in sight: snowcapped Mount Hermon.

It was sunset when Manaen halted near a grove of acacia trees. "You and Samu'el. You're tired. We'll camp here for the night."

Peniel nodded gratefully, aware that Manaen could have gone on alone and arrived at Yeshua's camp within hours if Samu'el and Peniel had not held him back. But Samu'el was, after all, the reason Manaen had remained behind to face the danger of Herodian killers. It was interesting to see how Manaen's restoration had turned his inner eyes from himself and toward the needs of others.

"We'll have a cold camp tonight in case they've followed us." Manaen passed around dried fruit, a bag of shelled almonds, and a crust of bread for each.

The boy ate and soon fell asleep.

"I'll stand watch," Manaen offered, drawing his sword. "If I shout, grab the boy and make a run for the acacia trees. Hide yourselves in the tall grass. They won't look long in the thorns of the acacia grove. Now get some sleep. A long hike yet for us."

Peniel's back rested against the rough granite of a stone. The spot on the hill was pleasant, the breeze a caress out of a clear sky.

He stared up at the distant spire of Mount Hermon. Above the summit of Zion waved a pink cloud banner in the face of the purpling twilight. Floating above the gleaming snow crown, Peniel thought he glimpsed a flash of red. An instant only, so it had to be his imagination. All the same, squinting his eyes, Peniel thought he recognized the image of a golden lion rampant on a crimson flag.

As night fell and cooled the air he covered himself with his cloak. Tucking the lavender bud under his face he lapsed into the deep slumber of exhaustion.

Hours passed and darkness blanketed the land. He was dimly aware of Manaen's footstep near his head.

Peniel raised slightly. "Shall I take the watch?"

An amused whisper replied, *You? Peniel? Stand watch? No. You'd be of little use.*

"I could shout and wake you."

I've been awake now several centuries by your reckoning. The voice was familiar in Peniel's dreams.

"Mosheh? Is that you?"

It is.

"*Ulu Ush-pi-zin.* Welcome to our fireless camp. We're being pursued by Herod's soldiers."

Yes. A dangerous night.

"I feel it. Very dangerous, even though I'm dreaming. Yes, dangerous night. I'm glad to see you. I've been thinking of what you told me. Hoping you'd come speak to me. You know the rumors. What the Herodians are saying about Yeshua. About his mother. Some saying he's illegitimate. Others saying he's just the son of a carpenter."

We were watching. Waiting. Something important is about to happen. I haven't much time. The hour of battle is near.

The skin on Peniel's arms prickled. "Are we going to have a fight? Should I wake up?"

Sleep. Dream. Remember lessons you thought you forgot. The answers to mysteries are all there in your mind when you need them. Only the son of a carpenter, eh? The world is at a turning point.

"The sky was bloodred tonight. I saw a lion and a banner in the clouds."

Ah, the standard of the Lion of the tribe of Judah.

"I'm in need of a good dream."

A good time to talk.

"Will you tell me more about the time Pharaoh's men and chariots were all cast into the sea?"

No, not tonight. Tonight I was sent to speak to you of small details in Torah that contain great prophecies. Tiny mysteries of Sinai that have remained hidden and soon will be revealed about salvation through the Carpenter.

"Tell me then, please! I'm Peniel. You know me. I love a good mystery!"

Far away the rumble of thunder rolled over the land. Peniel stirred with excitement. Was it thunder, or a voice?

A storm was coming. A cloudburst that would wash away the dust of obscurity to reveal great gems of truth.

Mosheh spoke quietly, his words a mixture of wind and rushing water. *You, Peniel! You know our word for carpenter,* atz, *is the same as the word for* tree."

Peniel laughed. "Tree, and timber, and plank."

And wood.

"Point taken. Tree. Wood. All the same word as carpenter. *ATZ.* Carpenter, sawdust in his beard, is Tree. What a language Adonai invented! One word with so many meanings."

Well spoken, Peniel. It is no accident you camp beside the acacia grove. The shittim tree, as we called it in my day. Shittim grows in spite of desolation. Wood so hard it is called "indestructible." Branches filled with thorns. Shittim means "pierce" or "scourge." And yet it is the wood Yahweh commanded be used for building the Tabernacle and also for the Aron HaKodesh, the Ark of the Covenant.

On Sinai from the cloud, Yahweh instructed me:

Mosheh! Make a chest of shittim wood. Overlay it with gold, inside and out. Then put in it the Ark of the Testimony, which I will give to you. Make an atonement cover of pure gold and two cherubim of hammered gold at the ends of the cover. The cherubim must face one another. Place the atonement cover on top of the ark. There, above the cover between the two cherubim that are over the Ark of Testimony, I will meet with you and give you all my commands for the Israelites.[60]

Oh, the long talks we had in that place over the years that followed! There, at the seat of the Mercy of the Lord, blessed be His Name forever, the Messiah, the Anointed One.

He who was

and is

and yet will be,

spoke plainly to me face-to-face. In words I could understand. With a voice as clear as my voice. As a man speaks to a man.

And so everything he instructed me to do was done exactly as He directed. Because everything, even the smallest detail in His Word, has eternal significance!

The Ark! Aron HaKodesh. Lined with pure gold on the inside. Covered with pure gold on the outside. Yet buried in the heart of shining glory is a simple chest carved from shittim wood.

Within the Ark is contained the Law, the broken tablets of Sinai.

Two omers of manna, the bread sent from heaven.

The rod belonging to Aaron, my brother the high priest, the letters of whose name are identical with the word for ark. *And this name,* Aron, *comes from the word that means "conception or pregnancy." This is important to remember.*

So the salvation of mankind was conceived. The Ark of the Covenant became like a womb, pregnant with the truth of eternal life. It contained the promise of our Redeemer who descended from heaven to be born as a baby in Beth-lehem.

Peniel spoke at last. "I know that much of the story. Zadok told me plainly. I know the mother of Yeshua too. A good lady. I know and I'm glad to be alive to see this day!"

It is not all glad tidings, Peniel. In the simplicity of a word Yahweh reveals an eternal mystery.

The Anointed One you love above all embodies all truth that was conceived and carried within the womb of the Ark, the Aron HaKodesh, as the Son of El Olam, the Eternal God.

Messiah is Torah, the Living Word of Yahweh.

Messiah is Manna, the Bread of Life sent from heaven.

Messiah is the Staff of Authority, the High Priest, who enters the Holy Place to pour out His own blood as the atonement for our sins.

The gold atonement covering speaks of Messiah's kingship. Yet plain acacia wood—shittim atz—speaks of Messiah's love for us.

Wood, atz, *says Carpenter.*

Acacia, shittim, *says scourge, thorn, pierce, suffer!*

The shittim atz. *Scourge . . . Carpenter. Gallows . . . Carpenter. Pierce . . . Carpenter. Suffer . . . Carpenter. Thorn . . . Carpenter. Do you see? Within the Holy of Holies even the acacia wood bears witness that in His humanity the Carpenter will be scourged and hung upon a tree and pierced and wear a crown of thorns. He will hang upon the wood He carries to the place of the skull where Adam is buried. There He will be pierced and suffer and die for the sins of all the children of Adam. And the final atonement will be provided.*

Only a carpenter? No, the Messiah, the Anointed One of Israel! From Mount Sinai every detail Yahweh commanded for the construction of the Tabernacle foretells His human identity! In the Living, sacred Word of Torah it is declared that He would be a carpenter! He is indeed the Lamb of Yahweh who takes away the sins of the world! The blood of His sacrifice will be poured out upon the mercy seat as an atonement for many.

Peniel tried to awaken. He did not like this part of the dream. He never liked it when the truth spoken by the Ushpizin turned to suffering. "Please, don't tell me more. I can't bear to hear it. No more. It can't be true! Let me wake up now."

This and more are true, Peniel. And you will see it with your own eyes. If you do not wish to hear more, I will leave the mysteries unspoken and unexplained. Your memory of Scripture and of all that is past in my day will teach you what is yet to come!

I leave you only this: Prophecies revealed on Sinai, The Mountain of the Thorn, now will be fulfilled!

Who do men say that He is? Those who mock the Carpenter and do not comprehend the significance of The Name. Think on these true words, Peniel, and eternal wisdom and understanding will bring you to your knees!

"No more! All right. All right! Yeshua is the Carpenter! I don't want to know it if he's going to be hurt! Don't tell me!" Peniel forced his eyes to open. Mosheh's voice resounded in his mind.

Manaen crouched beside him. "Peniel, you're dreaming. Wake up. You all right? Quiet all night. No one coming or going on the road. Very peaceful. Not a soul out but us. About an hour till daylight. Samu'el's wide-awake. Eager. We can be back in Caesarea Philippi, in Yeshua's camp, in three hours if we leave right now. Are you up for it?"

Peniel sat up and glowered toward the dark acacia grove. *Scourge. Pierce. Thorn. Tree.* "Yes. Yes. Let's get out of here."

26

CHAPTER

S amu'el, fast asleep, rode into the camp of Yeshua's seventy talmidim atop Manaen's shoulders. It was a secluded spot, hemmed in with trees, within sight of the Pool of Pan. No one but Zadok noticed the arrival of Peniel, Manaen, and Samu'el.

Zadok met them at the head of the trail. The big shepherd grasped Manaen by both shoulders. Neither man spoke.

Peniel knew that it was enough that they were here. Yes, it was enough.

Susanna rose from the campfire she shared with Yeshua's mother. Taking Samu'el down from Manaen's shoulders, she cradled him for a while beside the warmth of the flames.

After a time Samu'el awoke—confused at first and worried. Mary offered him a breakfast of bread, juice, and a boiled egg. Porridge simmering over the embers of a fire across the camp was not quite finished cooking. Samu'el, ashamed of his disfigurement, ate his boiled egg behind his hand, holding his tiny palm across the split in his features.

Susanna embraced Manaen, rubbing his neck and kissing him. She stood close to him and peered playfully into his eyes, then shook her head in joyous amazement as he looked back into her eyes, seeing her. At last they had awakened from a long nightmare.

Mary summoned Manaen and Susanna and brought Samu'el to Yeshua.

Peniel gnawed on a hunk of barley bread as he watched. Was anyone else in the camp aware of what was taking place? John chopped wood. Levi fed the fire. Women dished out porridge and flatbread to the talmidim.

Above them, on the ramparts of Caesarea Philippi, a pair of Philip's soldiers strolled on morning patrol. The city was coming to life, yet no one within the walls was aware that Life had come to their city.

Only a handful of Yeshua's talmidim and other followers who went about their morning tasks had even noticed the arrival of the little boy with the cleft lip.

The ordinary workings of the world continued on, undisturbed by the extraordinary wonder about to take place.

But Peniel knew what was coming. Each occasion he witnessed a miracle it was like experiencing his own all over again. Never old or commonplace. Each encounter varied. Every wound and hurt and longing was unique. And always, always, Yeshua embraced each person. He met every need as if there had never been a life so important as the one He held in His gaze that very moment.

Blessed art thou, O Lord God, King of the Universe, Who performs wondrous deeds.[61]

First Yeshua probed the human heart. Illuminated the darkness of a soul. He found and extracted the arrow of loneliness or shame or longing that pierced the soul. That was the first miracle. Only after healing the heart did He turn His attention to healing the broken body.

Yeshua rose from His meal to greet Manaen and Susanna and Samu'el. He embraced them, clapped Manaen on the back. *Well done! Well done!* Then He knelt eye to eye with Samu'el. Unspoken understanding passed between them.

The child threw His arms around Yeshua's neck and clung fiercely to Him. Yeshua bent His forehead to touch Samu'el's. They remained head to head for minutes, as if nothing else in the universe mattered. Then Samu'el's grip unlocked from around Yeshua's neck. Fingers fluttered to His lips. Backing up a pace, the boy turned. Clearly, distinctly, he spoke his first words: "Look! Look what he did for me!"

Few in the camp had noticed the need. Only a handful understood exactly how the need had been met.

John, axe poised over a log, glanced up to see what had happened. It was clear to Peniel that John saw only a child like any other child. Nothing remarkable in that. Heads around the encampment raised for one instant of curiosity and then activities resumed.

The woman who ladled porridge stopped long enough to ask her companion what all the shouting was about. A shrug. And then porridge sloshed into Thomas' bowl. And Ya'acov's bowl. And Philip's bowl. And Nathaniel's bowl. Judas' bowl.

But Peniel had seen it all. Samu'el, who had never smiled before, was smiling.

It was a very good story indeed.

The tang of autumn hung in the air. It seemed to Zahav that the tangible end of summer arrived each year on the first day of the Jewish month called Tishri. From now on the air would grow colder; the days would be shorter. The snows that had melted away from the heights of Mount Hermon would begin to fall again soon.

Today, beginning at sunset, was Rosh Hashanah, New Year.

In the seventh month, on the first day of the month, you shall observe complete rest, a sacred occasion commemorated by loud blasts![62]

Referred to in Torah as *Yom Teruah*—the Day of Sounding the Shofar—it marked the beginning of the autumn cycle of three High Holidays.

Ten days after New Year came *Yom Kippur*, "The Day of Atonement." Immediately after that was the Festival of Tabernacles.

Each year on Rosh Hashanah Zahav dressed in white as though she were a bride. But the Bridegroom of Israel never came.

Needle and thread in hand, Zahav studied the names on Messiah's prayer shawl. She had imagined presenting him with the gift at the start of the three festivals.

She whispered the prayer for the day:

"Blessed are you O Eternal—the Most High God who bestows gracious favors, possessor of all, who remembers the pious deeds of the patriarchs and will bring a Redeemer to their remotest posterity in love!" With her finger she traced the names on the fabric of the tallith. "He will be called, King, Helper, Savior, and Shield! Blessed are you, O Eternal! The Shield of Avraham! You are mighty forever, O Adonai! Reviving the dead, you are all-powerful to save! You reanimate the dead in abundant compassion. Support the fallen. Heal the sick. Release those who are bound. . . ."

She faltered and fell silent. Today was supposed to be a day for remembering, wasn't it?

She remembered Hero, sick and bound.

Alexander, fallen.

And herself, dead inside.

No life. No love. No children. No future. No hope. Barren as the barren earth.

How she had longed for a new beginning as the moan of the shofar announced Rosh Hashanah. But the Messiah depicted in this festival prayer—He who could raise the dead and heal the sick and loose the captives—had not appeared.

She looked around the stone walls of her room.

A tomb. Yes.

Perhaps the gift of the tallith, made for the Bridegroom of Israel who never came, would be her shroud one day.

Papa called for her. "Zahav! Come on! Hurry! So much to do! We visit Mama's grave today! We cast our sins into the sea! We eat! We sing! The children are all waiting for you!"

How Papa loved this day! A day of remembering. He had lived his life already.

Zahav forced herself to sound cheerful. "Coming, Papa." Folding the prayer shawl, she laid her cheek upon it. "Where are you now?" she whispered to Messiah. "Where? Do you know we wait?"

A quick comb through her hair, then she fixed the veil over her face and descended. The table was spread with a lavish family feast for later.

Papa hefted the box stacked with bread crumbs tied up in kerchiefs. "These sins are a heavy burden to this old man." Papa teased. "Micah has written: '*The Lord will again have compassion,*' eh? '*He will hurl our iniquities into the sea.*'[63] But we should hurry or the river will be clogged with bread crumbs for everyone else, and there won't be room for ours!"

There was one kerchief for every member of the family. By tradition, the bread, representing sins of the past year, would be cast into the river at the foot of a high waterfall flowing from Jordan's springs. There was no sea nearby, but Papa always said the Jordan eventually ended up in the Dead Sea, so this was close enough.

He kissed her cheek. "You look so beautiful today, Daughter. Like a bride. Maybe today Messiah will come." He paused a moment and inclined his head toward the overflowing table. "There, Zahav. That basket of apples. The jar of honey. A gift for your friend, Alexander. And for his little son, eh?"

"Papa!" She turned away quickly, hoping he did not see the emotion in her eyes.

"It came to me as I meditated on the berakhot. A vision you might say. And the Lord said in my heart, *Take those nice red apples and a little honey to the apostate and his son.* After all, this is their first Rosh Hashanah since he lost his wife."

Zahav did not comment that it was highly unlikely Alexander knew anything at all about the holiday. It was just another day to him and all those outside the Jewish Quarter. She clutched the jar of honey and basket of fruit to her. On each apple Zahav had engraved tiny Hebrew letters: *Ketivah tovah:* "May you be inscribed in the Book of Life."

Papa's clouded eyes followed her. "Zahav, daughter, you think I don't see. You think I don't know. But I do. Such a kind heart you have. I take a lesson from you. A mitzvah to the lost sheep of Israel. So, we will all go together. Your sisters. Brothers. The grandchildren. All of us will make the gift together. Wish them Shanah Tova. That their names also be inscribed in the Book of Life."

Alexander watched Hero playing on the floor, piling blocks of wood. At the boy's side was a single shining apple. Hero took no bite from the fruit, but in the midst of stacking he occasionally paused to rub the red globe against his cheek and peer at the engraving in the crisp red skin. Then he resumed his building.

The pot of honey sat on the sideboard next to the basket of apples. Alexander wished he knew the meaning of the Hebrew letters painstakingly inscribed on each.

A plate of slowly browning apple slices was stuck to the counter.

The shop was closed and shuttered. Outside the curtain of twilight veiled the new moon marking Rosh Hashanah. The celebration was also known as *Yom ha-Zikkaron*, "the Day of Remembering," and *Yom Teruah*, "the Day of Trumpets."

Deliberately timed to mark the sunset, the trumpet call broke the evening stillness.

A long note.

Three quavering notes.

Nine staccato alarmed notes.

A single sustained blast.

Hero raised his head.

Alexander stared at his son without seeing him. His thoughts were swimming in the *what-if* questions of being an apostate Jew. How would his life have been different *if* his grandfathers had not been so interested in fitting into a Gentile world? What would his life be like *if* he was still part of the Jewish community of believers? He remembered Zahav's family clustered at his door earlier today, smiling happily as he accepted their gift with surprise and pleasure. Zahav, her eyes brimming with emotion as she stood in the midst of her clan. So many. Bound together not only by blood but by love and faith and creed.

How Alexander envied them.

A second trumpet call repeated the pattern again. The air sobbed with the crying notes, groaned with the quavering ones.

Hero lifted his chin, turned his head toward the window, then resumed his play when the last note faded. He touched the apple shyly to reassure himself it was still there.

Alexander searched his memories for an explanation of the trumpet volleys. What had his father said? "Those Jews"—not "we Jews"—"take their creed and stick it in your face. Listen to the trumpet insisting: *One! Hear, O Israel! The Lord our God, the Lord is One God! One!*"[64]

Alexander's father had been adamant that tolerance for the Greek way of thinking was more important than insistence on a creed; besides, anything else was bad for business.

The third time the air was shattered with the sound Alexander was still looking directly at Hero when the boy's head jerked upright.

Alexander was transfixed with a sudden revelation: Hero acted as if he heard the trumpets! Was it possible? Could it be that the boy heard the shofar?

He knelt beside his son. Throughout the shofar's reverberation Hero gazed at the window. The child's face was suffused with intense longing. When the last note of the ram's horn faded, Hero turned back toward his toys.

Was the trumpet speaking to the boy's ears, or somehow directly to his heart? Or was the voice actually for Alexander, and Hero sensed what longing was inside his father?

Taking Hero by the hand, Alexander led him out into the deserted streets. Hero clutched his apple to his heart as if it were a precious treasure. With eager steps Alexander led the way into the Jewish Quarter, the shofar drawing them on: *Hear, O Israel!*

Every house they passed blazed with light and laughter. Every stray gleam from humble cottage to terraced mansion represented families, clans gathered for the Holy Day of Remembrance and Renewal.

Outside the synagogue Alexander stooped down beside Hero as a plaintive cry seemed to call the boy: *"HEAR, O Israel . . ."*

"O . . . Hero." Had Hero heard his name in the words? Had he heard a voice? "Hero? Hero! Hear O Israel . . . it doesn't mean us. The One God is not ours."

The child held up his apple, extending it like a gift offered to the beam of light that shone from a high window.

"Oh, Hero." Alexander buried his face against his son and wept.

The distant haunting call of a shofar died away. And so it was Rosh Hashanah, the celebration of creation, when the seventy talmidim pitched their camp beside the springs feeding the headwaters of the Jordan River.

The cliff face, where the idols of the Pantheon glowered over the pool, was within view of the encampment. From the heights of the city a casual observer would have looked down and seen an ordinary pilgrim band.

Yeshua sternly warned His talmidim not to speak to anyone about their presence in Caesarea Philippi. It was not yet time for Him to reveal Himself to the Israelites in the northernmost territory of Eretz-Israel.

The peak of Mount Hermon blocked the northern horizon.

The light of Caesarea Philippi sparkled on the plateau above them. Peniel searched the night sky. Tonight it seemed especially bright, etched with constellations.

Old Zadok was surrounded by his three small boys, a grandson, his daughter, and son-in-law. The aged shepherd called to Peniel, Manaen, Susanna, and little Samu'el: "Come share our fire! *Hayom barat ha-olam*, my friends! Today is the birthday of the world!"

Peniel wondered if Zadok remembered another birth day some thirty years earlier, by which so many lives had been changed.

Manaen glanced to where Yeshua stooped to breathe dying embers into flames and said to his wife, "*Hayom barat ha-olam.* Yes, I believe it. I do believe. The birth of creation."

There was wonder in Manaen's voice, Peniel noted. And why not? It had not been so long since Peniel had gained his sight. He, like Manaen, lived in wonder! He drank in every color, every glimmer of light that shone in through the window of his eyes. He shared that miraculous sense of new birth with Manaen now. Two blind men, blind for different reasons, both living in darkness, had been given a new beginning.

Tonight their supper was quail. Thomas and Levi had come upon a colony of over three hundred birds, which, with the help of the children in the camp, had been trapped and prepared for roasting over the ten open fires that crackled in the clearing.

"*Hayom barat ha-olam.*" Peniel sat cross-legged among Zadok's boys. Their fire was near to that of Yeshua, His mother, and the Twelve of the inner circle.

Yeshua blessed their meal and then, as quail sizzled over the flames, tinging the air with delicious aroma, He taught them. His face glowed with joy. His silhouette loomed large on the rock behind Him. Shim'on sat at His left, Mary on His right.

"Look up." Yeshua raised His right hand skyward.

Every eye searched the heavens. Stars and stars. The Milky Way was a highway. Planets spun and double stars danced around one another in distant pink vapors.

Peniel saw it. There was more in one square inch of sky than he had ever seen before. Perhaps it was the high clean air of the mountains. Or perhaps it was the presence of Yeshua that brought it so near. Peniel thought that tonight the universe gleamed more brightly than at any time since creation!

Yeshua said, "Today we remember the birthday of the world. The beginning of time. There was no time before this world was created, nor will there be time in *olam haba*, the world to come. Everything that was, or is, or will be, is written for you in Torah. Listen! Here is a curiosity! The Torah reading for Rosh Hashanah isn't the story of creation! No! Today in every synagogue we study the story of a firstborn child! The miraculous birth of a long-awaited child! The story of Yitz'chak! The son promised to Avraham by Yahweh. The true story about a barren woman longing for a firstborn son to open the womb. Waiting for the birth of a beloved son."

Yeshua touched His mother's hand. She beamed up at Him.

Manaen, as though reminded of the baby Susanna carried, put his arm around her and pulled her close to him.

Yeshua continued the lesson. "Today we remember the sixth day of creation, not the first. We remember the day Adam was created. The beginning of mankind marks the real beginning of creation. That day is the beginning of man's history and the expression of God's love. The beginning of a relationship between mankind and my Father in heaven. Rosh Hashanah affirms the importance of every human life to the Lord. Even one single birth is equal in the sight of the Father to the creation of the whole world! And my Father's promise to Avraham was this: Through one life all mankind will be redeemed."[65]

Thus ended the first lesson.

The quail was eaten. The hymn of creation was sung. Then Yeshua began to teach again. He quoted the story of Abraham and Sarah from memory. Peniel was certain Yeshua had not misplaced one word in the recitation. And then came the commentary.

What rabbi ever spoke as Yeshua spoke?

"For all who read the story of Avraham, Sarah, and Yitz'chak, the image of Sarah is as important as the image of Avraham raising his knife to sacrifice his beloved son. When the three angels visited Avraham at his home they asked him, 'Where's your wife, Sarah?'

"And Avraham answered, 'There in the tent.'

"And the Angel of Adonai said, 'I'll return to you when life is due, and your wife, Sarah, shall have a son!'

"Sarah was listening behind the tent flap. When she heard the promise she laughed. But Adonai spoke directly to Avraham; Sarah heard Adonai's words only indirectly. She laughed because she could not believe Adonai's promise.

"She thought, *Why wait ninety years to let me have a baby?*

"Why not bring salvation to mankind at the beginning of the world instead of the end? Why wait until so many have suffered and died before the world is redeemed?

"Sarah believed in Yahweh, and yet she couldn't believe His promise of redemption was meant for her."[66]

At this Yeshua paused to reflect. "You say you believe my words and you see my deeds. Yet like Sarah, you listen to Adonai's voice speak to another and don't believe He speaks to you. You hear the promise from behind the tent flap of your doubts. You are Sarah. In spite of the evidence, you don't trust. Give us a sign, you say. Yet who among you has the faith of Avraham? Avraham. He trusted completely! Believed that even if his beloved Yitz-chak perished, Yahweh would raise his only son up to life again! Who among you will walk beside the only Son of God? Who will travel up the mountain with knife held high to sacrifice your own cherished desire and ambition on the altar of the Lord? Who will believe the promise?"

Yeshua searched the faces of His talmidim for even one who believed.

The waters of the Jordan's springs rushed from their source. Wind rustled the trees overhead. The smoke of the campfires obscured the bright stars. Shim'on munched his second quail.

And Yeshua asked them straight-out, "Who do men say that I am?"

Judas answered first. "They used to think you were the Deliverer of Israel. The one who would lead our armies and conquer all our enemies."

Levi cleared his throat. "The Herodians think you're Yochanan the Baptizer back from the dead. You oppose Antipas and Herodias. You shame the Pharisees and Sadducees. You preach repentance."

John spoke up. "Elijah. They say you could be the Elijah we've been looking for. Elijah didn't die. He raised the widow's son. He made miraculous provision of food. He opposed Ahab as you oppose Herod Antipas. They wait to see if you'll call down fire from heaven."

John's brother, Ya'acov, jumped in. "Rabbi, they're thinking you may be Jeremiah. Like him, you pronounce curses on the hypocrites.

You cleansed the Temple like Jeremiah. You have no wife. You speak about the bad shepherds of Israel. And the murder of the babies of Beth-lehem was prophesied by Jeremiah."

Other possibilities were murmured among the seventy before Yeshua raised His hand in a request for silence.

And then He asked The Question:

But who do . . . you . . . say that I AM?

Silence blanketed the gathering. Peniel wanted to answer, but he did not want to get it wrong. Messiah? Yes. But everyone had a different idea about what that meant.

Shim'on, nearest Yeshua, licked his fingers, drew in his breath, and exhaled the answer. "You are the Messiah. The Anointed One we've been looking for. You are the only Son of the Living God. The promise. Our miracle. Like Yitz'chak."

Mary nodded once in affirmation. She smiled briefly, then gazed up at the stars.

Yeshua smiled. "Well spoken, Shim'on. You're blessed, Shim'on bar Jonah, because my Father in heaven has revealed this to you. You didn't learn this from any human being. From now on, you are Peter."

Peniel's eyes widened as he considered the declaration of Yeshua. In Hebrew the word *peter* meant "first to open the womb." And the Rosh Hashanah lesson was about firstborn sons!

Peniel remembered his dream visit from Mosheh. The first high priest's name, *Aaron*, meant "conception." Now Yeshua had announced Shim'on's new name as "firstborn." Did He mean that what had been waiting to be brought into the world since Mount Sinai was being birthed here, now, with Shim'on's declaration, at the foot of Mount Hermon?

But perhaps Yeshua also had another meaning in mind as well. To those who spoke Greek, *petros* meant "little rock."

Yeshua glanced toward the cliff and beyond it toward the citadel that towered over the source of the Jordan. The idols of the pagans were tucked into niches in the stone.

Yeshua looked back at Shim'on, now called Peter. "Upon *this rock* I'll build *my* fortress, and all the powers of hell won't conquer it!"[67]

Peniel heard a rumble like thunder in Yeshua's declaration. The earth trembled. For an instant he heard the shattering of stone, the falling of ancient idols as they tumbled into the waters.

Yeshua had reclaimed the source of the River of Life. And now He raised His voice above the roaring in Peniel's ears. "And Peter, I'll give you the keys of the Kingdom of Heaven. Whatever you lock on earth will be locked in heaven, and whatever you open on earth will be opened in heaven."[68]

So the name was a double pun. Yeshua had called Peter "the one who opens" as well as "the rock."

There was no place better in all the world for Yeshua to declare His true identity. He had issued the challenge that rang throughout creation. He had reclaimed the Jordan. He had thrown down the false gods of the pagan nations. He, Anointed One, Son of the Promise, firstborn Son of the Living God of Israel, descendant of Avraham, Yitz'chak, and Ya'acov, had come to this spot to openly claim the throne of David as His own. Redemption—salvation—had come at last.

Immanu'el, God, was with us!

The Evil One, who from the beginning of creation had marred the history of man, trembled in terror at the sound of Yeshua's voice.

From Dan to Beersheba, throughout all Eretz-Israel, Yeshua the Messiah vanquished the enemy with truth.

Three days had passed since Peter's startling declaration. The Messiah, revealed only to a handful, commanded silence about His identity. "Tell no man I AM!"

Zadok pleaded, "But, Master, the rest of my family? So near. Waiting so long. May I not bring them at least?"

The reply was "Not yet. Soon, but not yet."

The camp of seventy plus the Twelve and The One remained secluded. Above them, in the city of Caesarea Philippi, no one guessed that Yeshua of Nazareth was so near. The Messiah could see the lights of their houses; He breathed in the aroma of breakfasts cooking in the Jewish Quarter.

"Upon this rock . . . but for now tell no one who I AM!"[69]

Beneath the camp, on the long plain, pilgrims flowed south like the river descending toward Jerusalem.

Yom Kippur, the solemn feast known as the Day of Atonement, was

near. Pilgrim children asked their fathers, would Messiah be in Jerusalem this year? Would He enter through the Eastern Gate?

Time was running out. The rumors of Messiah had reached the far
North and great cities in the East. Jews from all over the known world
whose families had not made the journey to Jerusalem in decades
crowded the highways. They had not heard of Herod Antipas' edict.

"Will Messiah be there, you think?"

"Will we see him?"

They moved beneath the shadow of Mount Hermon as though the
wind pushed them forward.

And if . . . *if* . . . *if* they ever looked up to the smoke of fires on the
mountain, *if* they glimpsed the tall, lean figure of a man perched like a
hawk on the boulders? Well, they did not imagine—could not have
dreamed—that the very One they had come looking for watched them
from above.

Their longing would have plucked Him out of the sky and compelled Him to go with them into the Holy City!

But here in the North, the other mountain of Zion awaited
Yeshua's ascent!

The intervening days between the New Year and the Day of Atonement were called the Days of Awe.

Awe. Yes. And so they were. Awe-filled, awful, terrible, wonderful
days of Yeshua's teaching about Himself and about the purpose of His
coming to earth, which no one wanted to hear or to believe!

Beginning with Peter's declaration about Messiah, accompanied by
the blast of the shofar on Rosh Hashanah, Yeshua began to prepare His
disciples for everything. He taught that soon He must go to Jerusalem
and suffer many things at the hands of the chief priests and teachers of
the law. Many things.

Could He mean it? Not possible! What? Messiah killed? On the
third day rise again?

They did not believe Him. Who could blame them, after all. He
was, they assured themselves, speaking in some sort of metaphor,
showing them a middle light along the path that did not illuminate
either the beginning or the end of meanings.

And yet the heartrending trail winding through Scripture to the
Cross seemed plain enough when He pointed it out to them. The progress was steady. Onward, onward toward the suffering of Moriah!

Yeshua taught them:

"Just as Avraham offered his only son on Mount Moriah . . . Yahweh-Yireh! On that very mountain Yahweh will provide the sacrifice of his only Son in an eternal covenant of Mercy to prove his love for mankind through the seed of Avraham, Yitz'chak, and Isra'el![70]

"You remember the Passover lamb, firstborn, whose blood was The Sign upon the doorposts of your fathers in Egypt. So I AM your Passover Lamb. My blood will cover your sins upon the altar of my Father.[71]

"And Mosheh, the deliverer, ascended Mount Sinai to receive the tablets of the Covenant between Yahweh and men.[72]

"Of course it is clear when Isaias speaks of the Suffering Servant he prophesies that by the lashes of the whip upon Messiah's back the sins of many will be atoned for.[73]

"So I AM the manna, the bread sent down from heaven to feed the souls of all who hunger and thirst after righteousness! And my body will be broken for you. But on the third day the Son of Man will rise and you will see him alive."[74]

Each day the Good Shepherd led His little flock deep into the harsh desolation of prophecies foretelling the atoning death of the Anointed One. The Lamb of God who would soon take away the sins of the world fed His sheep on bitter, indigestible truth.

Only His mother, listening to her son speak of His approaching passion, fully believed Him, completely understood the purpose of His life. And Mary wept.

Others grew sullen. Resentful. Confused.

"Surely," John asked, "just as the voice of the Angel of the Lord stopped the hand of Avraham from killing Yitz'chak on Mount Moriah . . . surely the Lord would not let his Son, our Messiah, die!"

Yesua answered, "After Yochanan baptized me, I came up out of the water of the Jordan and the Spirit descended on me like a dove and the voice of ELoHiYM spoke. Then the Spirit led me out into the wilderness, and I fasted forty days and forty nights. I came to Mount Sinai, where Mosheh received the ten words of the covenant carved in stone by the finger of Yahweh. I was hungry. Satan came to me at the moment of my greatest weakness and taunted me. If I was the Son of God I should prove my power. Turn the stones of Sinai into bread, into manna from heaven. Pervert the provision Yahweh made to feed Israel to satisfy myself and prove a point! Prove that I am equal to Mosheh, who delivered the commandments, inscribed on stone by the finger of God! But it is written that man does not live by bread alone but by every living word which proceeds from the mouth of God![75] You shall worship the Lord your God and him only shall you serve!

"Satan appeared to me a second time and took me to the highest pinnacle in the Temple on Mount Moriah."

Peniel knew Mount Moriah well. This was the Temple Mount where, in days of old, Abraham offered to sacrifice his only son to Yahweh. In that place Yahweh promised to provide a substitute sacrifice.

Yeshua taught plainly. "From that peak Satan tempted me with this question: 'Surely if you really are the Son of the Most High, you can throw yourself down and not be hurt. For it is written that you will not dash your foot on a stone.' And so, the temptation on Mount Moriah demanded I should test the love of my heavenly Father! Like Yitz'chak, Avraham's only son, wouldn't I be spared suffering? Yet, it is written, on Mount Moriah Yahweh will provide himself a sacrifice. It is written, do not put the Lord your God to the test! You shall worship the Lord your God and him only shall you serve![76]

"A third time I was tempted by Satan. Right here. Up there, is the third mountain of temptation."

Peniel looked up at the summit. Mount Hermon had been set apart as holy to Yahweh. And yet the *Book of Enoch* recounts that rebellious angels descended to earth from this very mountain to lead mankind astray! This dark wilderness legend said that Pan, half goat and half man, enemy of mankind, the Accuser, Father of Lies, had taken root like a shittim tree and grown up to pierce men's hearts with thorns of whispers, doubts, and despair! From this location evil commanded men to build altars and offer their babies as sacrifices to counterfeit no-gods. So Satan had brought Yeshua up to his lair!

Yeshua was calm as He related the event. "And the adversary, enemy of The Most High God and of man, showed me all the kingdoms of the world spread out below. He didn't taunt me with doubts about my identity any longer. Satan and his demons are certain I AM. They know why Messiah was sent to this world. They tremble because they know the end. But Satan showed me all the kingdoms of the world in an instant. He swore a false oath that if I would only bow down and worship him, he would give all the kingdoms of his dark empire to me.

Satan forgot in that moment that all power has already been given to the Redeemer of Israel by his Father in heaven. It is only a matter of time before the command is issued from the throne, banishing all powers of darkness EL HaYaM! Into the sea! And this will be accomplished when the Redeemer is lifted up on a cross! So I answered Satan, 'Away from me, Satan! For it is written: "Worship the Lord your God and serve him only!" '

"Then Satan fled from me. And angels came and attended me."[77]

Thus ended the lesson.

But what did it mean? A knot of disciples crowded around one another to discuss the significance of the story.

Surely Yeshua did not actually mean die when He said die.

He did not mean suffer when He said suffer.

He could not mean that He was the literal provision, the sacrifice of Moriah that Yahweh had promised Avraham would be the substitute for his beloved son.

Could He? Did Yeshua mean that?

Peniel stepped back to observe.

Thomas doubted. Judas declared a dead king was no use at all to anyone. Levi made notes. John wrung his hands and said nothing.

Peter, confident of his recent designation as first-to-say-it, rock-solid Peter, keys-of-the-kingdom Peter, volunteered to speak with Yeshua. Everyone agreed. Someone had to say something. Enough was enough. Hadn't Yeshua noticed His mother crying? This talk about dying as an atonement for sin was depressing!

The fellows patted Peter on the back. Urged him on. He squared his shoulders and approached Yeshua. With a manly hand clasp, Peter led Yeshua to one side.

"Why're you talking of such things now that you've admitted plainly who you are? You'll rule as king in Yerushalayim! Feed the hungry with bread you create out of thin air! With a snap of your fingers you can lead armies and conquer Rome! We'll be your administrators. Govern all the people. Cleanse the Temple once and for all. You can have all the kingdoms of the world at your feet! You're the Messiah! Never will you die in such a way, Lord! This won't ever happen to you!"

There was a long silence before Yeshua turned His back on Peter. His voice was a whisper. "You! Get behind me, Satan! You're a stumbling block to me! You don't have in mind the things of God, but the things of men!"[78]

When He looked again at the observers, Yeshua's eyes burned fiercely. He stared every man to shame. There was no gentleness when He spoke to them—only a challenge.

"If any of you would come after me, you must deny your own ambitions, deny yourself, take up your cross, and follow me. Whoever among you wants to save your life will lose it! Whoever loses your life for my sake will save it!" Yeshua gestured up at the peak of Mount Hermon. "The whole world, is it? Tell me! What good will it be for a man if he gains the whole world, yet forfeits his own soul? What will a man give in exchange for his soul? What value do you put on your eternal soul? For the Son of Man *is going to come* in his Father's glory with his angels, and then he will reward each person according to what he has done!"[79]

At that, Yeshua looked into John's eyes, then at John's brother Ya'acov. With a withering gaze He cowed Peter.

At last Yeshua pinned Peniel in place with a glance. Peniel felt himself blush. He ducked his head. He had not meant to be any part of a challenge to Yeshua's teaching.

Yeshua addressed all the talmidim: "Listen to me now! I tell you the truth. Some who are standing here *will not taste death* before they see the Son of Man coming in his kingdom."[80]

Before dawn on the morning before Yom Kippur Zahav finished the final embroidery on Messiah's prayer shawl:

El Shaddai.

Almighty. Omnipotent. All-Bountiful. All-Embracing. All-Sufficient. All-Merciful. The One who nourishes as a mother nurses a child at her breast.

Such love in the name! Such comfort!

In Ya'acov's final, prophetic blessing over Joseph, the patriarch said, "From El of your father there shall be help to you. And with Shaddai there shall be blessing unto you."[81]

As the sun rose, Zahav kissed the fringes and tucked the gift away, doubting He would ever receive it. Nine days had passed since Tishri's new moon marked the New Year. Six days had passed since Rosh Hashanah. Sunset tonight would usher in Yom Kippur, the Day of Atonement. Neither carrying burdens, building a fire, nor cooking meals was permitted after dark.

Because Yom Kippur was a time of fasting and repentance, there was much to accomplish during the day. Zahav interrupted Papa in his own preparations to be certain he stopped long enough to eat breakfast. Then she delivered a large number of new prayer shawls. These had been specially requested for services beginning this afternoon before sunset with the singing of the Kol Nidrei.

Somehow time got away from her. It was already past eight in the morning before Zahav rushed across the flagstone-lined courtyard toward the entrance to the women's mikveh bath.

In that courtyard beside the synagogue a number of worshippers were preparing in their own ways for the Day of Repentance. The elderly bar Yehuda brothers took turns lying facedown on the ground. The upright sibling beat the prostrate one three times with a stalk of papyrus cane while each time reciting from the psalms: "Yet God was kind. He kept forgiving their sins and didn't destroy them."[82] Thirteen words recited three times over totaled thirty-nine . . . exactly the required number of lashes in the strictest punishment.

The aged brothers suffered more from the unyielding stone surface under their brittle bones than from the feeble blows, but the tradition had existed since the Exile to Babylon.

In the Temple of Jerusalem, two goats had been chosen for the atonement sacrifice. Tomorrow lots would be cast, deciding which would live and which would die. One goat would be killed, its blood poured out as an atonement for sin by the high priest who entered the Holy of Holies. The other, the scapegoat, would be taken into the wilderness and set free, symbolically carrying away the transgressions of Israel.[83]

Zahav's own preparation for Yom Kippur was a trip to the ritual baths with several hundred other women.

Rebecca waved to her from the middle of the long queue. "Here. Here. I saved your place. You're late!"

Zahav threw up her hands and rolled her eyes as she joined her sister and apologized to resentful women in line behind her. "As always."

On opposite sides of the terrace were identical entrances to belowground changing rooms and bathing pools for men and women. Beginning at sunset last night the entire Jewish community had begun the ritual of baptism, which symbolized repentance. There were among familiar faces also hundreds of Jewish pilgrims, men, women, and children, traveling to and from Jerusalem for the autumn holy days.

Everywhere the gossip was about Yeshua of Nazareth. He had not been seen in Jerusalem this year. Would He show up at the Temple during Yom Kippur as He had last year? Would He and His disciples build their sukkahs on the slopes of the Mount of Olives during the coming Feast of Tabernacles?

The authorities had spies everywhere. They could not find Him.

"Who is he? A prophet? Elijah?"

"Can't be Elijah."

"A holy man, certainly."

People searched for Him in Judea. In the Galil. But He was not to be found.

"But who is he?"

"Who does he claim to be?"

"Son of man? What's that?"

"I heard he's the illegitimate son of a Roman named Panterra."

The sick asked for Him. The dying cried out for Him. But no one knew where He was.

"A bastard child. His mother raped by a Roman. That's the rumor in Yerushalayim. They say . . . you know . . . he casts out demons by the power of the Lord of Flies. Or so the Pharisees say."[84]

Papa would not approve of such talk. Zahav and Rebecca turned away. Wasn't slander one of the sins for which the sacrifice of the atonement was made?

This time of year the ritual bath was the single religious duty Zahav hated. Strangers at the mikveh who did not know her story saw her face without the veil.

Undressing behind the screen of a curtained alcove, Zahav used the shallow stone tank at the top of the steps for washing her hands and feet. She felt the furtive stares of other women. Their eyes drank in the crimson stain. Like millstones they crushed her dignity with whispered accusations.

Who had sinned to cause such a permanent disfigurement on her face?

A child pointed and asked loudly. The mother shushed her and whispered she would explain later.

Rebecca, her usually mild expression a mask of controlled anger, nudged Zahav. "I felt cleaner before."

Zahav nodded, steeling herself against the frank stare of disgust on the face of the little girl clinging to her mother's hand. Zahav looked away. "Never mind. Never mind. Next year we come before sunup. While everything is still dark, eh?"

With Rebecca in the adjacent pool, Zahav descended the three stair treads and knelt in the waist-deep water of the mikveh. She prayed: *Though my sins be as scarlet, O Adonai, you can make my heart as white as snow. If only you would come. They accuse you, though you are without blemish. Surely your heart hears their accusations against you. Against your mother. Though the mark on my face brands me forever in the eyes of strangers, can you make my heart pure?*[85]

She immersed herself. The water was cold—not icy, but still chilly enough to make Zahav hurry. It was said that the spring feeding the mikvehs in the Jewish Quarter came straight from the snows of Mount Hermon. It had never descended to the level of the Pool of Pan but was pure and undefiled.

And so the humbling ordeal ended. Had Yahweh heard her prayer?

Zahav dried herself, put on the white dress she had made especially for the day. Hoping Messiah would come. Hoping she would see him face-to-face. Almond flowers, to remind her that God was always watching, ever awake and mindful of her, were embroidered on hem and sleeves and bodice. At the waist Zahav had woven four fringes like those on Messiah's prayer shawl.

Two knots. Ten wraps.

Two knots. Five wraps.

Two knots. Six wraps.

Two knots. Five wraps.

Two knots.

She and Rebecca parted company outside Papa's house.

Zahav entered to the urgent sound of Papa's voice speaking to her uncle. "Zadok! He's here? But how long? For how long?"

"Since Rosh Hashanah . . . teaching the seventy . . . now he's sent me into the city to call y' out to meet him. You and your kin."

"But . . . so few. How?"

"Need to keep it a secret."

"Kol Nidrei this afternoon . . . everyone . . . my children. All of my congregation. A secret? Such a thing a secret? A few more, Zadok. Only a few more or less. What can it hurt? The cantor. The sexton. Zahav's boys chorus. All hoping he would come . . . looking for him . . . just as we are."

Zakok stroked his beard for a long minute. "Y' could tell a few, I suppose." He gave a nod of assent.

Days of rest, together with Zahav's excellent provisions, had restored much of Alexander's strength. Hero regained his lost weight as well. The gaunt, angular faces of both father and son fleshed out, and the hollows around their ribs filled in. What's more, even without the poppy medicine, the boy was calm, though still very withdrawn.

Alexander was finally able to give proper consideration to the news Zahav had brought with the food.

So a healer in the Decapolis cast out evil spirits in the name of Yeshua of Nazareth? Nefesh, Zahav said his name was, and he was supposedly one who had been possessed but was now set free.

The priests of Pan had failed. Doctors had offered nothing except a means to prolong Hero's misery . . . or to end his life.

But what if the underlying cause of Hero's suffering could be eliminated? Hope rose in Alexander, hope as nourishing to his soul as Zahav's provisions had been to his body.

The Decapolis was no more than three or four days' journey from Caesarea Philippi. Alexander would carry his son if need be.

Alexander reflected on how severely the Sadducee elders had reacted to Hero. Yeshua of Nazareth, a rabbi of the Jews, might refuse to even touch Hero, the child of an idol worshipper, let alone cure him. But another Gentile as a healer! Now indeed there was room for hope.

Alexander studied Hero in the soft light of morning. The face so like Diana's, a mirror of all their love and dreams. Alexander owed it to Diana to make every effort to free Hero from whatever it was that kept him bound. Gathering the things they'd need for a week's journey— money, cloak, and walking stick—Alexander didn't forget to include what remained of Zahav's excellent bread.

Stuffing the bread into his knapsack, he thought of the Jewish woman. Was there a way to let her know of his decision? To go again in person to the synagogue might embarrass her, or worse. Could he send a message to her before they left?

Rummaging around his workbench, Alexander retrieved a torn scrap of parchment on which he'd been recording fingering patterns for a new flute design. Turning it to its unused side he wrote Zahav a brief note with a bit of charcoal. Now to get it to her . . .

Hero was sitting quietly on the floor beside the workbench, stacking wooden blocks, knocking them over, and assembling them again. The boy would be fine for a few minutes alone.

Alexander bent close. Waving for the child to watch closely, Alexander mimed that Hero should continue playing. "I'll be right back," he mouthed. Aloud, he added, "And then we're going on a journey together. You and I will find Nefesh and see if he and the name *Yeshua of Nazareth* can be the answer we seek."

Alexander's courtesy to Zahav was more difficult to complete than he expected. Instead of the usual number of Jewish passersby on the street outside the shop, there were none. He expanded his search to the next block and then turned the corner of the market square.

Still no luck.

It was a quarter hour before Alexander spotted the shawl and head covering of an observant Jew.

The man Alexander finally encountered would barely even speak to him, let alone carry a message for him. "The Eve of Yom Kippur is like a Sabbath!" the Jew returned tersely. "No carrying burdens!"

Of course! That explained it. On their Holy Days Jews did not travel far from home and synagogue. No work was permitted.

Fumbling in his pocket, Alexander located a pair of copper coins. The shoemaker's apprentice, a gangly youth with a shock of unruly brown hair, was delivering a new pair of sandals to the charcoal seller's house. Alexander called to him, "You, boy. Can you go a little out of your road on your way back to your master?"

The apprentice replied suspiciously, "Why?"

Alexander passed over the pennies. "Here's money. Take this note to the Jewish synagogue. Ask someone to give it to the choir director. Zahav is the name. Can you remember that?"

The boy accepted coins and message and darted off down the street. Alexander whistled as he returned to his home.

He pushed open the door without noticing it was not latched. Just inside, his pack and staff were in readiness for the journey. "Let's go, Hero," he called joyfully, thinking how remarkable it would be if soon the boy could actually hear! "We'll bring some of your toys," Alexander offered as he reentered the workshop. "Hero?"

The wooden blocks lay abandoned beside the workbench. Hero was nowhere to be seen.

"Hero?" Alexander called again, stooping to look beneath the table. Grabbing hold of the wicker baskets of ivory and olivewood from which he carved his instruments, Alexander dragged them aside. Sometimes the boy liked to play under things, as if hiding in caves or making a den for himself.

But this time he wasn't there.

Into the bedroom. Alexander was not yet alarmed, but frustrated. The excitement about meeting the healer urged haste, not this unnecessary delay!

Look under the bed; not there.

One of the storage chests was open, but Hero was not inside it. Nor was the boy in any of the other corners or cubbyholes.

Panic seized Alexander's heart. A horrifying idea came to him. Had the cook fire been completely out before he left?

Run to the kitchen area.

The fire ring was cold, and Alexander gave a sigh of relief. But he still had not located his son.

Behind the pot on the tripod over the hearth was a shallow recess in the wall that served as a chimney. Knocking over the clay vessel, Alexander thrust both hands into the flue. He seized a double armful of soot and grease . . . but no Hero.

Outside?

Alexander flung wide the door, then caught himself before he dashed off down the street. *Stop and think it through.* The door had been ajar, but Hero never went outside alone. The boy was too easily frightened, especially since his encounter with the bullies.

What other possibility existed?

Which god to pray to? From where would help come? Did any powerful being care about such an insignificant matter? Would the One God of the Jews respond to Alexander's plea, or was this a delayed revenge for apostasy?

Or was it Pan's revenge?

There was a commotion in the direction of the market square, but Alexander ignored it, urging himself to concentrate. Where would Hero go?

Not to Aunt Flavia, that much was certain.

Not to any of their neighbors either. Since Diana was no longer around to calm the boy, Hero was unwelcome in their orderly lives.

Alexander was struck by the notion that Hero, missing his father, had gone to look for him.

Or for Zahav? Was it possible the child would try to locate the most comforting presence he'd lately felt? The Jewish district lay on the other side of the crowd milling about in the market square.

Could Hero have gone toward the smells of the bakeshops around the corner? Recently awake and perhaps hungry, maybe the boy followed his nose?

Alexander took three steps toward the bakery, then hesitated. One direction seemed as likely as another.

But if he guessed wrong? How far away would Hero be? How far from home could a four-year-old get?

At least if he located Zahav she would help him search. Alexander was certain of that much kindness, even if no other existed in Caesarea.

Turning about again, Alexander set out resolutely to pass through the throng in the plaza. More people ran toward the center of the turmoil. Calls of alarm, calls for help, punctuated the day.

Suddenly Alexander ran also, shoving people out of his way, forcing himself deeper into the pack until . . .

His physician friend, Castor, knelt beside the stone trough next to the well. On the ground next to it was a small unmoving form, straw-colored hair darkened and slicked back with water, arms limp and pasty white.

"Hero!" Alexander cried, his voice breaking. He threw himself down at Hero's side. "O Adonai ELoHiYM! Help him!"

The throng stepped back, leaving father, son, and physician in a ring of stunned watchers.

Castor's hands pumped Hero's stomach, lifted his shoulders, turned the boy over, and pummeled his back.

"What? Castor, what?"

The doctor shook his head. "I didn't see it, but they say he went straight to the edge. Never stopped at all, just jumped in. A lucky throw of the rope holding the waterskin snagged him; otherwise . . ."

"Will he live?"

As if to answer for himself, Hero gasped, coughed, spat out water. There was no sign of recognition on the boy's tightly crimped face, but instinctively he crawled toward his father. Curling up in a ball in Alexander's lap, Hero pressed his head against his father's heart.

"Just take him home," Castor advised. "Dry him off. Keep him warm, and . . . and there is nothing else."

28

I n the early afternoon Zahav walked with all her family among the hundreds who climbed the narrow path toward the upper camp of Yeshua of Nazareth on the lower slopes of Mount Hermon. So many had joined them that the gathering had ended up something like Papa's "small" suppers. No one left out.

Word among the congregation in Caesarea Philippi had spread like fire driven by a wind. Pilgrims at the mikveh heard. Travelers in the caravansary. No Jew who wanted to come to the mountain and meet Yeshua face-to-face had been excluded. There were skeptics as well as true believers in the throng. But all had come seeking an answer to the questions: *What is Yeshua all about? Why has he come here? Who is he really?*

Zadok and Papa set the pace. Papa carried the Torah scroll. Zahav's arm was linked with Papa's arm. The tallith of The Name, which she had made for Messiah, was in a satchel over her shoulder. Heli brought the scroll of Jonah.

With the ease of a practiced shepherd, old Zadok hefted the two youngest children of Rebecca and Heli. Zadok's three young shepherd boys helped guide children even younger than themselves. Others steadied the elderly, carted the sick on litters, encouraged those who lagged behind. And so the pilgrims of the synagogue flowed inexorably up the grade toward Yeshua.

Even here, in a semiprotected swale on one of the lower shoulders of The Mountain Set Apart, the icy breeze swirling down from the summit was crisp. Huddling in their cloaks, searching among the boulders for scraps of brushwood to feed the struggling fires, the seventy disciples and the others who traveled with them labored to keep warm. They built shelters of branches as if for the Feast of Tabernacle.

As the pilgrims from Caesarea Philippi topped a rise, they paused to overlook the swale where Yeshua's camp was pitched. The air swirled with the pleasant scent of woodsmoke.

Where was Yeshua? Zahav searched for a towering giant among the men below. No one stood out. They all seemed so ordinary, one man like another, as they scrambled to collect wood and stoke the fires before the services began.

Zahav asked Zadok, "Which one? Who is he?"

Zadok inclined his head, indicating a man carrying a bundle of firewood across His shoulders. "Aye. There. That's him. Yeshua. His mother's there near him tending the fire."

Ordinary. Nothing about Yeshua distinguished Him from His followers at first glance. He was neither taller nor shorter than the others. Not older. Not younger. Not more handsome. Had no appearance of royalty. Wind whipped Yeshua's brown hair. He stacked the wood beside a firepit and pushed a lock from His dark eyes. His mother gestured toward the ridge where the congregation assembled. When He glanced up, Yeshua's expression beckoned a welcome to Zadok.

And in that one look Zahav saw how genuinely happy Yeshua was to see that so many had returned with the old shepherd. And in her own heart, she heard Yeshua's welcome:

Come on! I've been waiting for you! Exiles. Wanderers! Lost sheep of Israel! Come into my camp and rest! All you whose souls toss like the restless sea! Like waves, breaking, breaking, breaking, lap the shores of eternity. In this liquid moment of your existence, see my face and hear my voice and touch the firmness of heaven! Know that the world that waits ahead for you is tangible and safe! Fear not! Be warm! Stretch out your hands! Comfort yourself and rest awhile beside the fire kindled with wood I bore on my own shoulders. Come on! I'm waiting!

Yeshua waved broadly to Zadok. "Shalom!"

Zadok passed the children into the arms of Rebecca, then gave a shout. "Hallelujah! All the congregation's come up, Lord! As y' said they would!"

Papa's face beamed. Tears of joy streamed from his clouded eyes and streaked his face and clung to his beard. "So is it him? Himself? All grown up. After so many years! So many! Tell me!"

"Aye." Zadok exhaled relief. "It is himself, Eliyahu."

Papa's fingers gripped Zahav's arm. "Tell me, Daughter, what's he look like?"

All along the rise a ripple of excitement passed through the crowd. Yes. Finally. There He was. Nothing like Zahav expected. His arrival into the territory of Dan had not been heralded with trumpets and armies of great hosannas. The Anointed One, looking every inch a common shepherd, had been proclaimed by the shepherd Zadok.

How could Zahav answer Papa? "Papa. He looks like your little son would have looked if he had lived and grown to be a man. Yes, Papa. He looks like the son you lost."

Papa nodded. "That's the whole point of it, isn't it? Every man's only son. Take me to him."

"Papa? He's looking at you. Papa! Papa! His arms are out to embrace you."

Papa could barely speak. "Zadok? I would like to touch his face!"

Zahav self-consciously checked her veil as she and Papa shuffled down the path behind Zadok. The multitude followed. Zahav guided Papa's hand onto Yeshua's arm but kept a respectful distance as Yeshua embraced the old rabbi and kissed him on both cheeks.

Yeshua exclaimed, "Shalom, Eliyahu bar Mosheh! Old friend! Shalom! Mother! Look! Look here who's come to meet us! And all his family and congregation with him!"

And so it was a sort of family reunion. The thirty-year-old bonds of miracles, joy, and grief that had welded the shepherds of Beth-lehem with Mary and Yeshua, were unbroken. It was like any family coming together for a holiday after years of separation. There were missing faces, missed and asked after. Tears and laughter. Children met and embraced. So much to catch up on.

And the people kept coming! So many! All beloved by Papa! Honored that their rabbi knew this one whom some called the

Anointed One! They came in every size and shape and personality, all coming near to Papa, standing at his elbow. Waiting until one finished talking and the opportunity was open to interrupt. Shy or emotional, wise or foolish, awkward or confident. Smiling. Bowing. Taking Yeshua's hand.

Zahav did not crowd forward like the others. She stood behind Papa while the roll was called. The tallith in her satchel seemed almost warm. Would she have a chance to give it to Yeshua? What could she say? That she had been waiting for Him? wondering about Him? loving Him her whole life? She kept her eyes fixed on the back of Papa's head as she listened to voices she knew well bubbling up like a spring, telling Yeshua everything.

Her courage failed. How could she speak to Him? Everyone wanted His attention. What would she say? How could she ever offer this gift to Him when everyone wanted to tell Him something, give Him something?

And then a gentle hand rested on her shoulder. A woman's voice asked, "You must be Zahav?"

Zahav turned to face Yeshua's mother. Such warm eyes. Brown eyes with flecks of gold. An oval face framed with graying hair. A kind face, interested. "Yes. Rabbi Eliyahu's daughter. Only that."

"Much more."

"Only Zahav."

A smile. She grasped Zahav's hand. "I'm Mary. Yeshua's mother. I knew your mother well."

"Mama? You knew her then?"

"All the months she carried you. And long before that. Yes. We were great friends, she and I. So much in common. My son and your brother were babies together. She hoped she'd have a daughter."

"She had three." Zahav felt herself blush as Mary stared at the veil.

"Your mother wrote me many years after and told me . . . everything that happened."

"I am the firstborn daughter and the least. Never married. Have no children. Never will."

Mary tilted her head slightly as she listened. Her brow creased with compassion as though she heard something deeper. "She said how beautiful you are and that you love to sing. That you're your father's companion in Torah study. That you are a maker of prayer shawls."

Zahav loosened the veil and let it fall. "And this?"

Mary shook her head and kissed the birthmark. "You were all joy to her after so much sorrow."

Zahav, not able to believe such a statement, fumbled for the package containing the prayer shawl and put it in Mary's hands. "I made this for your son. So many people. All needing something. I'll never get close enough. Would you?"

Mary took her hand. "Come on. Give it to him yourself." She guided Zahav through the sea of people surrounding Yeshua. She caught His eye. Over the heads of a group of Torah schoolboys, He grasped Mary's hand and pulled her close.

No words were needed. Yeshua's gaze searched Zahav's unveiled face and seemed almost to know her, to embrace her. His eyes, so warm—a friend's eyes. Brown with golden flecks, like His mother's. So filled with compassion and interest in her.

Two hundred people crowded in, and yet it felt to her that He saw no one but Zahav.

Mary's arm remained around Zahav's shoulder.

Zahav, horribly aware of her disfigurement, tucked her chin in embarrassment and bit her lip.

Yeshua nodded and smiled expectantly. She had brought a gift for Him and He knew it.

She could not speak, for fear she would break open. Tears brimmed.

Mary urged her on with a squeeze to the back of her arm.

Zahav nodded. She would have spoken, but she could not. *Yes. Here it is. For you.* Shyly she extended the package to Yeshua.

He took it from her with obvious pleasure. He unwrapped it partly and peeked in. *Yes! Yes! Beautiful! Yes!* Then He unwrapped it entirely and showed His mother.

Mary said in an awed whisper, "Have you ever seen such a fine tallith, Son?"

Yeshua stroked the fabric. "I haven't seen the like. Not since Yoseph's coat of many colors."

He hummed approval at the gift as He studied the embroidery, the titles of Messiah, on the still-folded fabric. The fringes bearing the knots and wraps of The Name pointed neatly from each corner toward the center of the square.

Yahweh!   *Yahweh!*
Yahweh!   *Yahweh!*

Yeshua cupped Zahav's cheek in His right hand and asked in a voice so quiet no one else could hear, "What gift will I give you, Zahav?"

She swallowed back her emotion and found courage. "Oh, nothing for myself! There's nothing I need or want, Lord! But there's a child, a little boy who lives in the city with his father. Hero is the little boy's name . . . and though his father has strayed far from the truth, I see in his eyes how much he loves his son!"

With a slight motion of His head Yeshua summoned old Zadok. "It's a long walk back to the city, Zadok. But one small lamb was left behind. It will be dark coming back to camp. Zahav will need your protection."

No need to say more. Zadok brandished his staff as if to say no lion or jackel or bandit would dare to come near.

Yeshua squeezed Zahav's hand. "Bring the boy and his father to me."

In the late afternoon Peniel watched as throngs of people continued to arrive at the camp of the talmidim. They came from Caesarea Philippi, from across Gaulinitis, Galilee, and Syria. The booths improved from simple huts to more elaborate structures.

Manaen faced the other way, staring up the slope after Yeshua's receding form.

"Something wrong?" Peniel asked his friend.

Manaen fingered the hilt of the sword at his side. "All these people. So many strangers. Certainly there are spies in the crowd. Killers too, maybe? And now Yeshua, almost alone, way up there . . ."

"You're worried about him?"

Manaen shrugged. "Let's just say this time he didn't tell us to stay here. He only said he was taking Peter, John, and Ya'acov. I'm going to follow . . . at a distance, of course, as a sentry."

Peniel made up his mind. He grasped his sword manfully. "Me too. Two sets of eyes are better than one, eh? 'Specially ours. You going to tell Susanna first?"

"Already did. She agreed."

The path wound around the folds of the mountain, revealing at each turning a different vista. Apricot and fig orchards were below them. The glimpse of a terraced hillside on a lower slope gave lonely testimony to the efforts of men to subdue the mountain.

Oaks had replaced the fruit trees of the lower, warmer climes. These in turn surrendered to solitary sentinels of pine trees.

Ever ascending, the trail at first followed a stream, then climbed a natural stone staircase beside a waterfall. At the top of the steep scramble Manaen noticed Peniel gasping for breath and allowed a short break. "Air's thin up here. Don't push too hard."

Thin air was a new concept for Peniel, who had never previously climbed any slope steeper than the steps to the Temple Mount, nor been at any higher elevation than Jerusalem. Now he was a mile and a half up the side of a mountain.

He panted, "Don't . . . lose them. Go on . . . if you . . . need to."

Manaen clapped his friend on the back. "No need. I know now where they're going. Climbed here myself years ago. A natural hollow just below Zion peak. Here, let me carry your sword for you."

"Won't I need it?"

Manaen grinned and slung the harness across his shoulders. "If I hand it back, it means you need it."

Upward they went again, following a ridgeline so narrow that Peniel could see down both sides at the same time. The height made him feel dizzy. This was a new aspect of having sight he'd never imagined. The jagged edge of the crag was bare rock, but in the hollows lay dirty ice, bristling with pine needles. Arrowheads of snow, tips uppermost, marking canyons and crevasses, pointed inexorably toward the peak.

The gorge through which they passed had sheer cliffs on both sides. Peniel swayed slightly and grasped a boulder to steady himself. Manaen remarked, "Far as we go. No one can get past this point without coming through here. Devil's Gate, it's called. From a ledge up above we can see all over. Have plenty of warning."

There had been plenty of daylight when Peniel and Manaen set out to follow Yeshua. Now the yellow sun was sliding down the western curve of the bright blue sky.

From the rocky outcropping on which they perched Peniel saw

sunlight glint on a distant patch of pale greenish yellow enclosed by brown and green hills.

"Sea of Galilee," Manaen remarked.

"So far?" Peniel was amazed.

Manaen grasped Peniel's shoulders and faced him eastward. Hermon's vast shadow, a black pyramid shape that swallowed up the landscape, grew visibly larger. Manaen guided Peniel's view along his right index finger. "Seventy miles. Damascus."

Then, drawing his sword, Manaen held it at arm's length and swung it in an arc from north to south. "Syria. Parthia. Trachonitis. The Decapolis. Perea. Nabatea."

He stopped with the steel blade aimed toward the far southwestern horizon along a line of low crests paralleling the Jordan River. "See the farthest dark bump? Squint."

Peniel nodded.

"Yerushalayim. They used to light signal fires here and relay them . . . blaze upon blaze . . . Dan to Chorazin to Tabor to Gilboa to Ebal to Gerazim . . . to Benjamin . . . to Judah . . . all the way to the Holy City. King David used it. So did Solomon."

It was as if Peniel viewed all the kingdoms of the world from this one spot. A Pan-orama . . . the all-encompassing view. Peniel shivered. "This is not a place that feels altogether right to me."

Manaen frowned his understanding. "I sense it too. Some ancient evil. An old uncleanness needing to be purified."

Alexander cradled Hero across his left arm.

The boy slept, head back, mouth open, elbows cocked. When he breathed in, a high whistle sighed through the room, the exhale rattling slightly from the water he'd ingested.

He was serenely beautiful . . . and Alexander could barely stand to look at him. Today had nearly been the end for the child. Hero had only been out of Alexander's sight for a short time. How long would it be before whatever had driven Hero to throw himself into the well forced him headfirst into another fire? or urged him to pull over a steaming cauldron?

It was not possible for Alexander to watch him every minute of every day. Even now Alexander could barely keep his eyes open from exhaustion. What would happen to the son when the father drifted off to sleep?

Should Hero be chained to the bed? or locked in a cage?

Alexander couldn't bear it, and there was no one he could ask for help. Everyone else agreed Hero would be better off dead.

Alexander unclenched his right fist, revealing the blue vial, recently refilled by Castor. Though no further words had been exchanged about the use of the poppy juice, Castor's knowing gaze had penetrated into Alexander's heart.

He knew now what he had to do—what he should have realized long before. He and Hero would leave this life together. They would go to wherever Diana was. If Hero's life wasn't worth living, then neither was Alexander's.

Plain and simple conclusion, but there it was.

The bottle was as full of relief as Alexander's heart was full of grief. It was a simple exchange. Who was left to mourn?

Alexander had a momentary twinge when he thought of Zahav. This planned exit seemed a churlish way to repay her kindness.

Hurriedly Alexander tucked that thought away behind a mental wall of rationalization. There was no future for a woman already marked for derision connected with an apostate man and a disintegrating child.

Nor was there any hope for Hero's healing. That had been a foolish notion at best, a fantasy to postpone the painful reality. Might as well try to hang on to the dream that Diana still lived as to imagine that any power on earth could cure Hero.

Around the same circuit Alexander's reasoning tumbled again. He convinced himself he would feel guilt the rest of his days if he took the easy way out. He could not poison Hero to remove the inconvenience of dealing with the child, while remaining alive himself.

Alexander raised the bottle and held it up to the light. Viewed through the flask of oily fluid, the lamp's orange flame danced and changed. The white outline of a laughing face appeared amid flickering blue tongues of fire.

When Alexander lowered the glass the illusion vanished, leaving only the shrinking glow of the dying illumination.

This was a waste of time, he realized. He was merely postponing what he'd already decided. There was no longer any reason to put off what had to be done.

Crossing his right arm over his chest, Alexander pulled the cork from the bottle. When he did so he jostled Hero and the boy snorted and jerked once at the disturbance.

Best hurry then. Alexander did not want Hero to wake up; he could not bear the thought of wrestling with the child to force the draught down him.

A quarter of the bottle for his son, his only son, and the rest for himself. That should be more than ample to his purpose.

Outside the sky was already dark. The Jewish Day of Atonement had begun. But there would be no atonement, no mercy, no escape for Alexander or Hero . . . only oblivion.

Alexander pressed the bottle to Hero's lips.

There was an incessant pounding at the door and shouts of "Alexander! Alexander!"

Zahav! He'd have to send her away.

"Alexander! We've found him! It's true! Yeshua is the Messiah. Open up! Alexander!"

True? Alexander stared at the blue vial, corked it, and concealed it in his fist. With Hero still cradled in his arms he answered the door.

Zahav, radiant, bubbling with excitement, stood in the shadow of a tall, grizzled, lean old fellow with a patch over one eye.

She cried, "We've found him! No need to go to Nefesh. Yeshua is here!" And then, "This is my uncle Zadok. He came with me to fetch you back."

Zadok bowed slightly. "Shalom. My niece told me all about it on the way here. Yes. Y' should come with us."

Alexander gaped at the smooth expanse of unmarred skin on both Zahav's unveiled cheeks. "Your . . . your face!"

She breezed past him, not seeming to know or care that the angry red mark that had set the boundaries for her life was gone! "Alexander! Come on! Bring Hero! He told me to come for you both! A coat! Hero needs a coat! It's cold! They were all singing Kol Nidrei! I heard the shofar behind me! Hurry!"

"What happened to your face?" He blinked dumbly at her.

"Do you understand what I'm saying, Alexander?" Joy overflowed. "He sent me to fetch you!"

"Your cheek. Zahav. The mark . . ."

And then Zadok. "Zahav! Your face! Y' were on my blind side. I didn't notice."

She shrugged, "I lost my veil somewhere. But who cares? Alexander! You have to come now!"

Alexander was stunned. "The veil is gone. Is that all you can say? But don't you see?" He turned her toward the polished brass cymbal hanging on the wall that served as a mirror. "The mark! It's gone!"

She stared at herself as though she was seeing someone else. Swallowing hard, she examined her reflection. A quiet *Oh* of astonishment escaped her lips. She croaked, "Alexander, I didn't know. He just . . . he just . . . you know. My face in his hand and . . . look! He told me to bring you. That was what I asked for! My uncle Zadok and I have come back to find you and Hero! Come on. Come on. It's cold up there. Your warmest cloak."

Zahav looked up and knew a beautiful sunset was ahead. How many times in her life had she gazed at the mountain at twilight and imagined the altar of heaven?

Three sparks of light always remained as Zion's trio of peaks caught and held golden fire long after the rest of the earth plunged into shadow. Three candle flames. Two nearly equal in height and no more than the length of the Temple Mount apart. The third, the center spire, a mere hundred feet lower but separated from its brothers by an intervening chasm.

The first image presented by the three peaks was of a man's arms spread wide above his head as if to embrace the world, his feet planted solidly together as though nailed in place. As the light changed, the vision became like the two cherubim kneeling above the Ark of the Covenant, their golden wings covering the mercy seat, where for forty years the presence of the Lord had come to speak with Mosheh in the wilderness tabernacle!

Though the followers of pagan gods claimed the majestic heights were thrones of evil deities, Zahav's soul disputed this dark blasphemy with every sunset and sunrise she had witnessed. Even so, for fear of being defiled, neither she nor any Jew in Papa's congregation, had ever traveled this far up the incline with the intention of staying the night.

This day she was certain they were safe. No unholy creature would dare remain in the presence of Messiah.

Peniel continued up the path alone. He looked back over his shoulder once to see Manaen perched like a lion on the outcropping of Devil's Gate above the pass.

Manaen's hand remained on the hilt of his sword. His face was stone. Resolute in duty, Manaen would make certain no man intending harm to Yeshua would pass while he still breathed.

So Peniel would be the last line of defense in case Manaen fell. A wry smile played on his lips as he fingered the cold hilt of his weapon. A sword was of little use in his hand, but it made him feel useful nonetheless.

He could at least shout a warning before an enemy slit his throat. Oh, yes. If he heard the clash of battle below, Peniel had a voice to cry out, *Run!*

Up and up the trail ascended into the barren heights of Zion.

A cliff face of red-hued stone reared from the rubble of a narrow plateau to form a natural amphitheater just beneath the three jagged pinnacles that crowned the mountain.

Yeshua's confident strides took the grade in great bites. Peter was close on His heels. John and his brother, Ya'acov, struggled to keep up.

Meanwhile, Peniel, one hundred feet beneath them on the switch-back, labored to breathe. It was cold, but Peniel was sweating.

Yeshua, Peter, John, and Ya'acov were plainly visible as they emerged onto the west-facing plateau. Peniel ducked beneath a ledge as Peter peered over the rim into the darkening pool of the world. Gravel rained down on Peniel's head as he panted and thumped his searing chest.

Peter's voice, reflected by the curving cliff face, was as plain as if he shouted in Peniel's ear. "The whole world is spread out at our feet, Rabbi! Have you ever seen such a sight!"

Yeshua did not reply.

The two brothers joined in exclamations as they identified the light of far distant cities gleaming up like stars from the murky world. In the east true night had fallen. The sky was purple. Constellations appeared one star at a time.

Yet in the west the sun still had not vanished behind the gentle curve of the earth. It shimmered like a coin of molten gold about to pour into the distant sea.

It flashed over Peniel how exactly, perfectly the scene being enacted mirrored the story about Mount Sinai he'd heard from Mosheh: The elders of Israel had been seventy in number, just like Yeshua's talmidim.

Twelve pillars represented the twelve tribes, just as Yeshua had the twelve members of His inner circle.

Aaron, whose name meant "conception," had his counterpart in Peter, the "one who opened the womb."

And the Zebedee brothers matched Nadab and Abihu, brothers who also accompanied Mosheh up the mountain.

Peniel trembled. What was about to happen here on this mountain must be of enormous importance to require the closing of a circle begun so many hundreds of years before, symbolizing a new beginning.

Yeshua draped His prayer shawl over His head and shoulders and called the three for the evening prayer of Yom Kippur.

Peniel joined them in a quiet whisper.

Blessed, glorified, extolled, and exalted be The Name of the supreme King of Kings, the Holy One, blessed be he who is the first, the last, and besides whom there is no other God.

Far away on the wind, Peniel heard the flurry of panicked wings, a shrill cry of terror. Like the shriek of a bird of prey.

Extol the Anointed One who soars above the ethereal plains by the will of Yahweh, and exult in his presence, whose Name is elevated beyond all blessing and praise!

Peniel stammered. What was that? A second tremor of fear coursed through the air from east to west toward the crimson surface of the great sea.

Yeshua's victorious voice led His companions in the prayer that was more like a shout of victory:

Blessed be the Name of the Glory of his kingdom forever and ever!

And now the ethereal tremor mutated into a deep moan of agony! A wail of defeat from ten thousand voices emanated from the very stones of the mountain!

He comes!
Messiah! The Anointed One!
The end!
It is . . . the end!
Yahweh! Yahweh comes!
Yeshua! Messiah! Please!
Do not cast us into . . .
We beg!
We implore you!
Not yet! Not now!
Not time yet! Why have you come?
We are doomed!
He is here!
He who is!
Son of the Living God!
He who was!
You who will be!
Do not cast us into the sea!
Into the Abyss!
Lord of Hosts! Not the Abyss!
Yahweh! Messiah! Yeshua! Adonai! Not the Abyss!

Peniel coughed, choking on fear beyond expression! He crouched down and covered his head with his cloak as the voices of evil swooped around him like birds startled from the nest.

And still Yeshua prayed with the three, unperturbed by the roaring.

Blessed are you, O Eternal, our God! King of the Universe, at whose behest the evening darkens, who in wisdom opens the gates of heaven, and whose understanding varies the seasons and arrays the stars in their watches in the firmament according to his will. Eternal of Hosts is his Name!

Drop by drop light flowed away and with it the shouts of the dark ones as they were sucked down by the whirlpool of fire and light. One shining sliver remained. And then a flash of blue green radiated up and out from the horizon! The day was truly gone. And the air of the mountain was silent except from the voices of Yeshua and His three disciples.

Blessed are You, O Eternal, who creates the dusk of evening. With ever-enduring love you have loved your people of the House of Israel!

If Yeshua noticed Peniel quaking, wheezing, and weeping in fear, He did not acknowledge his presence. Nor did He point him out to the others.

Had Peniel been the only one on the mountain to hear the shouts of terror as the dark inhabitants had been banished?

Peniel tried to stand. Fear turned his legs to mush.

It was night anyway. He sank down onto the ground and told himself, *Not safe to continue up the path even for a fellow who had formerly lived his life in darkness.*

He would stop here. He would be the rear guard. No one could get past him here, once he got his strength back. No human creature anyway. He could take on a human army one at a time. Drop stones down on enemy heads. This was a good place to start an avalanche if required.

If only he could catch his breath.

When Alexander, Zahav, Zadok, and Hero reached the plateau north of the city an orange glow illuminated the entire night sky. An army of campfires stretching from horizon to horizon illuminated the base of Mount Hermon. Alexander marveled at the sight, wondering if the eve of battle between Antiochus and Ptolemy had boasted so large an encampment as this expanse of booths contained.

Hundreds of worshippers sang hymns, chanted psalms, and carried on the Ma'ariv service under the dome of the starry sky.

"Hear, O Israel, the Lord our God is One Lord!"

"Baruch Shem Kavod Malkuto . . . Blessed be the Name . . . Honored and Majestic."

Alexander also marveled at Zahav, her face radiantly alight with joy and expectation. He was overwhelmed by her compassion. She was more concerned for Hero, more eager for his healing, than exultant in her own miraculous cure.

"There's Papa!" Zahav exclaimed, leading the way toward family and friends grouped around a roaring bonfire.

Alexander was suddenly afraid. These were true believers, sons and daughters of the covenant. What if they drove him away? He fingered the blue vial in the pocket of his robe. It could not be! It must not be!

Rabbi Eliyahu met them.

Zahav took Hero from Alexander, cradled him, and rocked him. She asked urgently, "Yeshua? How soon can we see him?"

"He's not here, Daughter," the rabbi said. "Gone up the mountain with just three others."

Imploring in words what Alexander was shouting inside, Zahav pleaded, "But when? When will he return?"

"A day. Two days. He didn't say," Papa explained.

Despite the massive glow of the fires, gloom closed in around Alexander. Was this the end then? Would Hero die before Yeshua returned?

A trio of small boys and a red-coated dog gathered around Zadok. One of the boys, head covered in a profusion of red curls, piped, "He said wait here. What's wrong with your son? Is he sick? Yeshua's talmidim have been healing other people while he's away."

Alexander stared.

"Get one of them," Zahav ordered.

The boy returned a short while later to Alexander and Zahav with not one but *three* of Yeshua's followers: Levi, Judas Iscariot, and Thomas.

Alexander explained the situation to them, concluding with "He's always been like this, but much worse since his mother died. It's like some *thing* is trying to kill him."

Thomas bit his lip and shook his head slowly. "I . . . I'm not sure anymore. Ever since Yeshua spoke so plainly about death . . . his death . . ."

Judas' nose wrinkled. "Pan worshipper?" he repeated. His tone suggested everything Alexander feared: Hero was not worth saving; Alexander was getting a just punishment.

Levi did not act that way. Calling for Zahav to bring him the boy, he sat on the ground and laid Hero across his lap. At his touch Hero's eyes opened, sought and found Alexander's face. Then the boy lay unmoving.

Above them something was happening on Mount Hermon. Sparks of light darted in and out of a cloud hovering just above the peaks. Levi focused on the spectacle for a time, then prayed aloud. "O Adonai ELoHiYM, on this Day of Atonement, come to us, unworthy as we are, and grant us our requests."

At the name of God Hero stiffened, becoming rigid as a plank of acacia wood.

"In the name of Yeshua of Nazareth, heal this boy."

At the mention of Yeshua Hero writhed in Levi's arms. His back spasmed, neck arching. He moaned and shook. His eyes rolled back in his head and foam appeared on his lips.

"Send healing to this child!"

It looked to Alexander as if a giant pair of hands was kneading his son's tiny body like a lump of dough. Contractions seized Hero's chest, then his stomach, then bent head and knees together.

Moans became low growls, interspersed with panting breaths and choking sobs.

Zahav grabbed a finger-sized smooth branch from a pile of firewood and forced it between Hero's jaws.

At the next paroxysm the branch was bitten in two.

Zahav snatched up another stouter piece, forced it in place.

"Stop! Stop! You're killing him!" Alexander begged Levi. "Enough! Stop this!"

In the valley far below the peak of Zion, pilgrim watch fires floated on the dark earth like distant stars in the heavens. It seemed to Peniel as though the universe had turned upside down. There was no earth remaining, only pinpoints of light above and below. All creation sailed like night ships on a vast sea, searching for safe harbor. All. All. Everyone. Everything. Waiting for the great rising of First Light on eternity.

Suspended between heaven and earth, Peniel heard Yeshua's voice, praying, soothing like a mother's heartbeat soothes a baby in the womb:

You are mighty forever, O Father! Reviving the dead you are all-powerful to save! You cause the wind to blow and the rain to descend. You sustain the living in mercy and abundant compassion! You support the fallen and heal the sick and release those who are bound. You establish your faithfulness to those who sleep in the dust!

By starlight Peniel saw Yeshua clearly. So ordinary. So like every man's brother. Every man's son. Approachable. It was not surprising people wondered who He was. What He was.

No wonder people doubted when they saw Him.

Messiah. How could Messiah be so ordinary?

Son of David. King of Israel.

Could a cup fashioned from such common clay contain everything written in the Law and the Prophets?

Peter, John, and Ya'acov stood some distance from Him as Aaron and his two sons must have waited apart from Mosheh the day the Lord descended to Sinai.

Had it been on this very plateau that Satan had showed Yeshua the whole world and laid every kingdom at Yeshua's feet? From this precipice had Satan tempted the Messiah, encased in such ordinary humanity, to forsake God's covenant? to exchange the role of Isaiah's suffering Redeemer for all the glory and all the power of the temporal world?

As Satan tempted every human with his lies, so he had tempted Yeshua: "All this will I give you if only you bow down and worship me!"

Tonight, perhaps, Yeshua had returned to claim the heavenly kingdom of men's hearts for all eternity! Yeshua continued His prayer:

What does it profit a man if he gains the whole world and forfeits his soul?[86] I have come down to defend the afflicted among the people and save the children of the needy!

Wrapped in the prayer shawl embroidered with the names of God, Yeshua stretched out His arms as if to summon pinwheels of light and splashes of unnamed color from the far ends of the sky. From the four corners of His tallith the letters encoded into knots and wraps of the fringes sparked with cold blue fire!

Had he imagined it? Peniel shuddered with apprehension as the wind from Zion seemed to speak the names of the Most High in the branches of the trees. The stones of the mountain resounded with the echos of creation.

Yahweh-Roi! "The Lord, our Shepherd!"
ELoHiYM! God Almighty! Creator! Three in One!
Adonai!
Yaweh-Yireh! "God Who Provides!"
Redeemer!
Savior! Prince of Peace! Wonderful! Counselor! Lamb of God!
El Olam! "Ancient of Days!"
El'Elyon! "God Most High!"
Yahweh-Shammah! "Lord of Hosts!"
Yahweh-Rophi! "The Lord our Healer!"
El Shaddai! "God Who Embraces!"
Son of God! Son of Adam! Son of David!
Yeshua! Messiah! Shepherd! Savior! Redeemer! Anointed One!
Immanu'el! "God-with-us!"
The heavens declare the glory of Yahweh!

Then as Peniel watched, Yeshua's face gradually brightened. Illuminated to a glistening opacity. Bright. Brighter! Peniel gasped. It was not as though a beam of light shone down on Him. No! Not that! Nothing like a candle flame or a lamp or an ember or the flaming brand of a fire.

There was no counterpart on earth for what was happening! Yeshua's body was transformed as if molten silver gleamed from His core! Fingers. Hands. An awesome inner power altered His appearance until He was . . . something else . . . something more than human! More than angelic. The ground around Him was bathed in a mist of unearthly light. Beneath His feet was a pavement of sapphire. Dazzling! Radiant! He turned His head toward His three talmidim.

His eyes were the blinding flash of sunrise reflected on calm waters!

The tallith of The Name over His head and shoulders grew whiter than the snows of Mount Hermon!

Peter, John, and Ya'acov reeled back, grasping at one another, tripping, tumbling to the ground. Clinging to one another in astonishment!

From his hiding place on the path beneath the plateau, Peniel flattened himself against the boulder and covered his head with his cloak.

Above him, whispers! Distinct male voices.

Holy One of Israel!
Lamb of Yahweh!
To you alone is glory, Son of the Most High God!
To you alone all honor, Son of David!

Peniel peered out from beneath his cloak as two men emerged from thin air. Solid flesh now, they walked solemnly toward Yeshua.

Peniel blinked in disbelief! He knew these fellows; these were the Ushpizin of his dreams! They reflected the light that radiated from Yeshua. His light illuminated their path.

Mosheh and Elijah!

Mosheh, the priest-lawgiver! White-bearded, strong like a bull. Eyes like a hawk. Staff in hand. Mosheh! Alive and real as any man!

Elijah, the prophet, bearded, broad-shouldered, dressed in rugged homespun. Hair and beard as black as a raven's wing! Elijah, who had never died but had been taken to heaven in a whirlwind! Yes! *That Elijah! The Elijah who would come to proclaim Messiah!*

The trio stood close together, like old friends meeting on a long journey.

The prophet—confirming all that had been written about Messiah.

The priest—confirming the covenant of blood made between God and Israel!

Yeshua, the King, the fulfillment of everything written in the Law and the Prophets.

Mosheh touched hand to brow and bowed deeply before Yeshua. They did not speak, but Peniel felt their words.

The heavens praise Your wonders, O Lord![87]

A cool breeze blew against Peniel, entering his thoughts, pulsing through his blood.

Elijah stepped forward, bowed and touched his heart. *Who in the skies can compare with You?*[88]

Peniel recognized the greeting from the psalm of God's covenant with David.

Each of the Ushpizin whispered in turn.

Mosheh first. *Who is like You among the heavenly beings?*

Elijah followed. *You are mighty, O Lord!*

Your faithfulness surrounds You.

You rule over the surging sea!

> *When its waves mount up, You still them.*

The heavens are Yours

> *and Yours also the earth!*

You founded the world

> *and all that is in it!*

You created north and south.

> *Tabor and Hermon sing for joy at Your name!*[89]

The Ushpizin spoke openly with Yeshua about His coming death in Jerusalem.

"His Exodus," Mosheh said.

The blood of the Lamb of God who takes away the sins of the world applied once and for ever to the doorposts of the hearts of men.

The Pharaoh of this world forced at last to release his slaves.

EL HaYaM . . . into the sea with the powers of darkness.

No doubting, no second-guessing, no protesting that such a fate could not await the Messiah!

Mosheh exulted in a triumph, not a defeat.

Elijah agreed. Shame and torment and death in Jerusalem—a victorious conclusion to the mission of Messiah, the Anointed One, the Holy One of Israel, the Redeemer of All Mankind.

Wavering on his knees, it was as if Peter hadn't heard any of it. Batting back the glare, he squinted and called out, "Lord! Lord! Look! It's good for us to be here to see this! The Ushpizin! If you want, I'll put up three tabernacles. One for you! One for Mosheh! And one for Elijah![90] You can camp here for the Feast of Tabernacles."

While Peter was still speaking, a bright cloud descended, enveloping them. Not a rain cloud. No, Peniel knew rain clouds. On the Temple steps Peniel had heard enough about The Cloud to know.

The Shekinah Glory of Sinai blanketed them.

Peniel's heart raced. Dangerous energy crackled around him. He could not see. The air was heavy, weighing him down. He could barely breathe. Wrapping his arms over his head, he pressed himself against the hard ground.

Why had he followed? Why? Foolish. More foolish than Peter shouting to heavenly beings about staying around for the Feast of Tabernacles! At least Peter had been invited onto the mountain.

Peniel was an intruder! Too far! Too far up the path! Too far! Holy ground! Heat in the earth beneath his hands and knees. The presence of the Almighty God surrounded him and he was not holy! There was no escape! No place to run!

He ran anyway.

Granite ledges turned boglike; he sank into them.

Gravel beneath his feet shattered, scattered, as if the mountain were being pulverized around him.

Light pulsed behind him, the throbbing heartbeat of eternity.

Scrambling, clawing, desperate for breath, Peniel ran. But there was no end to the rolling, the shaking.

A voice like thunder flowed from the cloud, brandishing him. It crushed him into the dust of the earth, boomed in his chest, rattled his bones.

This is
    my only Son
whom I love.
    I AM well pleased
with him![91]
        Listen!
           To him!

Peniel, born blind, ran unseeing, heedless of dark, height, danger. Not in panic, not in unreasoning fear, but in utter, hopeless comprehension of his own unworthiness.

Solid earth vanished.

He tumbled, screaming. Peniel plunged into . . .

Darkness.

30 CHAPTER

F ar above those who watched and waited on the slopes that night, an unseen battle raged.

On the peak of The Mountain Set Apart, darkness was shattered by Messiah's presence. The thick cloud radiated light from within.

This is my only Son whom I love. I am well pleased with him! Listen to him! ELoHiYM commands!

A voice in the thunder rumbled words of admonition, mercy, and victory!

Ancient gods of darkness who had distorted every truth and oppressed mankind with hopelessness, fear, and despair, writhed in terror! Like granite boulders breaking loose from the summit, demons shrieked as they fell from their self-proclaimed heights!

The unseen legions of the Evil One trampled one another like stampeding swine trying to escape the presence of **ELoHiYM! EL HaYaM! Be cast into the sea!**

Alexander and Zahav rested on a knoll a short distance outside the glow of the fading fires. Cocooned in a blanket, Hero lay on the ground between them. The boy moaned in his sleep as if unable to escape a nightmare in which he was trapped.

Alexander reached out to rest his hand on Hero's shoulder and the boy relaxed again. How much longer could he keep this up? Alexander thought. How many more exhausting nights? How many more tortured spasms before Alexander turned again, finally, to the poppy juice?

Inside the pocket of his robe Alexander fingered the blue vial. It was cold to his touch.

Sensing Alexander's thoughts, Zahav murmured, "Don't despair. He'll be back . . . I know he will."

Alexander released his hold on the bottle as if it had suddenly burned him.

The top of Mount Hermon was alive with lightning that danced from peak to peak. Flashes illuminated the cloud bank resting on the summit. Crashes of thunder tumbled down the slopes and canyons like volleys of stones unleashed against a besieged fortress.

An unseen battle raged on the mountaintop, or rather, once begun on the peak, spread outward across the earth.

A fierce battle raged in Alexander's heart too. Hope raised and then dashed. Help for others all around, but not for Hero? Sitting out on this cold, lonely hillside . . . for what?

Zahav grew sleepy. Leaning protectively over the top of Hero, she rested her head against Alexander.

Slowly, uncertain how it would be received, Alexander stretched his arm around her. Zahav curled closer to his side. With one hand she held on to his embrace. "Don't give up," she whispered drowsily.

He gazed down at her. How he wished . . .

But it could never be. How could he inflict more heartache on one who had suffered so much already?

A tiny flame burned to the end of a log and flared. The flickering light dancing on Zahav's face made Alexander study her again.

She was beautiful! Alexander had always seen her as beautiful, but now the loveliness of her heart suffused her entire face as well. Gone was the reminder of evil's imprint on her life . . . removed while she had sought only to bless someone else.

Gone without her even asking it for herself.

Zahav truly deserved this miracle.

Alexander looked at his son once more before he also drifted off to sleep. For his sake . . . by Zahav's wish . . . Alexander would not despair. God help him, if he could make it through one more dark night, he would attempt to face one more heartbreaking day.

"Peniel?" From far away someone called him back. "Peniel. Breathe."

Peniel inhaled deeply, drawing morning into his lungs. A hand rested on his head. "Wake up. Peniel."

Yeshua.

Every man's son.

Every man's brother.

Speaking in a voice that any man with ears could plainly hear, as if the disguise of earthly existence was the reality. "Another breath. Deep. That's it."

A shudder. A groan. Peniel's own. He did not want to wake up. "So tired."

"Peniel. Open your eyes."

Peniel obeyed. It was before dawn. Cold. The sky ripening to crimson. He lay on his back in the dirt and listened to the sound of a brook. Yeshua, brown eyes concerned, was kneeling beside him. A quartet of worried faces—Manaen, Peter, John, Ya'acov—blinked down.

Peniel coughed, stirred, wiped gravel from his cheek and mouth. Tried to remember what had happened. The Light. The voices. The Ushpizin. Not a dream, but real. Yeshua. The Cloud descending, covering Him. The indescribable force emanating from its core—holy, perfect, all-knowing, all-powerful. It was the essence of holiness—holy, perfect, beyond possibility of human comprehension! Peniel remembered the overwhelming sense of his unworthiness to remain in such a presence! Running blindly, blindly, down the path. And then . . .

"Where am I?"

"You fell." Yeshua helped him sit up. Plucked pine needles from his hair. Brushed dirt from his back.

The world spun around once, then righted itself. Peniel recognized the rivulet of a stream near the place he had left Manaen on guard at Devil's Gate. He was far below the peak where *it* had happened. Had he fallen so far? "I don't remember."

Manaen, ashen-faced, wiped his mouth with the back of his hand.

"Looked like lightning on the mountain. A great storm. Then something came crashing and howling over the cliff last night. It was you. What happened?"

Peter scratched his head and scowled. "Little idiot. Up there in the dark. What were you doing up there prowling around? Up there in the dark?"

Peniel resented the tone. Who was Peter to call anyone an idiot? "Collecting branches. To build a tabernacle."

Peter straightened abruptly. Narrowed his eyes defensively. Crossed his arms. Peered at Peniel with suspicion.

Yeshua laughed. "Well, you're all right now. That's the important thing. Nothing broken." He clasped Peniel's hand and helped him to his feet.

They walked toward the encampment, with Yeshua at the fore. The three talmidim, somber and silent, were behind Him. Peniel and Manaen took up the rear.

Manaen whispered, "What happened up there?"

Peniel shook his head. "Nothing. Nothing."

"Why were you running?"

"I was scared. That's all."

"Of what?"

Peniel waved him off and shook his head. He removed the lavender bud from his pocket and held it to his nose. He inhaled and remembered what Yeshua said about one grain of truth being worth a whole wagon of colored sand.

How could he answer Manaen's question? How could he explain to Manaen the complexity of his terror?

Peniel had frightened Peniel. He had seen himself as he really was, compared to the Almighty God. All self-delusion shattered. Self-righteousness vaporized. Nothing was as he had imagined it. Peniel was not really who Peniel thought he was.

He realized he had drastically overestimated his ability to achieve righteousness through keeping the laws of Torah. Compared to the righteousness of God, Peniel's goodness fell short by the distance from earth to the farthest star!

Peniel had seen Yeshua as He *really* was.

He had heard the voice of the Omnipotent God bearing witness to His Beloved Son.

The Voice of the Almighty, the Creator of the Universe, had thundered from the Cloud of Unknowing, commanding all mankind to listen to Yeshua!

But who really listened to Yeshua? Who? Really?

Everything He had said had been in plain language. Nothing complicated. Peniel had heard Yeshua say it a hundred times over the summer. All the Law and the Prophets summed up in the commands *"Love the Lord your God with all your heart, soul and mind, and your neighbor as yourself."*[2]

But who fully lived out that command? No one. No one.

On top of terror came the height of human absurdity! Peter, volunteering to erect three huts for the Feast of Tabernacles. As if the point of Mosheh and Elijah and the Shekinah descending to the mountain was to camp in a hut Peter built for a family visit during the Holy Days!

Just try to cram the Most High God into anything built with human hands!

Peniel shuddered. He was certain that neither he nor Peter, John nor Ya'acov would ever grasp the magnitude of Who and What they had just encountered!

It was unfathomable. Humbling. From now on, even as he walked and talked of other things, Peniel's soul would remain on its knees!

And so for all these reasons—and more besides—Peniel was afraid. Rightly. Correctly. Truly. Terrified.

Peniel stared at Yeshua's back as they descended. It seemed to be the back of an ordinary man. But Peniel knew better.

Who would imagine by looking at Him . . .

There were no words to answer the unending questions: *Who is He? Carpenter? Rebel? Prophet? Healer? Magician? Messiah?*

So far, even the ones who called Him Lord and proclaimed Him Messiah had not figured it out. Not fully.

Yeshua. *He had come to earth like the great treasure of a king, beyond value, hidden in straw, packed into a common clay jug, shipped to earth among the cargo of a river scow.*

No one really knew. Those who thought they knew still could not fully comprehend the meaning of Immanu'el, "God-with-us."

Yeshua. *First Light. The great red dawning that rises over the mountains of all eternity. The shining bridge of stars that arches up and up to give mankind a path from earth into heaven's throne room.*

Yeshua. *Carrying the message of eternity across the vast gulf of all time to mankind! Chesed! Mercy! Forgiveness! Eternal Life!*

Yeshua. *Fulfillment of every promise and prophecy recorded in the Law and the Prophets. He was the great mystery that, after every revelation made to mankind, was still defied, doubted, and denied by those who witnessed His power with their own eyes!*

Even now. Even after so much. So many. So often. Even after everything.

And so Peniel was afraid.

How much longer would The Lord of All the Angel Armies, the Great King of all Eternity, Messiah, God-with-us, put up with us?

That was the question.

Freedom. Zahav's fingers explored the smoothness of her unmarred cheek. All reproach gone. A world of possibilities opened for her.

Alexander and Hero had moved inside the cedar-bough shelter with Zadok and his three boys. The red dog guarded the entry. Zahav wondered if Alexander had given the child poppy juice. Hero rested peacefully through the night.

Strange lightning had danced upon the summit, but no rain fell on the hundreds of brush tabernacles erected by pilgrims in the swale.

Praying, Zahav had remained outside with Papa to watch until the luminous cloud lifted slowly from the mountain and vanished in the predawn light. Most among the congregation had grown weary of the sight and wandered off to bed. But not Zahav. Not Papa.

People in the camp were awake and stirring now. The sun would rise soon. Messiah would come down from the mountain and teach them. It would be a new beginning.

"What do you think, Papa?" She sighed with contentment.

The old man, wrapped in layers of blankets like a child, stretched his hands to the warmth of the fire. "Daughter, we have waited a very long time to see the sun rise on this day."

"Soon he'll be here, Papa." Light glowed behind the brow of the hill where Yeshua's seventy and their families were already up and about.

Papa mused, "I was thinking of your mama, may she rest in peace.

Wishing she were here. Here to see your cheek as smooth and white as a blossom."

Zahav tucked her chin self-consciously and then, remembering she had nothing to hide, raised her head. "Mama would like him."

Papa poked at the embers with a stick. "Yes, Mama would like him. He's a very nice fellow. Very lonely, eh? Bright, I think. He will learn our ways quickly. His family was distinguished once. His great-grandfather helped erect the synagogue. I looked it up in the records. He will make a fine husband once he learns the Shema and grows his beard."

"Yeshua?"

"Ah. No. Yeshua has a fine beard, knows the Shema, and will not take a wife. Alexander. I meant Alexander. Alexander is the man you have loved for a long time, eh, Daughter?"

She blushed. Hugged her knees. "Mama would like him better if he had a beard like a Jew."

"So. The beard will grow without our help. But there are other things to take care of first. This and that. That and this. Education. Bar mitzvah. But Messiah is with us. The reproach is gone; everything will be restored. There will be forgiveness and mercy. And a breaking of chains. All things are possible with God. And the boy . . ."

"Hero."

"Yes. Poor little fellow. Living in such a lonely house. A cage. But, Daughter, it is the Year of Jubilee. The Year of Freedom. I knew he would come. As it is written by the prophet Isaias, *'The Spirit of the Lord is upon me, because he has anointed me to preach good news to the poor. He has sent me to proclaim release to the captives, recovery of sight to the blind, to set at liberty those who are oppressed, to proclaim the acceptable year of the Lord.'*"[93]

"A good hope. Hero is . . . ill."

"More than that. Yes. You know it. The mountain. The grotto. Things we will not speak of by name, Daughter. But the boy is more than ill."

Zahav nodded then glanced up as ten strangers entered the camp from the trail on the downward slope. They loitered by a fire. Engaged a pilgrim in conversation.

"Scribes, Papa. Pharisees. Look. Can you see them? A minyan. Ten. Dressed in the style of Yerushalayim."

Papa did not bother to look. "A minyan. On official business, then.

Sanhedrin I would guess. The edict Zadok told us about. Against Yeshua. I knew they would come eventually."

Behind them Zadok emerged from the shelter, stretching and yawning. "Eliyahu? Did I hear my name blasphemed?"

Zahav pointed toward the newcomers. "Shalom, Zadok. Zadok? Look. Ten of them."

Zadok was an oak unmoved by wind. His presence gave Zahav a sense of peace.

The shepherd adjusted his eyepatch, crossed his arms, and scowled. "I've seen them around Yerushalayim. Underlings. Arrogant know-nothings. Low rank. Relatives of Caiaphas mostly. Troublemakers."

Alexander unfolded himself from the shelter, stepped over the dog. Rumpled, with the stubble of beard just sprouting, he smiled at Zahav and rubbed his head.

So this is what he would look like in the morning, Zahav mused.

"The boys are all still sleeping. Like a pile of puppies. Hero hasn't slept so well since his mother died," Alexander said. And then, "What is it? Trouble?"

Papa explained, "Scribes from Yerushalayim by the look of them. Likely delivering an edict. Official religious document condemning Yeshua of Nazareth as a fraud and a Shabbat breaker."

Alexander frowned. "They're coming here? But what does it mean?"

Zadok's three boys crept out, leaving Hero sleeping alone on the pallet.

Zadok embraced his drowsy boys and explained the edict. "The religious officials can accomplish what the political powers can't."

The Pharisees had entered Philip's territory unopposed, under the authority of the religious rulers. Though soldiers of Herod Antipas were not welcome in Philip's territory, Philip would not ban officers from the Sanhedrin. And now they were in the right place at the right time.

The attempt to challenge and discredit Yeshua openly among Papa's congregation began immediately.

The minyan approached. A round-faced, rich young Pharisee with a thin beard bowed perfunctorily and addressed no one in particular. "Shalom. We have come by edict of the Sanhedrin and *Cohen Hagadol* Caiaphas of Yerushalayim."

Unearthly laughter erupted from inside the shelter.

The eyes of the official grew wide. Nervous. "We . . . we . . . are . . . looking for the imposter, Yeshua of Nazareth."

A scream followed Yeshua's name.

"As I was . . . saying . . . Yeshua of Nazareth. The Carpenter—"

This time the shriek drowned out his voice. It was as though the name of Yeshua was a firebrand, torturing Hero.

Throughout the encampment, heads turned. Morning chores, washings, and prayers came to a standstill as a third high, shrill scream shattered the quiet morning.

Alexander dove to Hero's aid. Zahav followed. On the floor Hero was convulsing, blood and froth on his lips.

So Yeshua, after revealing the glory of Who *He Was*, *He Is*, and *He Will Be*, descended from the mountain where Satan had once offered Him all the kingdoms of the world.

Yeshua entered the dimension of ordinary time and ordinary men once again.

And that descent, for the sake of conquering the darkness that oppressed men's hearts, is what was so extraordinary.

Human imagination could never invent a myth or a god or a love that would not be instantly eclipsed by the Truth of what He laid aside for the sake of that great love.

Even so, Immanu'el, Yeshua, Son of the Most High God, came down again to face petty men with hearts infused with darkness.

For if He had not come down, how could His Light have conquered the Prince of Darkness?

The voices from the camp drifted up before Yeshua's small group reached the final turning of the path. Yeshua understood the battle He faced was more fierce than that of merely the unseen world.

For the greatest two lies the Father of Lies had ever whispered were that He did not exist and that evil could not be defeated.

But The Lord of All the Angel Armies,
incarnate in ordinary human flesh,
came down to fight the battle
for the kingdom of men's hearts.

And so the story is written and recorded for all time as it really happened. One seeing this detail, another adding what he noted, a third witness offering more of the deliverance of the boy and his grieving father from bondage to the Prince of Darkness, who sought to kill them both.

Take their souls.

The Enemy used religious men in the first wave of his attack.

The shouts. The curses. The fury of the Pharisees reared up like waves of the sea, smashing hope against the base of the mountain.

Failure everywhere. Hopelessness. Who could help Hero? Who really cared? Hero had become nothing more than an object lesson, an example of failure. Was there no one who could set him free?

No one.

They said so.

Not Yeshua. Not His talmidim. It had all been a waste of time.

They said so.

The crowd multiplied to thousands.

Zahav, hoping, praying, trained her eyes on where the path emerged from between two boulders.

When would Yeshua return?

Next to her was Alexander, his life as hollow as a house gutted by fire. He held his only son in his arms and, half afraid to hope, he hoped all the same. He dared to hope, this one last time, for a miracle!

Why did Yeshua not return?

All around them strangers, religious teachers from Jerusalem, quarreled with Yeshua's talmidim over details Alexander could neither comprehend nor care about.

"If Yeshua is the Son of God . . ."

"Who does he think he is?"

"Who?"

"Son of a carpenter!"

"Illegitimate! Everyone knows that!"

"Son of God? Who does he think he is?"

"You're supposed to be his talmidim!"

"You learn the incantations from him. Why can't you cast out the demon?"

In the broken life of his son, Alexander also held up the fragments of himself. The wounds, the grief of father and son, were inseparable.

There was not one without the other. Both were captive, both trussed up for slaughter.

Did the One God of his fathers have a voice to call them home again?

How Alexander longed to hear the voice speak! But the enemy of his soul told him it was too late. Too late. How could the Eternal God of the thunder and the Law and the covenant ever care for him? He had held up his child to the false god of this world!

And yet Alexander's heart cried out to God for mercy. For the sake of his only son, Alexander, the apostate, cried out!

Who are you? Who? Are you the All? The Great Everything of Eternity? Once I dreamed I saw your light before I was born. You told me to listen and you would whisper to my heart. Was it a dream? I'm listening. Are you the First, the Last, the All? The One who knows me better than I know myself? Do you lean over the rim of heaven and see our broken lives, Hero and me? Sweep up the fragments of our lives, even broken, useless! O God of my fathers! I long for us to belong to you. Hero and me. I yearn for you to hold us in the hands of your heart. Here we are, Hero and me. Broken. My boy. All our pieces mixed together, his and mine. Waiting. Needing. Asking. Who are you? Can you sort us out?

It was at that moment extraordinary love entered his life. Father and son. Alexander and Hero. Stepping from the shadows of the boulders into the light of the open field He seemed so ordinary. Who would have guessed?

Zahav grasped Alexander's sleeve. "There he is! Alexander. There! The one in the center. He's wearing a prayer shawl over his shoulders. Let me take Hero. Run! Run to him, Alexander! Run ahead before the people see him!"

Alexander passed Hero into Zahav's arms. "Bring Hero! I'll try to reach Yeshua!" He raced across the field with a number of Yeshua's followers.

Then voices everywhere among the thousands began to cry in joy at the sight of Yeshua!

"*It's him!*"

"*There!*"

"*Hurry!*"

The tide turned, surging toward Him. They pushed, shoved, stalled—a sea of need surrounding Yeshua.

Yeshua asked Philip and Levi, "I heard you arguing in the field with the Pharisees. What is this about?"

Alexander recognized from Yeshua's tone that the Teacher already knew. He knew what it was about. He knew the truth of whose voice was raised in accusation against Him. Many throats it seemed to be, but all one voice.

Alexander leapt onto a stone before they could answer. He called over the heads of a hundred people: "Teacher! Rabbi! Over here! Teacher! I brought you my son!"

Yeshua fixed His gaze on Alexander. With a gesture of His hand the crowd parted like the sea.

Alexander made his way to Yeshua.

He dropped to his knees. Was lifted up until he was face-to-face with Yeshua. Salvation. Yeshua. At last.

And Yeshua knew everything about Alexander in an instant. Alexander saw the knowing, the compassion, clearly in His eyes. He understood the whole truth about Alexander and yet asked, "Tell me, Alexander. Tell me about your boy."

The anguish of Hero's torment gushed from Alexander like blood from a heart wound.

And all the dark unseen world hovered above the scene, whispering doubt to those who listened.

And all creation groaned, waiting to see if Immanu'el, God-with-us, would help a man who had once stood on the brink of the Jordan's headwaters and offered his infant son to the Prince of Darkness.

Would Yeshua turn him away?

"And so," Alexander finished, "Zahav brought us back. You were gone when we arrived. I asked your followers to help us. They tried, but they couldn't."

Yeshua pressed His lips together as though considering carefully what to say to His talmidim. Quietly, sadly, He addressed them. "Oh. Oh. Unbelieving generation. How long will I stay with you? How long shall I put up with you?" And then to Alexander, "Bring your child to me."[94]

Bring your child to me!

Oh, Lord, were there ever words so full of hope for a grieving parent longing for an answer for their child? There was no other answer. No other solution. None.

What breaking heart, helpless to help their dearest one, would not obey such a command? And so Yeshua's answer resounded like the echo of creation:

Bring your beloved to me.

Zahav, who had waited so patiently, gave Hero to Alexander.

And now the Enemy of Man, seeing imminent defeat, marshalled all his powers.

Despair! He cried out at the sight of Yeshua and seized Hero, throwing him to the ground in a convulsion!

With a gentle hand Yeshua stopped Alexander from taking the boy up again. This was Yeshua's battle now. "How long has he been like this?"

"Since infancy." Yes. It had always been this way. Never good. Growing worse by the day. Alexander choked with emotion. Wrung his hands. Instinct compelled him to do something. Anything. But Yeshua's hand stayed him, urged him to tell everything. "It has thrown him into fire and into water to kill him." The child writhed at their feet now, foaming at the mouth. Alexander, breaking, breaking inside, cried out, "But . . . if . . . you can . . . do anything! Lord! Take pity on us and help us!"

Yeshua repeated Alexander's words. "If . . . you . . . can?" He winced. "Everything is possible for him who believes."

Immediately Alexander, ashen-faced, exclaimed, "Lord! I do believe! Help me overcome my unbelief!"[95]

And so it was that Yeshua, the incarnate Word of ELoHiYM, spoke:

You spirit of evil!
The word of
ELoHiYM commands you,
EL HaYaM!
Into the sea!
Come out of him!
Leave him!
And never enter him again!

The spirit shrieked, convulsed Hero violently, and came out.

Hero lay on the ground—still, pale, drenched in perspiration. He looked like a corpse. The crowd hissed that he was dead. *Despair!*

Alexander, gripped with fear, covered his face with his hands.

Zahav touched his shoulder as if to console him.

Yeshua knelt beside the boy, brushed back a damp lock of hair, tenderly wiped the child's battered face with His cloak. "Hero?"

A long moment passed. Yeshua's hand on Hero's head. The little chest heaved, inhaling the morning, breathing in life.

"Hero?"

Eyes fluttered open at Yeshua's whisper.

A moan of relief passed through the multitude. The news was relayed, *"He is alive!"*

"Alive!"

"The boy's alive!"

Alexander cried out with joy and fell to his knees, sobbing. "My son! Hero! My boy! I thought I'd lost you!"

Hero turned to smile into his father's eyes. Reaching out, the child wiped away the tears that streamed down Alexander's cheeks. "Papa," Hero said. "Papa."

Later, in private, Yeshua's talmidim came to Him and asked why they had not been able to drive out the demon. Peniel and Manaen and Susanna and Zadok were among them. Levi wrote down Yeshua's reply:

"Because you have so little faith." Yeshua raised His hand to the summit of Mount Hermon, where long generations had worshipped false gods. "I tell you the truth, if you have the faith as small as a mustard seed, you can say to *this* mountain, 'Move from here to there,' and it will move. By the power of my name you can cast every mountain of evil into the deepest sea, and the sea of God's mercy will cover it forever. With faith, nothing will be impossible for you."[96]

Thus ends the lesson.

Yeshua and His mother remained for a time in the house of the chief rabbi of Caesarea Philippi. Yeshua attended the wedding of Alexander and Zahav. It is remembered by all how when Alexander played his flute, Yeshua danced for joy with young Hero high upon His shoulders.

The story of how that family served the Lord with great courage in the times of trials is recorded for everyone to read. And later, is it not written how the man, Hero, and his brothers, carried the Good News to the far ends of the earth? Are all these and other stories as well not found faithfully recorded in the A.D. Chronicles?

Elijah went before the people and said, "How long will you waver between two opinions? If the Lord is God, follow Him; but if Baal is God, follow him."

"But what about you?" He [Jesus] asked. "Who do you say I am?"

MATTHEW 16:15

Digging Deeper into
THIRD WATCH

Dear Reader,
First-century Jerusalem is sizzling with tension. The people have waited so long for the promised Messiah that they wonder if He's still coming—or if it's all just a fable. Every morning they cast an eye upon Mount Zion, hoping for a sign of the arrival of the only One who can right the wrongs of their world. But secretly, in the third watch of the night, the dark period just before dawn, they wonder, *Is our hope in vain?*

What about you?

Have you ever felt like Zahav—a person rooted in her faith yet filled with intense longing for what she can't have? A woman who spends her time fulfilling everyone else's dreams . . . but never experiences fulfillment herself?

Or Alexander, who has lost so much that he seems to exist only in life's shadows? And because of his hopelessness and grief, his grip on life is growing weaker and weaker.

Or Susannah, who loves much but cannot break through to the person she loves the most?

Or Manaen, who struggles against the bitterness of a life rerouted by insurmountable obstacles that changed the very core of who he is?

Then Yeshua steps in. "Who do you say that I am?"

Such a simple question. But very few seem to be sure. Even those who follow Him waver. And yet it's the single most important question of all time.

Following are six short studies designed to take you deeper into the answers to your questions. You may wish to delve into them on your own or share them with a friend or a discussion group.

Who is Yeshua really?

As you hear Him speak through *Third Watch*, may He come alive to you . . . in more brilliance than ever before.

1 | UNFULFILLED LONGINGS

"So much unfulfilled in my life. O Lord, I am lonely! Longing for something. I don't know what it is, but I ache inside. . . . My heart lies buried. Can you, Yahweh-Yireh, provide for me?"
  —ZAHAV (p. 209)

If you could snap your fingers and have one—but only one—of your longings fulfilled, what would that be? What seems unattainable?

_____

_____

_____

Why is this one particular dream so significant to you?

_____

_____

_____

Every person on earth is waiting for something, longing for something. Perhaps you, like Zahav, are good at hiding your longing. You keep busy with a great job, a wonderful family, lots of friends, and a schedule of endless activities. Everything looks good from the outside.

That was Zahav. As the revered rabbi's daughter, she had a godly home, her papa's and the community's respect, and high praise for her creative job of making beautiful talliths. She was the kind aunt who took care of her sisters' children and directed the community children's choir. She appeared to be a saintly woman who had it all together.

But in the third watch of the night she struggled. She longed for someone to love her, for a child of her own to hold. She had no doubt she was her father's treasure, but "she felt more like ore imprisoned in the granite of his life" (p. 66).

She was the "odd woman out" at family gatherings. Her married sisters talked about children, their pregnancies, and marital things she didn't understand. Clearly she "would never fit. She was resigned—buried in the only life she'd ever have. Guilt at ever wanting more pushed hope far, far down" (p. 188). Yet Zahav couldn't deny her heart's longings—or the envy she felt when others had what she did not have.

Is the first century so different from now? Whether we dream for a spouse (or the "right" spouse), a child, the perfect job, a different family, a healthier (or better-looking) body, or any other number of things, we *all* have desires.

READ

Delight yourself in the Lord
and he will give you the desires of your heart.
　—PSALM 37:4

Praise the Lord, O my soul,
and forget not all his benefits . . .
who satisfies your desires with good things.
　—PSALM 103:2, 5

ASK

What was your first thought when you read these verses from Psalms? Why?

- *Yeah, right. God hasn't done anything about it yet. And I sure don't see him moving in that direction.*
- *I made a big mistake earlier in my life, so I don't deserve to have that desire fulfilled. I've blown it for good.*
- *I'm not important enough for God to notice me—much less care about what concerns me.*
- *If I can just hang in a little longer . . . pray a little harder . . .*
- *I've given up a long time ago. Now I'm just living in limbo.*
- (Fill in the blank)_____

Zahav understood what it's like to live in limbo: "Her existence was spent waiting in a corridor of unopened doors. Life was unfolding behind the doors, but not for Zahav" (p. 65).

It was always "somebody else's son. Never Zahav's. Somebody else's wedding canopy. Never, never Zahav's. . . . She could not admit it to anyone, but she was lonely. . . . Her arms were empty; she felt empty. Lonely. Dead before she died; buried though still walking around" (pp. 6–7). Is that sometimes how you feel too?

What Zahav longed for more than anything was so far out of reach. Even if she hadn't been born with the birthmark that excluded her, by rabbinic law, from having a husband and children, the man she was drawn to was off limits. Alexander was an apostate Jew—he had turned away from his godly heritage. And Zahav was the daughter of a rabbi, no less! Showing interest in Alexander would result in rejection by the Jewish community.

READ

Yahweh-Shalom, God of Peace, there is no peace in my heart. No peace in my life. I'm fooling everyone, aren't I? So capable, so willing. My moments of tranquility are disrupted by the needs of everyone else. If you are Yahweh-Shalom, then where are you in my storm?
   —Zahav (p. 79)

Zahav's life, even in the womb, had begun as a storm. The scene is horrific. A pregnant woman hides in a well with her young son for safety. But one whimper from the child reveals them, and the son is killed! The mother's heart breaks as she fights futilely. The slap to her cheek becomes a slap to the infant within her womb.

The little girl is born with a birthmark on her face that resembles the slap of a Herodian hand. Every time the mother sees the girl's face, she will remember the horror of that night. Is it any wonder she wanted to call her child *Zarev*, "like the melted wax of a candle, because all light had melted from her soul" (p. 4)?

However, the father intervenes and names the little girl Zahav. But throughout her life she feels nothing like the meaning of her name: "'Shimmering like Gold,' just as the golden promise in your Torah shimmers like a bright star to guide us!" (p. 5).

ASK

Which parts of Zahav's prayer can you identify with (whether in the past or present)? Why?

_____

_____

_____

What personal storm is creating havoc in your life right now?

_____

_____

_____

There's a saying: "Sometimes He calms the storm. Other times He calms His child." Have you seen ways—even small ways—in which God has done this in your life? (For example, brought a break in the storm, introduced you to a person who's gone through what you have, revealed encouraging Scriptures, etc.)

_____

_____

_____

If you do all the "right things" spiritually, do you think *some* or *all* of your desires will or should be fulfilled? Why or why not?

_____

_____

_____

Proverbs 13:19 says, "A longing fulfilled is sweet to the soul." How satisfying it is to have dreams come true! But because this world is not our final destination, it's also not our place of final fulfillment. In fact, the unfulfilled things in life (as frustrating, painful, or unsatisfying as they are) bring our focus continually back to the ultimately fulfilling place—heaven, where there will be no sickness, sadness, or pain.

But how do we live in the meantime? That was the question Zahav—and each of us—needed to answer.

READ

Today she had crossed the line of propriety. No respectable Jewish woman would speak one word to a man like Alexander, let alone kneel in the dust and attend to the child of a pagan. And yet Zahav felt so sorry for the man and his son (p. 109).

Zahav was a woman in need. Her soul was aching. She had a choice to make: focus on herself and wallow in self-pity, or do what she felt in her heart was right. The risk was great. Just bringing Alexander and Hero soup and bread meant she was breaking the command to not work on Shabbat (pp. 120–122). Worse, she was "fraternizing with the enemy"—that's how others in her community would see it.

But Zahav chose to act in compassion. She put aside her unfulfilled longings for a time . . . and was granted fulfilled dreams beyond her wildest wishes!

ASK

If you could set aside all your unfulfilled longings for one week, what would you do with the time and energy you'd have left? Be specific.

_____

_____

_____

WONDER . . .

"Have mercy on those whose hearts are aching even more than mine."

    —Zahav (p. 231)

The world and its desires pass away, but the man who does the will of God lives forever.

    —1 John 2:17

As you live "in the meanwhile," what new desires is God placing in your heart? To whom can you extend mercy?

2 | LIVING IN THE SHADOWS

"My heart is broken. Broken. But it isn't just my heart. We're all waiting here, in the shadow of the mountain."
—ZAHAV (p. 231)

If you could go back and do something over, what's the first thing you'd choose?

_____

_____

_____

How has that situation or event affected your relationship—or lack of relationship—with God?

_____

_____

_____

In what ways has it changed your view of yourself?

_____

_____

_____

The *what-if*s. The *might-have-been*s. The *if-only*s.

These are the things that wake us up in the middle of the night. What if my father wouldn't have died? If I had acted when I should have, what might my life be like today? If only I hadn't said what I did to my friend. If only I knew then what I know now. . . .

Such thoughts steal our dreams and force us into the shadows, away from the light of Yeshua's love. They allow us to see only the mountain before us, but not over it to the beautiful blue sky beyond.

And yet we all have periods of living in the shadows.

READ

Their lives had overflowed with so many dreams. . . . Alexander tried not to think of what might have been. If Hero had not been born flawed. If Diana had lived. And yet what-ifs and might-have-beens taunted him, breaking his heart over and over again (pp. 9, 119).

If anyone "lived in the shadows," it was Alexander and Diana. Their married life had begun so blissfully, with heady dreams of home and family. But "five stillborn babies over twelve years had nearly destroyed Diana's ability to hope" (p. 9). Then, to their joy, their son, Hero, was born.

ASK

Put yourself in Alexander's and Diana's shoes. Your long-awaited child has just been born. You can't wait to pass on your love of music. Then you find out your child is deaf. What thoughts would run through your mind about yourself? about the child?

_____

_____

_____

Now factor in this information: Alexander is an apostate Jew. He has a Jewish heritage, but over generations that heritage has been neglected; now the only "religion" he has is cultural. He no longer knows what a personal relationship with a loving God looks like. And the only examples he sees are the holier-than-thou types.

If you were Alexander, what would think about God now, as you saw your beloved wife die? when you knew that there was no healing available for your troubled son?

_____

_____

_____

READ

Alexander's responses were swift—and honest.

"The truth? Castor! You don't know how badly I wanted to become smoke. To drift away with her! I know! I know what he's feeling."
—ALEXANDER (p. 88)

Life was hard and confusing. Why live it then? Why continue to hope? Because the uncertainty of death was more frightening (p. 58).

ASK

Have you ever wanted to "become smoke" and "drift away" because of the pain in your life? Describe the circumstances . . . and what kept you from doing just that.

_____

_____

_____

Castor the physician said, "We . . . face reality when it must be faced. Pragmatism, not sentiment, is true mercy. If there's no hope . . ." (p. 89). Do you agree with his statement? Why or why not?

_____

_____

_____

If you glimpsed Alexander's and Hero's suffering, what would your first response be (your *honest* response, not the way you *think* you should respond)? Why?

- *Poor man. Poor boy. They have nothing left to live for.*
- *I wonder what I can do, if anything, to help. . .*
- *It serves Alexander right—walking away from the faith that way. He deserves everything he gets.*
- *I know what it feels like to be rejected. I feel their pain.*
- (Fill in the blank)_____

READ

As Alexander watches Hero suffer, he agonizes. Should he end Hero's pain by a swift overdose? But then he agonizes further:

> *What if there's nothing to go to? What if I let go of your hand and you slip away from me and everything is darkness on the other side? Ending like the day. A night without stars. Nothing at all. Or worse: an eternity of terror* (pp. 119–120).

> *Do not let your hearts be troubled. Trust in God; trust also in me. In my Father's house are many rooms; if it were not so, I would have told you. I am going there to prepare a place for you. And if I go and prepare a place for you, I will come back and take you to be with me that you also may be where I am.*
> —JOHN 14:1-3

ASK

Which "place" or places do you believe exist after death? A great nothing. A eternity of terror. A beautiful world called heaven, where you'll be with Yeshua forever.

_____

_____

_____

In what ways do your views of death and any afterlife affect how you live now?

_____

_____

_____

Although Alexander does not believe in God, there is a lingering nudge in his soul as he walks by the synagogue where Zahav practices with her choir. He longs for the peace and safety of that community and wonders what it would be like to be part of God's family. But he isn't willing to give up his other gods yet, and he believes Satan's lie that he isn't welcome in God's kingdom (pp. 206–207).

Yet Alexander holds on, choosing life for his son, even when it seems impossible for them to go on. Finally, burdened by a horrible weight of dread and despair, surrounded by evil, he calls out to the God he doesn't know, the God his family has forgotten. "Oh! Help . . . us . . . God of . . . Zahav! Nameless . . . One I don't know! One God! Help . . . me! Help us! Find . . . us! Save us!" (p. 255).

READ

> This is the confidence we have in approaching God: that if we ask anything according to his will, he hears us.
> —1 JOHN 5:14

> Commit your way to the Lord;
> trust in him and he will do this. . . .
> Be still before the Lord and wait patiently for him.
> —PSALM 37:5, 7

ASK

Have you ever called on God for help in your desperate hour? Describe the circumstances.

_____

_____

_____

Did anything change in your relationship with God after that point? Why or why not?

_____

_____

_____

READ

He has sent me to bind up the brokenhearted,
to proclaim freedom for the captives
and release from darkness for the prisoners,
to proclaim the year of the Lord's favor.
—ISAIAH 61:1-2

"It is written that when Messiah comes, he will be a light also for the Gentiles."
—ZAHAV (p. 270)

At his darkest moment, when he feels he can't go on, Alexander hears the news—that Yeshua is near and there is hope even for those outside God's fold—and sees Zahav's healed face. Once again he experiences her compassion (she's so excited about Hero's possible healing that she is barely aware of her own!).

ASK

Do you have compassion for those living in the shadows? for those who believe differently than you do? Or are you God's "snarl and frown of disapproval" (p. 56)? Explain by giving examples of your actions from the last month or two.

_____

_____

_____

What things have you learned—or are learning—in your own days of shadow? For example, is your own pain making you more compassionate toward others? Do you think more "long-term"?

_____

_____

_____

WONDER . . .

"You are a candle. And when you call upon The Name of the God of Israel for help and guidance, the sun will shine down so brightly on you that not a shadow will remain!"
— YESHUA (p. 224)

Yeshua bids you with a welcoming smile: *Come on! I've been waiting for you! Exiles! Wanderers! . . . Come into my camp and rest! All you whose souls toss like the restless sea! . . . See my face and hear my voice and touch the firmness of heaven! Know that the world that waits ahead for you is tangible and safe! Fear not!* (p. 350).

Why not take Yeshua up on His offer?

3 | THE WHISPER OF EVIL

On the day before Yeshua arrived in the Decapolis, unseen whisperers who served the Prince of Darkness knew The Light was coming to their shore. They had seen Him in heaven and remembered how He, The Lord of All the Angel Armies, had cast them out. They trembled because of it. . . .

They hissed in terror to one another. The end of their dominion was threatened. They must band together to fight!

—PROLOGUE (p. ix)

Have you ever felt that those who serve darkness have gathered to fight you? If so, in what situation(s)?

_____

_____

_____

What thoughts ran through your mind during that time? Are any of these familiar to you?

- *God, why me?*
- *I'll never be useful to anybody again.*
- *Might as well give up.*
- *Things can't get worse.*
- *What did I do to deserve this?*
- (Fill in the blank)_____

As long as we live on this earth we will be affected by Satan's dark presence. The Bible makes it clear that he is always around:

The Lord said to Satan, "Where have you come from?"
Satan answered the Lord, "From roaming through the earth and going
back and forth in it."
    —Job 1:7

Satan roams freely and he's always busy. A little discouragement here, a little blame there; some anger here, a white lie that becomes a bigger lie there. A dose of self-pity, a betrayal, a feeling of uselessness. Yes, Satan is busy. And he's tenacious about hitting the bull's-eye on what really discourages you.

In his blind and depressed state, Manaen bar Talmai listened intently to the voices of darkness until "even his soul had become blind. What good was he now? He was nothing! Helpless!" (p. 39).

Is Manaen, the former wrestler, a "depressive type" by nature? No. But this man was used to taking the world by storm . . . and now the storm threatened to overtake his life. *Why go on living?* he wondered. *Why prolong the agony? What, if anything, is there left to believe in? Certainly not God . . . if He cared, He'd never allow this. And not myself . . . not anymore.*

Is Manaen alone in his despair over evil?

No. Even the great prophet Elijah admitted, *"Despair. My greatest enemy"* (p. 183). Peniel was comforted to know that even Elijah got discouraged and ran from his problems.

Has so much changed in the thousands of years since Elijah walked the earth?

READ

Peniel shuddered. "I've felt evil come near me at times. Heard a sort of whisper, calling me. A feeling like everything is falling apart. My whole life, useless. Falling like rotten apples. Of no use to anybody. Might as well give up and die. Well, you know all about that, Lord."

"Yes. I know the lies the devil shouts in men's hearts to drive them from Adonai's love. When you hear it, speak the promises of Torah out loud. Answer the devil's accusations with the living words of the Living God. When darkness is confronted by light it flees."

"It's just my own mind. Feelings. My own thoughts. Nothing, really."

"It's more than that, Peniel. The Prince of Darkness, the Prince of this world, is as real as this apple tree. The rotten fruit is his doing, not mine."
    —Yeshua and Peniel (pp. 199–200)

For our struggle is not against flesh and blood, but against the rulers, against the authorities, against the powers of this dark world and against the spiritual forces of evil in the heavenly realms.
—Ephesians 6:12

ASK

Evil is constant and sneaky. But we need not be caught off guard if we're aware of evil's influence. Which statements of Peniel's above can you identify with? Why?

_____

_____

_____

Why does the devil shout in men's hearts?

_____

_____

In what ways does the "internal drama" of your life (see p. 218) make so much racket that it's hard for you to understand or trust Yeshua's promises?

_____

_____

_____

Many think of Satan as the ineffectual, almost comical "devil in a red cape with a pitchfork." But that doesn't give this fallen angel enough credit. Satan is a powerful force, and he's out to make your life miserable because you are created and loved by God. Satan has already targeted you as God's child. His greatest desire is to separate you from your heavenly Father. He accomplishes that through a web of lies that keep you trapped and mired in anger and self-pity.

READ

Today the darkness said, "So this is what Manaen the wrestler has become! It used to be, not so very long ago, that men would step out of his way when he passed. Handsome, wealthy Manaen. Women would stare at him in admiration. Now a frail old man leads him!" (p. 40).

"Believing the lies of the Accuser blinds your soul to the true light of life."
    —YESHUA (p. 311)

ASK

If you were Manaen, how would you respond to life's changing winds?

_____

_____

_____

Manaen had a reason to ask why. By the whim of a jealous, sick brother and an evil ruler, Manaen was imprisoned and his eyes viciously put out with a firebrand.

When Manaen touches his scarred eyes, his wife, Susanna, says, "Demos only stole your sight."

Manaen's response? "He may as well have taken my life" (p. 15). How honest!

Until Yeshua returns in all His glory, this world will be sick and evil. Bad things *will* happen. That certainty will not change. However, it's up to *us* to choose our response.

READ

"Why are you anxious about lies the world believes? . . . Peniel! You have seen the face! Why tremble because of half-truths and lies when you have seen . . . with your own eyes . . . the face! You have seen . . . the Truth. Why do you cringe when they speak? Are not my Word and my Truth and my Light more powerful?"
    —YESHUA (p. 196)

"Praise him if you like, old man. But don't praise him in my presence. I'm chained in a prison. There aren't stars in this night. And the sun will never rise for me again."
  —MANAEN (p. 40)

ASK

Think honestly about your response to evil this past week. Is it more similar to Peniel's: *Teach me, Yeshua. Help my unbelief*? or to Manaen's: *Why me? I can't believe this is happening to me*? Why?

The Father of Lies "claims all mankind for himself. He rules by fear. . . . Many choose to believe his lies rather than trust in Adonai's love" (p. 199).

  What will you choose to believe in? Why?

The instant you believe in Yeshua, all the whisperers hovering at your shoulder "scream in terror and spin away" (p. 224). That means, with God's assistance, you have the power to banish evil! Satan will still come prowling, but he will no longer have dominion over your soul!

READ

> *Take up the shield of faith, with which you can extinguish all the flaming arrows of the evil one.*
>   —EPHESIANS 6:16

Remember Ephesians 6:12? God doesn't leave us defenseless. Read the surrounding verses:

Be strong in the Lord and in his mighty power. Put on the full armor of God so that you can take your stand against the devil's schemes . . . so that when the day of evil comes, you may be able to stand your ground, and after you have done everything, to stand.
—Ephesians 6:10-11, 13

ASK

In what area do you need to "stand your ground" against Satan?

_____

_____

_____

WONDER . . .

"The mountain of evil in whose shadow . . . we live is a dangerous place for us until Messiah is revealed in his glory. Messiah will come to Mount Hermon one day soon, I pray. He will ascend to the third peak. On Zion, by mercy and truth He will be revealed as the Holy One, Savior and Redeemer. This will happen on the very mountain where the Father of Lies and his army of Watchers lured the souls of mankind to destruction with empty promises and sorcery."
—Papa (pp. 212–213)

"By the power of my name you can cast every mountain of evil into the deepest sea, and the sea of God's mercy will cover it forever."
—Yeshua (p. 386)

Just think . . . someday Messiah will return to the very place where man was lured into evil in the first place. On that day He will remove every trace of evil and establish Himself as the true King. He will forever destroy the greatest two lies the Father of Lies ever whispered—that God does not exist, and that evil cannot be defeated (see p. 381).

In the light of that reality, how will you choose to live today?

4 | THE LAND OF THE HEART

"If you can make eyes for me, I believe somehow your inner light will beam into the darkest corners of men's hearts."
—PENIEL, THE ONCE-BLIND BEGGAR, TALKING TO YESHUA (p. 200)

Think about two people you see frequently. One you enjoy spending time with and walk away from feeling refreshed. And the other? It's a chore—something to check off your to-do list.

What specific characteristics and attitudes in the two people make the difference?

_____

_____

_____

Reflect on your own heart attitude. If Yeshua's light beamed into the dark corners of your heart, what would He see? (The dust of anger or disbelief? sadness? regret? bitterness? self-pity? jealousy? something else?)

_____

_____

_____

Heart attitude can make all the difference not only in how we feel about ourselves and our future, but in the way we relate to others.

Susanna and Manaen are good examples. For so long they had dreamed solely of being together. That goal kept them focused on the end product—their marriage—even when the consequences were dire. Susanna was banished and almost became the wife of Manaen's perverted brother,

Demos. Manaen was imprisoned, blinded, and then exiled, thinking he would never see Susanna again.

Yet they were brought together miraculously—and freed to marry. You would think they would settle into marital bliss. But both struggled with a deep sense of loss.

READ

Like weeds in a garden, bitterness and self-pity had taken root in his heart. There was no room for anything or anyone else to grow there. . . . What was lost had become the god of his idolatry, everything he longed for. The one thing in life forever unattainable was the one thing he longed to possess.
—MANAEN (p. 153)

Finding some way to make him whole again was all she dreamed of these days. Restoring his happiness had become her goal, her one desire, the god of her idolatry. . . . Her heart was a leaf tossed by the wind of his mood.
—SUSANNA (p. 154)

ASK

Have you ever felt "tossed by the wind" of another person's mood? If so, describe the situation and how you feel/felt about it.

_____

_____

_____

Has the situation been resolved in any way? If so, how has the other person changed? How have *you* changed?

_____

_____

_____

What would you like to see changed?

_____

_____

_____

Susanna longed for Manaen to see himself as she saw him—the man she had fallen in love with. At first she thought her love should be enough to make him happy (see p. 115). Then she realized that she couldn't "fix" him with her love. Manaen needed something more—he needed someone to enter the land of his heart. He needed someone who could till the soil.

READ

> A farmer went out to sow his seed. As he was scattering the seed, some fell along the path, and the birds came and ate it up. Some fell on rocky places, where it did not have much soil. It sprang up quickly, because the soil was shallow. But when the sun came up, the plants were scorched, and they withered because they had no root. Other seed fell among thorns, which grew up and choked the plants. Still other seed fell on good soil, where it produced a crop—a hundred, sixty or thirty times what was sown.
> —MATTHEW 13:3-8

ASK

List the three kinds of "soil" in Yeshua's parable.

_____

_____

_____

What kinds of people do these soils represent (read Matthew 13:18-25)?

_____

_____

_____

Which kind of soil are you? Why?

_____

_____

_____

READ

"Pride. Is that what you mean? You mean, that's what keeps us from seeing ourselves? from seeing you? from knowing you as you are? from being like you?"

"Pride. All evil springs from it. All . . . every sin! Pride is the soil. Pride is the seed. Pride is the sun. Pride is the water."

—CONVERSATION BETWEEN PENIEL AND YESHUA (p. 200)

> Pride goes before destruction,
> a haughty spirit before a fall.
> Better to be lowly in spirit and among the oppressed
> than to share plunder with the proud.
> —PROVERBS 16:18-19

ASK

Why do you think the Bible warns so much against the sin of pride?

_____

_____

_____

Has pride marked your life in any way? In what areas of your life? Work? Relationships?

_____

_____

_____

No one is immune to pride. It's human nature to think we can control the universe . . . and that what we want to happen is what ought to happen. Manaen and Susanna had a mental picture of what their life would be like. But when life doesn't happen as they wanted, both grow resentful, angry, and disillusioned.

First Susanna fights against what Manaen has become. Then she tries to fix him. When these attempts fail, she gives up and weeps. (Interestingly, when Susanna finally gives up, it is Manaen who decides that they should find Mary, Yeshua's mother.)

Then there's Manaen, who falls completely into the angry, bitter, self-pity trap. He becomes so chained by the darkness that surrounds him that he no longer values his own life (p. 43). Nor does he value the lives of those around him. In essence he becomes blind in heart too.

Sadly, neither Susanna nor Manaen sees any way out of their predicament.

It's "easier to blame everyone else, even God, than accept that you can't change—won't be changed—until you humble yourself before your Creator" (p. 200).

Do you agree with this statement? Why or why not?

_____

_____

_____

Just when all seems hopeless, things change for Susanna and Manaen. They make a hard and risky choice—to try to find Yeshua. To try to find hope. To try to find answers.

READ

For it is by grace you have been saved, through faith—and this not from
yourselves, it is the gift of God—not by works, so that no one can boast.
—EPHESIANS 2:8-9

"There are some who fight self-delusion," Yeshua answered. "Today there
was a man near the back. . . . He needed real hope today. And he drank The
Word down like cool water. He chose to believe me."

"Chose? Can a person choose to believe?"

"Of course . . . it's the only way your faith can grow. . . . You act on the
word I have spoken. Then you discover that what I told you really is the
truth. Faith in the Eternal One, in Adonai, isn't about what you feel. Feelings deceive. Trust in me and live out my words."
—YESHUA TO PENIEL (pp. 223–224)

ASK

What did it take for Susanna and Manaen to come to the end of themselves?
to be willing to pursue Yeshua and His truth?

_____

_____

_____

When faced with difficult situations, do you tend to trust your feelings or
God's truth? Give an example.

_____

_____

_____

READ

Romans 3:10 says, "There is no one righteous, not even one." Compared to
God, we are all dressed in rags. We are all needy. Yet the wonder of it all is
this:

The Lord of All the Angel Armies,
incarnate in ordinary human flesh,
came down to fight the battle
for the kingdom of men's hearts (p. 381).

And the joy of it:
"Each grain in a man's heart is weighed and counted and known by
Adonai" (p. 194).

ASK

If Yeshua looked into your heart today, after you've gone over this study,
what would He see? What, if anything, has changed in your perspective?

_____

_____

_____

WONDER . . .

"The ancient war between the Prince of Darkness and Yahweh is fought to
redeem one soul at a time. I wasn't sent at this time to rule an earthly kingdom. First I must establish my kingdom in men's hearts."

"The heart. There's a dark land to conquer."

"Guarded by a fierce, unseen enemy. The Father of Lies. He claims all
mankind for himself. He rules by fear. By making people doubt the love of
the Father for his children. Many choose to believe his lies rather than trust
in Adonai's love for them."

—CONVERSATION BETWEEN YESHUA AND PENIEL (p. 199)

What will you choose to believe in?

5 | GOD REVEALED?!

"Those coming to Yeshua are like a tide never turning. The people are all asking, 'Who is he?' Some say he is even more than we dreamed Messiah would be. This may be why many can't believe him. Some say he's more than a prophet. More than a priest. More than a king! You must go to him. . . . See for yourself!"
— JOANNA (p. 157)

If someone asked you right now, "Who is Yeshua?" what would you say?

- *He was a nice man who walked around helping people.*
- *He's the Son of God.*
- *It's a good story, but I don't think He really existed.*
- *He was a good man, but He was not the Messiah. The Messiah hasn't yet come.*
- *He is the one sent by God to save us, if we accept His sacrifice on the cross.*
- *He, like Buddha, is one of many paths to heaven.*
- *(Fill in the blank)_____*

Imagine a man walking around the earth, supposedly healing people. Crowds surround him, myriad TV interviews focus on him, and excited eyewitnesses tell miracle stories. "He's the One!" they claim, "the One sent from God to save us!"

What would your reaction be? Why?

_____

_____

_____

Do you need a Savior?

Everyone responds to this question differently. Some think, *I'm not really that bad. I haven't murdered anyone or had an affair.* Others despair: *I've done so many wrong things in my life. There's no way God wants me in heaven.* Still others think, *Sure, nature seems to have an order, but that doesn't mean somebody's watching over it. Someday it's all going to just end.*

Others are sarcastic. *There is no God. How can there be, with all the horrible things happening? And the whole afterlife thing? A figment of someone's imagination so we'll feel better about life.* And some simply think, *I know I can't do life on my own. I need help. But how will I know which way to God is the right way?*

Still others know, deep within their soul, that they not only need God, but they have found Him.

READ

Yeshua of Nazareth tossed out the question one evening as He camped with His talmidim. They hardly glanced up from the flames as they replied, "No one knows for sure who you are. Prophet. Liar. Lawgiver. Rebel. Rabbi. Heretic. Good Man. Bad Man."

Such bland, insignificant definitions were like shadows on the rocks. No substance. No strength. After all, it took no commitment to call Yeshua "a good man."

But upon His *next* question the gates of eternity hinged. "Who do *you* say that I am?"

—PROLOGUE (p. vii)

"I am the way and the truth and the life. No one comes to the Father except through me. If you really knew me, you would know my Father as well. From now on, you do know him and have seen him."
—JOHN 14:6-7

ASK

Imagine sitting around the campfire with Yeshua. What would He look like? What would His voice sound like?

_____

_____

_____

If Yeshua could perform one miracle to make you believe He is "the One sent from God," what would it be? Why?

_____

_____

_____

If you saw the following things begin to happen (p. 17), would you believe that Yeshua was the Messiah? Why or why not?

- a cripple walking without a limp
- a little girl raised from the dead
- a blind man healed
- relatives you thought were dead suddenly showing up at your door

_____

_____

_____

We humans are, in general, skeptical. "Prove it to me," we say. But how much proof do we need? Would any one miracle—or a host of miracles—be enough to make us believe the Messiah of the world has arrived?

Or is it something else—perhaps several somethings—that blocks us from believing?

READ

"Everybody wants a miracle of their own, Lord."

"That's why I was sent. A miracle for everyone. One miracle at a time."

"They want bigger proof. Proof you are. Proof you can. Proof you will do . . . what they want and when they want it."

"That would prove I AM who I AM? . . . I've heard those words before. He never gives up. He's beaten and he knows it, but he never gives up."

—CONVERSATION BETWEEN PENIEL AND YESHUA (p. 197)

Some people are like seed along the path, where the word is sown. As soon as they hear it, Satan comes and takes away the word that was sown in them.
    —MARK 4:15

ASK

Why do you think everyone wants a miracle of their own? Why is that so important?

_____

_____

_____

Consider yourself a "seed along the path." Why do you think Satan would care, or bother, to "take away the word" from you?

_____

_____

_____

In what ways *has* Satan taken that word away from you in different times of your life?

_____

_____

_____

It's fascinating that Shim'on (soon to become Peter, "the rock" of the church) confessed who Yeshua is at a very significant spot—near Caesarea Philippi, near the Pool of Pan, which was located in the very heart of evil, Satan's lair. But it is not until we open our hearts to God (as Alexander finally did when he felt weighed down—even passed out—from fear) that we truly sense that evil.

Satan, who disguises himself as an angel of light (see 2 Corinthians 11:14), is as crafty now as he was back in the Garden of Eden. He knew what would tempt Adam and Eve, and he knows what will tempt you. Just as he knew what would tempt Manaen and Zahav.

READ

Even if Yeshua was capable of such deeds, would He perform a wonder like that for Manaen?

In examining his past life, Manaen was brutally honest with himself. Before he was blind he had given no consideration to spiritual matters. He had lived for himself alone, for pleasure, and for the moment. The Almighty owed him no favors on that accounting.

And in the months since he became sightless? . . . Hadn't he continued to live for himself alone, absorbed in his own inner struggle, without regard to needs of others?

Maybe Manaen had merely gotten what he deserved. Perhaps this was justice (pp. 301–302).

"Are you myself? Looking for answers when there are no answers? . . . But life is what it is. . . . We have a lot in common, you and I. We are alone tonight. Calling on the name of a God who doesn't answer. . . . Perhaps the One we're looking for doesn't care to be found by the likes of us."
—ZAHAV (pp. 57–58)

ASK

Have you ever felt like Manaen, who thought God wouldn't want to forgive him? that he had merely gotten what he deserved? If so, describe why.

_____

_____

_____

Can you identify with Zahav's questions—whether in the past or now? What questions do you have about God and how (or if) He's working in your life?

_____

_____

_____

Then there's the claim that could change the world. It happened on an ordinary day, around an ordinary campfire, when Yeshua and His disciples were having a simple dinner. Even more, it was Shim'on, an uneducated, rough-around-the-edges former fisherman, who made the declaration.

READ
"You are the Messiah. The Anointed One we've been looking for. You are the only Son of the Living God. The promise. Our miracle."
　　—Shim'on (p. 331)

The demons asked Yeshua if they could go into the swine.
　　The townsfolk asked Yeshua to leave them and go away.
　　But Nefesh—restored, healed, in his right mind—wanted just to be allowed to stay near Yeshua forever.
　　—Prologoue (p. xvii)

ASK
Everyone responds differently to Yeshua, yet it is clear that no one can deny His presence:

- The Madman shouts, "What do you want with me, Yeshua? What? You who are bar El Olam, bar El'Elyon, bar ELoHiYM. The Son of the Most High God" (p. xiv).
- Even the assassin Eglon admits, "Yeshua of Nazareth is more than just a man" (p. 31).
- The pious Sanhedrin refuse to acknowledge His name (pp. 17–18).
- The crowds flow toward Him for healing (p. 18).
- Caiaphas declares indignantly, "Who does this Yeshua think he is? Who?" (p. 19).

- Judas wonders when Yeshua will declare Himself king and take over the world (p. 24).
- Herodias, Antipas, and Caiaphas plot rumors to try to destroy Yeshua's reputation (pp. 150–151).
- Peniel refuses to deny he's been healed, even if it means he is excommunicated—no longer able to live in the world of his people (p. 17).

Does your response to Yeshua resemble any of the above responses? If so, how?

_____

_____

_____

If you truly believed the following words of Jesus from John 17:3, how would your life change? *"Now this is eternal life: that they may know you, the only true God, and Jesus Christ, whom you have sent."*

_____

_____

_____

WONDER . . .

At the name of Jesus every knee should bow, in heaven and on earth and under the earth, and every tongue confess that Jesus Christ is Lord, to the glory of God the Father.
—PHILIPPIANS 2:10

Look! Yeshua approaches the shore and calls out The Question! You do not answer Him, yet the boat draws nearer. Its keel scrapes onto the sand. He steps into the water, wades to shore, takes your hand, looks you in the eyes and asks: "Who do you say that I am?"

Eternal destiny depends on the answer.
—PROLOGUE (p. viii)

For every soul that moment will come. What will your response be? Will you leave, like the doubting Amos, and pursue your own way? Or will you choose to say, like Peniel: "No. No. I can't leave him. Not after what he's given me" (p. 139)?

6 | A HEALING TOUCH

"The wait is over. The true Balm of Gilead, who can heal our wounds, has come at last. He will heal his people!"
—ZADOK (p. 82)

Think of a person you know who is "wounded" in some way. What kind of scars does this person have? How have these scars affected his or her life?

_____

_____

_____

What "wounds" wake you up in the third watch of the night? What scars follow you throughout your day?

_____

_____

_____

We are all wounded in some way. We all carry scars. They might be physical—ones others can see. Or emotional—ones that affect our psychological well-being and sidetrack or destroy our relationships. Or mental—thoughts that torture us and keep us in Satan's dark clutches.

Many characters in this book have some type of scar, or even multiple scars. Samu'el tries to hide his cleft lip and palate behind his hand. Hero is not only deaf, but also possessed by forces that constantly strive to destroy him. Alexander's life has been turned upside down. He grieves intensely. He was not able to save his wife; now it seems he cannot save his son. The Madman is lost in a life of insanity, evil, and desperation. Zahav's face is scarred with the mark and memory of evil. But that isn't her only wound. Her heart cries out in loneliness; her mind reels with questions.

They are questions we must all face.

READ

Immanu'el! "God-with-us!"

Are you coming soon? Zahav's heart cried out. *Do you walk, unnoticed, through the streets of a great city? Do you speak to a lonely man beneath a tree? or feed an abandoned child huddled in a doorway? O, Immanu'el! God-with-us! I am watching for you! Speak to me!*

— ZAHAV (p. 35)

ASK

Have you ever wondered where God is in the midst of your pain? if He is really present and watching? if He does care or is merely a dispassionate creator? if the Bible's claims are true—that Yeshua is returning someday to earth to right all wrongs? In what situation(s) do you wonder these things?

_____

_____

_____

What questions or doubts stir in your soul right now?

_____

_____

_____

READ

Manaen was thinking about a lot of things. About the brother he had killed. About the serving girl whose life he had ruined when he was old enough to know better. About lies too many to count. About the rage and curses he had hurled at Susanna as she wept and asked him why. . . .

Manaen winced. He remembered small Samu'el with his cleft lip and palate, who could not utter a word. And how he had cuffed the boy hard the morning he and Susanna left his estates.

Yeshua asked, "Manaen bar Talmai, does your life have value?"

It was exactly the issue with which Manaen had wrestled ever since he lost his eyes. How did Yeshua know? Manaen wondered (pp. 309–310).

He himself bore our sins in his body on the tree, so that we might die to sins and live for righteousness; by his wounds you have been healed. For you were like sheep going astray, but now you have returned to the Shepherd and Overseer of your souls.
—1 PETER 2:24-25

ASK

Do you, like Manaen, ever struggle with regret? long for emotional healing? In what areas of your life?

_____

_____

_____

Have you ever wondered if your life has value? What made you feel that way?

_____

_____

_____

What steps would take you back to the Shepherd of your soul?

_____

_____

_____

READ

Madman's body quivered from the top of his Medusa-like locks to the horn-hard soles of his bare feet. Spasms that began at opposite black and jagged fingernails met in the middle of his scarred back. Madman's spine arched. Then he sagged, like a sail when the wind dies away.
—PROLOGUE (p. xv)

Seated beside Yeshua, bathed, dressed, sandals on his feet, eating a meal of bread and broiled fish, was the former madman. Ignoring the stares and speculation, Nefesh engaged Yeshua in earnest conversation.
—PROLOGUE (p. xvii)

ASK

If you saw the Madman of Gadara leaping crazily from rock to rock and yelling wildly, and then saw Nefesh sitting by Yeshua, would you believe it was the same person? Why or why not?

_____

_____

_____

Look deep within those hidden places no one but God sees. Do you need psychological or mental healing? In what areas?

_____

_____

_____

What connections (see Proverbs 15:30) do you see between your physical condition (i.e., depression, stomachaches, fingernail biting) and the psychological or mental healing you long for?

_____

_____

_____

Take courage! Nefesh, healed Madman, was able to smile, even if some sorrow still remained in his eyes (p. xviii).

Were the consequences of his past life completely removed? No, his back was still scarred (p. xv). And he would probably always be the source of gossip and colorful stories for the rest of his life. But none of that matters to Nefesh, because he has been forever changed by Yeshua not only physically but *spiritually*. As 2 Corinthians 5:17 says, "Therefore, if anyone is in Christ, he is a new creation; the old has gone, the new has come!"

Kuza too will bear the scars of his beating for the rest of his life (notice that in Kuza's case, unlike the Madman's, the scars are not his fault; they result from the sin of others). But Yeshua tells him: "You're free now. The scars. They're an honor, not a shame" (p. 310).

Think about your own scars. How can you see them as "an honor, not a shame"?

_____

_____

_____

READ

From the boat a luminous beam flashed skyward, up from His right hand like a sword, deflecting a forked spike of descending fire and piercing the underbelly of the storm! And then the retreating wind howled like a thousand demons. Towering waves shuddered and collapsed under the weight of His command. Clouds splintered and broke, rolling back at His roar: "Shalom! Peace!"

And there was peace.

"*Raphah!* Be still!"

Tranquil silence.

"And know that I AM."

— PROLOGUE (p. xii)

"Can the storm of a soul be calmed by him?"

"His voice is oil on troubled waters for some. Peace. Yes. Hope. I feel it, although I'm afraid. We're hoping for something, but we don't know what."

— CONVERSATION BETWEEN SUSANNA AND JOANNA (p. 156)

ASK

The Madman's soul was calmed. Manaen's soul was calmed. Zahav's soul was calmed. And that's only a few of the lives transformed in *Third Watch*. Along with many physical healings came mental, emotional, psychological, and spiritual healings.

Susanna tells Manaen, "No matter to me if you can see or if you can't see. As long as you are well, *inside* yourself. Well and whole in your soul" (p. 309). Keep in mind that this was *before* Manaen's healing, when neither knew that his physical circumstances would change.

What about you? Are you "well and whole in your soul"? Why or why not?

_____

_____

_____

READ

"Peniel, put out your hand. I brought a gift for you. . . ."
"A gift for me?"
"One of many. There is always a gift to meet every need."
—Conversation between Yeshua and Peniel (p. 194)

"I was looking for you every day. With my heart I was looking for the Light. Longing for the Light. And when you did come, it was like your Word promised. Quietly. When I was in my solitude, there you were. That you saw me sitting in the dust and cared enough to stoop and speak to a beggar like me? That was my miracle."
—Peniel (p. 198)

ASK

Yeshua says that God has a gift to meet every need. If Yeshua is indeed the Tsori, the great Healer, what gift would you ask Him for?

_____

_____

_____

In Peniel's case, the gift of one lavender bud (p. 194) reaffirmed God's love at a time when Peniel felt the heavy weight of fear, discouragement, and rejection.

What "lavender buds" have you experienced recently? (Perhaps an encouraging e-mail from a friend, financial help from a surprising source, a good doctor's report when all seems dark, etc.)

_____

_____

_____

How does Peniel's definition of a miracle change your perspective on your own "life happenings"?

_____

_____

_____

Are you, like Nefesh, ready to say, "Lord, Yeshua, Son of the Most High God. You can count on me" (p. xviii)? Why or why not?

_____

_____

_____

WONDER . . .

I . . . tried to heal myself with every earthly cure. Nothing worked. I was discovered. Cast out. At last, when I had no place else to turn, I made my way to the one Jeremiah wrote of, the true Healing Balm, the *Tsori* of Gilead. Yeshua—"God is Salvation"—is his name. And Yeshua, the Tsori, healed the wounds of this *tsara*. Nor does he heal only bodies! He is true balm for corruption of the soul.

—SIMON (p. 83)

"You can be my witness here. Go home. Tell everyone how much God has done for you today."
—YESHUA (p. xviii)

In what ways can you share God's miracles—from lavender buds to life transformations—with others who long for healing?

Dear Reader,

You are so important to us. We have prayed for you as we wrote this book and also as we receive your letters and hear your soul cries. We hope that *Third Watch* has encouraged you to go deeper. To get to know Yeshua better. To fill your soul hunger by examining Scripture's truths for yourself.

We are convinced that if you do so, you will find this promise true: "If you seek him, he will be found by you." —1 CHRONICLES 28:9

Bodie & Brock Thoene

Scripture References

1 Mark 8:27-29
2 Isa. 45:23
3 Ps. 84:10
4 Exod. 2:3-4
5 Exod. 2:5-10
6 Joel 2:28
7 Luke 12:33-34
8 John 21:25
9 Jer. 8:18-22
10 Isa. 53:3
11 Jer. 7:11; Matt. 21:13; John 2:16
12 Jer. 7:11
13 Zech. 12:10
14 Exod. 20:8
15 *The Complete Jewish Bible*
16 *The Complete Jewish Bible*
17 *The Complete Jewish Bible*
18 Exod. 20:12
19 Matt. 21:33-41
20 Matt. 21:42-44
21 Micah 5:2
22 Isa. 7:14
23 Exod. 16:1-34
24 Exod. 34:29-35
25 Ps. 66:1-2
26 Mal. 4:5
27 1 Kings 17:1–18:46
28 1 Kings 19:1-18
29 1 Kings 17:2-6
30 1 Kings 19:7-18
31 2 Kings 2:1-18
32 1 Kings 16:29-33

33 1 Kings 21:1-13
34 Matt. 2:16-18
35 Ps. 4:2
36 Ps. 4:3
37 Ps. 4:6
38 Ps. 4:8
39 Gen. 6:4
40 Ps. 89:9, 12
41 Isa. 59:20
42 Jer. 30–33
43 Matt. 4:3
44 Matt. 4:4
45 Matt. 7:9-11
46 Ps. 8:1
47 Ps. 8:1-2
48 Ps. 8:3-4
49 Num. 24:15-17
50 Micah 5:2
51 Gen. 49:10
52 Exod. 19:3-6
53 Exod. 19:9
54 Exod. 19:24
55 Isa. 64:6
56 Lev. 10:1-2
57 Ps. 24:3-4
58 Deut. 18:17-19
59 Exod. 23:20-21
60 Exod. 25:10-11, 17-22
61 Ps. 86:10
62 Lev. 23:24
63 Micah 7:19
64 Deut. 6:4
65 Gen. 12:2-3; 17:4-7

66 Gen. 18:10-15
67 Matt. 16:13-18
68 Matt. 16:19
69 Matt. 16:20
70 Gen. 22:1-18
71 Exod. 12:1-13
72 Exod. 19:3–20:21
73 Isa. 53:1-12
74 Exod. 16:1-32; John 6:32-33, 48-51
75 Matt. 3:13–4:4
76 Matt. 4:5-10
77 Matt. 4:8-11; Luke 4:5-8
78 Matt. 16:23
79 Matt. 16:24-27
80 Matt. 16:28
81 Gen. 49:25-26
82 Ps. 78:38
83 Lev. 16:5-22
84 Matt. 12:24
85 Isa. 1:18-20
86 Luke 9:25
87 Ps. 89:5
88 Ps. 89:6
89 Ps. 89:6-12
90 Matt. 17:4
91 Matt. 3:17; Luke 3:22
92 Matt. 22:37-40
93 Luke 4:18-19; Isa. 61:1-2
94 Matt. 17:17
95 Mark 9:24
96 Matt. 17:19-20

Authors' Note

The following sources have been helpful in our research for this book.

- *The Complete Jewish Bible*. Translated by David H. Stern. Baltimore, MD: Jewish New Testament Publications, Inc., 1998.

- *iLumina*, a digitally animated Bible and encyclopedia suite. Wheaton, IL.: Tyndale House Publishers, 2002.

- *The International Standard Bible Encyclopaedia*. George Bromiley, ed. 5 vols. Grand Rapids, MI.: Eerdmans, 1979.

- *The Life and Times of Jesus the Messiah*. Alfred Edersheim. Peabody, MA: Hendrickson Publishers, Inc., 1995.

About the Authors

BODIE AND BROCK THOENE (pronounced *Tay-nee*), who worked with John Wayne in their early years, have written over forty historical novels. Their novels have sold more than 10 million copies and have won eight ECPA Gold Medallion awards, affirming what readers have already discovered—that the Thoenes are not only master stylists of historical fiction but experts at capturing readers' minds and hearts. From the classic Zion Chronicles and Zion Covenant series and *The Twilight of Courage* to tales of the West, such as *The Saga of the Sierras* and *The Wayward Winds*, to The Shiloh Legacy series and *Shiloh Autumn*, poignant stories about the American depression, to the dramatic portrayal of the Irish 1840s famine in The Galway Chronicles, to their most recent Zion Legacy series, the Thoenes have made their mark in modern history. Now, with the A.D. Chronicles series, they step seamlessly into the world of Jerusalem and Rome, in the days when Yeshua of Nazareth walked the earth.

The Thoenes have four grown children—Rachel, Jake, Luke, Ellie—and five grandchildren. They divide their time between England and Nevada.

For more information visit www.thoenebooks.com.

THE NEW BEST-SELLING SERIES
FROM BODIE AND BROCK THOENE...

A.D. CHRONICLES™

BOOK ONE
First Light

In their most dramatic historical series to date, Bodie and Brock Thoene
transport readers back in time to first century A.D., to the most critical
events in the history of the world. // ISBN 0-8423-7507-4 • SOFTCOVER • US $14.99

BOOK TWO
second touch

This moving story will draw readers down the path of discovery to the
understanding that we all need the hope of Yeshua's touch upon not only
our bodies, but our souls. // ISBN 0-8423-7509-0 • HARDCOVER • US $22.99
SOFTCOVER AVAILABLE WINTER OF 2005: ISBN 0-8423-7510-4

BOOK THREE
third watch

"Who do they say that I am?" From the wilderness of Sinai to Mount
Hermon the question of Yeshua of Nazareth's identity resounds across the
ancient land of Israel. Even evil waits to hear the answer. It is in the very
air, the storm, and the sea. // ISBN 0-8423-7512-0 • HARDCOVER • US $19.99

WATCH FOR BOOK 4 IN THE BEST-SELLING
A.D. CHRONICLES SERIES AVAILABLE SPRING 2005!

Unabridged audios are available on CD from Tyndale Audio and Luke Thoene
Productions. Performed by actor Sean Barrett for your listening enjoyment.
FIRST LIGHT UNABRIDGED AUDIO CD • ISBN 0-8423-7508-2 • US $49.99
SECOND TOUCH UNABRIDGED AUDIO CD • ISBN 0-8423-7511-2 • US $49.99
THIRD WATCH UNABRIDGED AUDIO CD • ISBN 0-8423-7514-7 • US $49.99

The dramatic audio of *First Light* is also available in cassette and CD from
Tyndale Audio and Luke Thoene Productions.
CD • ISBN 0-8423-8291-7 • US $24.99 • CASSETTE • ISBN 0-8423-8292-5 • US $24.99

DISCOVER THE
TRUTH
THROUGH
FICTION™

suspense with a mission

TITLES BY

Jake Thoene

"The Christian Tom Clancy"
Dale Hurd, *CBN Newswatch*

Shaiton's Fire

In this first book in the techno-thriller series by Jake Thoene, the bombing of a subway train is only the beginning of a master plan that Steve Alstead and Chapter 16 have to stop . . . before it's too late.
ISBN 0-8423-5361-5 SOFTCOVER
US $12.99

Firefly Blue

In this action-packed sequel to Shaiton's Fire, Chapter 16 is called in when barrels of cyanide are stolen during a truckjacking. Experience heart-stopping action as you read this gripping story that could have been ripped from today's headlines.
ISBN 0-8423-5362-3 SOFTCOVER
US $12.99

Watch for the exciting third book in the series available winter 2004.

for more information on other great Tyndale fiction,
visit www.tyndalefiction.com

Other Books by
BODIE AND BROCK THOENE

Second Touch

First Light

The Zion Legacy Series

Shiloh Autumn

The Twilight of Courage

The Zion Covenant Series

The Zion Chronicles Series

The Shiloh Legacy Series

The Saga of the Sierras

The Galway Chronicles

The Wayward Winds Series

Writer-to-Writer

the middle east

FIRST CENTURY A.D.

Mount Hermon +

GALILEE

Mediterranean Sea

• Caesarea Philippi

Chorazin •
Capernaum •   • Bethsaida
Magdala •
Sea of Galilee
• Tiberias

Jordan River

SAMARIA

PEREA

Jericho •
Jerusalem • + Mount of Olives
• Bethany
Bethlehem •
• Herodium

JUDEA   Dead
           Sea

IDUMEA

← to Alexandria, Egypt

CB 9/06

MG 5/06